IN ME MEA SPES OMNIS

THE
LITTLE
GOLDEN CALF

THE
LITTLE
GOLDEN CALF

A Satiric Novel

ILYA ILF and EUGENE PETROV

FREDERICK UNGAR PUBLISHING CO.
NEW YORK

Translated from the Russian by
CHARLES MALAMUTH

Look up and down before you cross the street . .

Contents

CONTENTS

Characters

ANTELOPIANS

OSTAP IBRAGIMOVICH BENDER, *the great schemer and commander of the Antelopians*
SHURA BALAGANOV
MIKHAIL SAMUILOVICH PANIKOVSKY } *his aides and associates*
ADAM KAZIMIROVICH KOZLEVICH

HERCULEANS

COMRADE POLYKHAYEV, *the democratic and public-spirited chief of the Herculeans*
SERNA MIKHAILOVNA, *his secretary*
YEGOR SKUMBRIEVICH
ADOLF NIKOLAIEVICH BOMZE
BOOKKEEPER BERLAGA
SAKHARKOV
DREYFUS
TEZOIMENITSKY
MUZYKANT
CHEVAZHEVSKAYA
KUKUSHKIND
BORISOKHLEBSKY
LAPIDUS JR.
ALEXANDER IVANOVICH KOREIKO, *the millionaire clerk*
HEINRICH-MARIA SAUSE, *a German specialist*

RESIDENTS OF MAGPIE VILLAGE

LUZZIA FRANZEVNA PFERD
CHAMBERLAIN MITRICH
NIKITA PRYAKHIN
GIGIENISHVILI
NOBODY'S GRANDMOTHER
AUNTIE PASHA

ix

X CHARACTERS

Dunya
Vasisualy Andreyevich Lokhankin
Varvara, *his wife*

PASSENGERS ON A SPECIAL TRAIN

Palamidov
Gargantua
Lavoizian
Ukhudshansky
Navrotsky
Photographer Menshov
Lev Rubashkin
Jan Skameikin
Heinrich, *erstwhile lieutenant of the Imperial Austrian Army*
Mr. Hiram Burman, *an American Zionist*

UNORGANIZED MINORITIES

Kuszakowski
Moroszek } *priests of the Roman Catholic Church*
Valiadis
Funt } *who wear piqué vests*
Ptiburdukov I, *an engineer*
Ptiburdukov II, *a physician*
Khvorobyov, *of the Crooked Little Log House*
Sinitsky, *a puzzle-maker*
Zosya Adamovna Sinitskaya, *his grand-daughter*
Ivan Osipovich Trikartov, *formerly a maître d'hôtel*
Engineer Talmudovsky, *a chronic deserter*

ALSO

Inmates and Keepers of an Insane Asylum, Members of the Communist Party and of the League of Communist Youth, Neighbors, Students, Motorists, Pedestrians, Orators, Auditors, Clerks, Constables, Lecturers, Nurses, Kazaks, Workmen, Peasants, Tractors, Camels, etc., etc.

Place: U.S.S.R.
Time: The Present

Part One

ANTELOPE'S EQUIPAGE

Chapter One

OF HOW PANIKOVSKY VIOLATED THE PACT

Pedestrians should be loved.

Pedestrians make up the greater part of humanity. More than that—its best part. Pedestrians have created the world. It was they who built cities, reared many-storied buildings, put through canalization and the water system, paved the streets and lighted them with electric lamps. It was they who spread culture throughout the world, devised printing, invented gunpowder, flung bridges across rivers, deciphered Egyptian hieroglyphics, introduced the safety razor into common usage, destroyed the slave trade, and determined that one hundred palatable, nourishing dishes may be prepared out of soya beans.

And when everything was ready, when our native planet assumed a comparatively well-ordered appearance, motorists appeared.

It must be noted that automobiles were also invented by pedestrians. But it seems that the motorists immediately forgot about it. Gentle and wise pedestrians began to be pressed. The streets created by pedestrians passed into the power of the motorists. Pavements became twice as wide, while sidewalks narrowed to the limits of an Internal Revenue stamp. Then frightened pedestrians began to edge against the walls of houses.

In a large city pedestrians lead a martyr's life. A certain transport ghetto has been introduced for their benefit. They are permitted to cross the street only at the crossing; that is, precisely in those places where traffic is thickest and where the

3

hair on which usually hangs the life of a pedestrian may be most easily severed.

In our spacious country an ordinary automobile intended, according to the pedestrian's idea, for the peaceful transportation of men and merchandise has assumed the threatening proportions of a fratricidal projectile. It knocks out of formation entire ranks of trade union members and their families.

Should the pedestrian happen to succeed in fluttering out alive from under the silver nose of the machine, the militia [1] fines him for violating the rules of the traffic catechism.

And in general the authority of the pedestrian has been greatly shaken. They who have given the world such remarkable people as Horace, Boyle-Mariotte, Lobachevsky and Gutenberg, Meyerhold and Anatole France, are now forced to grimace in a most disgusting fashion simply to remind people of their existence. Oh, God, oh, God (who dost not really exist), to what straits hast thou (who indeed dost not exist) brought the pedestrian?

Here he comes from Vladivostok to Moscow, along the Siberian highway, holding in one hand a banner with the inscription, "Let Us Reconstruct the Life of the Textile Workers," and holding on his shoulder a stick on the tip of which dangle reserve sandals of the "Uncle Vanya" brand, and a tin teapot without a cover. This is a Soviet pedestrian-physical-culturist who in his youth departed from Vladivostok, and who, in his declining years, at the very gates of Moscow, will be crushed by a heavy autocar, the number of which he will not have time to notice.

Or another, a European Mohican of pedestrian traffic. He is walking on foot around the world, rolling a barrel before him. He would have gladly gone as he was, without a barrel,

---

[1] Although there is an outward resemblance between the functions performed by the militia of a proletarian state and our police, the two should not be confounded because of fundamental differences. To the Soviet citizen the word "police" connotes oppression and persecution. C. M.

but then no one would notice that he was really a pedestrian
out for a long-distance record and nothing would be written
about him in the newspapers. So for the rest of his life he is
obliged to push before him the damned keg on which, moreover (shame, shame!), a large yellow sign praises the incomparable virtues of an automobile oil entitled "The Chauffeur's
Dream."

Thus has the pedestrian degenerated.

It is only in small Russian cities that the pedestrian is yet
respected and loved. There he is still the master of the street,
wanders carefree over the pavement and crosses it in any
direction in the most involved manner.

A citizen in a cap with a white top, the kind worn for the
most part by managers of summer gardens and masters of
ceremonies at vaudeville theaters, undoubtedly belonged to
the greater and best part of humanity. He moved through
the streets of the town of Arbatov on foot, looking around
him with tolerant curiosity. In one hand he held a small
obstetrician's bag. Apparently the town had in no way amazed
the pedestrian in the artistic cap.

He saw about fifteen azure, mignonette-colored, and pale
rose church bells. His eyes beheld the molting Caucasian gold
of church cupolas. A strawberry flag snapped over the official
building. At the white-towered gates of the provincial Kremlin
two severe old ladies spoke French, complained about the
Soviet government, and exchanged reminiscences about their
favorite daughters. A wave of cold came from the church
cellar—a sour wine odor belched forth. There, apparently, potatoes were stored.

"Potatoes have saved the temple," the pedestrian said
quietly.

Passing under a veneered arch with a fresh lime slogan:
"Greetings to the Fifth District Conference of Women and
Girls," he found himself at the beginning of a long lane called
the Boulevard of Youthful Talents.

"No," he said anxiously, "this is not Rio de Janeiro. This is much worse."

On nearly all the benches of the Boulevard of Youthful Talents sat lonely young women with open books in their hands. Ragged shadows fell on the pages of their books, on their bare elbows, on their pathetic bangs. When the new arrival entered the cool lane there was noticeable movement on the benches. The girls, hiding behind the books of Gladkov, Eliza Orrzeszko and Seyfullina, cast timid glances at the visitor. He stalked officiously past the agitated readers and came to the building of the Executive Committee—the goal of his journey.

That very minute an izvozchik came around the corner. Beside him, clinging to the dusty crumbling edge of the carriage and waving a bulging portfolio with a stamped inscription "Musique," ran a man in a long *tolstofka* shirt. He was expostulating heatedly with the passenger, an elderly man with a nose that hung like a banana, who pressed a suitcase with his feet and from time to time thumbed a fig in the face of his opponent. In the heat of the argument his engineering cap, the band of which glistened with the green velvet of a divan, slid threateningly to the side. Both contending sides frequently and with special sonority pronounced the word "emolument."

Soon other words were heard.

"You'll take full responsibility for this, Comrade Talmudovsky!" shouted the long-shirted one, brushing away from his face the engineer's thumbing gesture.

"But I tell you that under such conditions not a single decent specialist will come to you," answered Talmudovsky, attempting to return his thumbing gesture to its former place.

"If you mention emolument again, I shall have to charge you with graft!"

"To hell with emolument! I'll work for nothing!" shouted the engineer, in his agitation drafting all sorts of diagonals with his thumbing gesture. "If I want to, I'll retire altogether on a pension. Forget this serfdom. They themselves write everywhere 'Liberty, Equality, Fraternity,' and yet they try to make me work in this rat hole!"

At this point Engineer Talmudovsky quickly opened the fist with which he had thumbed and began to count on his fingers:

"The apartment—a pig-sty. No theater. The emolument . . . Izvozchik! Off to the station!"

"Whoa-a!" the long-shirted one screamed, fussily running in front of the horse and catching it by the bridle. "I, as secretary of the Section of Engineers and Technicians . . . Kondrat Ivanovich! But the factory will remain without specialists . . . Shame on you! . . . Our public opinion will not permit it, Engineer Talmudovsky. . . . I have a complaint in my brief case. . . ."

And the Secretary of the Section, planting his feet apart, quickly began to untie the ribbons of his "Musique."

This indiscretion decided the argument. Seeing that the road was clear, Talmudovsky rose to his feet and with all his might cried out:

"Off to the station!"

"Where? Where?" babbled the secretary, running after the carriage. "You are a deserter from the labor front!"

From the "musique" portfolio flew out sheets of tissue paper with "Resolutions" in purple ink.

The new arrival who had watched the incident with great interest stood for a minute on the deserted square and said with conviction:

"No. This is not Rio de Janeiro."

A moment later he was knocking at the door of the private office of the chairman of the Executive Committee.

"Whom do you want?" asked the secretary who was sitting at a table next to the door. "Why do you want the chairman? What's your business?"

Evidently the visitor had a subtle knowledge of how to
deal with secretaries of governmental, economic and public
organizations. He made no attempt to prove that he had
arrived on pressing government business.

"Private," he said dryly, without looking at the secretary,
and pushed his head into the doorway. "May I come in?"

And without waiting for an answer he approached the desk.
"Hello, don't you recognize me?"

The chairman, a black-eyed, large-headed man in a blue
coat and trousers to match stuffed into boots with high, wing-
foot heels, looked at the visitor rather absentmindedly and
declared that he did not recognize him.

"Is it possible that you don't recognize me? And yet many
people think that I am remarkably like my father."

"I also resemble my father," the chairman answered impatiently. "What do you want, comrade?"

"The whole point is in the father," the visitor remarked
sadly. "I am the son of Lieutenant Schmidt."

The chairman became confused and rose. He quickly remembered the far-famed image and pale mustached face of
the revolutionary lieutenant in his black cape buckled with
bronze lions. While he was gathering his thoughts in order
to ask the son of the Black Sea hero a question deserving of
the occasion, the visitor regarded the furniture of the office
with the look of a discriminating purchaser.

A long time ago, in the days of the Tsar, the furnishing of
public places was standardized. A special pedigree of official
furniture was bred: flat wooden benches with six-inch polished
seats, tables on billiard legs, and oaken parapets that separated
the officials from the restive outer world. In the course of the
Revolution this breed of furniture became almost extinct, and
the secret of its production was lost. People forgot how the
quarters of official personages should be arranged, and there
appeared in the offices of civil servants objects that until then
had been the inseparable property of private apartments. Gov-

ernment offices now boasted the divans of lawyers, with springs and a mirrored shelf for seven porcelain elephants which presumably bring luck, cupboards for dishes, little cabinets, special leather chairs for rheumatics, and azure Japanese vases. To the private office of the chairman of the Arbatov Executive Committee, in addition to the usual writing desk, two small pillows upholstered in pink silk had attached themselves, also a striped settee, a velvet screen with a Fujiama and a cherry tree in blossom, and a cheap, machine-made Slavic cupboard with a mirror.

"The cupboard is of the type 'Hey, you Slavs!'" thought the visitor. "There isn't much to get here. Nope, this is not Rio de Janeiro."

"Very glad you dropped in," the chairman said finally. "I suppose you're from Moscow."

"Yes, passing through," replied the visitor, examining the settee and becoming increasingly convinced that the financial affairs of the Executive Committee were in a bad way. He preferred Executive Committees furnished with the new Swedish furniture of the Leningrad Lumber Trust.

The chairman wanted to ask about the purpose of the lieutenant's son's visit to Arbatov, but, unexpectedly even for himself, he smiled weakly and said:

"Our churches are remarkable. People have come here from *Glavnauka*. They intend to restore them. Tell me, and do you yourself remember the rebellion on the battleship 'Ochakov'?"

"Dimly, dimly," the visitor replied. "In those heroic times I was extremely small. I was an infant."

"Excuse me, but what is your name?"

"Nicholas . . . Nicholas Schmidt."

"And . . . your patronymic?"

"Ach, that's bad," thought the visitor, who did not know the name of his father.

"Ye-es," he drawled, evading a direct reply. "Nowadays many people don't know the names of heroes. The pernicious

NEP! The old enthusiasm is lacking. To tell the truth, I came to your city quite by accident, got into difficulties on the way, haven't a kopek to my illustrious name."

The chairman was glad of the change in conversation. It seemed shameful to him that he had forgotten the name of the "Ochakov" hero.

"Really," he thought, looking lovingly at the inspired face of his guest. "We get lost in work. We forget the milestones of history."

"What did you say—not a kopek? That's interesting."

"Of course, I could have approached any private person. Anyone would give it to me. But, you understand, it's not altogether convenient for political considerations. The son of a revolutionist, and suddenly he asks money from a private person—a Nepman. . . ."

The lieutenant's son pronounced the last words tearfully. The chairman listened with anxiety to the new intonations in the voice of his visitor. "And suppose he's an epileptic," he thought. "There'll be no end of trouble with him."

"You did very well not to have gone to a private trader," said the chairman, finally involving himself completely.

Then the son of the Black Sea hero, softly and without pressure, turned to business. He asked for fifty rubles. The chairman, limited by the narrow frames of the local budget, could give him only eight rubles and three meal tickets to the coöperative restaurant "The Stomach's Erstwhile Friend."

The hero's son put the money and the tickets in the deep pocket of his wornout gray dotted coat and was about to rise from the pink cushion, when stamping and the forbidding cry of the secretary were heard outside the door of the private office. The door was opened hurriedly and on the threshold appeared a new visitor.

"Who's in charge here?" he asked, breathing heavily, his knavish eyes scouring about.

"Well, let's say I am," said the chairman.

"Greetings, Chairman," barked the new arrival, stretching forth a shovel-shaped palm. "Let's be acquainted. Lieutenant Schmidt's son."

"Who?" asked the city chief, his eyes bulging.

"Son of the great, unforgettable hero, Lieutenant Schmidt," repeated the new arrival.

"But the Comrade sitting there is the son of Comrade Schmidt—Nicholas Schmidt!"

And in utter confusion the chairman pointed to the first visitor whose face suddenly assumed a somnolent expression. In the lives of the two crooks dawned a ticklish situation. At any moment the unpleasant sword of Nemesis might suddenly gleam in the hands of the modest and gullible chairman of the Executive Committee. Fate granted only one second of time for concocting means of rescue. Horror appeared in the eyes of Lieutenant Schmidt's second son. He was clad in a Paraguay summer shirt, sailor trousers and bluish canvas slippers. His figure which a moment ago had been sharp and angular began to melt, lost its threatening contours and no longer inspired respect. A wicked smile appeared on the face of the chairman.

And just when it seemed to the second son of Lieutenant Schmidt that all was lost and that the terrible anger of the chairman would roll in a moment on his red head, rescue came from the pink cushion.

"Vasya!" cried the first son of Lieutenant Schmidt, jumping up. "My own little brother! Don't you recognize your brother Nick?"

And the first son embraced the second son.

"Of course, I recognize you!" exclaimed Vasya, seeing the light. "Of course I recognize my brother Nick!"

The happy meeting was marked by such stormy caresses and such unusually strong embraces that the second son of the Black Sea revolutionist emerged with a face pale with pain. In his transports of joy Brother Nick had pummeled him pretty strongly.

While embracing, both brothers looked out of the corner of their eyes at the chairman on whose face remained a vinegary expression. In view of this the means of rescue had to be developed right there, augmented by intimate details and new materials about the uprising of the seamen in 1905 which had escaped the party historians. Holding each other's hands, the brothers sank onto the settee and, their flattering eyes constantly on the chairman, lost themselves in reminiscences.

"What a remarkable meeting!" exclaimed the first son sententiously, inviting the chairman with a glance to join the family celebration.

"Yes," said the chairman in a frozen voice. "It happens, it happens."

Seeing that the chairman was still in the claws of doubt, the first son stroked his brother's locks, red as a setter's, and asked caressingly:

"When did you come from Mariupol? Where did you live there—at grandmother's?"

"Yes, that's where I lived," muttered the lieutenant's second son. "With her."

"Why did you write me so rarely? I was frightfully worried."

"I was busy," the redhead answered sulkily.

And fearing that his indefatigable brother would immediately become interested in what he had been busy with (and he had been busy principally with sitting in houses of correction of various autonomous republics and districts), the second son of Lieutenant Schmidt snatched the initiative and turned questioner.

"And why didn't *you* write?"

"What do you mean I didn't write?" the brother answered unexpectedly, feeling an unusual wave of gayety. "I sent you registered letters. I have piles of receipts."

And he dived into his side pocket from which he actually pulled out a multitude of papers. But for some reason, he showed them not to his brother but to the chairman of the Executive Committee—and that from a distance.

However strange it may seem, a view of the papers somewhat quieted the chairman, and the recollections of the brothers took a livelier turn than ever. The redhead became thoroughly adjusted to his surroundings and fairly sensibly, albeit rather monotonously, he retold the contents of a popular edition of the pamphlet "The Uprising on the 'Ochakov.'" The brother embellished his dry exposition with such colorful details that the chairman, who had apparently begun to quiet down, again pricked up his ears.

However he let the brothers go in peace, and they ran out into the street feeling much easier.

Around the corner of the Executive Committee's building they stopped.

"By the way, speaking of childhood," said the first son. "When I was a child I used to kill guys like you right on the spot. With a sling."

"Why?" joyfully inquired the second son of the famous father.

"Such are the implacable laws of life. Or, to put it briefly, life dictates to us its implacable laws. What made you come to the private office? Didn't you see that the chairman was not alone?"

"I thought . . ."

"Oh, so you thought! In other words, there are times when you think. Are you a thinker? What is your name, Thinker? Spinoza? Jean Jacques Rousseau? Marcus Aurelius?"

The redhead was silent, crushed by the just indictment.

"Well, I forgive you. You may live. And now let's get acquainted. Say what you like, we're brothers, and kinship has its obligations. My name is Ostap Bender. Permit me to learn your original surname."

"Balaganov," the redhead presented himself. "Shura Balaganov."

"I'm not asking about your profession," Bender said respectfully. "But I can guess. I'm sure it must be something intellectual. Have you been tried many times this year?"

"Twice," Balaganov answered freely.

"Now that's bad. Why do you put your immortal soul in bondage? No man should come to trial. That's an ugly occupation. I'm referring to theft. Setting aside even the fact that stealing is sinful—I'm sure that when you were a child your mother made you familiar with such a doctrine—it is moreover an aimless waste of strength and energy."

Ostap would have developed his views on life interminably if he had not been interrupted by Balaganov.

"Look," he said, pointing into the green depths of the Boulevard of Youthful Talents. "Do you see that man in a straw hat?"

"I see," Ostap said haughtily. "What of it? Is he the governor of Borneo?"

"That is Panikovsky," Shura said. "A son of Lieutenant Schmidt."

Along the lane in the shadow of the august lime trees, slightly bent to one side, moved a citizen no longer young. A hard straw hat with a scarred brim sat awry on his head. His trousers were so short that they revealed the ragged edges of his underwear. Under the mustache of this citizen, like the fire of a cigarette, glowed a golden tooth.

"What! Another son?" said Ostap. "This is getting funny."

Panikovsky came to the building of the Executive Committee, thoughtfully described a figure eight at the entrance, lifted his hat by the brim with both hands and set it correctly on his head, pulled his coat all around, and, sighing lugubriously, moved toward the entrance.

"Lieutenant Schmidt had three sons," Bender remarked.

"Two were wise, but the third was a fool. He must be warned."

"Don't bother," said Balaganov. "He'll know next time how to violate a pact."

"What pact are you talking about?"

"Never mind. I'll tell you later. He's entered, he's entered."

"I am an envious man," Bender confessed. "But there's nothing to envy here. Have you ever seen a bull fight? Come, let's watch."

The friendly children of Lieutenant Schmidt went around the corner and came to the window of the chairman's private office.

The chairman sat behind the foggy, unwashed glass. He was writing rapidly. Like the faces of all who write, his face was mournful. The door was flung open and into the room entered Panikovsky. Pressing his hat to his greasy coat, he stopped before the table and for a long time moved his thick lips. Then the chairman jumped up in his chair and opened his mouth wide. The friends heard a prolonged cry.

With the words "General retreat," Ostap pulled Balaganov after him. They ran to the boulevard and hid behind a tree.

"Hats off!" said Ostap. "Bare your head. Presently the body will be carried out."

He made no mistake. No sooner did the rolls and reverberations of the chairman's voice become still when in the portals of the Executive Committee building appeared two hefty committeemen. They were carrying Panikovsky. One held him by the hands, the other by the feet.

"The body of the deceased," commented Ostap, "was carried out on the hands of kinsmen and friends."

The committeemen carried out the third and foolish son of Lieutenant Schmidt and began to swing him slowly. Panikovsky was silent, piously gazing at the azure sky.

"After a short civil ceremony . . ." began Ostap.

At that very moment, having given the inert body of

Panikovsky sufficient swing, they threw him out into the street.

". . . the body was interred," Bender finished.

Panikovsky slapped to the earth like a frog. He rose quickly and, leaning to one side more than ever, he ran along the Boulevard of Youthful Talents with incredible swiftness.

"Well now," Ostap pronounced. "Tell me how this viper violated the pact and what sort of a pact it was."

Chapter Two

THE THIRTY SONS OF LIEUTENANT SCHMIDT

THE busy morning came to an end. Ostap Bender wanted to eat.

"You, of course, are on the verge of financial disaster," he said to Balaganov.

"Are you speaking of money?" Shura inquired. "I haven't had any for a week."

"In that case, you'll end badly, young man," Ostap chided him. "Financial disaster is the most grievous of all that may befall you in life. Well, never mind. Don't worry. I managed to carry away three meal tickets in my beak. It was a case of love at first sight with the chairman of the Executive Committee."

But the foster-brothers were not able to take advantage of the city chief's kindness. On the doors of the restaurant "The Stomach's Erstwhile Friend" hung a large lock covered with something that looked like a mixture of rust and buckwheat grits.

"Of course," Ostap said bitterly. "While they're taking an inventory of schnitzels the restaurant is closed forever. We must offer our bodies to the lacerations of private traders."

"Private traders love cash money," Balaganov objected in a dull voice.

"Well, well, I shan't torture you. The chairman showered me with a golden rain of eight rubles. But, bear in mind, most respected Shura, that I have no intention of feeding you gratis. For every vitamin you receive I shall demand of you a number of minor services."

17

However there were no private owners in town and the brothers dined in a coöperative summer garden where special placards announced to the citizens the latest Arbatov regulation in the field of popular dietetics:

> BEER IS SOLD ONLY TO MEMBERS OF
> TRADE UNIONS

"Kvass will do," said Balaganov.

"Besides," added Bender, "the local kvass is manufactured by a coöperative of private owners who sympathize with the Soviet régime. And now let's hear how the depraved Panikovsky got in wrong. I delight in stories of petty cheating."

Having eaten his fill, Balaganov looked gratefully at his saviour and began his story. The tale lasted for two hours and contained exceedingly interesting information.

In all the departments of human endeavor the supply and demand of labor is managed by appropriate organizations. Everything is regulated, flows along smooth channels, and returns to its starting point in complete conformity with the law and under its protection.

And only the market of a special category of swindlers who called themselves the children of Lieutenant Schmidt remained in a chaotic condition. Anarchy rent the fraternity of the lieutenant's children and they could not derive from their profession its natural perquisites.

It is difficult to find a more convenient field of operations for all sorts of pretenders than our expansive country, filled either with exceedingly suspicious or exceedingly gullible administrators, managers and social workers.

Throughout the land, extorting and begging, move the spurious grandchildren of Karl Marx, the non-existent nephews of Friedrich Engels, the brothers of Lunacharsky, the cousins of Clara Zetkin, and, if the worst comes to the worst, the descendants of the famous anarchist Prince Kropotkin. Detachments of mythical kinsmen assiduously exploit the natural wealth of the land: goodheartedness, foolishness, servility, and cringing.

From Minsk to the Bering Sea, and from Nakhichevan to Franz Josef Land, the kinsmen of great men enter executive committees, detrain at station platforms, and anxiously ride in cabs. They hurry. They have much to do.

At one time the supply of kinsmen exceeded the demand and a depression hit this unique market. A need for reforms was strongly felt. Gradually the grandchildren of Karl Marx, the Kropotkinites, the Engelsites and their like ceased their activity, with the exception of the stormy fraternity of Lieutenant Schmidt's children, which, like the Polish Sejm, was constantly torn by anarchy. The children appeared to be coarse, greedy, refractory, and interfered with each other's golden harvest.

Shura Balaganov, who considered himself the lieutenant's first-born, was seriously worried about the new state of affairs. With increasing frequency he had to meet members of the fraternity who had completely ruined the fertile fields of the Ukraine and the salubrious heights of the Caucasus where he had been accustomed to work profitably.

"And so you feared the increasing difficulties?" Ostap inquired jeeringly.

But Balaganov did not notice the irony. Sipping the lavender kvass, he continued his narrative.

There was only one way out of this strained situation and that was a convention. Balaganov had worked at it throughout the winter. He corresponded with the competitors of his acquaintance. To those he did not know he extended invitations through the courtesy of Marx's grandchildren he met on the way. And finally, in the early spring of 1928, nearly all the known children of Lieutenant Schmidt gathered in a

Moscow saloon near the Sukharev Tower. The quorum was rather large—it developed that Lieutenant Schmidt had thirty sons, ranging in age from eighteen to fifty-two years, and four daughters, rather silly, rather old, rather unprepossessing.

In a short introductory speech Balaganov expressed the hope that the brothers would reach an understanding and would finally work out a pact, the necessity of which was dictated by life itself.

According to Balaganov's project, the entire Union of the Republics should be divided into as many exploitational districts as there were delegates. Each district was to be granted in fee simple to each of the children for ninety-nine years. No member of the fraternity had the right to cross the borders and invade the territory unassigned to him for purposes of profit.

No one objected to the new principles with the possible exception of Panikovsky, who even then had announced that he could manage to live without a pact. However, during the division of the land most disgraceful scenes developed. The high contracting parties called each other names from the very first minute and addressed each other exclusively with insulting epithets.

The argument was caused by the distribution of districts.

No one wanted to take university centers; no one wanted to take the well-known prospects of Moscow, Leningrad and Kharkov. All of them were unanimous in refusing the German Republic along the Volga.

"What's the matter? What's wrong with that republic?" Balaganov asked innocently. "It seems a very good place to me. The Germans, a cultured people, cannot fail to lend a helping hand."

"You don't say!" cried the excited children. "Try and get something out of the Germans!"

It seems that more than one member of the gathering had been imprisoned by the suspicious German colonists.

"I shouldn't mind taking it in installments if I could afford to, but I need it all immediately."

Balaganov wanted to jest about the last remark, but raising his eyes to Ostap, he stopped short. Before him sat an athlete with the regular features of a face stamped on a coin. A slender white scar cut his tanned throat. His eyes glistened with austere joy.

Balaganov suddenly sensed an irresistible impulse to spring to attention. He even had the desire to clear his throat, as happens with people of middling responsibility when conversing with one of the high-placed comrades. And actually clearing his throat, he asked in embarrassment:

"Why do you need so much money. . . . And right away?"

"As a matter of fact, I need more," said Ostap. "Five hundred thousand is my minimum. Five hundred thousand genuine rubles for orientation. I want to go away, Comrade Shura, very far away, to Rio de Janeiro."

"Have you relatives there?" Balaganov asked.

"Why? Do I look like a man who could have relatives?"

"No, but it seemed to me . . ."

"I have no kinsmen, Comrade Shura. I'm all alone in the world. I had a father once who was a Turkish subject, but even he passed on in horrible convulsions. But that's not the point. Ever since I was a child I have wanted to go to Rio de Janeiro. You, of course, are not aware that such a city exists."

Balaganov mournfully shook his head. Of the world homes of culture, in addition to Moscow, he knew only Kiev, Melitopol and Zhmerinka. And anyway he was convinced that the earth was flat.

Ostap flung on the table a page torn out of a book.

"This is a clipping from the Little Soviet Encyclopedia. Listen to what it says here about Rio de Janeiro: 'Population one million three hundred and sixty thousand' . . . So . . . 'a considerable number of mulattoes . . . at the large bay in

The distant Eastern districts, sunk in sands, enjoyed also a very bad reputation. They were accused of being ignorant, and of being unfamiliar with the fame of Lieutenant Schmidt.

"Do you take me for a fool!" Panikovsky screamed. "Let me have the central Russian plateau and I'll sign the pact!"

"How's that? All of the plateau?" Balaganov taunted. "And why not add Melitopol, or perhaps Bobruisk?"

At the mention of Bobruisk the entire convention moaned painfully. Everybody was ready to go to Bobruisk immediately. Bobruisk was considered a splendid, highly cultured place.

"Well, if not all of the plateau," insisted the greedy Panikovsky, "then half of it. After all, I am a family man; I have two families."

But he didn't get even half of it.

After prolonged cries it was decided to distribute the districts by lot. Thirty-four pieces of paper were cut and on each one a geographical name was inscribed. Fruitful Kursk and dubious Kherson, almost untouched Minusinsk and almost hopeless Ashkhabad, Kiev, Petrozavodsk and Chita—all the republics, all the districts lay in somebody's rabbit hat with ear muffs and waited for its master.

Joyous exclamations, dull groans and oaths accompanied the drawing of the lots.

Panikovsky's evil star exerted its influence on the course of affairs. He was rewarded with the fruitless and vengeful republic of the Volga Germans. Beside himself with anger, he nevertheless signed the pact.

"I'll go!" he cried. "But I warn you that should the Germans treat me unkindly I'll violate the pact! I'll cross the border!"

Balaganov, who drew the golden Arbatov district close to the German republic, became disturbed and immediately announced that he would not tolerate any violation of exploitational norms.

"And you yourself, Bender, saw how this viper has violated the pact," Shura Balaganov finished his exposition. "He's been crawling about my district for some time, but I haven't been able to catch him until just now."

Contrary to the narrator's expectations, Panikovsky's wicked act evoked no censure from Ostap. Bender sprawled on his chair, looking idly before him. On the high rear wall of the restaurant garden trees were drawn, thick-leaved and regular like on pictures in text books. There were no real trees in the garden, but the shadow of the wall yielded sufficient coolness to satisfy the citizens. All of these were evidently members of trade unions because they drank only beer and ate not a thing.

To the gates of the garden, constantly groaning and spitting, drove up a green automobile on the door of which was written a white, arched sign: "Hey, let's ride!" Below it was the tariff: three rubles an hour; other terms by agreement. There were no passengers in the machine.

The beer-drinkers began to whisper anxiously. For about five minutes the chauffeur looked pleadingly through the garden wicket. Then, evidently losing all hope of securing a passenger, he cried out with the defiance of desperation:

"The taxi is free! Please take a seat!"

But none of the citizens expressed any desire to sit down in the automobile "Hey, let's ride!" As a matter of fact, the very invitation of the chauffeur affected them strangely. They sulked and attempted not to look in the direction of the automobile. The chauffeur shook his head and slowly drove away. The doleful glances of the Arbatovites followed in his wake. Five minutes later the green automobile sped madly past the garden in the opposite direction. The chauffeur jumped up and down in his seat and cried something unintelligible. The automobile was as empty as ever.

Ostap followed it with his glance and said:

"So then, Balaganov, you are a fop. Don't be offended. I

merely want to indicate the place that y the sun."

"Go to the devil!" Balaganov said rudel

"So you have taken offense after all. In ot ing to you the occupation of being a lieute foppery."

"But you yourself are a son of Lieut Balaganov cried out.

"You are a fop," Ostap repeated. "And And your children will be fops. Don't be a curred this morning is not even an episode incident, the caprice of an artist, a gentle a ten-spot. It's not in my character to res tricks. And what sort of a profession is it, A son of Lieutenant Schmidt! Very well, year. All right, two! But then what? Then will begin to get thin and you'll simply be

"What am I to do then?" Balaganov wor to find my daily bread?"

"You must think," Ostap replied severely am fed by ideas. I don't stretch my paw fo of some Executive Committee. My aim is h I see that you are in love with money for i me, what sum would appeal to you?"

"Five thousand," Balaganov answered pro

"A month?"

"A year."

"In that case, our ways part right here. I thousand, and, if possible, immediately an ments."

"Wouldn't you take it in installments?" vindictively.

Ostap looked attentively at his interlocutor seriousness:

the Atlantic Ocean' . . . Here, here! . . . 'in the wealth of stores and the grandeur of buildings its main streets rival those of the largest cities of the world.' Can you imagine that, Shura? Rival! Mulattoes, bay, export coffee! In other words, coffee dumping. A charleston entitled 'My Girl Has A Little Thing,' and . . . But what's the use of talking? You can see for yourself what's going on. One and a half million people, and all of them to a man in white trousers. I want to go away from here. In the course of the last year grave differences have developed between the Soviet government and me. The government wants to build socialism but I am not interested. The building of socialism bores me. What am I—a stone mason? A stone mason in a white apron? . . . Now do you understand why I need so much money?"

"But where will you get five hundred thousand?" Balaganov asked quietly.

"Wherever you like," Ostap answered. "Show me a rich man and I'll take his money away from him."

"What! Murder?" Balaganov asked in a quieter voice than ever and glanced at neighboring tables where the Arbatovites were drinking each other's health.

"Do you know," Ostap said, "you shouldn't have signed that so-called Sukharev pact. That mental exercise, it seems to me, has exhausted you frightfully. You are becoming sillier before my very eyes. Note this: Ostap Bender never killed anyone. He has been killed. That happened. But he himself is pure before the law. I admit that I'm no cherub, of course. I have no wings. But I respect the criminal code. This is my weakness."

"But how do you propose to take the money away?"

"How do I propose to take it away? The taking away or the expropriation of moneys varies according to circumstances. I personally have four hundred comparatively honest means of expropriation. But that's not the point. The point is that nowadays there are no rich people. And herein lies the whole horror of my situation. Another man would, of course, attack some defenseless organization. But that is not within my rules. You are aware of my respect for the criminal code. And it doesn't pay to rob a collective. Give me a rich individual. But he's not to be had, that sort of an individual."

"Come on," Balaganov exclaimed. "There are very wealthy people."

"But do you know them?" Ostap said immediately. "Can you give me the name and exact address of one Soviet millionaire? And yet they exist! There must be some! As long as any type of coinage wanders over the country, then there must be people who have a lot of it. But how can I find such a clever fellow?"

Ostap sighed. Apparently the dreams about a rich individual had been disturbing him for a long time.

"How pleasant it would be," he remarked thoughtfully, "to work with a legal millionaire in a well-organized bourgeois state with ancient capitalistic traditions! There a millionaire is a popular figure. His address is known to everybody. He lives in a private house somewhere in Rio de Janeiro. You go to him to keep an appointment, and in the hall itself, after the very first greetings, you take some money away from him. And all of this, bear in mind, is done in a kindly way, politely: 'Hello, sir. Excuse me, I'll have to trouble you a bit. All right. That's all.' And that *is* all! Culture. What could be simpler? A gentleman in the society of other gentlemen transacts his little business. Only you must not fire at the chandeliers. That's not necessary. But with us . . . God, God, what a cold country we live in! With us everything is secret, everything is underground. Even the Commissariat of Finance with its all-powerful taxing apparatus cannot find a Soviet millionaire. And yet the millionaire may be sitting at this very moment in this so-called summer garden, at the adjoining table, and drinking a forty-kopek bottle of Tip Top beer. That is what hurts!"

"In other words," Balaganov asked after a pause, "it is your opinion that if such a secret millionaire could be found, then . . ."

"Don't continue. I know exactly what you want to say. No, not that. Nothing of the kind. I will not choke him with a pillow, or beat him over the head with a black jack. And in general there will be no foolishness. Oh, if I could only find such an individual! I'll arrange things so well that he'll bring his money to me himself, on a little saucer with a blue border."

"That's very good," Balaganov smiled incredulously. "Five hundred thousand on a little saucer with a blue border!"

He rose and began to walk around the table. He clicked his tongue mournfully, stopped, opened his mouth as if wanting to say something. Saying nothing, he sat down, but again rose to his feet. Ostap followed Balaganov's convolutions with perfect equanimity.

"He'll bring it himself?" Balaganov asked suddenly in a screechy voice. "On a little saucer? But suppose he doesn't bring it? And where is that Rio de Janeiro? Is it far? It's impossible that all should wear white trousers! Don't try to tell me that, Bender! On five hundred thousand you can live well, even here."

"I don't doubt it, I don't doubt it," Ostap said gayly. "It's possible to live on it. But don't count your chickens before they're hatched. You haven't got the five hundred thousand."

A deep wrinkle marked the placid, unplowed brow of Balaganov. With uncertainty he glanced at Ostap and muttered:

"I know such a millionaire. Something may come of this."

In a flash Bender's face lost its liveliness. It hardened immediately and again assumed the contours of a coin.

"Go on, go on," he said. "I apply only on Saturdays. Don't waste my time."

"Word of honor, Monsieur Bender . . ."

"Listen, Shura, if you have definitely decided to use the

French language, then don't call me *monsieur* but *citoyen*, which means "citizen." By the way, what is your millionaire's address?"

"He lives in Chernomorsk."

"Why, of course, just as I thought. Chernomorsk! There, even in pre-war days they called a man with ten thousand a millionaire. While now . . . I can well imagine! No, that's nonsense!"

"But no, let me tell you. This is a genuine millionaire. You see, Bender, not long ago I had the occasion to spend some time in the local house of correction . . ."

Ten minutes later the foster brothers left the coöperative summer garden in which beer was served. The great schemer felt like a surgeon on the eve of a very serious operation.

"That's just my luck," Bender said, his eyes shining. "I must begin an enterprise of millions with a painful lack of cash on hand. All of my capital for investment, operation and reserve is represented by five rubles. . . . What did you say was the name of your underground millionaire?"

"Koreiko," Balaganov answered.

"Yes, yes. Koreiko. A splendid name. But are you certain that no one knows about his millions?"

"No one besides myself and Pruzhansky. But Pruzhansky, as I have already told you, will sit in jail for another three years. If you could only see how he worried and wept when I was getting released. He seemed to feel that I should not tell anyone about Koreiko."

"The fact that he disclosed the secret to *you* is nonsense. That isn't why he worried and wept. What he evidently sensed was that you would tell *me* about it. And that is really a direct loss for poor Pruzhansky. By the time Pruzhansky gets out of jail, Koreiko will be finding solace in the banal proverb: Poverty is no sin."

Ostap flung off his summer cap and swinging it in the air asked:

"Have I any gray hair?"

Balaganov pulled in his stomach, moved his toes apart to the width of a rifle butt, and in the voice of the soldier on the right flank, replied:

"No, sir!"

"There will be! Great battles are ahead of us. You, too, will become gray, Balaganov!"

Suddenly Balaganov giggled in a silly manner:

"How did you put it—he'll bring it to you himself on a little saucer with a blue border?"

"For *me* on a little saucer," Ostap said. "For *you* on a little plate."

"But how about Rio de Janeiro? I want to have white pants too."

"Rio de Janeiro is the delicate dream of my childhood," the great schemer answered severely. "Don't you touch it with your dirty paws. Now, to business! Send the troops of the line for my disposal. The military units must arrive in the city of Chernomorsk in the shortest possible time. Service uniforms. Bugle 'advance'! I will command the parade!"

Chapter Three

YOUR GASOLINE——OUR IDEAS

O NE year before Panikovsky violated the pact by penetrating into someone else's exploitational territory, the
first automobile had appeared in Arbatov. The founder of the
automobile business was a chauffeur by the name of Kozlevich.

He was brought to the steering wheel by his decision to
begin a new life. Adam Kozlevich's life had been full of
iniquity. He had continually violated the criminal code of the
R.S.F.S.R., and particularly Article CLXII which deals with
the secret seizure of the property of others (theft).

This article has many paragraphs. But sinful Adam had
nothing to do with Paragraph A (theft committed without
the application of any or sundry technical means). This was
altogether too primitive for him. Paragraph E, which punished with loss of liberty up to five years, did not appeal to
him either. He did not relish the prospect of wasting too
much time in prison. And because since childhood he had
been technically inclined, he devoted himself with all his
heart to Paragraph C (the secret seizure of the property of
others committed with the application of technical means,
either repeatedly or after preliminary agreement with other
persons on railway stations, docks, steamships, trains, and in
hotels).

But Kozlevich met with disaster. He was caught whenever
he applied his beloved technical means, and also when he
managed without them. He was caught on railway stations,
docks, on steamships and in hotels. On trains he was also

caught. He was caught even when, in utter desperation, he began to appropriate the property of others after previous agreement with other persons.

Having spent the sum total of three years in prison, it began to occur to Adam Kozlevich that it is more convenient to occupy oneself with the open accumulation of one's own property rather than with the secret seizure by appropriation of the property of others. This brought solace to his stormy soul. He became a model prisoner, began to write self-castigating verses for the prison newspaper "The Sun Rises And Sinks," [1] and assiduously worked in the machine shop of the house of correction. The penitentiary system produced a beneficial effect on him. Kozlevich, Adam Kazimirovich, 46 years old, by descent a peasant of the former Chenstokhov county, single, repeatedly arraigned, came out of prison an honest man.

After two years of work in a Moscow garage, he bought by accident an automobile so old that its appearance on the market could be explained only by the liquidation of an automobile museum. This rare specimen was sold to Kozlevich for one hundred and ninety rubles. For some strange reason, an artificial palm in a green tub was offered with the automobile. So he bought the palm also. He didn't mind the palm so much, but he had a lot of trouble with the automobile. He had to find missing parts at the bazaars, patch up the seat, install a new electrical system. The overhauling was crowned by painting the machine a lizard green. The make of the machine was unknown, but Adam Kozlevich insisted that it was a Lauren-Dietrich. As proof, he attached to the radiator of the automobile a small brass plate with a Lauren-Dietrich insignia. All he had to do now was to realize his fond dream and go into the car-for-hire business.

On the very day that Adam Kozlevich decided to bring his child out into the world for the first time, a sad event affected

[1] This is the first line of a famous Russian prisoners' song. C. M.

all the private chauffeurs. A hundred and twenty small black
Reno taxis that looked like Browning guns arrived in Moscow.
Kozlevich did not even attempt to compete with them. He
left the palm for safekeeping in the izvozchik's tearoom "Ver-
sailles" and went to work in the provinces.

Arbatov, devoid of automobile business, appealed to our
chauffeur as a virgin field, and he decided to settle there for
life.

Adam Kazimirovich imagined how lovingly, happily, and
principally how honestly he would work in the field of auto
hire. He imagined how early of an arctic morning he would
be on watch at the railroad station awaiting the Moscow
train. Tucked in a red cowhide, the aviator's goggles lifted
on his brow, he would amicably treat the porters to cigarettes.
Far in the back, the freezing drozhky drivers huddled together. They wept with the cold and shivered in their thick
blue-skirted coats. But lo! he hears the alarm of the station
bell. This gives him notice of the train's arrival. The passengers come out on the station platform and with pleased expressions on their faces stop before the machine. They had not
expected that the idea of auto hire had penetrated into the
wilds of Arbatov. Honking his horn, Kozlevich would speed
his passengers to the House of the Peasant.

There is work for the entire day. Everybody is glad to take
advantage of the services offered by the mechanical equipage.
Kozlevich and his loyal Lauren-Dietrich are indispensable
participants in all the city's weddings, excursions and celebrations. But most of the work is in the summer. On Sundays
entire families go out of the city in Kozlevich's car. The innocent laughter of children resounds. The wind tugs at scarves
and ribbons. Women chatter gayly. Fathers of families gaze
with respect at the leather back of the chauffeur and ask him
about the condition of the automobile business in the United
States of North America. (Is it true, by the way, that Ford
buys himself a new car every day?)

This is how Kozlevich imagined his splendid new life in Arbatov. But in the shortest space of time the aircastle constructed by Adam Kazimirovich's imagination, with all its turrets, drawbridges, weathercocks and banners, crashed.

In the beginning it was the train schedule that played him false. Extra-fare and express trains passed by the station of Arbatov without stopping, snatching the mail bag off the rod at full speed and dropping only special mail. The ordinary trains came only once a week. For the most part they brought the less important people, pilgrims and other foot passengers. As a rule the ordinary passengers did not use the automobile. There were no excursions or celebrations, and Kozlevich was not invited to the weddings. For marriage ceremonies the Arbatovites were accustomed to hire izvozchiks who, on such occasions, would weave paper roses and chrysanthemums into the horses' manes. This appealed especially to the donor of the bride.

There was however a multitude of town jaunts, but they were not the kind imagined by Adam Kazimirovich. There were neither children, nor fluttering scarves, nor gay chatter.

On the very first evening, illumined by the dim kerosene street lamps, four men approached Adam Kazimirovich who had spent a fruitless day standing at the Spaso-Coöperative Square. They stared at the automobile long and silently. Finally one of them, a hunchback, asked hesitatingly:

"Can anybody ride?"

"Anybody," replied Kozlevich, surprised at the timidity of Arbatov's citizens. "Five rubles an hour."

The men began to whisper. The chauffeur heard passionate sighs and the words: "Comrades, shall we take a ride after the conference? But is it quite all right? A ruble twenty-five per man is not high. Why isn't it all right?"

And for the first time the roomy machine took Arbatovites unto its calico bosom. For several minutes the passengers were silent, crushed by the speed of movement, by the hot odor of the gasoline and the whistling of the wind. Later, plagued by a dim foreboding, they began to sing quietly: "Swift as the waves are the days of our life." [2] Kozlevich increased his speed. The machine dashed out past houses into a clear field, into moon-drenched spaciousness.

"Every day ever shorter the path to our grave," the passengers chanted lugubriously. They began to pity themselves and to regret that they had never been college students. They performed the chorus with sonorous voices:

"A glass apiece, a little glass, tirlim-bom-bom, tirlim-bom-bom."

"Stop!" the hunchback cried suddenly. "Turn back! My soul is aflame!"

In town the occupants of the car secured a number of colorless bottles that looked like rolling pins and a broad-shouldered townswoman. They made a bivouac in a field, drank vodka with their supper, and then, without music, danced a coquettish polka.

Wearied by the adventures of the night, Kozlevich dozed all day over the wheel at his stand. Toward evening the same company appeared, already gay, again sat down in the machine and drove all around town throughout the night. The same thing was repeated on the third day. The night revelries of the gay company under the leadership of the hunchback continued for two weeks on end. The joys of motoring exerted a strange influence on Adam Kazimirovich's clients: their faces became swollen and white in the darkness, like pillows. The hunchback with a piece of sausage hanging from his mouth resembled a werewolf.

They became fidgety and at times would weep in the midst of their revelry. On one occasion the mischievous hunchback brought a sack of rice in a droshky to the automobile. At dawn they took the rice to a village, exchanged it for very strong home brew, and throughout that day did not return

[2] The first line of a famous pre-Revolutionary student drinking song. C. M.

to the city. They drank eternal friendship with the muzhiks, sitting on hayricks. At night they lighted camp fires and wept with particular mournfulness.

On the following gray morning the Railroad Workers' Co-operative "Lineyets," of which the hunchback was manager and his gay comrades members of the managing board and the store commission, closed down to take stock of the merchandise. To the bitter surprise of the inspectors, they found in the store neither flour nor pepper nor the soap that should have been there, nor the troughs of the peasants nor textiles nor rice. Shelves, counters, boxes and vats—everything was stripped. Only, on the floor in the middle of the store, two gigantic hunting boots, size 49, with yellow cardboard soles, stretched forth to the ceiling; and dimly gleaming in a glass cage was an automatic National Cash Register like the nickeled bust of a lady sewn with multi-colored buttons. As for Kozlevich, he found in his room a notice from the People's Investigator; the chauffeur was asked to appear as a witness in the case of the Lineyets Coöperative.

The hunchback and his friends appeared no more, and the green machine was idle for three days.

The new passengers, like their predecessors, appeared under the cover of darkness. They also began with an innocent jaunt out of town, but the thought of vodka struck them before the automobile had made its first half-kilometer. Evidently the Arbatovites could not imagine how one could use an automobile while sober, and considered the horseless carriage of Kozlevich a nest of lechery in which one must perforce behave boisterously amid unnecessary cries and generally lead a fast life.

Only then did Kozlevich understand why the men who passed his stand in the daytime would wink at each other and smile unpleasantly.

Everything went on contrary to Adam Kazimirovich's presuppositions. Throughout the nights he sped with lighted headlights past the surrounding groves, hearing behind him the drunken racket and the wails of his passengers, while in the daytime, drunk from lack of sleep, he would sit in the offices of investigators in the capacity of a witness. The Arbatovites, for some reason, lived their fast lives on moneys that belonged to the government, to the public and to the co-operatives. And again, against his will, Kozlevich sank into the morass of the criminal code, into the world of the third chapter, which edifyingly instructs about the crime of embezzlement.

The trials began. In all of them Adam Kazimirovich appeared as the chief witness for the prosecution. His truthful stories would knock the defendants off their feet, causing them to choke and snivel and confess to everything. He annihilated a multitude of establishments. His last victim was the branch of the District Motion Picture Organization which was filming in Arbatov the historical film "Stenka Razin and the Princess." The entire branch was tucked away for six years, while the film, which was merely of legal interest, was turned over to the Museum of Material Evidence, which already contained the hunting boots from the Lineyets Co-operative.

Then came the crash. People began to fear the green automobile like the plague. The citizens would walk far away from the Spaso-Coöperative Square on which Kozlevich had erected a striped post with a sign: "Automobile Exchange." In the course of several months Adam did not earn a kopek and lived on the savings made in the course of the nocturnal jaunts.

Then he decided to make a sacrifice. On the door of the automobile he traced a white inscription that seemed to him exceedingly enticing: "Hey, let's ride!" and lowered the price from five to three rubles an hour. But even then the citizens did not change their tactics. The chauffeur would

wheel his car slowly through the city, would ride up to establishments and shout at the window:

"What fine air! Come on, let's take a ride!"

Official persons would stick their heads out into the street
and through the thunder of Underwoods would reply:

"Ride yourself, cutthroat!"

"But why a 'cutthroat'?" Kozlevich would expostulate, on
the verge of tears.

"Cutthroat you are!" the office workers would answer.
"You'll trick us into a special session of the court!"

"Ride on your own!" the chauffeur shouted vehemently.
"On your own money!"

At these words the official personages would look at each
other humorously and close the window. A jaunt in an automobile on one's own money seemed utterly ridiculous to
them.

The owner of "Hey, let's ride!" quarreled with the entire
city. He wasn't even on bowing terms with anybody, became
irritable and increasingly angry. Beholding some Soviet official in a long Caucasian shirt with sleeves like rubber bulb
syringes, he would drive up behind him and shout with bitter
laughter:

"Swindlers! In a jiffy I'll get you into an exhibition trial [3]
according to Article 109!"

The Soviet official would quiver, nonchalantly adjust his
belt, studded with the silver trinkets which usually decorate
the harness of truck horses, and, making believe that the
shouts did not apply to him, would quicken his pace. But the
vengeful Kozlevich would ride at his side and would tease
his enemy with a monotonous reading from a pocket edition
of the criminal breviary:

[3] An exhibition trial is an open court trial, elaborately staged, for the par-
tial purpose of making a public example of the prisoners at the bar. Recent
famous trials of this kind were the Shakhty trial in the summer of 1928, a
trial of a group of engineers headed by Ramzin in November, 1930, and the
trial of the Mensheviks early in 1931. C. M.

"The appropriation by official persons of money, valuables or other property under his stewardship, in accordance with his official position, is punishable . . ."

The Soviet official would make a futile gesture and a cowardly escape.

"Imprisonment," Kozlevich would shout after him, "for a term up to three years."

But whatever satisfaction this may have brought to the chauffeur, was merely of the moral variety. His financial affairs were in a bad way. His savings were drawing to an end. He had to take steps. Things could not go on in this way.

One day when prospects seemed blackest Adam Kazimirovich sat in his machine looking with disgust at the foolish striped post that supported the "Automobile Exchange." He began to understand dimly that an honest life had not profited him, that the Messiah of Motoring had come before his time, and that the citizens refused to believe in him. Kozlevich was so sunk in his mournful ruminations that he did not even notice the two young men who had been admiring his machine for some time.

"An original construction," one of them said finally. "The dawn of motoring. Do you see, Balaganov, what can be made out of a simple Singer Sewing Machine? A slight adaptation— and you would have an excellent bailing machine for a collective farm."

"Go away," Kozlevich said sullenly.

"What do you mean 'Go away'? Why then did you brand your threshing machine with the invitation, 'Hey, let's ride!'? Perhaps my friend and I desire to make a business journey, or perhaps we desire precisely to 'Hey, let's ride!'"

For the first time in the Arbatov period of his life a smile appeared on the face of the martyr to motoring. He jumped out of the machine and adroitly cranked the heavily knocking motor.

"If you please," he said. "Where may I take you?"

"This time, nowhere," Balaganov remarked. "There is no money. Can't do anything about it, Comrade Mechanic. Sheer poverty."

"Never mind, get in!" Kozlevich cried out in desperation. "I'll take you for nothing. Promise only not to drink, not to dance naked by moonlight. Hey, let's ride!"

"Well, what do you say? Let's accept this hospitality," Bender said, sitting down next to the chauffeur. "I can see that you are an excellent fellow. But what makes you think that we are capable of dancing in the nude?"

"They're all like that here," answered the chauffeur, bringing his machine out into the main street. "Federal criminals."

He longed to unburden his grief-laden heart to someone. Best of all, of course, would have been to tell of his sufferings to his tender, wrinkled mother. She would pity him. But, unfortunately, Madame Kozlevich had died of grief when she learned that her son Adam had begun to acquire fame as an habitual thief. So the chauffeur told his new passengers the entire history of the fall of the city of Arbatov, under the ruins of which at this very moment, floundered his green automobile.

"Where can I go now?" Kozlevich finished mournfully. "Where shall I turn?"

Ostap deliberated, looked significantly at his redheaded companion and said:

"All of your troubles come from your being a truth-seeker. You are a lamb, almost a Baptist. It's very sad to notice among chauffeurs such decadent moods. You have an automobile, yet you don't know where to go. Our affairs are worse off—we have no automobile. Nevertheless we know where to go. Would you like to go with us?"

"Where?" asked the chauffeur.

"To Chernomorsk," Ostap said. "There we have a small, intimate business. We'll find work for you, too. In Chernomorsk antiques are appreciated and people are pleased to ride in them. What do you say?"

At first Adam Kazimirovich merely smiled as if he were a widow who had lost all faith in life. But Bender was not stingy with the paint. He unrolled before the embarrassed chauffeur wonderful vistas and right there painted them in pink and azure colors.

"While in Arbatov you have nothing to lose but your spare chains," he argued. "You'll not go hungry on the road; this is my responsibility. The gasoline is yours, the ideas are ours."

Kozlevich stopped the machine and, still objecting, said sullenly:

"There's not enough gasoline."

"Is there enough for sixty kilometers?"

"There's enough for eighty."

"In that case, everything is in order. I've already informed you that I never have a dearth of ideas and thoughts. Precisely at the end of sixty kilometers, directly on the road, a large iron barrel of aviation gasoline will wait for you. Do you like aviation gasoline?"

"I like it," Kozlevich replied, blushing.

Life suddenly seemed to him easy and gay. He wanted to go to Chernomorsk immediately.

"And what's more," Ostap concluded, "you will receive this barrel completely gratis. I'll say more: they will beg you to accept this gasoline."

"What gasoline?" Balaganov whispered. "What are you raving about?"

Ostap glanced with utter contempt at the orange freckles scattered over the face of his foster-brother and coolly answered:

"It is the moral duty of every citizen to kill on the spot people who do not read newspapers. They are utterly unnecessary. I grant you your life only because I hope to re-educate you."

Ostap did not explain the connection between the reading of newspapers and the large barrel of gasoline which presumably lay on the road.

"I hereby announce the opening of the great automobile race from Arbatov to Chernomorsk," Ostap said solemnly. "I appoint myself commander of the race. The driver of the machine is . . . what is your name? . . . Adam Kozlevich. I appoint Citizen Balaganov to the position of mechanic and upon the latter are placed all duties of servicing. Only, my dear Kozlevich, the sign 'Hey, let's ride!' must be immediately blocked out. We are in no need of distinguishing marks."

Two hours later the machine, a fresh dark green spot on its side, slowly rolled out of the garage and for the last time drove through the streets of the city of Arbatov. Hope gleamed in the eyes of Kozlevich. At his side sat Balaganov. With a little rag he fussily polished the brass parts, conscientiously carrying out his new duties of mechanic. The commander of the race sprawled in the rusty seat, glancing from time to time with satisfaction at his new subordinates.

"Adam!" he cried, outshouting the grinding of the motor. "What do you call your wagon?"

"Lauren-Dietrich," Kozlevich answered.

"That's a hell of a rotten name! An automobile, like a battleship, must have its own name. Your Lauren-Dietrich is distinguished by remarkable speed and a noble beauty of line. Therefore I propose that we give to the machine the name Antelope-Gnu. Any objections? Unanimous!"

The green Antelope, all its parts screeching, sped along the outer runway of the Boulevard of Youthful Talents and dashed out on the market square.

There the Antelope equipage was presented with a picture of everyday life. From the square toward the highway, bending over, ran a man with a white goose under his arm. With his left hand he pressed to his head a hard straw hat. Behind him ran a large crowd, shouting. The runaway frequently looked around and at such moments one could discern on his well-shaped actor's face an expression of horror.

"That's Panikovsky running!" Balaganov cried.

"The second stage is the theft of a goose," Ostap remarked coldly. "The third stage will begin after the culprit is caught. It is accompanied by sound thrashings."

Panikovsky had evidently surmised the approach of the third stage, because he ran with all his might. Out of sheer fright he convulsively clutched the goose, which provoked the most dire irritation on the part of his pursuers.

"The 116th Article," Kozlevich quoted by heart. "'The secret and simultaneously open seizure of large stock from the toiling agricultural or/and stock-breeding population.'"

Balaganov laughed. He was tickled by the thought that the violator of the pact would receive his just deserts.

The machine made its way to the highway, cutting through the irate mob.

"Save me!" Panikovsky cried when the Antelope caught up with him.

"God will help you," Balaganov answered, hanging out of the machine.

The automobile covered Panikovsky with clouds of raspberry dust.

"Take me!" Panikovsky pleaded with his last strength, keeping up with the machine. "I'll be good!"

The voices of the pursuers came together in one general, ominous roar.

"Shall we take the viper?" Ostap asked.

"Don't," Balaganov answered cruelly. "He'll know better next time than to violate a pact."

But Ostap had already arrived at a decision.

"Drop that bird!" he cried to Panikovsky. And, turning to the chauffeur, added, "Slow down."

Panikovsky immediately submitted. The goose rose from

the ground with displeasure, scratched itself and, as if nothing had happened, nonchalantly waddled back to the city.

"Crawl in," Ostap suggested. "The devil take you! But sin no more or I shall pull out your arms by their roots."

Panikovsky, moving his feet rapidly, caught onto the body, then fell with his stomach on the rim of the door, flung himself heavily into the car like a swimmer into a boat, and, his starched cuffs rattling, fell to the bottom.

"Full speed ahead," Ostap commanded. "The session continues."

Balaganov pressed the rubber pear, and out of the brass horn tore gay, old fashioned sounds that broke sporadically:

> "Matchish a splendid dance is
>   Ta-ra-ta . . .
> Matchish a splendid dance is
>   Ta-ra-ta . . ."

And Antelope-Gnu dashed out into the wild field to meet the barrel of aviation gasoline.

Chapter Four

AN ORDINARY LITTLE SUITCASE

A MAN without a hat, in gray canvas trousers, leather sandals, which he wore monk-fashion on his bare feet, and a white shirt without a collar, bending his head to one side, walked out of the wicket of house No. 16. Finding himself on a sidewalk of bluish stone, he stopped and said quietly:

"This is Friday. That means I must go to the station."

Having said these words, the man in sandals suddenly turned around. It seemed to him that behind his back stood a citizen with the zinc face of a snooper. But there was no one else in the Street of Little Worries.

The June morning was only beginning to form. The acacias quivered, dropping on the flat stones a cold leaden dew. The street birds twittered some gay rubbish. At the end of the street, below, beyond the roofs of the houses, flamed the molten heavy sea. Young dogs, looking around sadly and scratching with their claws, scrambled up trash cans. The hour of the janitors had passed; the hour of the milkwomen had not yet begun.

It was that interlude between five and six o'clock when the janitors, having had their fill of swinging twiggy brooms, had disappeared into their respective shacks. The city was light, clean and quiet, like the inside of a bank. At such a moment one wants to weep and believe that clabbered milk is indeed more beneficial and tastes better than vodka; but already you hear a distant thunder—the interurban trains are unloading milkwomen with their milk cans. Presently they will attack the city and on the landings of dark stair-

44

ways they will begin their customary brawls with house-wives. Workmen with lunch baskets will appear and immediately disappear within factory buildings. Smoke will break out of factory chimneys. After a while, jumping angrily up and down on night stands, a billion alarm clocks will ring out their triple alarums, while sleep-sodden Soviet employees will bellow, falling out of their crowded beds. The hour of the milkwomen will end and the hour of the office workers will begin.

But it was early yet. The office workers were still asleep. The man in sandals passed through the city, meeting almost no one in his path. He walked under the acacia trees which, in Chernomorsk, carried out certain civic functions: on some of them hung blue mail boxes with the official insignia of an envelope crossed by a streak of lightning; to others were attached little tin tubs with water for dogs.

The man in sandals arrived at the Seaside railroad station at the very moment when the milk women were coming out of it. Bumping several times against their cast-iron shoulders, he went up to the checkroom and presented a receipt. The checkroom clerk glanced at the receipt with the unnatural severity peculiar to Soviet railroad employees and immediately flung a suitcase at the man who had presented the receipt. The latter, in his turn, opened a leather purse, extracted from it with a sigh a ten-kopek piece and placed it on the baggage counter which was made out of six old rails polished by elbows.

Finding himself at the station square the man in sandals placed the suitcase on the pavement, examined it solicitously on all sides and even touched with his hands its little brief case lock. It was an ordinary little wooden suitcase covered with fabricoid.

In such trashy little suitcases slightly younger passengers keep cotton socks, two changes of *tolstofka* shirts, hair bands, trunks, a pamphlet entitled "Problems of the League of Communist Youth in the Village," and three crushed hard-boiled eggs. Moreover, in the corner there is the inevitable bundle of dirty linen, wrapped in the newspaper "Economic Life." Passengers who are older keep in such suitcases a full suit of clothes with an extra pair of checkered trousers, famous under the name "the 100th Anniversary of Odessa," suspenders on rolls, house slippers with tongues, a bottle of triple strength eau de Cologne, and a white Marseilles sheet. It must be noted that in such cases the corner contains something rolled up in "Economic Life." But this is not dirty linen; it is a pale boiled chicken.

Satisfied with the rapid examination, the man in sandals put the suitcase under his arm and entered the white tropical street car which brought him to the other end of the city—to the Eastern Railroad station. Here his activity was in direct contrast to that which he had just performed at the Seaside station. He surrendered his suitcase for safekeeping and received a receipt from the officious checkroom clerk.

Having performed these maneuvers, the owner of the suitcase left the station precisely at the time when the most exemplary office workers appeared on the streets. He lost himself in their uneven columns, which deprived his garb of all its originality. The man in sandals was an office worker, and nearly all the office workers of Chernomorsk dressed in the same indescribable fashion: a nightshirt with sleeves rolled up above the elbow, light orphan-asylum trousers, the same type of sandals or canvas slippers. No one wore hats and only rarely a cap, but for the most part there were black rearing shocks of hair and frequently a sun-flecked bald spot would gleam like a melon in a melon patch, enticing one to write at least one word on it with an indelible pencil.

The establishment in which the man with sandals worked was called HERCULES and was located in a former hotel. The swinging glass door with its brass rails pushed him into a large vestibule of pink marble. The information bureau was lo-

cated in the elevator after it had become stationary. A laughing feminine face already looked out of there. Running several
steps by inertia, the man stopped before the old doorman who
wore a cap with a golden zig-zag on its visor, and asked with
spirit:

"How about it, old man? About time for the crematory?"

"It's time, little father," the doorman answered, smiling
joyfully. "To our Soviet columbarium!"

He even waved his hands. His kindly face reflected his utter
readiness to give himself up at once to burial by fire.

It had been proposed to build in Chernomorsk a crematory
with the necessary room for urns, that is, a columbarium,
and this novelty which had been suggested by a sub-depart-
ment of the cemetery, for some reason intrigued the citizens
exceedingly. Perhaps they were amused by the new words—
crematorium and columbarium—and perhaps they were especially entertained by the thought that a man might be consumed like a log. But they always accosted all old men and
old women in streetcars and on the street with cries: "Where
are you going, old woman? Are you hurrying to the crematory?" or, "Make room for the old man. It's time for him
to go to the crematory." And strange to say, the idea of burial
by fire appealed to the old folks exceedingly, so that these
gay jokes evoked their complete approval. And in general,
conversations about death, which hitherto had been considered
improper and impolite, began to rate in Chernomorsk on a
par with anecdotes about Jewish and Caucasian life.

Circumventing at the foot of the stairs the naked marble
girl who held an electric torch in her outstretched hand, and
glancing with displeasure at the placard "The Housecleaning
of HERCULES Is About To Begin, Down with the Conspir-
acy of Silence and Shirking of Responsibility," this office
worker passed to the second floor. He worked in the financial
accounting department.

Although there were still fifteen minutes before starting

time, Sakharkov, Dreyfus, Tezoimenitsky, Muzykant, Chevazhevskaya, Kukushkind, Borisokhlebsky and Lapidus Jr. were already at their desks. They repeatedly assured each other that they were not at all afraid of the house cleaning; but recently, for some reason, they had begun to come to work as early as possible. Taking advantage of the few minutes of free time, they boisterously talked with one another. Their voices buzzed in the large hall which in former times had been the hotel restaurant. Of this they were reminded by the ceiling with carved moldings and frescoed walls on which somersaulted horribly smiling mænads, naiads and dryads.

"Have you heard the news, Koreiko?" Lapidus Jr. asked of the man who entered. "Haven't you really heard it? You don't say! I bet you'll be surprised!"

"What's the news? How do you do, comrades," Koreiko said. "How do you do, Anna Vasilyevna."

"But you can't even imagine!" Lapidus Jr. said with pleasure. "Bookkeeper Berlaga has entered an insane asylum!"

"What did you say—Berlaga? But he's perfectly sane!"

"Until yesterday he was the sanest. But beginning to-day he has become the most insane," said Borisokhlebsky. "It's a fact. His wife rang me up about it. He's in the most serious psychopathological condition—disorder of the *medulla oblongata.*"

"We ought to be surprised that all of us haven't a disorder of the same kind," old man Kukushkind remarked ominously, looking at his fellow employees through oval steel spectacles.

"Stop your croaking," said Chevazhevskaya. "You're always making people feel bad."

"Still, I'm sorry for Berlaga," responded Dreyfus, turning around on his revolving stool and facing the gathering.

The gathering silently agreed with Dreyfus. Only Lapidus Jr. smiled enigmatically. The conversation passed to the theme of the behavior of the insane. They began to speak of maniacs, and several remarkable stories about famous madmen were told.

"I, for example," exclaimed Sakharkov, "had an insane uncle who imagined himself to be simultaneously Abraham, Isaac and Jacob. Can you imagine what noise he would raise?"

"We ought to be surprised, rather," old man Kukushkind said in a tinny voice, slowly rubbing his glasses with his coat tail. "We ought to be surprised, rather, that all of us haven't yet imagined ourselves to be Abraham," the old man wheezed, "Isaac . . ."

"And Jacob?" Sakharkov asked jeeringly.

"Yes, and Jacob!" Kukushkind yelped suddenly. "And nobody else but Jacob! We live in such nervous times. . . . For example, when I worked in the banking office of Sikomorsky and Tsesarevich there was no house cleaning . . ."

At the mention of house cleaning Lapidus Jr. started, took Koreiko by the hand and led him to a tremendous window on which two Gothic knights were designed in multi-colored bits of glass.

"You don't know yet the most interesting thing about Berlaga," he whispered. "Berlaga is as healthy as a bull."

"How's that? Do you mean to say that he's not in an insane asylum?"

"No. He *is* in an insane asylum." Lapidus Jr. smiled subtly. "That's the whole point. He was simply scared of the house cleaning and decided to stay away during the troubled times. He is feigning madness. At this very moment I'm sure he is roaring with laughter. There's a smart fellow for you! I even envy him."

"What's the matter? Is there something wrong with his parents? Were they merchants or some other foreign element?"

"Of course, not only is there something wrong with his parents, but, between you and me, at one time he had a drug store. Who could have known that some day there would be a revolution? People made their way in the world as best they could; some managed to get a drugstore, and there were people who even had a factory. Personally, I don't see anything wrong with it. Who could have known?"

"He should have known," Koreiko said coldly.

"That's just what I say," Lapidus caught up the tune quickly. "There is no place for the like of him in a Soviet establishment."

And looking at Koreiko with bulging eyes, he returned to his table.

The hall had already filled with the clerks. Metallic folding rulers, gleaming like silver herrings, were pulled out of boxes. After these emerged abacuses with palmwood beads, thick books edged with pink and blue lines, and a multitude of other large and small office supplies. Tezoimenitsky tore yesterday's leaf off the calendar, and the new day began. One of the employees had already sunk his young teeth into a long sandwich of minced ham.

Koreiko also sat down at his table. Setting his tanned elbows on the writing table, he began to make entries in a current account book.

Alexander Ivanovich Koreiko, one of the least important employees of HERCULES, was a man in the last trench of youth. He was thirty-eight years old. On his red sealing wax face squatted wheaten brows over white eyes. His English-style mustache was the color of ripe grain. His face would have seemed altogether young were it not for the coarse corporal's chevrons that crossed his cheeks and neck. On the job Alexander Ivanovich carried himself like an exemplary soldier. He did not reason why, carried out orders, was indefatigable, ever ready to serve, and somewhat stupid.

"He is such a timid one," the chief of the financial accounting department would say of him. "He is a bit too humble, a bit too devoted. As soon as a subscription to a loan is announced, there he is offering a month's salary. He is the first to subscribe. And his whole salary is only forty-six rubles. I would like to know how he manages to exist on such money."

Alexander Ivanovich had a remarkable gift. With lightning speed he could multiply and divide in his mind large three-digit and four-digit figures. But this did not redeem him from the reputation of being a rather dull fellow.

"Say, Alexander Ivanovich," a neighbor would ask in the midst of his work, "how much is 836 by 423?"

"353,628," Koreiko would answer, pausing for a fraction of a second.

And the neighbor would not bother to check the result of the multiplication, for he knew that the rather stupid Koreiko never erred.

"Another man in his place would make himself a career," Sakharkov and Dreyfus and Tezoimenitsky, Muzykant and Chevazhevskaya, and Borisokhlebsky and Lapidus Jr., and the old fool Kukushkind, and even the Bookkeeper Berlaga who had run away to the insane asylum, would say. "But he is just an idiot. He'll sit here the rest of his life on his forty-six rubles."

And, of course, all of Alexander Ivanovich's fellow job-holders, and even the chief of the financial accounting department, Comrade Arnikov, and not only he, but even the chief of the entire HERCULES, Comrade Polykhayev and his personal secretary, Serna Mikhailovna, well, in a word, they would all have been exceedingly surprised if they had found out that Alexander Ivanovich Koreiko, the lowliest of clerks, for some strange reason, less than an hour ago, had dragged from one railroad station to another a suitcase in which lay neither trousers known as "the 100th Anniversary of Odessa," nor a pale chicken, nor a pamphlet entitled "The Problems of the League of Communist Youth in the Village," but ten million rubles in foreign *valuta* and Soviet coinage.

In the year 1915 Sasha Koreiko was a twenty-three-year-old idler among those who in all justice had been dubbed "retired gymnasium students." He had never graduated from the middle school, had no occupation, wandered over the boulevards and lived on his parents. His uncle, who was the executive secretary of the chief of the military district, freed him from military service and therefore he could listen without terror to the cries of the half-mad newsboy: "Latest news! Our army advancing! Thank God! Many killed and wounded! Thank God!"

In those days Sasha Koreiko imagined his future thus: suddenly, while walking along the street, in the gutter of the drainpipe covered with zinc stars, right near the wall, he would find a cherry-colored leather billfold that squeaked like a saddle. In the billfold there would be much money—two thousand five hundred rubles—and after that all would be well. He had imagined so frequently how he would find the money that he knew exactly where it would happen—on Victory of Poltava Street, in the asphalt corner created by a promontory of the house, right in the starry gutter. There his leather benefactor would lie, slightly covered with the dry blooms of acacia, and next door neighbor to a flattened cigarette butt. Sasha would go every day to Victory of Poltava Street, but to his extreme surprise he found no billfold there. He would poke the trash with his walking stick and look stupidly at the enameled sign "Tax Inspector U. M. Soloveysky" which hung over the adjoining front entrance. Then Sasha would wander home like a madman, throw himself on the red plush divan and dream of wealth, deafened by the blows of his heart and pulse. His pulses were small, spiteful, restive.

The Revolution of 1917 chased Koreiko off the plush divan. He discovered that he could become the happy heir of rich men with whom he was not acquainted. He sensed that throughout the land there was at this time a great quantity of shelterless gold, precious things, superb furniture, pictures and rugs, furs and dinner services. He simply must take advantage of the opportunity and seize this wealth—the sooner the better.

But in those days he was still young and foolish. He seized a large apartment, the owner of which had wisely departed on a French ship for Constantinople, and began to live in it openly. Throughout an entire week he accustomed himself to the rich life of the merchant who had disappeared, drank the muscat he found in the sideboard, ate with it the finest herring, dragged various bric-a-brac to the market, and was extremely surprised when he was arrested.

Five months later he left prison. He did not abandon the thought of becoming a rich man, but he understood that this enterprise required dissimulation, canniness and secrecy. He had to put on protective coloring; and that came to Alexander Ivanovich in the shape of high ocher boots, deep blue riding breeches, and the long military coat of a commissary worker.

In those unquiet times everything made by the hands of man functioned worse than formerly: houses did not protect from cold, food did not fill, electricity was turned on only on the occasion of a mass attack against deserters and bandits, the water system gave water only to the lower floors, while the streetcars did not operate at all. At the same time, the elements became angrier and more dangerous: winters were colder than formerly; the wind was stronger; and colds that formerly would lay a man up in bed for three days now killed him in three days. And young people of uncertain occupation would wander in droves through the streets, recklessly singing a song about money that had lost its value:

> "I run into an eating place,
> Not a kopek to my face,
> Change ten milli-ions for me."

Alexander Ivanovich noticed with anxiety that the moneys that he earned with great cunning turned to nothing.

Typhoid toppled people over by the thousands. Sasha traded in medicaments stolen from the government stores. The typhoid epidemic netted him five hundred million, but in a month the exchange rate converted this to five million. In sugars he made a billion. The rate of exchange turned this money to dust.

During this period one of his most successful enterprises was the stealing of the regular supply train bound for the Volga. Koreiko was the commandant of the train. The train left Poltava for Samara, but never reached Samara and never returned to Poltava. It was lost on the road without a trace. With it disappeared Alexander Ivanovich.

Chapter Five

THE UNDERGROUND KINGDOM

THE ocher boots turned up in Moscow toward the end of 1922. With them appeared a short green leather jacket lined with golden fox. The raised sheepskin collar, which at first glance resembled a quilt, protected the dashing fellow's mug and its Sebastopol whiskers from the frost. On Alexander Ivanovich's head rested a splendid curly Caucasian fur hat.

In those days Moscow was already overrun by new motors with crystal headlights. The newly-rich moved over the streets in sealskin caps and in coats lined with fur in a pretentious lyre design. Pointed Gothic boots and brief cases with the straps and handles of suitcases had become fashionable. The non-committal greeting "citizen" began to crowd out "comrade." Some young people who had quickly comprehended in what consisted the joy of life were already dancing in restaurants the one-step "Dixie" and even the fox-trot "Flower of the Sun." In the city rang out the shouts of dashing izvozchiks, and in the large house of the Commissariat of Foreign Affairs the tailor Zhurkevich was working night and day on swallow tails for Soviet diplomats about to depart abroad.

Alexander Ivanovich noted with surprise that his raiment, which in the provinces was a mark of manliness and wealth, here in Moscow appeared a remnant of antiquity and cast an inconvenient shadow on its possessor.

Two months later a new establishment under the sign "Industrial Artel Revanche" opened on the Sretensky Boulevard. The artel had two rooms at its disposal. In the first hung a portrait of the founder of socialism, Friedrich Engels, under which, smiling innocently, sat Koreiko himself in a gray English suit stitched with red silk thread. The ocher boots and the coarse whiskers had disappeared. The cheeks of Alexander Ivanovich were smoothly shaven. The production end was in the back room. There stood two oaken barrels equipped with manometers and measuring glasses, one on the floor, the other on a shelf. The barrels were connected by a thin rubber tube through which a liquid ran, gurgling importantly. When all of the liquid had passed from the upper container to the lower, a boy in felt boots would appear in the production room. Sighing in a manner not customary to children, the boy would remove the liquid from the lower barrel in a bucket, drag it to the shelf and pour it into the upper barrel. Finishing this complicated industrial process, the boy would go into the office to get warm, while gurgles would again issue from the tubing—the liquid was going along its customary way from the upper reservoir to the lower.

Alexander Ivanovich himself did not know exactly what type of chemicals were manufactured by the artel "Revanche." He had no time for chemicals. His working day was sufficiently full without them. He drove from one bank to another, negotiating resources for expanding production. In trusts he concluded agreements for the supply of chemical products and received raw materials at a standard price. He also received financial aid. The resale of the raw materials to state factories at ten times the purchase price took a good deal of his time, and much energy was also consumed by *valuta* transactions on the Black Exchange at the foot of the monument to the heroes of the battle of Plevna.

At the end of a year the banks and trusts became desirous of learning what beneficial effects the aid in finances and raw materials had had on the development of the "Industrial Artel Revanche," and whether the promising private establishment was in need of further aid. The commission, properly decorated with learned beards, arrived at the "Revanche" in three carriages. The chairman of the commission stared for a long time into the unresponsive face of Engels, and for a long time knocked with his stick on the pine counter, challenging the management and the members of the artel to come forth. Finally the door of the production room opened and before the eyes of the commission appeared a weeping boy, bucket in hand.

From conversation with the youthful representative of "Revanche," they learned that production was in full swing but that the master had not appeared for a week. The commission did not spend much time in the production room. The fluid that had gurgled so importantly in the rubber tubing, by taste, color, and chemical contents resembled ordinary water, which it actually proved to be. Having determined this astounding fact, the chairman of the commission said "H'm," and looked at the members, who also said "H'm." Then the chairman glanced at the boy with a perturbed smile and asked:

"How old are you?"

"I'm past twelve," the boy answered.

And he began to weep so profusely that the members of the commission, jostling each other, ran out to the street, found their places in the carriages, and drove away in utter embarrassment. As for the artel "Revanche"—all of its operations were entered in the books of the banks and the trusts on the account of Profit and Loss, and particularly in that division of the account which does not mention a word about profits but is entirely dedicated to losses.

The very day that the commission carried on its significant conversation with the boy in the office of "Revanche," Alexander Ivanovich Koreiko issued from a sleeping compartment of an express train in a small grape republic about three thousand kilometers from Moscow.

He opened a window in the hotel room and saw a little

town in the midst of an oasis, separated from the burning
sands by a row of poplar trees, provided with a bamboo water
system and a trashy clay fortress, and full of Asiatic noise.

The very next day he learned that the republic had begun
to build an electric power station. He also learned that there
was a constant dearth of money and that the construction on
which depended the future of the republic might have to stop.

Then the altruistic private operator decided to help the
republic. Again he sank into his ocher boots, put on a Thibetan skull cap, and taking along a swollen portfolio advanced
upon the office of the construction works.

He was not greeted with particular courtesy. But he carried
himself with due dignity, asked nothing for himself, and
emphasized principally the fact that the idea of electrifying
backward parts of the country was especially dear to his heart.

"Your construction job," he argued, "lacks money. I'll get
it."

And he proposed to organize, in conjunction with the construction of the electric power station, a subsidiary company
that would yield a profit.

"What could be simpler? We'll sell postcards with views of
the construction, and this will bring us the means of which
the construction job is in such great need. Bear in mind that
you will give nothing; you will only receive."

Alexander Ivanovich slit the air with his palm decisively.
His words were convincing. The project seemed good and
advantageous. Armed with an agreement according to which
he would receive one-fourth of all profits from the post card
enterprise, Koreiko began to work.

First of all, there was the need of operating expenses. These
had to be taken from money assigned for the construction of
the station. There was no other money in the republic.

"Never mind," he soothed the builders. "Bear in mind,
from this moment on you will only receive."

On horseback Alexander Ivanovich inspected the canyon

in which already rose the cement parallelepipeds of the future power station, and with one glance estimated the picturesqueness of the porphyry cliffs. After him, in a buggy, photographers rolled into the canyon. They surrounded the construction with jointed, long-legged tripods, hid themselves under black shawls, and for a long time clicked the shutters of their cameras. When everything had been photographed, one of the photographers dropped the shawl to his shoulders and remarked meditatively:

"It would have been better, of course, to have built the station a bit more to the left with the monastery for background. That would be much more picturesque."

It was decided to build a proper establishment as soon as possible to print the pictures. The money, as before, was taken out of the building funds. For that reason certain operations had to stop at the electric power station. But everyone consoled himself with the fact that the profits from the new enterprise would enable them to make up for lost time. The printing establishment was built in the very same canyon opposite the power station, and soon, not far from the cemented parallelepipeds of the station appeared the parallelepipeds of the printing establishment. Gradually barrels of cement, iron rods, bricks and gravel wandered from one end of the canyon to the other. Later the workmen also wandered over across the canyon, because the wages on the new construction job were better.

A half year later at all the railroad stations appeared distributing agents in striped trousers. They traded in post cards depicting the grandiose construction that was being carried on among the cliffs of the great republic. In summer gardens, theaters, cinemas, on ships and in health resorts innocent young ladies turned the glass drums of charity lotteries. Everyone who played the lottery won something, the prize being a postcard with a view of the electrical canyon.

The predictions of Koreiko came true. Profits flowed in

from all sides. But Alexander Ivanovich did not let them out
of his hands. A fourth part he took unto himself according
to agreement. He appropriated an equal amount on the pretext that he had not yet received a complete accounting from
all of his agents, while the remainder he used for developing
his charity combine.

"You have to be a good manager," he would say quietly.
"First the business must be established properly, and only
then will the real profits appear."

By this time the Marion excavator which had been removed
from the station was digging a foundation for a new printing
building. The work at the electric station stopped. No one
appeared on the construction job except photographers and
black shawls.

The business developed, and Alexander Koreiko, from
whose face never disappeared an honest Soviet smile, began
to print postcards with the portraits of cinema actors.

One evening, in accordance with the regulations of the local
Workers' and Peasants' Inspection, a commission with full
powers drove up in a quaking machine. Alexander Ivanovich
lost no time, cast a farewell glance at the crumbling foundation of the electric power station, at the grandiose structure of
the subsidiary organization, flooded with lights, and took to
his heels.

"H'm," said the chairman of the commission, poking with
his stick the cracks in the foundation. "Where is the electric
station?"

Then he looked at the members of the commission who, in
their turn, said "H'm." There was no electric station.

But in the edifice of the printing establishment the commission found work in full swing. Violet lamps gleamed and
flat printing presses conscientiously flapped their wings. Three
of them painted the canyon one color, while out of the
fourth, the multicolored one, like cards out of the sleeves of
a magician, flew postcards with the portraits of an alleged

Douglas Fairbanks in a black half-mask on the mug of a samovar tippler, of the enchanting Lya de Putti and of a nice chap with bulging eyes, famous under the name of Monte Banks.

For a long time after this memorable evening open-air exemplary trials were held in the canyon. But Alexander Ivanovich had managed to add a half a million rubles to his capital.

His small restive pulse beat as impatiently as ever. He felt that right now when the old economic system had perished and while the new was only coming to life, it was possible to amass a great fortune. But he was aware that an open struggle for wealth was unthinkable in the land of the Soviets. And with a smile of superiority he looked at the pathetic remains of the Nepmen rotting under signboards: "Sale of the Merchandise of the B. S. Lyebedev Worsted Stuffs Trust," "Brocade and Utensils for Churches and Clubs," or "Grocery Store, X. Robinson and M. Piatnitsa."

Koreiko understood that at this time only an underground trade founded on the strictest secrecy was possible. All the crises that affected the young economy benefited him. All that the government lost brought him profit. He took advantage of every error in merchandising and carried away his hundred thousand. He dealt in grain products, cloth, sugar, textiles, everything. And he was alone, all alone with his millions. In various parts of the country various, divers, large and small, smart alecks worked, but they did not know that they were working for him. Koreiko acted only through intermediaries, and he was the only one who knew the channels through which money flowed to him.

Precisely at noon Alexander Ivanovich pushed aside his current account book and began his lunch. He took out of his box a peeled white radish and ate it sedately. Then he swallowed a cold soft-boiled egg. There is no more unsavory food than cold soft-boiled eggs and an honest, happy man will never eat them. But Alexander Ivanovich did not eat; he fed himself. He did not lunch; he went through the physiological process of introducing into his organism the necessary proportions of fats, carbohydrates and vitamins.

All of the HERCULES employees topped their lunch with tea. Alexander Ivanovich, however, drank boiled water with a bit of sugar. Tea excites excessive activity of the heart and Koreiko was preciously guarding his health.

The possessor of millions resembled a boxer who is calculatingly preparing his triumph. Alexander Ivanovich wanted to be young and fresh on the day when the old order would return and he would be able to emerge from underground and fearlessly open his ordinary little suitcase. Koreiko never doubted that the old order would return. He was saving himself for capitalism.

And that no one might guess his secondary and most important life, he led a penurious existence, trying not to live beyond the means of his forty-six rubles a month income which he received for petty and tedious work in the financial accounting department decorated with mænads, naiads and dryads.

Chapter Six

ANTELOPE-GNU

THE green box with the four knaves hopped, skipped and jumped over the smoking road.

The progress of the machine was that of a swimmer in a storm. It was suddenly knocked off its course by advancing ruts, sucked into holes, flung from side to side and drenched in waves of red dust.

"Listen, student," Ostap addressed the new passenger, who by this time had recovered from his recent shock and sat with perfect equanimity next to the commander. "How did you dare to violate the Sukharev pact—that honorable agreement emulating the League of Nations?"

Panikovsky pretended not to have heard and even turned away.

"And in general," Ostap continued, "you are butter-fingered. Just a moment ago we witnessed a disgusting scene. The Arbatovites, whose goose you had filched, pursued you."

"Pathetic, insignificant people," Panikovsky muttered angrily.

"Is that so?" said Ostap. "And I suppose you regard yourself as a doctor and a social worker, or perhaps a gentleman? In that case, this is what I'll tell you: if it should ever occur to you as a genuine gentleman to make notes on your cuff, you'll have to make them with chalk."

"Why?" the new passenger snarled irritably.

"Because your cuffs are absolutely black. Is it not due to unclean habits?"

"You are a pathetic, insignificant person," Panikovsky was quick to announce.

"And you say this to me, to your savior?" Ostap asked meekly. "Adam Kazimirovich, please stop your machine for a minute. Thank you. Shura, my dear fellow, please restore the status quo."

Balaganov did not understand the meaning of *status quo,* but he gathered its significance from the intonation with which these words were uttered. Grinning fiendishly, he seized Panikovsky under the arms, dragged him out of the machine and set him down in the dust of the road.

"Student, go back to Arbatov," Ostap said dryly. "There you are eagerly awaited by the owners of the goose. We are in no need of ruffians. We ourselves are ruffians. Drive on, lad."

"I'll never do it again," Panikovsky pleaded. "I'm very nervous."

"Get down on your knees," commanded Ostap.

Panikovsky dropped to his knees as quickly as if his legs had been chopped off.

"Good," said Ostap. "Your pose satisfies me. You're accepted conditionally until the first violation of discipline and charged with the duties of a servant to everybody."

Antelope-Gnu accepted the chastened ruffian and rolled further, swaying like a funeral car.

A half hour later the machine turned into the large New Rabbit tract and without decreasing its speed drove into a village. At a log house, out of the roof of which grew a bent and branchy radio mast, a crowd had gathered. From the crowd stepped a beardless man. In his hand the beardless one held a piece of paper.

"Comrades," he shouted angrily, "I solemnly declare the meeting open! Permit me, comrades, to regard this applause . . ."

He had evidently prepared his speech and was already look-

ing back into his paper. But noticing that the machine did
not stop, he ceased.

"All to the auto club," he said hurriedly, looking at Ostap
who had just come even with him at that moment. "Let us
install the uninterrupted production of Soviet autocars. The
iron steed is coming to replace the puny peasant horse!"

And outshouting the congratulatory din of the crowd, he
yelled the final slogan:

"The automobile is not a luxury but a means of conveyance!"

With the exception of Ostap, all the Antelopians were somewhat disturbed by this solemn reception. Not understanding
a thing, they squirmed in the machine like fledgling sparrows
in a nest. Panikovsky, who generally did not like any gathering of honest people in one place, guardedly squatted down
so that the villagers glimpsed only his dirty straw hat. But
Ostap was not a bit embarrassed. He took off his white-topped
cap and responded to the greeting with a proud wave of his
head to the right and to the left.

"Improve the roads!" he shouted in farewell. "Merci for
the reception!"

And the machine again appeared on the white road that
split the large quiet fields.

"Won't they chase after us?" Panikovsky inquired anxiously. "Why the crowd? What has happened?"

"The people have simply never before seen an automobile,"
said Balaganov.

"The exchange of impressions continues," Bender remarked.
"The driver of the machine has the floor. What is your opinion, Adam Kazimirovich?"

The chauffeur pondered, frightened a foolish dog by singing the "Matchish" to the accompaniment of the back-firing
Antelope, and expressed the supposition that the crowd had
gathered on the occasion of a church holiday. "Holidays of

that sort," explained the driver of the Antelope, "frequently occur among the villagers."

"Yes," said Bender, "now I see clearly that I have happened into the society of uncultured people—that is, tramps without a higher education. Oh, children, dear children of Lieutenant Schmidt, why don't you read newspapers? They should be read. Very frequently they reveal that which is wise, good, eternal."

Ostap took out of his pocket a copy of "Izvestia," and in a sonorous voice read to the Antelope equipage a notice about the automobile race Moscow-Kharkov-Moscow.

"At present," he summed up with self-satisfaction, "we are located in the line of the auto race, approximately 150 kilometers ahead of the front machine. May I suppose you have guessed to what I am referring?"

The lower ranks of the Antelope were silent. Panikovsky unbuttoned his coat and scratched his bare chest under his dirty silk necktie.

"Do you mean that you do not understand? It seems that sometimes even the reading of newspapers does not help. Very well then. I shall express myself with greater detail, albeit this is against my rules. First, the peasants have mistaken the Antelope for the leading car of the auto race. Second, we have no objections to this designation. Moreover, we shall require all persons and organizations to give us the coöperation that is our due, emphasizing our status of leading machine. Third . . . Anyway, two points will do for you. It is perfectly clear that for a certain time we shall keep ahead of the auto race, skimming the heavy cream, the light cream, and the other densities of cream that this highly cultured enterprise may yield."

The speech of the great schemer made a tremendous impression. Kozlevich threw the most worshipful glances at the commander. Balaganov smoothed his unruly red locks with the palms of his hands and resounded with laughter. Panikovsky, anticipating the satisfactions of a safe haul, shouted: "Hurrah!"

"Well, enough emotion," Ostap said. "In view of the advancing darkness, I declare the evening open. Stop."

The machine stopped and the tired Antelopians descended to earth. In the ripening grain *kuznechiki*[1] were forging their small joys. The passengers sat down in a circle at the edge of the road, while old Antelope gasped and gurgled. From time to time convulsive shudders shook the body of the mechanical steed and from its depths issued sporadic groans.

The amateurish Panikovsky started such a huge campfire that it looked like a village aflame. Roaring, the fire flung itself on all sides. While the travelers attacked the column of flame, Panikovsky, bending low, ran out into the field and returned, holding in his hand a warm, crooked cucumber. Ostap quickly snatched it from Panikovsky.

"Don't make a cult of eating!"

Whereupon he ate the cucumber himself.

They supped on sausage which had been brought from home by the provident Kozlevich and fell asleep under a blanket of star dust.

"Well," said Ostap to Kozlevich at the break of dawn. "Get ready properly. Your mechanical mare has never yet beheld, and will never behold again a day like the one that is ahead of us."

Balaganov seized the neat pail inscribed "Arbatov Maternity Home" and ran to the river for water. Adam Kazimirovich lifted the apron of the machine and, whistling, sank his hands into the motor, digging into its steel intestines.

Panikovsky leaned against a wheel and, becoming pensive, looked unblinkingly at the crimson segment of the sun that was rising over the horizon. His wrinkled face was marred by a multitude of details that indicated old age—pouches, swollen veins, and strawberry spots. Such a face usually belongs to a

[1] *Kuznechiki*, literally "little blacksmiths," are grasshoppers. C. M.

man who has lived a long, decent life, has mature children, faithfully drinks acorn health coffee every morning, and signs his effusions in his establishment's wall newspaper with the pseudonym "Anti-Christ."

"Panikovsky, shall I tell you how you will die?" Ostap inquired unexpectedly.

The old man quivered and turned around.

"This is how you will die: some day you will return to a cold and dreary room in the Marseilles Hotel (that will be somewhere in a county town whither your profession has led you), and you will feel unwell. Your legs will crumple under you. Hungry and unshaven, you will lie on the wooden floor and no one will come to you, Panikovsky; no one will take pity on you. Children, most likely, you have never had because of economy; and all your wives you have abandoned. For a week you will lie in torture. Your agony will be horrible. You will be long in dying and you will be thoroughly sick of it. But before you finally die, the bureaucratic manager of the hotel will write to the department of Communal Economy about issuing a free coffin . . . what is your name and surname?"

"Mikhail Samuilovich," the astonished Panikovsky answered.

". . . about issuing a free coffin to Cit. M. S. Panikovsky. But there is no need for tears because you'll manage to drag out another year or two. Now, to business! We must take care of the cultural and agitational aspect of our campaign."

Ostap took out of the automobile his obstetrician's bag and laid it on the grass.

"My right hand," said the great schemer, patting the bag's fat little sausage-shaped side. "Here I have everything that an elegant citizen of my years and my scope of interests might need."

Bender sat down over the little suitcase like a wandering Chinese magician over his bag of enchantments and began to extract one thing after another. First he pulled out a red arm band on which was embroidered in golden letters the word "Director." Then on the grass was laid a militia cap with a badge of the city of Kiev, four decks of cards with identical backs, and a package of documents with round crimson seals.

The entire equipage of Antelope-Gnu looked with respect at the traveling bag while new objects constantly appeared out of it.

"You are innocent lambs," said Ostap. "You, of course, will never understand that an honest Soviet itinerant seeker like myself cannot get along without a doctor's apron."

Then emerged a stethoscope.

"I am not a surgeon," Ostap remarked. "I am a neuropathologist, a psychiatrist. I study the souls of my patients, and for some reason I always happen to meet foolish souls."

Then into the light of day were introduced: an alphabet for the deaf and dumb, charity postcards, enameled badges, and a poster of Bender himself in loose trousers and a turban. The poster announced:

THE SEER HAS COME

The famous Bombay Brahmin (Yogi)
son of Krepysh
favorite of Rabindranath Tagore

IOAKANAAN MARUSIDZE

(Veteran artist of the Union Republics)

Performance of Sherlock Holmes experiments. Hindu fakir. The invisible hand. Lights of Atlantis. The tent of Hell. The prophet Samuel answers all questions propounded by the audience. The materialization of spirits and the distribution of elephants.

Tickets from 50k. to 2r.

In the wake of the poster appeared a greasy turban.

"I resort to this amusement very rarely," Ostap said. "Believe it or not, such worldly people as managers of railroad clubs fall hardest for a seer. The work is easy but disgusting. Personally I loathe being the favorite of Rabindranath Tagore, while the prophet Samuel is always asked to answer the same questions: "Why is there no butter on sale?", or, "Are you a Jew?"

Finally Ostap found what he sought—a tin lacquered box, honey-colored, containing little porcelain dishes and two brushes.

"The machine that leads the race should be decorated with at least one slogan," said Ostap.

And on a long strip of yellow cotton cloth out of the same traveling bag he printed an inscription in brown:

RACE AGAINST AIMLESSNESS AND
SLOVENLINESS

The banner was fastened on two sticks to the front of the automobile. As soon as the machine started, the banner bent under the force of the wind and assumed such a cocky appearance that there was not the slightest doubt of the need to race against aimlessness, slovenliness and even against bureaucracy. The Antelope passengers assumed a dignified mein. Balaganov covered his red head with the cap which usually reposed in his pocket. Panikovsky turned his cuffs inside out and carefully displayed no more than two centimeters of them. Kozlevich was more concerned about the machine than himself. Before the departure he washed it and the sun glittered on its dented sides. The commander himself winked gayly and teased his traveling companions.

"A village to the starboard, sir!" shouted Balaganov, peering sailor-wise under the palm of his hand. "Drop anchor, sir?"

"Behind us," said Ostap, "are five first-class machines. Meeting them does not enter into our plans. Gather ye rosebuds while we may, as a certain feudal poet has remarked. Wherefore, I indicate the city of Udoyev as our stop. There the barrel of gasoline and oil will await us. Speed, Adam Kazimirovich!"

"Shall we respond to greetings?" Balaganov asked anxiously.

"Reply with bows and smiles. I forbid you to open your mouths. Otherwise the devil only knows what you might say."

The village met the leading car hospitably, but its welcome was rather unusual. Apparently the villagers had been told that someone would pass, but who, and for what reason, they did not know. Therefore, to meet any eventuality, all the slogans and catchwords prepared during the last few years had been pressed into service. Schoolboys stood along the street with divers placards: "Hail League of Time and Its Founder, Dear Comrade Kerzhentsev"; "Public Nurseries Will Give Little Tots Their Chance To Live"; "We Fear No Bourgeois Threats—We'll Answer Kurzon's Ultimatum"; "Electricity + Soap = Revolution's Hope."

Besides these were numerous placards executed principally in old Church-Slavic script with one and the same greeting: "Hearty Welcome."

All of this flashed past the travelers. This time they waved their hats with self-confidence. Panikovsky could not contain himself and, despite the ban, sprang up and shouted incomprehensible and politically illiterate greetings. But fortunately the noise of the motor and the shouts of the populace drowned it.

"Hip, hip, hurrah!" Ostap cried.

Kozlevich opened the cut-out and the machine spat an

enormous cloud of blue smoke which caused the dogs that ran after the automobile to sneeze heartily.

"How about the gasoline?" asked Ostap. "Will it last till Udoyev? We have only thirty kilometers to make. Once there we'll take everything they have!"

"It *should* last," Kozlevich answered dubiously.

"Bear in mind," Ostap said severely to his army, "I will permit no marauding, no violations of the law. Remember that I command the parade."

Panikovsky and Balaganov looked embarrassed.

"The Udoyevites themselves will give us everything we need. Mark my words. Prepare the place for the offerings."

The Antelope made the next thirty kilometers in an hour and a half. During the last kilometer Kozlevich fussed a lot, fidgeting with the throttle and shaking his head ominously. But all his efforts and the shouts and taunts of Balaganov came to nothing. The brilliant finish that Adam Kozlevich had planned was frustrated by lack of gasoline. The machine stopped shamefully in the middle of the street, a hundred kilometers from the grandstand festooned with garlands in honor of the daring motorists.

Those who had gathered there rushed with loud cries to greet the Lauren-Dietrich that had come to them from the mists of the centuries. Laurels of fame immediately fell upon the noble brows of the vanguard. Impetuous rustic hands dragged the heroes out of the machine and wrung their arms as energetically as if they had been drowned and had to be resuscitated at any cost.

Kozlevich remained at the machine, but all the others were taken to the rostrum where, according to schedule, there was to be a three-hour impromptu meeting. A young man who looked like a chauffeur squeezed his way to Ostap and asked:

"How are the other machines?"

"Lagging behind," Ostap answered indifferently. "Punctures, breakdowns, the enthusiasm of the population—all these things cause delay."

"Are you in the commander's car?" the amateur chauffeur insisted. "Is Kleptunov with you?"

"I took Kleptunov out of the race," Ostap said with displeasure.

"And Professor Dvuptikh—is he in the Packard?"

"Yes, in the Packard."

"And the woman writer—Vera Cruz?" the demi-chauffeur wondered. "I'd like to have a look at her. I'd like to see her and Arapoport. Is he also with you?"

"Do you know," said Ostap. "I'm rather tired from the race."

"Are you in the Studebaker?"

"You may consider our car a Studebaker," Ostap snapped viciously. "But until now it has been called a Lauren-Dietrich. Are you satisfied?"

But the amateur chauffeur was not satisfied.

"I beg your pardon!" he exclaimed with youthful persistence. "But there are no Lauren-Dietrichs in the race. I read in the papers that there are two Packards, two Fiats and one Studebaker."

"Go to the devil's mother with your Studebaker!" Ostap yelled. "Who is this Studebaker? Is Studebaker related to you? Is Studebaker your father? Why do you annoy a fellow like this? I tell him in plain Russian that at the last moment a Lauren-Dietrich was substituted for the Studebaker, and still he bothers me! Studebaker! Studebaker!"

Long after the young man had been pushed away by the directors Ostap still waved his hands and muttered:

"Experts! Such experts should be shot! He *will* have a Studebaker!"

He did this to forestall dangerous inquiries once and for all.

In his speech of greetings the chairman of the welcoming committee introduced so many subsidiary clauses that he could not crawl out of the maze for half an hour. Through-

out this time the commander was greatly disturbed. From the
height of the rostrum he watched the suspicious activities of
Balaganov and Panikovsky who were moving about in the
crowd with too much liveliness. He cast terrifying glances
at them and finally his signals nailed the children of Lieutenant Schmidt to one spot.

"Comrades," Ostap responded. "I rejoice in the opportunity
to violate the patriarchal peace of the city of Udoyev with an
automobile siren. The automobile, comrades, is not a luxury
but a means of conveyance. The iron steed comes to take the
place of the puny peasant horse. We must work for the uninterrupted production of Soviet automobiles. We race against
aimlessness and slovenliness. This is all, comrades. After a bite
to eat we shall continue our long journey."

While the crowd pressed around the rostrum, drinking in
the words of the commander, Kozlevich developed considerable activity. He filled his tank with gasoline which, as
Ostap had promised, proved to be of the finest quality, shamelessly acquired three large barrels of reserve oil and gas,
changed the tubes and tires on all four wheels, requisitioned
a tire pump and, for good measure, a jack, thereby exhausting
the basic and operational supplies of the Udoyev Auto Club.

There were now sufficient supplies for the run to Chernomorsk, but of course there was no money. This, however,
did not disturb the commander. At Udoyev the travelers dined
magnificently.

"There's no use thinking about pocket money," said Ostap.
"It's waiting to be picked up and we shall pick it up as
the need arises."

Between ancient Udoyev, founded in the year 794, and
Chernomorsk, founded in the year 1794, lay a thousand years
and a thousand kilometers of paved and unpaved roads.

In the course of these thousand years various figures had
passed between Udoyev and the Black Sea. Over the roads
had moved traveling clerks with the merchandise of Byzan-

tine trading firms. Out of the murmuring forest Nightingale-the-Robber had galloped against them, a rough fellow in a caracul hat. He took away their merchandise and did away with the clerks. Over this road had wandered conquerors with their retinues, muzhiks chanting their songs, pilgrims begging their way.

The life of the land altered with every century. Garb changed. Weapons improved. The potato riots were quelled.

Men learned to shave their beards. The first balloon rose. The iron twins were invented: steamship and steam engine. Automobiles honked their horns.

But the highway remained as it had been in the days of Nightingale-the-Robber.

Humped, strewn with volcanic dust as poisonous as a powder made of bedbugs, it stretched past villages, towns, factories and collective farms—stretched in a thousand versts of snares. Along its sides in the yellowing polluted grasses lay the skeletons of wagons and tortured automobiles.

Perhaps the émigré going mad selling newspapers in the asphalt fields of Paris may recollect the Russian country road with its charms: the moon sitting in a puddle, the crickets praying sonorously, and the clatter of the empty pail tied to a muzhik's cart.

But of late moonlight has received a different assignment: now it may illumine paved roads only. Automobile sirens and klaxons will replace the tympanic rattle of the peasant pail, while crickets will be heard in reservations where special rostrums will be built, and citizens, prepared by the intro-ductory speech of some old gray cricket specialist, will enjoy the singing of their favorite insects.

Chapter Seven

THE SWEET BURDEN OF FAME

THE commander of the race, the driver of the machine, the mechanic and the all-around servant were in excellent spirits.

The morning was cool. The pale sun wound its way across the pearly sky. For twenty-four hours they had been racing ahead of the auto race. They were met with music and speeches. Children beat drums for them. Adults fed them with dinners and suppers, supplied them with auto parts, and in one hamlet they were presented with bread and salt on a cross-stitched towel in a carved oaken trencher. The bread and salt lay on the floor of the machine between the feet of Panikovsky who surreptitiously nibbled a mouse hole in it. After this the meticulous Ostap threw the bread and salt on the road. The Antelopians passed the night in a little village, basking in the solicitudes of its civic leaders. From there they carried away a large pitcher of warm milk and the sweet memory of the eau de Cologne odor of the hay in which they had slept.

"Milk and hay!" Ostap philosophized when Antelope was leaving the village at dawn. "What could be lovelier? You always think—I'll have time for that yet. There will be more milk and hay in my life. As a matter of fact, it will never be again. Mark my words. This was the best night of your lives, my poor friends, and you haven't even noticed it."

Bender's fellow travelers looked at him with awe. They exulted in the prospect of their new easy life.

"It's good to be alive," said Balaganov. "Here we are riding along, eating well. Perhaps happiness is waiting for us . . ."

"Are you firmly convinced of that?" asked Ostap. "You say that happiness is waiting for you on the road? Perhaps it is even waving its wings with impatience! 'Where,' it says, 'is Admiral Balaganov? Why is he so long in coming?' You're crazy, Balaganov. Happiness waits for no one. It wanders over the lands in long white garments, singing a nursery rhyme: 'Oh, America? *That's* a country! There people have a good time and drink endlessly!' But this naïve child must be caught. Her favor must be won. You must woo her. My dear Balaganov, you will never have an affair with that child. You're a tramp. Just see what you look like. A man dressed like you will never win happiness. And in general, all members of the Antelope equipage are disgustingly equipped. I am even surprised that you are taken for participants in the auto race."

Ostap looked at his fellow travelers with pity.

The fields continued to turn slowly on either side of the machine. A large red owl that sat at the edge of the road bent its head to one side, its foolish unseeing eyes bulging. Disturbed by the creaking of the Antelope, the bird spread its wings, passed over the machine, and flew away on its dull owlish business. Nothing else worthy of attention occurred on the way.

"Look!" Balaganov shouted suddenly. "An automobile!"

Ostap ordered the banner taken down on general principles. While Panikovsky was carrying out the order, the Antelope came close to the machine.

A gray closed Cadillac stood on the edge of the road. The Central Russian countryside which was reflected in its thick polished panes looked cleaner and more beautiful than it actually was.

A kneeling chauffeur was changing a tire. Three figures in dustcoats were standing about. Ostap addressed the chauffeur politely, but the latter raised his strained face and, saying nothing, resumed his work.

The Antelopians crawled out of their lumbering stage coach. Kozlevich walked around the splendid machine several times and, sighing enviously, finally squatted next to the chauffeur and wandered away with him into the realm of mechanics. Panikovsky and Balaganov examined the passengers with childish curiosity and noted that two of them had the haughty appearance of foreigners. The third, judging by the opiating odor of rubber that issued from his dustcoat manufactured by the State Rubber Trust, was a compatriot.

"Are you in trouble?" Ostap repeated, delicately touching the rubber shoulder of the compatriot, and at the same time casting a meditative glance at the foreigners.

The compatriot began to speak irritably about a punctured tire, but his muttering was wasted on the ears of Ostap. On the highway, a hundred and thirty kilometers from the nearest district capital, in the very center of European Russia, two juicy little foreign fledglings walked around their automobile. This stirred the great schemer.

"Tell me," he interrupted. "Aren't these two from Rio de Janeiro?"

"No," answered the compatriot. "They are from Chicago. And I am their interpreter from the Intourist."

"What are they doing here in the middle of the highway, in a wild ancient field, far from Moscow, the Red Poppy ballet, the Torgsin,[1] antique stores, and the famous picture by the artist Ryepin entitled 'Ivan the Terrible Murders His Double-dealing Son'? I can't understand it! Why did you bring them here?"

"I didn't bring them here; it was they who dragged *me* here," the interpreter whined. "We've been dashing around villages for three days as if running away from a prairie fire. They've worn me out! I've had much to do with foreigners, but I've never seen any like these!" And he waved his hand

---

[1] Stores established for foreigners and others who can pay for purchases in *valuta*—that is, any non-Soviet money. C. M.

in the direction of his rosy-cheeked fellow-travelers. "Most tourists behave as we make them: they run around Moscow, buy wooden things in handicraft stores. But these two went wild! They decided to travel through villages!"

"That's laudable," said Ostap. "The broad masses of the millionaires are becoming acquainted with life in the new Soviet village."

The citizens of Chicago wore silvery gray hats, immaculate collars and gleaming ox-blood shoes.

The interpreter looked indignantly at Ostap and exclaimed:

"Go on! They don't give a rap about the village! What they're looking for is village home brew!"

At the mention of home brew, pronounced emphatically by the interpreter, the gentlemen looked around and approached the two speakers.

"You see," said the interpreter. "They know *that* much Russian! They cannot hear that word with equanimity."

"I see. There must be some mystery here," replied Ostap. "Or a perversion of taste. I don't understand how anyone can like home brew when in our country there is such a large selection of noble strong drinks."

"It is all much simpler than you think," said the interpreter. "They're on the trail of a good recipe for home brew!"

"Why, of course!" Bender cried. "They have a dry law. Now I understand. Did you get them a recipe? Oh, you didn't get it! I'll tell you what's wrong. You should have come with three more automobiles . . . Can't you see that you are taken for commissars? I can assure you that you'll never get a recipe."

The interpreter began to complain about the foreigners:

"Believe me or not, they bother the life out of me. They insist that I tell them the secret of home brew. But I'm not a bootlegger! I'm a member of the Union of Educational Workers. I have an old mother at home in Moscow."

"And do you really want to go back to Moscow, back to Mother?"

The interpreter sighed pathetically.

"In that case, let's get down to business," Bender pronounced. "How much will your patrons give for a recipe? Will they give a hundred and fifty?"

"They'll give two hundred," the interpreter whispered. "But have you really got a recipe?"

"I'll dictate it to you immediately—that is, immediately after the receipt of the money. Any kind you like—home brew from potatoes, wheat, barley, apricots, from local berries, from buckwheat grits. You can make home brew even from an ordinary chair. Some people are crazy about chair home brew. Or, if you like, we can make it ordinary *kishmishevka,* or a *slivianka.* In a word, I can give you any of the hundred and fifty home brew recipes that I know."

Ostap was presented to the Americans. For quite a while politely raised hats floated in the air. Then the business meeting began. The Americans selected wheat home brew which attracted them because of the simplicity of production and the condition of the wheat market. For a long time they were busily writing it down in their notebooks. As a free premium Ostap told the American pilgrims the best way to construct a home brew apparatus that could be hidden inside a writing desk. The pilgrims agreed with Ostap that because of America's leadership in technology it would be quite easy to construct such an apparatus.

"You see," said Ostap after they had left the American machine in a cloud of dust, "everything turned out just as I predicted. On the road we found the money. I picked it up. Look, it's not even dusty." He rustled the package of banknotes. "As a matter of fact, there's nothing to brag about. It was very simple. What appeals to me most is that it was clean and honest. Two hundred rubles! In five minutes! And not only did I show due reverence for the law, but I have rendered service—I've done some good: the Antelope equipage

is provided with wherewithal; the old mother has her interpreter son back with her; and finally, I have quenched the
spiritual thirst of two citizens of a country which, at any rate,
has trade relations with us."

Dinnertime was approaching. Ostap studied the map of
the race, which he had torn out of an automobile journal, and
announced the approach of Luchansk.

"It's a very small town," said Bender. "That's bad. The
smaller the town, the longer the speeches of welcome. Wherefore, we shall request the kind hosts of this city to give us our
dinner first and our speeches later. In the intermission I shall
provide you with all the clothes you want. Panikovsky! You
are beginning to forget your duties! Restore the banner to its
erstwhile place."

Practiced in the art by now, Kozlevich stopped with a
flourish right in front of the rostrum. Bender limited himself to a brief greeting. It was agreed to postpone the meeting
until two o'clock. Fortified by a free dinner, the motorists
went to the store of ready-made clothes in excellent humor.
With due dignity the Antelopians carried the sweet burden
of fame that had fallen on their shoulders. Hand-in-hand they
walked in the middle of the street with the swinging step of
sailors in a foreign port. Redheaded Balaganov, who actually
looked like a young boatswain, began to sing a sea chantey.
The store "Clothes for Men, Ladies and Children" was under
a huge sign that covered the entire two-story house. On the
sign were a score of figures: lemon-faced men with fur coats
and thin mustaches, ladies with muffs in their hands, short-
legged children in sailor suits, girl *Comsomols* in red ker-
chiefs, and gloomy Soviet business executives sunk up to their
hips in felt boots. Against this background was a tiny piece of
paper pasted to the entrance door of the store:

```
NO PANTS
```

"Ugh, how crude!" cried Ostap, entering. "Wouldn't you know right away that you were in the provinces! They might have written 'No Trousers' as is done in Moscow. That would have been decent and honorable, and docile citizens could return to their respective homes."

The motorists did not stay long in the store, but they performed a miracle. Armed with a special order from the local executive committee, they bought for Balaganov a cowboy shirt in large green and canary checks and a Stetson hat with ventilating holes. Kozlevich had to be satisfied with a chrome yellow cap and a corduroy coat that glistened like pressed caviar. They took a long time with Panikovsky. The store could offer him only a fireman's parade uniform—a coat with gilt pumps in the buttonholes, hairy mixed wool trousers, and a blue-bordered cap. Panikovsky objected and jumped angrily up and down before the wavy mirror.

"I don't understand," said Bender, "why you object to a fireman's suit. It is infinitely superior to the suit of a king in exile which you are now wearing. Here, turn around, my boy. Excellent! I must tell you frankly that this is more becoming than the preacher's cutaway and hat that I intended to buy you."

They went out into the street in their new outfits. Ostap did not buy himself anything.

"I really need a dinner jacket, but I can neither buy nor use it here. I shall have to wait. Am I right, friend Fire Chief?"

Ostap opened the meeting in high spirits, without suspecting the storm that was advancing on the passengers of the Antelope. He jested, told comical adventures of the road and Jewish anecdotes, which particularly appealed to his audience. The end of his speech he dedicated to an analysis of the pressing problem of the automobile situation.

"The automobile," he exclaimed sonorously, "is not a luxury but . . ."

At this moment he noticed that the chairman of the welcome committee had taken a telegram from a boy who had just run up. Pronouncing the words, "not a luxury but a means of conveyance!", Ostap bent to the left and looked over the shoulder of the chairman. What he read astounded him. He thought that he had at least a day's leeway. In a flash his consciousness registered all the villages and towns in which the Antelope had taken advantage of the means and supplies belonging to others.

While the chairman was wriggling his mustaches, making an effort to comprehend the contents of the telegram, Ostap jumped down from the rostrum and pushed his way through the crowd. The Antelope was standing at the crossroad. Luckily, the passengers were sitting in their places, thoroughly bored, waiting for Ostap to tell them when to load the gifts of the city into the machine. This usually occurred after the meeting.

Finally the chairman caught the sense of the telegram. He raised his eyes and saw the running commander.

"These are crooks!" he shouted in a pained voice.

All through the night he had labored on his speech of welcome, and now his author's pride was stung.

"At them, boys!" The chairman's cry reached the ears of the Antelopians. They jumped into action. Kozlevich started the motor and with one swing flew back into his seat. The machine lurched forward without waiting for Ostap. In the excitement it did not occur to the Antelopians that they were leaving their commander in danger.

"Stop!" cried Bender, making gigantic leaps. "When I catch up with you I'll fire all of you!"

"Stop!" cried the chairman, addressing Bender.

"Stop, fool!" shouted Balaganov to Kozlevich. "Can't you see that we've lost our chief?"

Adam Kazimirovich pressed the pedals. The Antelope screeched and stopped. The commander flung himself into the machine with the desperate cry, "Full speed!" In spite of his cool and tolerant character, he disliked physical punishment. The mad Kozlevich shot into third speed; the machine started suddenly, and Balaganov fell out of the door that suddenly swung open. All of this happened in a flash. Before Kozlevich could jam on the brakes, the shadow of the advancing mob had already fallen on Balaganov. As powerful hands were stretching toward him, the Antelope backed up and the iron hand of the commander gripped Balaganov by his cowboy shirt.

"Go like hell!" screamed Ostap.

And then the inhabitants of Luchansk realized for the first time the advantages of mechanical transportation. Rattling with all its being, the Antelope darted forward, carrying the four lawbreakers away from their just punishment.

During the first few kilometers the rogues breathed heavily. Balaganov, who was extremely solicitous about his appearance, with the aid of a hand mirror carefully examined the raspberry scratches that he had received on his face when he fell. Panikovsky trembled in his fireman's suit. He feared the vengeance of the commander. And it came immediately.

"Was it you who sped up the machine before I had time to sit down in it?" the commander asked threateningly.

"So help me God . . ." Panikovsky began.

"No. No. Don't deny it. These are your tricks. In other words, you are also a coward. I find myself in the company of a thief and a coward. Very well. I shall demote you. Until now in my eyes you have been a fire chief. From now on you shall be a common fireman." And Ostap solemnly tore the golden pumps out of the red buttonholes—one by one.

After this procedure the commander revealed to his subordinates the contents of the telegram.

"We're in a bad way. The telegram orders the stopping of the green machine that is going ahead of the auto race. We must turn off to the side immediately. We've had enough of triumphs, palm leaves and free dinners. This strategy has had its day. We cannot turn off until the Gryazhsk highway, and that we shall not reach for three hours. I'm convinced that a hot welcome is being prepared for us at all the adjacent populated points. The damned telegraph has stuck its posts and wires everywhere. Panikovsky! Take good care of your helmet. You may need it."

The commander made no mistake. They were invited to stop at the very first village. Kozlevich drew unprecedented speed from the Antelope. For several yards they were pursued by the shouts of a hefty young fellow on an unsaddled mare—apparently the village constable.

Further along the road was a small town, the name of which the Antelopians never discovered but which they would have liked to have known in order to remember it occasionally with a wicked word. At the very entrance into the town the road was blocked by a heavy log. The Antelope turned and like a blind puppy tried to push in from the sides in search of a detour. But there was none.

"Back!" Ostap commanded.

At this point the four knaves heard the distant mosquito song of motors—the automobiles of the real auto race. It was impossible to go back, so the Antelopians moved forward.

Kozlevich frowned and swiftly brought the machine right up to the log. The citizens who stood around dashed away to all sides, expecting catastrophe, but Kozlevich unexpectedly cut his speed and slowly went over the obstacle. While the Antelope was passing through the city the pedestrians cursed the riders, but Ostap, usually sensitive to all forms of insult, did not even reply.

The Antelope reached the Gryazhsk highway with the ever-increasing drone of the yet-unseen automobiles pursuing them. Scarcely had they managed to turn off the main road and hide their machine around a bend in the darkness when they heard the roar of motors and in a blaze of light appeared the leading machines. The rogues hid themselves in the grass at the edge of the road and suddenly losing their usual effrontery, gazed in silence at the passing column.

The machines, the road ahead of them flooded by light, humming contentedly, sped past the humbled Antelopians. Dust flew from under their wheels. Their klaxons challenged the night insistently. The wind of their passing rushed from side to side. All of this went by in a flash, and only the ruby lantern of the last machine rose and fell in the darkness.

Real life raced by, joyously blowing its horn, its lacquered wings shining.

The adventurers were left with only the trailing odor of gasoline; and for a long time they sat in the grass, rubbing their eyes and sneezing.

"Yes," said Ostap at last. "Now I can see for myself that the automobile is not a luxury but a means of conveyance. Don't you envy them, Balaganov? I do."

Chapter Eight

THE LANDSCAPE CHANGES

IN the fourth hour of the night the hunted Antelope stopped at the edge of a cliff. Below on a little plate lay an unfamiliar city, cut evenly like a cake. Rainbow mists swayed over it. The Antelopians seemed to hear a wheezing and a faint whistling: were the citizens snoring?

"A valley in Paradise," said Ostap. "It is pleasant to rob such cities early in the morning before the sun begins to bake. Less tiring."

"It's early morning right now," remarked Panikovsky, looking ingratiatingly into the commander's eyes.

"Shut up!" Ostap shouted. "Can't you understand a joke?"

"What shall we do with the Antelope?" asked Kozlevich.

"Quite right," Ostap said. "It's impossible to drive into town with this green tub after what has happened. They *would* arrest us! I suppose we shall have to follow the example of the more advanced countries. In Rio de Janeiro, for instance, stolen automobiles are usually painted another color. This is done purely from humanitarian motives—in order that the former owner may not worry when he spies a stranger driving his machine. The sweet burden of fame that Antelope has earned itself has soured. With a change in taste, we must change the color."

It was decided to enter the city on foot, obtain paints and, in the meanwhile, to find an appropriate haven for the machine outside the city limits.

Ostap walked rapidly down the road along the cliffs and soon beheld a crooked little log house with little windows reflecting the blue of the river. Behind the little house stood a barn that seemed appropriate shelter for Antelope.

While the great schemer pondered upon the pretext that would most easily secure for him a domicile for the faithful Antelope, the door of the house burst open and out dashed an honorable gentleman, wearing a private soldier's underwear with black tin buttons. On his pale paraffine cheeks were most respectable gray sideburns. During the last century his would have been considered an ordinary physiognomy —the physiognomy of a loyal citizen who pledged his fealty to the State even unto his beard. But nowadays when under the sideburns there could be neither a blue parade uniform, nor a civil service medal on a moiré ribbon, nor the gold star of a privy councilor, his appearance seemed unnatural.

"Oh, Lord!" mumbled the denizen of the crooked little log house, stretching forth his hands to the rising sun. "God, God! The same dreams, the very same dreams!"

Having uttered this complaint, the old man began to weep and, shuffling, ran along the path around the house. An ordinary rooster, at that moment about to sing for the third time and who for that reason had come out to the middle of the yard and had already opened his beak, dashed away in fright. In the heat of excitement he took several hurried steps and even dropped a feather, but soon recovered, flew up on an empty trunk and having captured this safe position, he announced to the world the advance of the morning. There was a sense of alarm in his voice, however, a sense of uncertainty provoked by the ominous behavior of the denizen of the crooked little log house.

"Why must I dream only of the accurs'd ones!" Ostap heard the old man sob.

Bender, regarding with surprise and astonishment the strange man with sideburns—such as may be found nowadays only on the ministerial face of a museum doorman— thought to himself: "Who is this crawfish of a recluse?"

In the meanwhile the strange gentleman completed his circle, and sighing, "I ll go and try again," disappeared through the door.

"I'm fond of old men," Ostap whispered. "One never has a dull moment with them. I must wait and find out the results of his mysterious attempt."

Ostap did not wait long. Soon weeping and wailing issued from the depths of the crooked little log house and, backing out like Boris Godunov in Moussorgsky's opera, the old man stumbled into the yard.

"Don't touch me! Avaunt!" he exclaimed with Chaliapinesque intonations in his voice. "That curs'd dream again! Ah! Ah!"

He turned around and, stumbling over himself, walked straight at Ostap. The great schemer decided that it was time to act, and came out from behind a tree and caught the owner of the sideburns in a mighty embrace.

"What? Who? What's the matter?" cried the restless old man. "What?"

Ostap carefully released the old man, caught his withered old hand and shook it heartily.

"I sympathize with you!" he exclaimed.

"Really?" asked the denizen of the crooked little log house, sinking to Bender's shoulder.

"Of course. Really," Ostap replied. "I dream sometimes myself."

"Ah, but what do you dream?"

"Various things."

"No. You must tell me *what* you dream," insisted the old man.

"Well, various things. A melange. The sort of thing that the newspapers call 'News from Everywhere,' and in the cinemas, 'Topics of the Day.' The day before yesterday, for example, I dreamed of the Mikado's funeral, while last night, of the Anniversary of the Sushchvsk fire department."

"God!" the old man exclaimed. "God! What a fortunate man you are, how fortunate! Tell me, have you ever dreamed perhaps of a governor-general, or . . . at least a cabinet minister?"

Bender was not obdurate.

"Of course I have," he said gayly. "Why, of course! Governor-generals! Why, last Friday I dreamed of one all night. And I remember that beside him stood a chief of police in loose embroidered trousers."

"How I envy you!" cried the old man. "But have you ever dreamed of the entry of His Imperial Majesty into the city of Kostroma?"

"Did you say Kostroma? Why, of course I have! Wait a minute, when was it? Why, of course, of course! The third of February this year. There was the Emperor, and beside him, if I remember correctly, stood Count Fredericks. You know whom I mean, don't you?"

"Why, Lord help us!" the old man mumbled excitedly. "Why are we standing here? Do come in. But excuse me, are you sure you are not a socialist or a member of the Party?"

"What are you saying?" Ostap said good-naturedly. "How could I be a party member? I am a non-partisan monarchist. I am a servant to my Tsar and a father to my soldiers!"

"Wouldn't you like to have some tea?" muttered the old man, pushing Bender ahead of him through the door.

In the crooked little log house there was an entrance hall and one room. The walls were covered with portraits of gentlemen in formal attire. Judging by their boutonnières, these gentlefolk had at one time been officials in the Ministry of Public Instruction. The bed was in disorder, presenting convincing evidence that the person who usually slept in it spent there the most restless hours of his life.

And indeed the host confessed to his guest that such really was the case. The monarchist raved in his dreams. He told Bender that after great difficulty he had managed to persuade

the Commissariat of Education, in which he had been em-
ployed until recently, to grant him an old-age pension. This
enabled him to retire to the crooked little log house, but all
day long the memory of his experiences under the Soviet
régime pursued him. He had hoped to escape in sleep, in
dreams of the good old days. He wanted to forget the vulgar
comrades with their meetings, wall newspapers, loans, socialist competition, shock brigades, five-year-plans in four, in three,
in two and a half. These crude, mad innovations sent shivers
up and down his back. He was sick and tired of membership
dues, state farms, collective farms, the solemn opening of the
first socialized kitchen, of the chairman of the Society of the
Friends of Cremation. He did not want to see the friends of
cremation. But he *did* want to see the extreme Right deputy
of the State Duma Purishkevich, Patriarch Tikhon, Mayor
Dumbadze of the city of Yalta, or at least a simple little inspector of the lower grade schools. But this could not be. The
Soviet régime had invaded even the dreams of the monarchist.

"The same dreams," weepingly concluded Khvorobyov,
whom the Revolution had flung from the District Inspector-
ship of Schools to the depths of a chairmanship of the Method-
ological and Pedagogical Sector in the Proletcult of a small
town. "The accurs'd dreams!"

"You're in a bad way," said Ostap sympathetically. "As the
saying is: 'Existence determines the nature of consciousness.'
Since you live in a Soviet land your dreams are bound to be
Sovietic."

"I don't get a minute of rest!" Khvorobyov wept. "If I got
the tiniest mite I'd be ready to give up my ideals. Let's say,
if I can't have Purishkevich, let me have at least Miliukov!
He is at least a university man and a monarchist at heart.
But, no! All I am permitted to have are those Soviet Anti-
Christs!"

"I'll help you," Ostap said. "I've had occasion to treat many
of my friends and acquaintances with Freudian therapy. The

dream itself is nonsense. The main thing is to remove the cause of the dream." He leaned forward and confided with emphasis: "The principal cause is the very existence of the Soviet régime. But, for the present, I cannot remove it. I simply haven't the time. You see, I am a tourist and a sportsman and right now I have to overhaul my automobile a bit, and I would be very much obliged to you if you would let me roll it into your barn. And as for the cause, don't worry. I'll remove it on my way back. All I need is an opportunity to finish this trip."

The monarchist, drugged by nightmares, gladly permitted the nice, responsive young man to use the barn. He threw an overcoat over his night clothes, stuck his bare feet into rubber overshoes and followed Bender into the yard.

"So there is hope?" he asked, shuffling after his early visitor.

"Don't have a single misgiving," the commander answered earnestly. "You'll feel a lot better when the Soviet régime disappears. Mind my words."

A half hour later the Antelope was lodged in Khvorobyov's barn under the protection of Kozlevich and Panikovsky. Bender and Balaganov went to town for paints.

The foster brothers walked against the sun. Gray doves preened themselves on the cornices of the houses. The wooden sidewalks, sprinkled with water, were clean and cool.

When the foster brothers finally stopped before a chandlery, Balaganov whispered to Ostap:

"Aren't you ashamed of yourself?"

"Ashamed of what?" Ostap asked.

"Aren't you ashamed of paying real, live money for paint?"

"Oh, so that's what's on your mind!" Ostap said. "I must confess that I *am* a bit ashamed. I feel rather foolish about it, but what can we do? I can't very well run to the local executive committee and ask them to supply us with paints for the celebration of Skylark Day. They'd give it to me, of course. But before you could cut through the red tape you'd waste several days. And at this stage of our enterprise, time is money!"

The commander and the mechanic selected the paints with great fastidiousness.

"Black is too mournful," Ostap said. "Green will not do either. It is the color of lost hope. Lavender? No. Let the chief of the Criminal Investigation Committee ride around in a lavender machine. Pink? Vulgar. Azure? Banal. Red? Suspiciously loyal. I'm afraid we shall have to paint Antelope yellow. It's a bit bright but lovely."

"And what are you? Artists?" asked the salesman, whose chin was covered lightly with cinnabar dust.

"Yes, we are artists," Bender replied. "Battle-scene and marine painters."

"Then you should not have come here," said the salesman, removing the packages and the cans from the counter.

"What do you mean!" Ostap exclaimed. "Where then?"

"Across the street."

The clerk led the friends to the door and indicated a sign across the road. On it was portrayed the head of a bay horse, and under it, in black letters against a blue background: "Oats and Hay."

"That's all very well," said Ostap. "Hard and soft fodder for cattle. But what has that to do with us artists? I see no connection."

It appeared, however, that there was a connection, and a very real one. Ostap discovered it at the very beginning of the clerk's explanation:

This city had always loved the fine arts, and four artists, who had lived there a long time, had founded a group called "The Dialectic Bench-Worker." They painted portraits of responsible workers and placed them with the local museum of fine arts. In the course of time there was a considerable decrease in the number of responsible workers whose portraits had not yet been painted, which noticeably lowered the earnings of the dialectic bench-workers. That could still be tolerated. But the years of suffering began when a new artist, Feofan Kopytto, arrived in the city.

His first work created a sensation in the city. It was a portrait of the manager of the hotel trust. Feofan Kopytto hopelessly outdistanced the bench-workers. The manager of the hotel trust was depicted not in oils, not in water colors, not in charcoal, not in tempera, not in pastels, not in gouache, and not in lead pencil. He was depicted in oats! And while the artist Kopytto was transporting the picture in a droshky to the museum, the horse looked around restlessly and neighed.

In the course of time Kopytto began to use other cereals as well. Thunderous success attended portraits made of millet, wheat, and poppyseed, daring sketches in corn and buckwheat, landscapes of rice and still lifes of barley.

Now he was at work on a group portrait. The large canvas presented a section of the district planning committee. Feofan was fashioning this picture with beans and peas. But deep in his heart he remained faithful to oats, which had made his career and had dislodged the dialectic bench-workers from their positions.

"Of course, he is more talented in oats!" Ostap exclaimed. "And Rubens and Raphael were fools to have attempted their efforts in oils. We, also, are fools like Leonardo da Vinci. Give us some yellow enamel paint."

On the street the foster brothers beheld the dialectic bench-workers. All four of them, with the sad, wistful faces of gypsies, stood at the crossing. Beside them were their easels, folded like stacked rifles.

"Well, fellow-soldiers on the artistic sector, how are things? Pretty bad, eh?"

"Terrible, terrible!" groaned the artists.

"Feofan put one over on you, didn't he?" Ostap inquired, revealing thorough familiarity with the subject.

"Yes, he's painting his pot-boilers," replied one of the artists, who was so hairy that he might have been mistaken for Henry of Navarre. "In oats! He says he's returning to his old manner. He's complaining, the grain-dealer, about the crisis of the *genre!*"

"And where is the *atelier* of this shyster?" Ostap was curious to know. "I should like to have a look at it."

The artists, who had much free time, gladly led Ostap and Balaganov to Feofan Kopytto. Feofan was working in the open air, in his modest little garden. Before him on a stool sat the prominent comrade, Plotsky-Potseluyev—apparently a timid soul. Breathless, he gazed upon the artist, who, like the sower on a thirty-ruble banknote, seized handfuls of oats out of a bast-basket and flung them over the canvas. Kopytto was frowning. Sparrows were annoying him, impudently flying into the portrait and pecking out the finely-wrought details.

"How much will you receive for this picture?" Plotsky-Potseluyev inquired, blushing modestly.

Feofan stopped his sowing, cast a critical glance at his production, and answered thoughtfully:

"Who can tell! I hope the museum will give two hundred and fifty rubles for it."

"But that is too much!"

"Just try and get the oats!" Kopytto retorted contentiously. "Oats cost real money, nowadays."

"Well, now! How is the summer planting?" asked Ostap, pushing his head through the fence palings. "The sowing campaign, I see, is proceeding famously. Do you expect to fulfill a hundred percent of the plan? . . . But all this is nothing compared with what I have seen in Moscow. There one artist made a picture from hair, a large picture with many figures, and, note this, ideologically correct, although the artist used the hair of non-Party people. He *did* commit that sin. But, I repeat, ideologically, the picture was remarkably correct. It was called 'Grandfather Pakhom and the Tractor at

Home.' It was such a refractory picture that they simply did not know what to do with it. Occasionally the hair would stand on end. Then one fine day it turned gray, and not a trace remained of Grandfather Pakhom and his tractor. But the artist had managed to grab about fifteen hundred rubles for this invention. So don't be too high and mighty, Comrade Kopytto. The oats may suddenly begin to grow; your picture will expand into stalks; and never again will you have the occasion to harvest your crop!"

The dialectic bench-workers laughed sympathetically. But Feofan was not embarrassed.

"That sounds like a paradox," he remarked, renewing his sowing operations.

"Very well," said Ostap in farewell. "Sow that which is sensible, good, eternal, and the rest will take care of itself. And farewell to you, fellow-soldiers! Forsake your oils, turn to mosaics of bolts, spikes and screws. A portrait of screws! In our age of steam and electricity! A remarkable idea!"

All through the day the Antelopians painted their Antelope. By evening it was unrecognizable and glistened with all the shades of an egg-yolk.

When the next day dawned the transformed Antelope abandoned the hospitable barn and took a course due south.

"It's a pity that we did not bid adieu to our host. But he's sleeping so sweetly now that I didn't have the heart to awaken him. Perhaps at this very moment he is dreaming the long-awaited dream: the Metropolite Dvulogy blessing the officials of the Ministry of Public Instruction on the 300th Anniversary of the Romanov dynasty."

But at that very minute out of the crooked little log house behind them issued the heartrending sobs with which Ostap was already familiar.

"That very same dream!" howled old Khovorobyov. "God! God!"

"I've made a mistake," Ostap remarked. "Apparently he did

not dream of the Metropolite Dvulogy, but of an extended plenum of the literary group 'The Forge and the Farmstead.' However, the devil take him! Business calls us to Chernomorsk!"

Chapter Nine

THE LANDSCAPE CHANGES AGAIN

THROUGH the white glass door of the balcony could be seen blooming acacias, the patched roofs of houses and the sharp blue line of the sea's horizon. High noon blazed over Chernomorsk.

Worn out by his efforts, old man Sinitsky fell back in his chair and closed his eyes. He was already seventy years old. During fifty of those years he had composed rebuses, charades, problems and cross word puzzles. But never before did the honorable puzzlemaker find it so difficult to carry on his profession as nowadays. Losing step with life, he had become politically illiterate and his young competitors had easily outstripped him. They would bring the editor problems so splendidly grounded in correct ideology that the old man, reading them, would weep with envy. How could he ever hope, for example, to measure up to something like this:

AN ARITHMOMOIDICAL PROBLEM

There was an equal number of employees on the three stations Sparrowburg, Rooktown and Thrushton. At the Thrushton station there were six times fewer members of the Comsomol than on the two others together, while at Sparrowburg there were twelve more members of the Communist Party than at Rooktown. But in the latter there were six more nonpartisans than in the first two. How many employees were there at each station, and how many of them were members of the Communist Party and of the Comsomol?

Recovering from his mournful thoughts, the old man again took up his sheet of paper with the word DEBIT irrevocably stamped on it, but at that moment a girl with wet bobbed hair and a black swimming suit on her shoulder entered the room.

Silently she passed to the balcony, hung her damp suit on the dilapidated railing and looked down. The girl beheld the same impoverished yard that she had seen for many years on end—a pauper yard strewn with broken boxes, cats smeared with coal dust wandering about, and a tinsmith thunderously fixing a pail. On the lower floor housewives complained about their difficult life.

This was not the first time that the girl had heard such conversations. She knew all the cats by name, and it seemed to her that the tinsmith had been fixing the identical pail for several years on end. Zosya Sinitskaya returned to the room.

"It's the ideology that's spoiling everything," she heard her grandfather mutter. "Why should there be ideology in the puzzle-making business? The puzzle-making business . . ."

Zosya began to set the table for dinner. She passed from the cupboard with its cutglass candelabra to the table and set down the crockery. A porcelain soup tureen with a broken handle appeared, plates with little flowers and without little flowers, yellowed forks, and even a compote dish, although no compote was intended for dinner.

In general it might be said that the affairs of the Sinitskys were not enviable. Rebuses and charades brought into the house more worry than money. As for the home-cooked dinners which the old puzzle-maker supplied to citizens of his acquaintance and which were the chief source of income— things were no better. Podvysotsky and Bomze had gone away on vacation; Stulyan had married a Greek girl and had taken to dining in his new home; while Pobirukhin had been house-cleaned out of his job in accordance with regulations of the second category, so that from worry he had lost his appetite

and refused to dine altogether. Now he wandered through the
city, buttonholed his acquaintances and pronounced the same
phrase chockfull of hidden sarcasm: "Have you heard the
news? I've been cleaned out. Second category." And among
his acquaintances there were some who answered with sym-
pathy: "They've certainly started things—those old bandits
Marx and Engels." While there were others who answered
nothing, cast fiery glances at Pobirukhin and sped by, their
brief cases quivering. Anyway, in the end there remained
only one boarder and he had not paid for a week because
the payment of his salary had been delayed.

Moving her shoulders with displeasure, Zosya went into
the kitchen. When she returned she found at the dinner
table the last of the boarders—Alexander Ivanovich Koreiko.

Alexander Ivanovich boarded with the Sinitskys partly because their dinners were cheap and palatable. Besides, his
fundamental rule consisted in never forgetting that he was a
petty clerk. He paraded his pretended poverty before everyone, loved to talk about the difficulties of making a living in
a large city on a miserable salary. But for some time the price
and the palatableness of the dinners had lost for him that
abstract and significant meaning that he attached to them.
If he had been asked, and if he could do it openly, he would
pay for his dinners not sixty-five kopeks as now, but three
and even five thousand rubles.

Alexander Ivanovich, an ascetic who consciously tortured
himself with financial fetters, who had forbidden himself to
touch anything that cost more than half a ruble, and irritated,
because, fearful of losing millions, he could not spend openly
a hundred rubles—fell in love with all the irrevocableness of
which only a strong, silent man, baited by endless expectations, is capable.

On this day he had finally decided to declare his feelings to
Zosya and to take her hand in his hand with its small, spite-

ful, restive pulse, and lay it on his heart which beat in the cage of his self-imposed martyrdom.

"Yes," he sighed, "that's the way it goes, Zosya Adamovna."

Having communicated this, Citizen Koreiko seized from the table an ashtray on which was written the pre-Revolutionary slogan: "Husband, don't be angry with your wife," and began to study it attentively.

Here it is necessary to explain that there is not a girl in the world who does not know at least a week ahead about an impending declaration of love. Therefore Zosya Adamovna sighed wearily and stopped before the mirror. She had the athletic appearance which so many pretty girls have lately acquired. Making sure of this, she sat down opposite Alexander Ivanovich and prepared to listen to him. But Alexander Ivanovich said nothing. He knew how to play only two rôles: that of a poor clerk and that of an underground millionaire. He knew no other rôle.

"Have you heard the news?" asked Zosya. "Pobirukhin has been cleaned out."

"We're also having a house cleaning," Koreiko answered. "Many will get their walking papers. For example, Lapidus Jr. As far as that is concerned, Lapidus Sr. is also a pretty fine fellow . . ."

At this point Koreiko noticed that he was following the straight and narrow path of a poor clerk. Leaden pensiveness again possessed him.

"Yes, yes," he said. "That's how I live—in loneliness—without knowing pleasures."

"What's that? Not knowing what?" Zosya brightened up.

"Without knowing a woman's attachment," remarked Koreiko in a choking voice.

Seeing no encouragement on Zosya's part, he developed this thought.

He was old, that is, not exactly old but no longer young. And not exactly no longer young, but simply time flies, the years pass. The years go, and anyway, this movement of time inspires him with certain thoughts. About matrimony, for instance. People shouldn't think that he is such-and-such. He's not so bad in general. An utterly harmless man. He should be pitied, and it seems to him that perhaps he could even be loved. He is not a fop like others, and he doesn't like to cast his words to the wind. Honestly and sincerely. Why shouldn't some girl marry him?

Having expressed his thoughts in this timid form, Alexander Ivanovich glanced angrily at the granddaughter of the puzzle-maker.

"Do you really think that Lapidus Jr. may be cleaned out?" Zosya asked.

And meeting prolonged, stony silence, she turned to the subject under discussion.

She understands everything very well. Time really does go horribly fast. Not so long ago she was nineteen years old, but now she is already twenty. And in another year she'll be twenty-one. She has never thought that Alexander Ivanovich was such-and-such. On the contrary, she was always convinced that he was not so bad. Better than many. And of course he is deserving of everything. But precisely at this time, she is seeking something—what, she does not yet know herself. Generally speaking, for the present she cannot marry. Besides, what sort of a life would they have together? She is a seeker, while he, if one is to speak honestly and sincerely, has only forty-six rubles a month.

"What do you mean, forty-six rubles!" Alexander Ivanovich said suddenly in a terrible voice, rising to his full height. "I have . . . In my possession . . ."

He said nothing else. He was frightened. Here began the rôle of millionaire, and that could only lead to ruin. His fright was so great that he even began to mutter about happiness not depending on money.

"How dramatic!" Zosya exclaimed.

Then she put on her hat and left the room. Alexander Ivanovich followed her, though he realized that he should not go along. When they passed the long corridor of the communal apartment thickly stuffed with people and things, doors opened after them and the burning eyes of their neighbors gleamed in the murkiness.

On the street Zosya took Koreiko's arm and said:

"We'll still be friends, won't we?"

"It would be better if you would marry me," Koreiko mumbled frankly.

"There's a stubborn man for you!" laughed Zosya. "There's lots of time for that."

In the open stand of artificial mineral water were crowds of young men without hats, in white shirts with sleeves rolled up above the elbow. Blue siphons with metallic spigots stood on the shelves. Long glass cylinders of syrups gleamed with a drugstore sheen as they were turned around. Persians with grieving eyes roasted nuts and the choking smoke lured the pleasure-seekers.

"I want to go to a cinema," Zosya said capriciously. "I want some nuts! I want seltzer water with syrup!"

Koreiko was ready to do anything for Zosya. He would have dared even to violate his conspirative régime slightly and spend five rubles for a spree, but at that moment in a flat tin box which formerly contained "Caucasus" cigarettes, there lay ten thousand rubles in banknotes of no smaller denomination than two thousand five hundred rubles each. And even if he were to go utterly mad and decide to disclose even one such banknote he could not have it changed in a single cinema.

"They're holding up the pay," he said in utter despair. "We get our pay very irregularly, extremely irregularly."

At that moment out of the crowd of promenaders stepped a young man with excellent sandals on his bare feet. He saluted Zosya by raising his arm to an angle of forty-five degrees.

"Greetings, greetings," he said. "I have two passes to a cinema. Want to come, Zosya? Only you must decide immediately."

And the young man in the remarkable sandals lured Zosya under the dim cinema sign: "Kamo-Jyradeshi, née Quo Vadis."

That night the millionaire clerk did not sleep at all. Until early morning he wandered through the city, stupidly examining the photographs of nude infants in the showcases of photographers, digging his feet into the gravel of the boulevard, and gazing at the dark abyss of the port. There he heard the conversations of unseen steamships; he heard the whistles of policemen; and he saw the red beacon light turn.

"Accursed land," muttered Koreiko. "A land in which a millionaire cannot take his bride to a cinema!"

At this moment Zosya seemed to him already his bride.

Toward morning Alexander Ivanovich, pale from lack of sleep, wandered to the outskirts of the city. When he was passing Bessarabian Street it seemed to him that he heard the sound of the "Matchish." Astonished, he stopped.

Approaching him, a large yellow automobile was descending the hill. Bent over the wheel sat a tired chauffeur in a corduroy coat. Beside him slumbered a broadshouldered chap whose head in a Stetson hat with ventilating holes hung to one side. In the rear seat sprawled two other passengers: a fireman in full parade uniform, and an athletically built man in a yachting cap with a white top.

"Greetings to the first Chernomorskian!" shouted Ostap while the machine rumbled like a tractor past Koreiko. "Are the warm sea baths still going strong? Is the City Theater still functioning? Has Chernomorsk been declared a free city yet?"

But Ostap received no answer. Kozlevich opened his cutout

and the Antelope drowned the first Chernomorskian in a cloud of blue smoke.

"Well," said Ostap to Balaganov who had just awakened. "The meeting continues. Let me have your underground Rockefeller. I'll begin to strip him immediately. Oh, these princes and paupers!"

Part Two

TWO SCHEMERS

Chapter Ten

A TELEGRAM FROM THE BROTHERS KARAMAZOV

FOR some time the underground millionaire had felt some-one's relentless attention upon him. At first there was nothing definite. He had merely lost his habitual and peaceful sense of aloneness. Later he began to notice more alarming symptoms.

Once while Koreiko was bound for work at the deliberate pace habitual to him, an impertinent pauper with a gold tooth stopped him at the HERCULES building. Seizing Alexander Ivanovich by the hand he muttered rapidly:

"Gimme million, gimme million, gimme million!"

Then the pauper stuck out his thick, unclean tongue and began to talk utterly incomprehensible nonsense. He seemed an ordinary, weak-minded beggar, the kind frequently seen in southern cities. Koreiko was perturbed, nevertheless, as he walked up to his place in the Financial Accounting room.

All sorts of devilry followed this strange encounter. At three o'clock of a raw morning Alexander Ivanovich was awakened by a telegram. Shivering, his teeth chattering, the millionaire tore the seal and read:

"Countess altered appearance running pondward."

"What countess?" muttered the dumbfounded Koreiko, standing barefooted in the corridor.

But no one answered him. The messenger had gone. In the court doves moaned passionately. The lodgers snored. Alexander Ivanovich fingered the gray blank in his hand. The address was correct. So was the name.

"alexander koreiko 16 little worries countess altered face running pondward"

Alexander Ivanovich could make nothing of it. He was so upset, however, that he burned the telegram with the candle by which he had read it.

At two thirty-five in the afternoon of the same day a second telegram came:

"meeting continues stop million kisses"

Alexander Ivanovich turned pale with anger and tore the telegram to pieces. But that night there were two more telegrams:

"load oranges barrels brothers karamazov"

And the second:

"ice breaking stop eye command parade"

While Alexander Ivanovich was at work the next day, a regrettable and extraordinary incident occurred. Mentally multiplying 985 by 13 at the request of Chevazhevskaya, he gave her the wrong answer, something that had never happened before in his life.

But now he had no mind for arithmetic. He was preoccupied by the mad telegrams.

"Barrels," he whispered, staring at old man Kukushkind. "Brothers Karamazov. How stupid!"

He tried to allay his fears with the thought that these were probably pranks by some of his friends; but he soon had to abandon this theory. He had no friends. As for his fellow employees, they were serious people who played practical jokes only once a year, on the first of April. But even on that memorable day their gay and joyous mysteries consisted of one and the same pathetic jest; on a typewriter they forged a spurious order dismissing Kukushkind and placed it on his table. And, unfailingly, every April Fool's Day for seven years on end, the old man clutched his heart, evoking great merriment. Besides, they were not sufficiently well-off to spend money on telegrams.

A lull set in after the telegram in which the anonymous citizen had stated that he commanded the parade. For three days Alexander Ivanovich was left in peace. He had begun to accustom himself to the thought that all that had happened in no way concerned him, when a thick registered package arrived. He opened it and found in his hands a book entitled "Capitalist Sharks," with the subtitle, "Biographies of American Millionaires."

At any other time Koreiko would have been glad even to buy such an engaging book, but now the gift of it made him squirm with apprehension. The first sentence of the book had been underlined with a blue pencil:

"All the large contemporary fortunes in America were acquired in a most dishonest way."

For the time being Alexander Ivanovich decided not to go to the station for his precious suitcase. He was constantly in a state of panic.

"Most important of all," Ostap was saying, as he jauntily paced his spacious room in the Hotel Karlsbad, "is to create confusion in the camp of the enemy. He must lose all peace of mind. This is not difficult to achieve. In the final analysis, it is the incomprehensible that people fear most. There was a time when I myself was a solitary mystic, and I reached the point where I could be frightened by a simple little Finnish knife. Yes, yes. . . . The more mystery the better. I am convinced that my last telegram, 'twins in thought,' produced a disastrous impression on our colleague. All of this is superphosphate—fertilizer. Let him worry a bit. The defendant must be educated to the idea that he must surrender the money. He must be morally disarmed. His reactionary instinct for private property must be suppressed."

Bender glanced severely at his subordinates. Balaganov, Panikovsky and Kozlevich sat sedately in fringed and tasseled red plush chairs. They were ill at ease, embarrassed by the gilt lambrequins, by the colorful rugs, and by the engraving "Christ Appears to the People." They and the Antelope stopped at an inn and came to the hotel only to receive instructions.

"Panikovsky," Ostap said, "you were told to meet the defendant to-day and again ask him for a million, accompanying this request with idiotic laughter."

"As soon as he saw me, he crossed the street," Panikovsky answered complacently.

"Good. All is going well. The defendant is becoming nervous. He is now passing from stupid perplexity to unreasoning fear. I have no doubt that he jumps up in the middle of the night and pathetically calls for his Mamma. A little more, just a little, the last flick of the wrist, and he will be completely ripe. He will creep tearfully to the sideboard and take out a little plate with a blue border . . ."

Ostap winked at Balaganov, Balaganov winked at Panikovsky, Panikovsky winked at Kozlevich and, although the honest Kozlevich understood absolutely nothing, he also began to blink both eyes and the friendly winking continued for a long time in this room of the Karlsbad Hotel, accompanied by jests and clicking of tongues. They even bounced up and down in the red plush chairs.

"Enough gayety," Ostap reproved them. "The little plate of money is still in the hands of Koreiko, if it exists at all—that magic little plate!"

Then Bender sent Panikovsky and Kozlevich back to the inn, ordering them to keep the Antelope in readiness.

"Well, Shura," he said when he was alone with Balaganov, "no more telegrams are necessary. We may consider the preparatory work finished. Now we begin the active struggle. Presently we shall go and take a look at our precious little lamb and see how he performs his clerical duties."

Keeping in the diaphanous shade of the acacia trees, the foster brothers passed through the city garden where the thick stream of the fountain guttered like a candle, went past several pretentious beer saloons, and stopped at the corner of Mehring Street. Flower girls with faces as red as sailors' bathed their delicate merchandise in enameled bowls. Melting asphalt hissed under foot. From a blue-tiled creamery emerged citizens, wiping their *kefir*-fringed lips. The thick macaroni letters of gilded wood that composed the word HERCULES gleamed enticingly. The sun scintillated on the enormous panes of the swinging door. Ostap and Balaganov entered the vestibule and lost themselves in the crowd.

Chapter Eleven

THE HERCULEANS

DESPITE all efforts, the HERCULES management failed to divest the establishment of its hotel atmosphere. The old signs persisted through repeated coats of paint. In the Trading Department emerged "Private Dining Room"; "Maid on Duty" was decipherable on the frosted glass door of the Machinery Bureau; on the walls golden pointing fingers indicated "Pour Les Dames." The hotel was ineffaceable.

The less important clerks were in the one-ruble rooms on the fourth floor, where in their time had stopped minor civil service officials delegated to diocesan conventions, or petty traveling salesmen with diminutive Warsaw mustaches. Here lingered the odor of perspiration, and pink-enameled iron wash stands were still in evidence. In rooms somewhat cleaner, where billiard champions and provincial actors usually stayed, the department chief, the heads of sub-departments and their aides had placed their desks. Here stood plane-tree wardrobes with mirrors, and the floor was covered with brown linoleum. The management made its nests in sumptuous rooms with private baths and alcoves. In white bathtubs reigned a chaos of business papers, while in dim alcoves hung diagrams and charts that graphically portrayed the structure of HERCULES and also its connection with organizations on the periphery of Soviet economic life. Here silly little gilt settees had been preserved, rugs, and night tables with marble tops. In some of the alcoves even stood wrought-iron beds ornamented with round nickeled bulbs. These also held folders and current correspondence. This was very convenient, because thus all the papers were constantly at hand.

In one of these rooms, number five, the famous author Leonid Andreyev had stopped some time in 1911. All the Herculeans knew about it and room five had a bad reputation. All the responsible workers who arranged their offices there inevitably met with some misfortune. No sooner did room five begin to hum with business than it was abandoned and its occupant was demoted. It would not have been so bad had it happened without a reprimand, but it usually happened *with* a reprimand, sometimes with the publication of a notice in the press, and at times it was even worse—so much worse that it is unpleasant even to speak of it.

"Fiend's room!" the victims agreed unanimously. "But who could have known?"

And on the head of the writer, the author of the terrible "The Seven Who Were Hanged," fell the most horrible accusations that he, creator of the famous play "The Days of Our Life," was guilty because Comrade Lapshin had given jobs to six of his own heroic brothers, because Comrade Spravchenko in the collecting of wood bark relied on its own momentum and therefore failed miserably, and because Comrade Indokitaisky gambled away 7384 rubles 03 kopeks of government money. Despite Indokitaisky's wriggling, despite his attempts to prove to the proper persons that the 03 kopeks he had spent for the benefit of the State, presenting corroborating documents, nothing helped him. The shadow of the deceased writer was implacable, and one autumn evening Indokitaisky was taken away to serve his time. Undoubtedly, room number five was inimical.

The chief of the entire HERCULES, Comrade Polykhayev, a man of distinguished appearance, with close-cropped hair, had his office in the former winter garden; and his secretary, Serna Mikhailovna, flitted among the surviving palms and magnolias. There stood a table as long as a railway platform, covered with a raspberry cloth, at which were held the long and private conferences of the management. And now in room 262, where once a bar had been located, the house-cleaning committee of eight gray-eyed nondescript comrades sat in judgment. They came on time every day, and all of them read conscientiously from bits of paper.

As Ostap and Balaganov were going up the stairway, an alarm bell rang and all the employees jumped out of the rooms at once. Their feverish haste made one think of a ship's "All hands on deck!" But this was not "All hands on deck"; it was lunch time. Some of the employees hurried to the buffet in an effort to get the few sandwiches of salmon roe; others promenaded in the corridors, munching as they walked.

From the Planning Department emerged an employee of noble mien. A round youthful beard hung on his pale kind face. His limpid feminine eyes shone with goodness. In one hand he held a cold meatball which he examined attentively, repeatedly, each time he applied it to his mouth. The employee of noble mien expressed extreme annoyance when Balaganov interrupted this indoor exercise by desiring to know the location of the Financial Accounting Department.

"Comrade, can't you see that I am eating?" said the employee, indignantly turning away from Balaganov. And paying no more attention to the foster brothers, he abandoned himself to the examination of the last bit of meatball. After surveying it from all sides in the most meticulous manner, and even smelling it in farewell, the employee deposited it in his mouth, threw out his chest, brushed some crumbs off his coat, and slowly approached another employee who stood at the door of his department.

"Well now," he asked, looking around, "how does it go?"

"Don't ask, Comrade Bomze," the other answered, and, also looking around, added, "So you call this life? There is no room for individuality. Always one and the same thing: the Five-Year Plan in four years, the Five-Year Plan in three years!"

"Yes, yes," Bomze whispered. "It's simply horrible! I quite agree with you. That's it! There's no room for individuality, no incentive, no personal prospects. My wife, you know, is only a housewife, but even *she* says that there's no incentive, no personal prospects."

Sighing heavily and stroking his beard, Bomze went to meet another employee.

"Well?" he asked, already smiling mournfully, "how does it go?"

"I don't know how to tell you," the other answered. "This morning I returned from a government trip. I managed to see a state farm. Grandiose! Grain factory! My dear fellow, you can't imagine the significance of the Five-Year Plan, and what the will of the collective means!"

"Why, that's exactly, word for word, what I was just saying!" Bomze exclaimed excitedly. "That's it! The will of the collective! The Five-Year Plan in four years, even in three— Here is an incentive which . . . Take even my wife—just a housewife, and even she gives industrialization its due. . . . The devil take it, a new life is growing up before our very eyes!"

He shook his head joyously. A minute later he was holding the sleeve of the timid Borisokhlebsky and was saying:

"You're right! That's just what I think. Why build Magnitogorsk, state farms, all sorts of combines, when there is no personal life, when the individuality is suppressed?"

But a minute later his flat voice gurgled on the staircase landing:

"Why, that is exactly what I was just saying to Comrade Borisokhlebsky! Why weep over individualism and personal life, when before our very eyes grain factories are growing, Magnitogorsk, all sorts of combines, cement-mixers! When the collective . . ."

In the course of the lunch period, Bomze, who loved intellectual intercourse, managed to chatter with half a score of his fellow employees. The subject of each conversation could be determined by the expression of his face, where grief for the suppression of individualism gave way to the luminous smile of the enthusiast. But whatever the feelings that swayed Bomze, the expression of innate decency never left his face. And all, beginning with tried comrades from the local committee and ending with the politically immature Kukushkind, regarded Bomze as an honest man and, what is more important, as a man of principle. Indeed, *he* had a similar opinion of himself.

Another bell announced the end of "All hands on deck!" and returned the employees to their rooms. Work was resumed.

As a matter of fact, the words "work was resumed" had no direct bearing on the activity of HERCULES, which consisted, according to decree, of various trading operations in the field of lumber materials. During the last year, the Herculeans, casting aside all thought of dull timbers, planks, export cedars and similar uninteresting things, had devoted themselves to a most breathless occupation: they struggled for their domicile, for their beloved hotel.

It all began with a bit of paper which was brought in a receipt book by a messenger from the Department of Communal Housing.

On the paper was written: "With the receipt of this, we *request* that you vacate the premises of the former Hotel Cairo within one week, and surrender it and all its former hotel furnishings to the Hotel Trust. You are offered in exchange the former domicile of the joint stock company, 'Tin and Bacon.' Resolution of the city Soviet of the 12/11/'29."

One evening this little paper had been placed on the desk, right before the eyes of Comrade Polykhayev as he sat in the shade of electrically-lighted palms and magnolias.

"What!" cried the HERCULES chieftain nervously. "They write 'request' to me? To *me,* who am subordinate only to the

Center! Only to Moscow! What's the matter with them?
Have they gone crazy?"

"They might have even written 'order'!" Serna Mikhailovna
added fuel to the fire. "Boors! Louts!"

Immediately a most decisive reply was dictated: the HER-
CULES chieftain flatly refused to vacate the premises.

"Next time they'll know that I'm not some night watchman, and that they can't write any 'requests' to me!" muttered
Comrade Polykhayev, taking out of his pocket a rubber
stamp with his facsimile, and pressing his signature upside
down in his excitement.

And again a lazy messenger, this time one from HERCULES,
wended his way over the sunny streets, stopping at kvass
stands, butting into all the street scandals, and jauntily swinging his receipt book.

Three days later Serna Mikhailovna reported the arrival of
a comrade from the Communal Housing Department. This
comrade had been recently assigned from a county seat to
the center of culture here and did not yet understand proper
behavior. To avoid bureaucratic correspondence, he had decided to clear up matters by appearing in person.

"Hello there," he said, entering the palm hall and brushing
the leaves with his head. "What is all this nonsense about
your premises? This is a building of the hotel type, which
means that it should be a hotel, and that you must move over
to 'Tin and Bacon.' It's very conveniently situated."

"Comrade," the chief of the HERCULES answered importantly.
"I am not some night watchman. I'm not your subordinate,
and I will not give up these premises. You'd better act through
the Center in Moscow. And as for your 'requests' and 'orders'
—forget them. You're just starting a lot of red tape. I intend
to complain about you to the Control Commission."

The tactless comrade from the Communal Housing Department was so surprised by this unexpected turn of affairs that
he departed without saying good-by, almost overturning a

decorative plant as he was going out. And the next day HER-
CULES was *ordered* to move out of the hotel immediately. The
ultim:.tum was signed by the chairman of the city Executive
Committee.

"This is simply a joke," said Polykhayev, smiling darkly.

For a whole week the Herculeans discussed the new turn
of affairs. The employees agreed that Polykhayev would not
tolerate such undermining of his authority.

"You don't know our Polykhayev," said the fine fellows
from the Financial Accounting Department. "He's been
through the mill. You can't stump *him* with a mere ultimatum!"

One fine day Comrade Bomze came out of the chief's office.
In his hand was a list of selected fellow employees. He
walked from one department to another, bent over the person indicated on the list, and whispered mysteriously:

"A little evening party . . . three rubles apiece . . . farewell for Polykhayev."

"What!" the selected employees exclaimed in fright. "Is
Polykhayev leaving? Has he been discharged?"

"Of course not! He's going to the Center for a week to
arrange about the premises. Don't be late now. At eight sharp,
in my place."

The farewell party was very gay. The fellow employees
regarded Polykhayev loyally as he sat there, a glass of lafitte
in his hand. They beat the palms of their hands rhythmically
and sang:

> "Bottoms up, bottoms up, bottoms up,
> Bottoms up, bottoms up, bottoms up . . ."

They sang until their beloved chief had drained a considerable quantity of lafitte and many glasses of high-grade
Sebastopol vodka. Afterwards, in an uncertain voice, he began
the song: "On the old Kaluga Road at the forty-ninth *verst*
post." But no one found out what occurred at this particular

verst post because Polykhayev unexpectedly began another
song:

"On the street car passing by
Someone died—I don't know why.
Now the corpse is hustled out—
Oh, the lout! . . . Oh, the lout! . . ."

After Polykhayev's departure, the productivity of labor at
HERCULES slightly decreased. It would have been absurd to
work in full swing, not knowing whether they were going to
remain in those premises or whether it was going to be necessary to move to "Tin and Bacon" with all their office equip-
ment. But it would have been more absurd yet to work in full
swing after Polykhayev's return. As Bomze expressed it, he
came back with his shield. The place remained with HERCULES,
and the fellow employees devoted their office hours to derisive
remarks about the Communal Housing Department.

That defeated organization asked to be given at least the
wash stands and the metal beds, but Polykhayev, stirred by his
success, did not deign to reply. Then they clinched again with
renewed strength. Complaints flew to the Center. In order to
deny them, Polykhayev made other trips. More and more
often Bomze's room resounded with the victorious "Bottoms
up!", and fellow employees in greater number were drawn
into the work of fighting for the premises. Gradually the
lumber materials were forgotten. Whenever Polykhayev suddenly found on his table a bit of paper relative to export
cedars or planks, he would be so astonished that for a time
he would not understand what it was doing there. For the
present he was up to his ears in work, devoted to carrying out
an extremely important project: with offers of higher pay he
was luring to his establishment two of the most dangerous
members of the Communal Housing Department.

"You are fortunate," Ostap said to his companion. "You are
witnessing a very curious phenomenon. Ostap Bender is on

a hot trail. Learn to master yourself. A petty criminal like Panikovsky would have written a letter to Koreiko: 'Put six hundred rubles under the garbage can in the yard, otherwise it will go ill with you.' And below he would have drawn a cross, a skull and a candle. Golden-handed Sonya, whose good points I do not wish to disparage, would resort to an ordinary subterfuge which would bring her about one and a half thousand. That may be enough for a woman. Finally, let us take Lieutenant Savin of the Horse Marines. He's a talented peculator, *ne plus ultra,* or, as the saying is *"Chevalier sans peur et sans reproche."* But what would he have done? He would have come to Koreiko's room in the disguise of a Bulgarian king, would have begun a scandal at the office of the Housing Committee, and would have bungled the entire affair. But, as you see, I am in no hurry. We have been in Chernomorsk for an entire week, yet only to-day am I setting my eyes upon him for the first time. . . . Aha, here is the Financial Accounting hall. Well, Mechanic, show me the patient. I believe you are a specialist in Koreiko."

They walked into a hall full of cackling visitors. Balaganov led Bender to a corner where, behind a yellow partition, sat Chevazhevskaya, Koreiko, Kukushkind and Dreyfus. Balaganov had already raised his hand to indicate the millionaire, when Ostap whispered angrily:

"Why don't you shout with all your might, 'Here is the rich guy! Hold him!'? Composure! I shall guess myself. Let's see now: which of the four is it?"

Ostap sat down on the cool marble window sill and, swinging his legs like a child, began to speculate:

"The girl doesn't count. There remain three: the red-mugged time-server with white eyes, the little old man in steel spectacles who looks like a mushroom, and the solemn fat Fido. The little old man who looks like a mushroom I sweep aside contemptuously. Except for the cotton which he has stuck into his shaggy ears, he possesses no valuables. There remain two: Fido and the white-eyed toad. Which of these is Koreiko? I pause to ponder."

Ostap craned his neck and began to compare the candidates. He turned his head so rapidly that one might think he was intently following a tennis match, keeping his eyes on every ball.

"Do you know, Mechanic," he said finally, "the fat Fido is more likely to be playing the rôle of an underground millionaire than the white-eyed toad. Pay particular attention to the gleam of alarm in Fido's eyes. He cannot sit in one place; he is impatient; he wants to run home as soon as possible and sink his paws into the packages of *chervontsy*.[1] Of course, *he's* the one who gathers in karats and dollars! Can't you see that his fat filthy phiz is nothing but a democratic combination of Shylock, Scrooge, and Harpagon, while the other one with white eyes is a mere nonentity, a Soviet mouse? Of course, he has quite a fortune—twelve rubles in a savings bank! The limit of all his dreams is to buy himself a hairy coat with a calf collar. That's not a Koreiko. That's a mouse which . . ."

But at this point the brilliant speech of the great schemer was cut short by a shout which issued from the depths of the Financial Accounting hall and belonged to an employee whose right to shout in such a manner was undoubtedly indisputable.

"Comrade Koreiko! Where are the figures about the Communal Housing Department's indebtedness to us? Comrade Polykhayev wants them immediately."

Ostap hit Balaganov with his foot, but Fido continued to scratch peacefully with his pen. The face which bore the characteristic points of Shylock, Scrooge and Harpagon did not change. But the white-eyed toad, the nonentity, the Soviet

---

[1] The gold *chervonets*, equivalent to ten rubles, normally worth about a guinea or slightly more than five dollars, is the standard monetary unit of Russian currency. C. M.

mouse wrapped in his dream of an overcoat with a calf collar, displayed unusual activity. He slammed several drawers, seized a bit of paper and ran swiftly to answer the shout. The great schemer clicked his tongue and looked suspiciously at Balaganov. Apparently Lieutenant Schmidt's firstborn did not yet know the master he served. He began to laugh.

"Yes," said Ostap after prolonged silence. "This one will not bring the money on a little plate unless, of course, I plead with him insistently. He is an object deserving of respect. Now let us quickly get some air. An amusing scheme has just been born in my brain. This evening, with the help of God, we shall begin to milk Mr. Koreiko for the first time. You will do the milking, Shura."

Chapter Twelve

HOMER, MILTON, AND PANIKOVSKY

The instructions were very simple:

1. Accidentally meet Citizen Koreiko on the street.
2. Under no circumstances is he to be beaten or thrashed; in general, no violent persuasion is to be applied.
3. Confiscate everything that may be found in the pockets of the above-named citizen.
4. Report the results of the performance of duties.

Despite the extraordinary simplicity and clarity of the instructions issued by the great schemer, Balaganov and Panikovsky began to argue heatedly. The sons of the lieutenant were sitting on a green bench in the city garden, from time to time gazing significantly at the entrance to HERCULES. As they wrangled, they did not even notice when the wind bent the firehose stream of the fountain and sprayed them with a shower of water. They merely ducked, looked distractedly at the clear sky and continued to argue. Panikovsky, who because of the heat had changed his thick fireman's coat for a cotton shirt with an open collar, was haughty. He was very proud of the responsibility that had devolved upon him.

"Mere theft," he said.

"Mere robbery," objected Balaganov, who was also proud of the commander's confidence.

"You are a pathetic nonentity," declared Panikovsky, regarding his companion with disgust.

"And you're a cripple," remarked Balaganov. "Right now I'm the chief."

"Who's the chief?"

"I'm the chief. I'm responsible."

"You?"

"Yes, I."

"You?"

"And who else could it be? I hope you don't think it could be you?"

And the discussion passed into a realm that had nothing to do with the instructions. The foster-brothers became so excited that they began to slap each other and cry out: "Who do you think you are?" Such actions usually precede a free-for-all fight in which the opponents throw their hats on the ground, appeal to passersby to act as witnesses, and smear childish tears over their shaggy faces.

But there was no fight. When the opportune moment finally arrived for the first slap on the face, Panikovsky suddenly lowered his hands and agreed to regard Balaganov as his immediate superior. He no doubt remembered that he had frequently been beaten by single individuals and by entire collectives, and that those were very painful experiences. Seizing the power in his own hands, Balaganov immediately became indulgent.

"Why not rob him?" he said less insistently. "Is it so difficult? Koreiko walks in the street at night. It's dark. I come up on his left hand, you come up on the right. I push him from the left, you push him from the right. The fool stops and says: 'Bully!' to me. 'Who's a bully?' I ask. You also ask 'Who's a bully?' and shove him harder than ever from the right side. Here I swing at his jaw . . . No, we can't beat him!"

"That's just the point—we can't beat him," Panikovsky sighed hypocritically. "Bender doesn't permit it."

"I know it. . . . Anyway, I grab his hands and you pilfer his pockets. He begins to shout 'Police!' And here I . . . Ugh! the devil take it, we can't beat him! Anyway, we go home. Well, how do you like the plan?"

But Panikovsky evaded a direct reply. He took out of Balaganov's hand the carved health resort stick that had a spiked handle instead of a knob, and, sketching a straight line on the sand, said:

"Look! In the first place, we'll have to wait until evening. In the second place . . ." And Panikovsky drew a wavy perpendicular to form a right angle. "This evening he may not come out into the street at all. But even if he should come out, then . . ." Here Panikovsky connected the two lines with a third one so that something resembling a triangle appeared in the sand, and finished, "You can never tell. Maybe he will come out in the company of many others. What do you think?"

Balaganov looked with respect at the triangle. Panikovsky's arguments did not seem to him especially convincing, but he sensed such genuine hopelessness in the triangle that he wavered. Noticing this, Panikovsky lost no time.

"Go to Kiev," he said unexpectedly. "And then you will understand that I am right. I insist upon your going to Kiev."

"What do you mean—Kiev?" Shura muttered. "Why?"

"Go to Kiev and ask what Panikovsky was before the Revolution. I insist upon your asking."

"Don't bother me," Balaganov said sullenly.

"No, you *must* ask!" Panikovsky demanded. "Go there and ask. And they will tell you that before the Revolution, Panikovsky was a blind man. If it were not for the Revolution, do you believe I would ever descend to being the child of Lieutenant Schmidt? What do you think? Why, I was a wealthy man! I had a family. And on my table was a nickel-plated samovar. And how did I make my living? Blue glasses and a little stick!"

He took out of his pocket a cardboard box pasted over with silver-starred black paper and displayed his blue glasses.

"With these glasses," he sighed, "I earned my living for many years. In these glasses and with a little stick, I would go into the heart of Kreshchatik and ask some gentleman who looked a bit cleaner than the rest to help a poor blind man cross the street. The gentleman would take me under my arm and lead me off. By the time we reached the sidewalk, he was already minus a watch, if he had a watch, or his bill fold was gone for sure. Some people had bill folds in those days!"

"Why did you quit this business?" Balaganov asked, coming to life.

"The Revolution," said the former blind man. "In those days I used to pay the policeman on the corner of Kreshchatik and Proreznaya five rubles a month and no one touched me. The policeman even saw to it that no one insulted me. He was a fine man. His name was Nebaba, Semyon Vasilyevich. I met him the other day. He's a music critic now. But nowadays is it possible to establish any decent connections with the police? I've never seen worse people. They've become high-principled, apostles of civilization! And so in my old age, Balaganov, I had to become an impostor. But, for this special business, I could resort to my old glasses. It is much safer than robbery."

Five minutes later a blind man in blue glasses came out of the public lavatory. Holding his chin high and tapping before him with a health resort stick, he moved toward the exit from the garden. Balaganov was on his trail. Panikovsky could not be recognized. Bending back his shoulders and carefully placing his feet on the sidewalk, he walked right up to the houses, tapped his stick along the window bars, collided with the passersby and, looking through them, marched on. He worked so conscientiously that he even broke through a queue, the beginning of which rested on a little post inscribed "Auto Bus Stop." Balaganov marveled as he watched the brave blind man.

Panikovsky practiced until he noticed Koreiko come out of the HERCULES building. Balaganov became panic-stricken. At first he approached too close to the scene of activity, and then he retreated too far away. Finally he assumed a very convenient observation point near a fruit stand. For some reason he had a disgusting taste in his mouth, as if he had been sucking a brass door-knob for a half hour. But, glancing at Panikovsky's maneuvers, he quieted down.

Balaganov saw the blind man turn toward the millionaire, catch him by the foot with his stick and bump him with his shoulder. After this they seemed to exchange a few words. Then Koreiko smiled, took the blind man under his arm, and helped him down the curb. For greater verisimilitude Panikovsky belabored the stones with his stick and tossed back his head like one possessed. The next movements of the blind man were distinguished by such purity and exactness that Balaganov was actually jealous. Panikovsky embraced his companion's waist. His hand glided along Koreiko's left side and for a fraction of a second paused over the millionaire clerk's canvas pocket.

"Go on, go on!" Balagnov whispered. "Come on, old man! Come on!"

But just then panes of glass gleamed, a horn honked frantic warnings, the earth shook and a large white autobus that could not control itself on its wheels stopped with a shudder in the middle of the street. Two voices cried out simultaneously:

"Idiot! Can't you see the autobus!" Panikovsky screamed, jumping out from under the wheels, and waving his glasses threateningly.	"He is not a blind man!" Koreiko cried in astonishment. "You dirty pickpocket!"

Everything was veiled by blue smoke. The autobus rolled on. And when the smoke screen lifted, Balaganov saw that Panikovsky was surrounded by a small crowd of citizens. A good deal of excitement developed around the blind impostor. Balaganov ran up. An ugly smile quivered on Panikovsky's face. He was strangely indifferent to what went on, although one of his ears was so ruby-red that it seemed as if it would shine in the darkness, and one could develop photographic films by its light.

Pushing away the citizens who were running from all sides to the scene of the disaster, Balaganov dashed to the hotel Karlsbad.

The great schemer was sitting at a little bamboo table, writing.

"Panikovsky is being beaten!" Balaganov cried, appearing dramatically in the doorway.

"Already?" Bender asked in a business-like way. "Rather soon."

"Panikovsky's being beaten!" red-headed Shura repeated in despair. "Near HERCULES!"

"Why do you bellow like a white bear in hot weather?" Ostap asked severely. "How long have they been beating him?"

"About five minutes."

"Why didn't you say so in the first place! *There's* a silly old man for you! Well, let's go and have a look at him. You can tell me the rest on the way."

When the great schemer arrived at the scene of disaster Koreiko was already gone, but a great mob swayed around Panikovsky, blocking the entire street. Automobiles honked impatiently, pressing against the mass of humanity. Out of the windows of infirmaries leaned nurses in white aprons. Dogs with tails bent like sabers scurried back and forth. The fountain in the city garden had stopped. With a sigh of decision, Bender pushed his way into the mob.

"Pardon," he said. "Pardon. Excuse me, madam, didn't you lose a permit for jam there on the corner? Run along quickly. It's still lying there. Please let the experts through, man! Let me through, I tell you, you disfranchised kulak!"

Applying thus the policy of the whip and the cookie, Ostap made his way to the center where Panikovsky was languish-

ing. By this time the light that shone from the other ear of
the pact-violator was so bright that one could perform the
most minute photographic operations. Seeing the commander,
Panikovsky sank mournfully.

"This one?" Ostap asked dryly, kicking Panikovsky in the
back.

"That's the one!" a multitude of truth-lovers confirmed
joyously. "I saw him with my own eyes."

Ostap asked the citizens to calm down, took a note book
out of his pocket, and looking at Panikovsky, declared importantly:

"I shall ask the witnesses to indicate their names and ad-
dresses. Witnesses, please register."

It would seem that the citizens who had exhibited such
active interest in seizing Panikovsky would not hesitate to
appear as witnesses against the offender. As a matter of fact,
however, at the mention of the word "witnesses," all the
truth-lovers became sad, moved about sheepishly and began
to desert. Wide gaps formed in the crowd. It crumbled before
everyone's eyes.

"Where are the witnesses?" Ostap repeated.

A panic began. Working with their elbows, the witnesses
made their way out, and in a minute the street assumed its
customary aspect. Automobiles moved from their places. The
windows of the infirmaries slammed. Dogs resumed their
occupation of examining sidewalk piles. And in the city garden the fountain stream rose with the scream of charged
water.

Convinced that the street was clear and that no danger
threatened Panikovsky, the great schemer grumbled:

"Foolish old man! You crazy fool! Another great blind man
has been discovered—Panikovsky! Homer, Milton, and Panikovsky! The three blind men! And as for Balaganov! Like
a sailor from a wrecked ship! 'Panikovsky's being beaten!
Panikovsky's being beaten!' While he himself . . . Let's go to

the city garden. I'll create a little scene for you at the fountain."

At the fountain Balaganov immediately laid all the blame on Panikovsky. The guilty blind man pointed out that his nerves had been shattered through ill-starred years, and at the same time declared that the fault was Balaganov's—a person well-known to be pathetic and insignificant. Right here the brothers began to shove each other. Cries of "Who do you think you are?" were heard. From the eyes of Panikovsky dropped a large tear, that forerunner of a general fight. But the great schemer shouted "Break!" and separated the opponents like a referee in a ring.

"You will box on your days off," he declared. "A splendid pair! Balaganov the rooster and Panikovsky the chicken! However, gentlemen champions, you're a fine pair of bunglers! This will end badly. I'm likely to fire you, you know, because neither of you has any socially useful value."

Panikovsky and Balaganov, forgetting their quarrel, began to promise and persuade Bender that that very evening they would pick the pockets of Koreiko. Bender merely smiled.

"You'll see," Balaganov blustered. "A robbery in the street under the cover of nocturnal darkness. Am I right, Mikhail Samuilovich?"

"My honest and most honorable word," Panikovsky supported him. . . . "Shura and I . . . don't worry. You're dealing with Panikovsky."

"That's why I'm sad," Bender responded. "Although if you like . . . What did you say—under the cover of nocturnal darkness? All right, do it under cover. The idea, of course, is rather thin, and I'm sure it will be badly executed."

After several hours of watching in the street, all the necessary conditions were present: the cover of darkness, and the victim himself, who came out with a girl from the house in which the old puzzle-maker lived. The girl had not been considered in the plan. For the time being they had to follow the promenaders, who went in the direction of the sea.

The glowing fragment of the moon hung low over the cooling shore. On the cliffs sat black basalt couples who had embraced for eternity. The sea whispered of love unto death, of happiness without end, of the tortures of the heart and similar irrelevant details. Star spoke to star with the aid of the glimmering Morse code. The luminous tunnel of a searchlight connected the shores of the bay. When it disappeared, a black post remained in its place.

"I'm tired," Panikovsky whined, tagging after Alexander Ivanovich and his lady over the cliffs. "I'm old. I can't stand it."

He stumbled over gopher holes and fell, his hands catching on to dry cow dung. He wanted to go back to the inn, to the home-loving Kozlevich with whom it was so pleasant to drink tea and gossip about everything.

At the moment when Panikovsky had firmly decided to go home and to ask Balaganov to finish the business alone, he heard in front of him:

"How warm it is! Don't you swim at night, Alexander Ivanovich? Well then, will you wait for me here? I'll take a dip and be right back."

The sound of gravel falling down the precipice was heard. The white dress disappeared and Koreiko remained alone.

"Hurry!" Balaganov whispered, tugging Panikovsky by the hand. "I'll go in from the left and you from the right. But hurry up!"

"I from the left!" the pact-violator said timidly.

"All right, all right! You from the left? I'll push him from the left side, no, from the right, and you from the left."

"Why from the left?"

"For heaven's sake. . . . Well, from the right. He'll say, 'Bully!' And you'll say, 'Who's a bully?' "

"No, *you* talk to him first."

"All right. I'll tell Bender on you! Come on, come on! Remember, you from the left. . . ."

And the valiant sons of Lieutenant Schmidt, frightened to death, approached Alexander Ivanovich.

They deviated from the plan at the very beginning. Instead of coming from the right, in accordance with the disposition of forces, and pushing the millionaire from the right side, Balaganov stood stock-still and suddenly said:

"May I have a light?"

"I don't smoke," Koreiko answered coldly.

"Is that so?" Shura said foolishly, looking around for Panikovsky. "Can you tell me what time it is?"

"About twelve."

"Twelve?" repeated Balaganov. "H'm . . . I had no idea."

"It's a nice warm evening," Panikovsky said ingratiatingly.

There was a pause, during which the crickets cried hysterically. The moon turned pale and by its light one could observe that the shoulders of Alexander Ivanovich were well-developed. Panikovsky could not stand the strain. He went behind Koreiko's back and screamed:

"Hands up!"

"What?" Koreiko asked in astonishment.

"Hands up!" Panikovsky repeated in a faint voice.

Just then he received a short painful blow on the shoulder and fell to the ground. By the time he rose Koreiko had already clinched with Balaganov. Both breathed heavily, as if they were moving a grand piano. From below came the splashing and laughter of a naiad.

"Why are you beating me?" Balaganov shouted at the top of his quivering voice. "I merely asked you what time it was!"

"I'll show you what time it is," hissed Koreiko who was investing his blows with a rich man's ancient hatred of a robber.

On all fours Panikovsky made his way to the place of the massacre and both hands wandered into the pockets of the man from HERCULES. Koreiko kicked him with his foot, but it was too late. The tin cigarette box drifted from the left pocket into the hands of Panikovsky. From the other pocket a number of little papers and membership books dropped to the ground.

"Let's run!" Panikovsky shouted from somewhere in the darkness.

Balaganov received the last blow on his back.

A few minutes later Alexander Ivanovich, disheveled, excited, saw high above him two silhouettes against the moon. They were running along the crest of the hill in the direction of the city.

Refreshed, odorous with the iodine smell of the sea, Zosya found Alexander Ivanovich at a strange occupation. Crawling on his knees and frantically lighting matches, he was picking up papers from the grass. But before Zosya had time to ask what was the matter, he had already found the receipt of the little suitcase which at that moment was resting in the room for hand baggage between a wicker basket full of cherries and a roll of blankets.

"I dropped it accidentally," he said with a strange smile, and carefully put it away. Only when they were already entering the city did he remember the cigarette box labeled "Caucasus" containing the ten thousand rubles which he had not had the time to place in the suitcase.

While the momentous struggle went on at the seashore, Ostap Bender decided that to remain longer at the hotel might rouse general curiosity and make him a marked figure. He read the following advertisement in the Chernomorsk evening paper: "fr rnt splnd rm w cnvncs sv sng int bchlr," and understanding in a flash that this announcement meant: "for rent, a splendid room with all conveniences and a view of the sea, to a single, intellectual bachelor," Ostap thought:

"For the present I am apparently a bachelor. Not long ago

the Stargorod marriage bureau sent me an announcement that my marriage with Citizen Gritsatsue was dissolved on the basis of her complaint, and that I might assume my pre-marital name—O. Bender. What is to be done about it? I suppose I shall have to go back to pre-marital life. Therefore, I am a bachelor, single, and indisputably intellectual. The room will undoubtedly be mine."

And pulling up his cool white trousers, the great schemer went to the address indicated in the advertisement.

Chapter Thirteen

VASISUALY LOKHANKIN AND HIS RÔLE IN
THE RUSSIAN REVOLUTION

At precisely 4.40 in the afternoon Vasisualy Lokhankin declared a hunger strike.

He lay on an oil cloth sofa, his face turned from the entire world toward the sofa's bulging back. He lay in suspenders and green socks, which in Chernomorsk are also called *karpetki*.

Having starved in this position for twenty minutes, Lokhankin groaned, turned on the other side, and glared at his wife. In the course of this half-circle, his green *karpetki* described a small arc in the air. His wife was throwing all of her belongings into a handbag: figured perfume bottles, a rubber roller for massage, two dresses with trains and one old one without a train, a felt *shako* ornamented with a glass half moon, brass cartridges of lip-sticks, and knitted riding breeches.

"Varvara!" Lokhankin said through his nose.

His wife, breathing heavily, made no response.

"Varvara!" he repeated. "Is it possible that you are leaving me for Ptiburdukov?"

"Yes," answered his wife. "It must be!"

"But why? But why?" Lokhankin demanded with bovine passion.

His large nostrils dilated tragically. His pharaoh beard quivered.

"Because I love him."

"But what about me?"

"Vasisualy! But I told you about it yesterday. I don't love you any more."

"But what about me! I love you, Varvara!"

"That's your private affair. Vasisualy, I'm going to Ptiburdukov. It must be!"

"No!" Lokhankin exclaimed. "It must not be! No human being may leave another as long as that other loves him."

"He may so!" Varvara said irritably, looking at herself in a hand mirror. "And anyway, stop being a fool, Vasisualy."

"All right! I shall continue the hunger strike!" the unfortunate husband cried. "I shall starve until you return. A whole day! A week! I shall starve for a year!"

Lokhankin turned over again and pushed his fat nose into the slippery cold oil cloth.

"I shall lie thus in my suspenders until I die," came from the divan. "And the fault will be yours and Engineer Ptiburdukov's!"

The wife thought a moment, covered her shoulder with the shawl that had dropped, and suddenly began to scream:

"Don't you dare to say such things about Ptiburdukov! He's better than you are!"

Lokhankin could not tolerate this. He twitched as if a charge of electricity had gone through his entire body, from the suspenders to the green *karpetki*.

"You're a bitch, Varvara!" he whispered. "You're a street walker!"

"Vasisualy, you are a fool," his wife answered calmly.

"You are a she-wolf," Lokhankin continued to whine. "I despise you. You are leaving me for a lover. You are leaving me for Ptiburdukov. You loathsome creature, you are going away from me to that Ptiburdukov. That's what you're leaving me for! You want to wallow in lust with him. Besides, you're a loathsome old she-wolf!"

Reveling in his sorrow, Lokhankin did not even notice that

he was speaking in iambic pentameter, although he had never written verse before and did not even like to read it.

"Vasisualy, stop clowning!" said the she-wolf, closing the traveling bag. "I wish you could see what you look like. If you would only wash yourself! I am going away. It must be! Farewell, Vasisualy. I'm leaving your bread card on the table."

She picked up the bag and went to the door. But seeing that his exorcisms had been of no avail, Lokhankin quickly jumped off the divan, ran up to the table, and with a cry "Help," tore up the bread card. This frightened Varvara. In a flash she saw her husband emaciated by hunger, with slowing pulses and cold extremities.

"What have you done?" she said. "Don't you dare to starve!"

"I will!" Lokhankin declared stubbornly.

"It's foolish, Vasisualy. It's a revolt of individuality."

"And I am proud of it," replied Lokhankin in a tone that was suspiciously iambic. "You do not appreciate the significance of either individuality or of the intelligentsia as a whole."

"Public opinion will condemn you."

"Let it condemn me!" Vasisualy said decisively, and again fell on the sofa.

Exasperated, Varvara flung her handbag to the floor, quickly pulled the straw hat from her head and muttering, "The mad tomcat! Tyrant! Proprietor!" rapidly made a sandwich of chopped eggplant "caviar."

"Eat!" she said, pushing the food against her husband's crimson lips. "Do you hear me, Lokhankin? Eat at once! Well?"

"Leave me alone," he said, brushing her hand aside.

Taking advantage of the momentary opening of the hunger-striker's mouth, Varvara dextrously shoved the sandwich into the aperture between the pharaoh beard and the

little neatly-shaven Moscow mustache. But with a quick movement of his tongue, the hunger-striker pushed it out.

"Eat, you scoundrel!" Varvara cried in despair, frantically
jabbing at his face with the sandwich. "You intellectual!"

But Lokhankin moved his face away from the sandwich
with lightning speed, mooing negatively. Several minutes later
the excited Varvara, smeared with the green "caviar," beat a
retreat. She sat down on her bag and began to weep bitter
tears.

Lokhankin brushed the crumbs off his beard, carefully
glanced sideways at his wife, and sank into silence on his sofa.
He did not want to part with Varvara. In spite of a multitude
of drawbacks, Varvara had two real assets: a large white
bosom and a job. Vasisualy *never* had a job. A job would
have interfered with his ruminations about the Russian intelligentsia, of which social layer he considered himself a part.
Thus the profound thoughts of Lokhankin were all on such
pleasing and intimate themes as: "Vasisualy Lokhankin and
His Significance," "Lokhankin and the Tragedy of Russian
Liberalism," "Lokhankin and His Rôle in the Russian Revolution." He pondered these themes in peace and comfort,
pacing the room in his felt slippers—bought on Varvara's
money—and glancing now and then at his favorite bookcase
where gleamed the gilded backs of the Brockhaus Encyclopedia. For long minutes Vasisualy would stand in front of the
bookcase, his eyes moving from one volume to another. Here
also stood other excellent examples of the bookbinding art: a
large medical encyclopedia, Brehm's "Life of Animals," a
huge tome of "Man and Woman," and also Elise Reclus' "The
Earth and the People."

"With this precious thought," Vasisualy would meditate at
length, "one somehow becomes purer, one somehow grows
spiritually."

Having arrived at this conclusion, he would sigh joyously,
pull out from under the bookcase a copy of the magazine

"Fatherland" for the year 1899, in the binding that represented a breaking wave, and examine pictures of the Boer war, the announcement of an anonymous lady: "This is how I increased my bust by six inches," and other matters of prime interest.

Varvara's departure meant the disappearance of the material basis on which rested the well-being of a worthy member of thinking humanity.

Ptiburdukov came in the evening. For a long time he could not decide to enter the rooms of the Lokhankins. He wandered about in the communal kitchen among long-flamed Primus stoves and ropes stretched under the ceiling on which hung dry, plaster of Paris underwear streaked with blueing. The apartment became lively at once. Doors opened and shut, shadows glided by, the eyes of the lodgers glistened, and somewhere someone sighed passionately: "A man has come."

Ptiburdukov took off his cap, tugged at his engineer's mustache, and finally came to a decision.

"Varya," he pleaded, entering the room. "But we had agreed . . ."

"Feast your eyes, Sasha darling!" cried Varvara, seizing his hand and dragging him to the sofa. "Here he is! Lying down! The tomcat! The vile proprietor! Do you understand? This slaveholder has declared a hunger strike because I want to leave him!"

Upon beholding Ptiburdukov, the hunger striker immediately delivered himself of an iambic pentameter:

"Ptiburdukov, how I despise you! And don't you dare to touch my life's companion! You are a cad, Ptiburdukov, a scoundrel! What have you done to lure my wife away?"

"Comrade Lokhankin!" said Ptiburdukov in astonishment, tugging at his mustache.

"Away! Away! Oh, Lord, how I detest you!" continued Vasisualy, swaying like an old Jew at his prayers. "You are a loathsome and pathetic nit! Who said you were an engineer?

You are a boor! A scoundrel! Trash! A crawling reptile! And furthermore, a pimp!"

"You ought to be ashamed of yourself, Vasisualy Andreyich!" said the disgusted Ptiburdukov. "It's simply silly. Just think what you are doing! And this is the second year of the Five-Year Plan!"

"He dares to say to me that this is silly! Yes, he, the cad who steals my wife from me! Away, Ptiburdukov, or I shall scream!"

"Poor man!" said Ptiburdukov, trying to remain within the bounds of decency.

But Varvara could no longer contain herself within these bounds. She seized the dry green sandwich and advanced upon the hunger-striker. Lokhankin defended himself with the desperation of a man who resists castration. Ptiburdukov turned away and looked through the window at a horse-chestnut tree starred with blossoms like white candles. Behind him he heard the disgusting mooing of Lokhankin and Varvara's cries: "Eat, you low scoundrel! Eat, you slave driver!"

The next day, upset by the unexpected difficulties, Varvara did not go to work. The hunger-striker had a bad relapse.

"My stomach already gripes me," he announced complacently. "Later I will have scurvy because I don't eat, and then my hair and teeth will fall out. . . ."

Ptiburdukov brought his brother, a military surgeon. Ptiburdukov II applied his ear to the body of Lokhankin for a long time, listening to the activity of his organs with the attentiveness of a cat listening to the movements of a mouse that has crawled into the sugar bowl. During the examination Vasisualy regarded his chest, shaggy as an autumn overcoat, with tear-filled eyes. He was very sorry for himself. Ptiburdukov II looked at Ptiburdukov I and announced that the sick man did not need a diet, that he might eat everything: for example, soup, meat balls, compote; that he might also have bread, vegetables, fruits; that fish wouldn't hurt him either;

that he might smoke, but naturally within reason; that he did not advise the sick man to drink strong liquor but that it would not hurt to introduce into his organism a full glass of good port wine as an apéritif—in general, it might be said that the doctor did not do a good job in diagnosing the emotional conflict of the Lokhankins. Puffing majestically and stepping heavily, he went away, declaring in farewell that he also did not forbid the sick man to take sea baths and ride a bicycle.

But the sick man had no intention of introducing into his organism either compotes, or fish, or meat balls, or any other solid food. Nor did he take sea baths, but continued to lie on the divan, belaboring those around him in insulting blank verse. Varvara pitied him. "He is starving himself for my sake," she thought with pride. "After all, what passion he is capable of! I wonder if darling Sasha is capable of such exalted feelings?" And she cast uneasy glances at well-fed darling Sasha, whose appearance indicated that amorous experience would not deter him from regularly introducing into his organism both dinners and suppers. And once when Ptiburdukov left the room she called Vasisualy "her poor little boy." But the sandwich which appeared at the mouth of the starving man at the same time was again rejected. "A little more endurance," thought Lokhankin, "and Ptiburdukov will never see my Varvara again."

Later he listened with satisfaction to the voices in the adjoining room.

"But he'll die without me!" Varvara was saying. "We must wait awhile. Don't you see that I cannot leave right away?"

That night Varvara had a terrible dream. Vasisualy, emaciated by his exalted feelings, was hungrily gnawing the silver spurs on the boots of the military doctor. It was horrible. On the face of the doctor was the resigned expression of a cow that is being milked by the village thief. The spurs clanked, the teeth chattered. In fright Varvara awakened.

The yellow sun freshly imported from Japan shone intensely, wasting all its energy on illuminating such an insignificant detail as the cut-glass stopper of a vial of "Turandot" eau de Cologne. The oil cloth sofa was empty. Varvara looked around and beheld Vasisualy. He was standing at the open doors of the cupboard, his back to the bed, loudly smacking his lips. He was bending over in greedy haste, stamping his green-socked foot, while whistling and snuffling noises issued from his nose. Having emptied a tall glass of preserves, he took the cover off a pan and, dipping his fingers into cold *borshch,* pulled out a piece of meat. Had Varvara caught her husband thus occupied, even during the best period of their marital life, Vasisualy would have got it in the neck, to use the vulgar language of non-intellectuals. Now his fate was decided.

"Lokhankin!" she cried in a terrible voice.

The frightened hunger-striker dropped the meat which slapped back into the pan, lifting a spray of cabbage and carrot stars. He flung himself on the sofa with a pathetic whine. Varvara was dressing, silently, rapidly.

"Varvara!" he moaned through his nose. "Are you actually leaving me for Ptiburdukov?"

There was no answer.

"You she-wolf!" Lokhankin declared with lack of conviction. "I despise you! You are leaving me for Pt . . ."

But it was already too late. Vasisualy whimpered in vain of love, and of death by starvation. Varvara left him forever, dragging after her the traveling bag containing the colored breeches, the *shako,* the perfume bottles, and other feminine accouterments.

And the life of Vasisualy Andreyevich entered into a period of torturing thoughts and moral suffering. There are people who cannot enjoy suffering. Somehow nothing comes of it. When they must suffer, they try to make their period of suffering as brief as possible and unnoticeable to those around them. But Lokhankin suffered openly, majestically. He guzzled his grief; he got drunk on it. His great sorrow gave him another opportunity to ponder not only upon the significance of the Russian intelligentsia, but also upon the tragedy of Russian liberalism.

"But perhaps it must be," he thought. "Perhaps this is an atonement, and I shall come out of it thoroughly purified. Is this not the fate of all who stand higher than the mob, of all whose constitutions are delicate? Galileo! Miliukov! Kerensky! Yes, yes! Varvara is right! It must be!"

This spiritual depression did not prevent him, however, from placing an announcement in the newspaper about his desire to rent the other room.

"Anyway, it will help me financially for the time being," Vasisualy decided, and again sank into vague concepts about the suffering of the flesh and the significance of the soul as the source of the beautiful. He could not be detached from these ruminations even by the insistent declarations of his neighbors concerning the necessity of turning out the light after him in the communal lavatory. Suffering likewise from an emotional diarrhœa, Lokhankin constantly forgot; and his economical fellow-lodgers were incensed.

At the same time, it must be added that the denizens of the large Apartment No. 3 in which Lokhankin resided were people who had established a definite reputation for frequent scenes and vehement quarrels. Apartment No. 3 had even been dubbed "Magpie Village." Continual life together had toughened these people, and they knew no fear. The apartmental balance of power depended on blocs among the various lodgers. There were even times when all the residents of "Magpie Village" united against one lodger, and on such occasions that one was in a bad way. The centripetal force of barratry swept him up, sucked him into offices of jurisconsults, whirled him through tobacco-reeking court corridors, and thrust him into chambers of various trial courts. And long after that the unsubmissive lodger would be wandering in search of equity, finding his way finally to the All-Union Bailiff, Comrade Kalinin. To the day of his death the lodger would shower you with the legal terminology he had gathered in various public places, referring to himself not as Comrade Zhukov but as "the plaintiff," and pronouncing with particular expressiveness the words: "I filed suit." And his life, which even before had not flowed with milk and honey, would become utterly wretched.

Long before the family tragedy of the Lokhankins, aviator Sevryugov, who had the misfortune to live in Apartment No. 3, flew away to the North Pole at the urgent order of the Osoviakhim. The whole world was excitedly following Sevryugov's flight. A foreign expedition bound for the Pole had been lost; no word had come from them, and Sevryugov was despatched to find them. The world lived on the hope of the airman's success. The radio stations of all the continents talked to each other; meteorologists warned the daring Sevryugov against electric storms; short waves filled the ether with SOS.'s. And the Polish newspaper "Kurjer Poranny," which is close to the Ministry of Foreign Affairs, had already announced the expansion of Polish borders to the status of 1772. For a whole month the distinguished lodger of Apartment No. 3 flew over the icy wastes, and the rumble of his motor was heard throughout the world.

Finally Sevryugov did something which completely befuddled the newspaper that was close to the Polish Ministry of Foreign Affairs: he found the expedition among the blocks of ice, managed to communicate its precise location, and then immediately disappeared himself. This news filled the world with cries of admiration. The name of Sevryugov was pronounced in 320 languages and dialects, including the language of the Blackfoot Indians. The portrait of Sevryugov muffled in animal skins appeared on every spare piece of paper. In an interview granted to the press, Gabriele d'Annunzio declared that he had just finished a new novel and would immediately fly to the rescue of the daring Russian. A Charleston entitled "I'm Warm with My Sweetie at the Pole" appeared, and the veteran Moscow potboilers—Usyshkin-Werther, Leonid Trepetovsky, and Boris Amniakov, who had long been practicing literary dumping and were throwing their products on the market at cut-rate prices—were already writing a review under the title: "Aren't You Cold?" In a word, our planet was experiencing a great sensation.

But the sensation was even greater when the news reached Apartment No. 3, which was located in house No. 8 on Lemon Lane, and better known as "Magpie Village."

"Our lodger is lost!" rejoiced the retired janitor Nikita Pryakhin, drying his felt boot over the primus stove. "The poor fellow is lost. Shouldn't fly. Shouldn't fly. Man should walk, not fly. He should walk, he should walk."

And he turned the boot over the groaning fire.

"Well, he's come to the end of *his* flying, that jaundice-eyed bum!" muttered Grandma, whose name and surname no one knew. She lived in an attic over the kitchen, and although the whole apartment was lighted with electricity, in Grandma's corner there was a kerosene lamp with a reflector. She would not trust electricity. "Anyway, now we have a vacant room. More living space."

Grandma was the first to pronounce the word which weighed so heavily upon the inhabitants of Magpie Village. The room of the lost aviator was on the tongue of everyone, including the former Caucasian prince and now Eastern worker, Citizen Gigienishvili, and Dunya, who rented a cot in the room of Aunty Pasha, and Aunty Pasha herself, a quarrelsome, drunken derelict, and Alexander Dmitrievich Sukhoveiko, formerly a chamberlain in the court of his Imperial Majesty, now known in the apartment simply as Mitrich, and the rest of the apartment's small fry, headed by the responsible renter, Luzzia Franzevna Pferd.

"Well," said Mitrich, adjusting his gold spectacles as soon as the kitchen became full of lodgers. "As long as the comrade has disappeared, we ought to divvy up. For instance, I have had the right to additional space for a long time."

"What does a man need extra room for?" objected Dunya the cot-renter. "A woman needs it. Perhaps it will never happen again in my life that a man will suddenly disappear."

And for a long time she pushed her way through the gathering, adducing various proofs in her favor and frequently pronouncing the word "man."

At any rate, the lodgers agreed on one thing: the room should be taken over immediately by the apartment as a whole.

That very day the world quivered with a new sensation. The daring Sevryugov was found. Nizhni-Novgorod, Quebec, and Reykjavik had heard Sevryugov's SOS.'s. He was sitting on his crumpled chassis exactly on the 84th parallel. The ether quivered with messages: "The daring Russian feels fine"; "Sevryugov reports to the Præsidium of the Osoviakhim"; "Charles Lindbergh considers Sevryugov the best aviator in the world"; "Seven ice-breakers have gone forth to help Sevryugov and the new-found expedition."

In the space that was left between all these communications, newspapers printed nothing but photographs of chunks of ice and snow-bound wastes. There were endless reiterations of "Sevryugov, North Cape, parallel, Sevryugov, Franz Joseph Land, Spitzbergen, King's Bay, ice floes, gasoline, Sevryugov . . ."

The dejection which fell upon Magpie Village when this news reached them soon changed to quiet assurance. Ice-breakers move slowly, breaking through the fields of ice with difficulty.

"Take the room away and that's all there is to it," Nikita Pryakhin was saying. "He doesn't mind sitting there on the ice. But here, Dunya has a right to floor space. Moreover, according to law, a lodger cannot stay away longer than two months."

"Shame on you, Citizen Pryakhin," objected Varvara, at that time still Lokhankina, shaking a copy of "Izvestia." "He's a hero—at this very moment he's on the 84th parallel!"

"Whoever heard of such a parallel?" said Mitrich dubiously. "Maybe there isn't such a parallel. I've never heard of it— never studied about it in the gymnasium."

Mitrich spoke the honest truth. He had never studied in a gymnasium. He had graduated from the Imperial school of Court Pages.

"Can't you understand?" Varvara was agitated, bringing the paper right up to the nose of the former chamberlain. "Here's the article. Do you see? 'I'm in the midst of ice floes and icebergs.'"

"Eisbergs!" Mitrich jeered. "I can understand that. I haven't lived decently for ten years. All these Eisbergs, Weisbergs, Eisenbergs, Rosenbergs, and then all the Rabinoviches! Pryakhin is right. Take the room away, that's all! Besides, Luzzia Franzevna agrees about the law."

"And throw his things out on the stairway! To hell with them!" came the chesty voice of the former prince who was now the Eastern worker, Citizen Gigienishvili.

Varvara was soon completely routed and ran away to complain to her husband.

"And perhaps it should be like that," replied her husband, raising his pharaoh's beard. "Perhaps homespun truth speaks through the lips of the common peasant Mitrich. Only think of the rôle of the Russian intelligentsia, of its significance . . ."

On the momentous day that the ice-breaker finally reached Sevryugov's tent, Citizen Gigienishvili broke the lock on Sevryugov's door and threw all the hero's property into the corridor, including the red propeller that hung on the wall. Dunya moved into the room and immediately sub-let floor space to six people who brought their own cots. On the conquered territory an all night feast was held. Nikita Pryakhin played on his harmonica and Chamberlain Mitrich danced the national Russian dance with drunken Auntie Pasha.

If Sevryugov's fame, acquired by his remarkable flights to the Arctic, had been a trifle less than world-wide, he would never again have beheld his room. The centripetal force of barratry would have whisked him away, and to his dying day he would be known not as the brave Sevryugov, the hero of the North, but as "plaintiff." But on this occasion Magpie Village was thoroughly chastised. The room was returned (Sevryugov soon moved out to a new house), while the enterprising Gigienishvili spent four months in jail and returned as mad as the devil.

It was he who first informed the orphaned Lokhankin of the necessity of regularly turning out the light upon leaving the communal lavatory. When he spoke of this his eyes were diabolical. The absent-minded Lokhankin underestimated the importance of Citizen Gigienishvili's declaration and thus disregarded the beginning of a conflict which soon led to a horrible event, uncommon even in the experience of the lodgers.

The affair developed in this way: Vasisualy Andreyevich continued to forget to turn out the light in the commonly used cabinet. How could he be expected to remember such details of daily life when his wife had deserted him, when he had been left without a kopek, and when he had not yet definitely decided upon the variegated significance of the Russian intelligentsia? How could he have guessed that the pitiful, dim little light of an eight-candle-power lamp could provoke such violent feelings among his neighbors? At first he was warned several times a day. Later they sent him a letter composed by Mitrich and signed by all the lodgers. Finally they stopped warning him and sent no more letters. Lokhankin had not yet grasped the significance of what was happening, but he began to sense dimly that some ring was closing in upon him.

On Tuesday evening Auntie Pasha's little girl ran into his room and announced in one breath:

"Theysayforthelasttimeyoushouldturnoutthelights!"

But again Vasisualy Andreyevich forgot, and the little lamp glowed incriminatingly through the spider webs and the dirt. The apartment took a deep breath. A minute later Citizen Gigienishvili appeared in the doorway of Lokhankin's room. He wore blue cloth boots and a flat brimless hat of brown lambskin.

"Come on," he said, luring Vasisualy with a finger.

He grasped him firmly by the hand, led him along the dark corridor, which depressed Vasisualy for some reason and even caused him to buck a little, and with a blow on the back shoved him out into the middle of the kitchen. Lokhankin managed to maintain his balance by grabbing at the laundry ropes, and looked around in fright. The entire apartment had gathered, and stood in silence about Luzzia Franzevna Pferd. Ominous purple wrinkles scarred the mighty face of the responsible renter. At her side sat drunken little Auntie Pasha, humped sadly on the top of the stove. Barefooted Nikita Pryakhin smiled wryly at the intimidated Lokhankin. The head of nobody's Grandma peered from the attic. Dunya made signs to Mitrich. The former Court Chamberlain smiled, hiding something behind his back.

"What! Will I get a reprimand?" asked Vasisualy Andreyevich in a thin voice.

"You'll get it, you'll get it!" said Nikita Pryakhin, coming close to Lokhankin. "You'll get coffee, *kakawa!* Lie down!" he cried suddenly, breathing a mixed odor of vodka and turpentine into Vasisualy's face.

"In what sense do you mean 'lie down'?" asked Vasisualy Andreyevich, beginning to tremble.

"Why bother with this criminal!" said Citizen Gigienishvili.

And sitting down on his haunches, he began to fumble around Lokhankin's waist, unbuttoning the suspenders.

"Help!" Vasisualy whispered, his mad eyes staring at Luzzia Franzevna.

"You should have turned off the light," Citizen Pferd responded severely.

"We are not bourgeois; we don't waste electric energy," added Chamberlain Mitrich, dipping something into a pail of water.

"I'm not guilty!" Lokhankin squeaked, tearing himself out of the hands of the former prince who was now an Eastern worker.

"None of us is guilty," muttered Nikita Pryakhin, holding the quivering lodger.

"But I didn't do anything!"

"None of us did anything."

"I feel depressed!"

"We all feel depressed."

"Don't you dare to touch me! I'm anemic!"

"So are all of us! We're all anemic!"

"My wife has deserted me!" Vasisualy uttered with his last strength.

"Our wives have deserted all of us," replied Nikita Pryakhin.

"Come on, Nikitushko," Chamberlain Mitrich uttered in a business-like way, brandishing the shining wet birch twigs. "If we keep on talking, we won't get through till dawn."

Vasisualy Andreyevich was placed with his stomach on the floor. His white legs were exposed. Citizen Gigienishvili swung on him with all his might, and the birch twigs whistled thinly in the air.

"Mamochka!" screamed Vasisualy.

"Everybody has a Mamochka," Nikita informed him, pressing Lokhankin with his knee.

But suddenly Vasisualy stopped screaming.

"But perhaps it should be," he thought, twitching from the blows and examining the armored toe nails on the feet of Nikita. "Perhaps precisely in this lies salvation, purification, the great sacrifice."

And while he was being thrashed, while Dunya giggled in embarrassment, while Grandma yelled from her attic, "That's the way to teach the nitwit! That's the way to treat the angel child!", Vasisualy Andreyevich concentrated his thoughts on the significance of the Russian intelligentsia, and on the fact that Galileo also suffered for the truth.

Mitrich was the last to take the birch twigs.

"Give it to me. Let me have a try," he said, raising his arm for a good blow. "Let me lay a few strokes to make the fillet parts of his anatomy tender!"

But Lokhankin was not fated to know the chamberlain's stroke. There was a knock on the back door. Dunya ran to open it. (The front entrance of Magpie Village had been closed up long ago because the lodgers could never decide whose turn it was to wash the stairway; for a similar reason the bathroom was locked up.)

"Vasisualy Andreyevich, a strange man is asking for you," Dunya said, as if nothing had happened.

And all beheld in the doorway a strange man in a gentleman's white trousers. Vasisualy Andreyevich jumped to his feet quickly, fixed his clothes, and with an ingratiating smile turned his face to Bender.

"I hope I didn't disturb you?" the great schemer asked respectfully, blinking his eyes.

"Yes, yes," Lokhankin muttered, shuffling his feet. "Here I was—how shall I put it—a trifle occupied . . . but . . . I think . . . that I am free now."

And he looked appealingly around him. But there was no one left in the kitchen except Auntie Pasha who had fallen asleep on top of the stove. On the planked floor were scattered birch twigs and a white cloth-covered button with two holes.

"Come into my room," Vasisualy invited.

"But perhaps—are you sure that I'm not taking too much of your valuable time," asked Ostap, finding himself in Lokhankin's first room. "Are you quite sure? Very well then. Is it you who announced: fr rnt splnd rm w cnvncs sv sng int bchlr? And is it really splnd, and has cnvncs?"

"Absolutely right!" Vasisualy revived. "A splendid room, all the conveniences. And I don't want much. Fifty rubles a month."

"The price is quite all right," said Ostap politely. "But about the neighbors . . . What are they like?"

"Splendid people!" Vasisualy replied. "And besides, all the conveniences. And the price is cheap."

"But it seems they've introduced corporal punishment into this apartment."

"Ach!" Lokhankin said profoundly. "But when you come right down to essentials, who knows? Perhaps it ought to be. Perhaps precisely here lies the great homespun truth."

"Homespun?" Bender repeated thoughtfully. "Perhaps it may be hempen, home woven, fibrous and filamentiferous. H'm . . . H'm . . . By the way, would you tell me from which class of the gymnasium were you flunked out? From the sixth?"

"From the fifth," Lokhankin responded.

"Wonderful class! Then you didn't get as far as Krayevich's 'Physics'? And I suppose since then you have led an exclusively intellectual life. But after all, I don't care. Live as you like. To-morrow I shall move in."

"But . . . mm . . . the . . . mm . . . deposit?" the former gymnasium student asked.

"You're not in a church, so you won't be fooled," the great schemer said with conviction. "You'll get your deposit—in due time."

Chapter Fourteen

THE FIRST MEETING

O STAP returned to the Karlsbad Hotel. As he mounted the stairs, he noted with pleasure his endless reflections in the vestibule, stairway, and corridor mirrors with which establishments of this kind like to decorate themselves. He was astonished by the chaos that reigned in his orderly room. The red plush chair lay upside down on the floor, its short legs sticking up and disclosing a most unattractive jute cover. The gold-embroidered velvet cloth had slipped off the table. Even the picture entitled "Christ Appears to the People" hung awry, thus losing its original effectiveness. From the balcony blew a fresh sea breeze, rustling the banknotes that were scattered over the bed. Among them lay a tin box that had once contained "Caucasus" cigarettes. Clinched on the carpet, their legs jerking, Panikovsky and Balaganov rolled in silence.

The great schemer stepped contemptuously over the squabblers and went out on the balcony. Below on the boulevard promenaders chattered, gravel crunched underfoot, and the harmonious strains of the symphony orchestra were wafted over the black maples. In the dark depths of the port, lights glistened, and faint clangs resounded from the refrigerating plant that was being built. Beyond the breakwater an invisible steamship roared and demanded something—probably to be let into the harbor.

Reëntering the room, Ostap saw that the foster brothers had reached the stage of wearily pushing each other as they sat, and muttering, "Who do you think you are?"

"So you didn't divide up after all?" Bender asked, pulling the portière across the window.

Panikovsky and Balaganov quickly jumped to their feet and began to talk. Each of them claimed sole credit for the success of the enterprise, and berated the activity of the other. Having reached no previous agreement, they omitted unfavorable details about themselves and cited instead a large number of particulars which presented them in the best light.

"That's enough!" Ostap said. "Don't wear yourselves to a frazzle. The scene of battle is clear to me. You say there was a girl with him? Fine! And so the petty clerk carries in his pocket a mere . . . I think you have already counted the money? How much was there? Oho! Ten thousand! Mr. Koreiko's salary for twenty years of faultless service. It's a sight for the gods, as the smart editorials put it. But I think I disturbed you? It seems to me you were busy on the floor. Oh, it was money you were dividing? Pray, continue—I shall watch."

"I wanted it done honestly and fairly," said Balaganov, gathering the money from the bed. "An equal part for everybody. Two and a half thousand apiece."

And dividing the money into four piles, he stood modestly aside and explained, "You, I, he, and Kozlevich."

"Very good," Ostap remarked. "Now let Panikovsky divide. He seems to have his own opinion on the subject."

In support of his own opinion, Panikovsky undertook the business with alacrity. Bending over the bed, he smacked his thick lips, spat on his fingers, and deliberately moved the banknotes from one place to another, as if he were laying out the large Royal Patience. After all sorts of manipulations, three piles formed on the cover of the bed: one, large, of new clean bills; another of the same size, but of bills a little dirtier; and the third small, and of the dirtiest bills.

"You and I get four thousand apiece," he said to Bender. "And Balaganov two. He hasn't earned even those two!"

"But Kozlevich?" Balaganov asked, his eyes closing in anger.

"Why give anything to Kozlevich?" Panikovsky screamed. "That's robbery! Who is this Kozlevich that we should divide with him? I don't know any Kozlevich!"

"Have you finished?" asked the great schemer.

"Yes," replied Panikovsky, without removing his eyes from the pile of clean bills. "What has Kozlevich to do with it?"

"And now I shall show you how it should be done," said Ostap.

Unhurriedly he put all the piles into one, placed the money in the tin box, and the box in the pocket of his white trousers.

"All of this money," he announced, "will be immediately returned to the victimized Citizen Koreiko. Do you approve this form of division?"

"No, I don't!" broke from Panikovsky.

"Stop joking, Bender!" Balaganov said irritably. "Let's divide it up fairly."

"There will be no division," Ostap said coldly. "Furthermore, I have no desire to jest with you at this late hour."

Panikovsky threw up his purple old hands. He looked at the great schemer with dismay, and began to sulk in a corner. The old pact-violator effaced himself completely; only his gold tooth gleamed occasionally.

Balaganov's face immediately became as wet as if it had been roasted in the sun.

"What did we work for then?" he puffed. "That's not right!"

"To you," Ostap said courteously, "seeing that you are the favorite son of the lieutenant, I can repeat only what I said at Arbatov: I respect the criminal code. I'm not a bandit, but a high-principled fighter for currency. Robbery does not enter into my four hundred honest means of securing money. Somehow there's no room for it. And besides, we didn't come here for ten thousand. Of thousands, I alone need at least five hundred."

"Why did you send us then?" asked Balaganov, cooling down. "We tried . . ."

"In other words, you want to ask whether your most respected commander knows what aim he had in view when he undertook the recent enterprise? To this I can answer: yes, he knows. This is the point . . ."

At this minute, the light of the golden tooth in the corner went out. Panikovsky lowered his head, aimed his entire body, and with a cry of, "Who do you think you are?", desperately flung himself upon Ostap. Without changing his pose, without even turning his head, merely with a push of his hard-rubber fist, the great schemer returned the incensed pact-violator to his former place, and continued . . .

"The point is, Shura, that this was merely a test. Consider: a clerk with a salary of forty rubles has ten thousand rubles in his pockets. This is strange, to say the least, and presents us with great opportunities, permits us, in the language of marathon runners and other running bugs, to hope for a king's ransom. Five hundred thousand—that is really a king's ransom. And here is how we shall get it: I shall return the ten thousand to Koreiko and he will take it. I should like to see the man who will not take back his own money. And precisely here will come his downfall. He will be destroyed by greed. He will scarcely confess to his wealth, when I shall take him with my bare hands. Being a wise man, he will understand that a part is less than the whole, and he will give me that part for fear of losing all. And at this point, Shura, there will appear a certain little plate with a certain little border . . ."

"You're right!" Balaganov exclaimed. "Amazing!"

In the corner Panikovsky wept.

"Give me back my money!" he blubbered. "I am so poor!

I haven't had a bath for a year! And I'm old. Girls don't like me."

"I refer you to the Universal League of Sexual Reform," said Bender. "Perhaps there they will help you."

"Nobody loves me!" continued Panikovsky, shaking with sobs.

"How could anybody love you? Girls don't love the like of you. They love young, long-legged, politically literate ones. You'll die soon, anyway. And no one will write about you in the newspapers: 'Another comrade has killed himself with work.' And no beautiful widow with Persian eyes will sit on your grave. And no weeping children will ask, 'Papa, papa, do you hear us?' "

"Don't talk like that!" cried the frightened Panikovsky. "I'll outlive all of you! You don't know Panikovsky! Panikovsky will yet buy and sell you all! Give me back my money!"

"You had better tell me whether you want to go on working or not. I'm asking you for the last time."

"I want to," answered Panikovsky, slowly wiping his old man's tears.

Night, night, night lay over the entire country. In the port of Chernomorsk the cranes turned easily, dropped their steel feelers into the deep holds of foreign ships, and turned again to the quay to deposit, with the loving care of a mother-cat, pine boxes with machinery for the tractor factory. Sparks, like rosy comets, spurted from the high chimneys of silicate plants. Here gleamed the gathered stars of Dnieprostroi, Magnitogorsk, and Stalingrad. In the north the star of Krasnoputilovsk had risen, and behind it flared a great multitude of other stars of first magnitude. Here were factories, combines, electric stations, new construction; here blazed the entire Five-Year Plan, its illumination blocking out the old sky which once shone for the Egyptians.

And the young man who had sat for a long time with his sweetheart in the workers' club, quickly lit the electrified map of the Fve-Year Plan and whispered:

"Look at that red light! There is where the Sibcombine will be. We'll go there! Want to?"

And the beloved laughed quietly, freeing her hands.

Night, night, night, as we have already noted, lay over the entire country.

In his sleep the monarchist Khvorobyov groaned, dreaming of a huge trade union card. Engineer Talmudovsky snored in the upper berth from Kharkov to Rostov whither he had been lured by more salary. The American gentlemen rolled on the broad Atlantic wave, carrying a recipe for excellent wheat home brew to their "dry" country. On his sofa Vasisualy Lokhankin squirmed, rubbing the injured places with his hand. The old puzzle-maker Sinitsky burned electricity in vain while he composed for the magazine, "The Water-Main Business," a puzzle picture entitled: "Where is the chairman of this general meeting of workers and clerks who have gathered to elect the local committee of the pumping station?", and tried not to make any noise so as not to awaken Zosya. Polykhayev lay in bed with Serna Mikhailovna. Other Herculeans slept fitfully in various parts of the city. Alexander Ivanovich Koreiko could not fall asleep, tortured by thoughts of his wealth. If this wealth had not existed at all, he could have slept peacefully. What Bender, Balaganov and Panikovsky were doing is already known. And only concerning Kozlevich, the driver and owner of Antelope-Gnu, will nothing be said right now, although he was already in hot water of an extremely political nature.

Early in the morning Bender opened his obstetrician's bag, extracted a policeman's cap with the insignia of the city of Kiev, and shoving it in his pocket, went to call on Alexander Ivanovich Koreiko. On the way he collided with the milk women, for the hour of these canny women had already arrived, while the hour of the office-workers had not yet begun. He hummed to himself the words of the song: "And the joy of the first meeting no longer stirs my blood." The great schemer's behavior belied his words. He was excited at the prospect of the first meeting with the millionaire clerk. Entering house No. 16 on the Street of Little Worries, he put on the official cap, and, knitting his brows, knocked on the door.

Alexander Ivanovich stood in the middle of the room. He was in his sleeveless undershirt and had had time to put on the orphan-asylum trousers of a petty employee. The room was furnished with the exemplary penury of pre-Revolutionary orphan asylums and similar organizations under the patronage of the Empress Marie Feodorovna. Here were three objects: an iron hospital bed, a kitchen table with little doors that were closed by the wooden latch typical of summer-cottage outhouses, and a dilapidated chair. In a corner lay Indian Clubs and two large weights—the sport of an indoor athlete.

At the sight of the policeman, Alexander Ivanovich stepped forward heavily.

"Citizen Koreiko?" Ostap asked, smiling radiantly.

"Yes," responded Alexander Ivanovich, likewise expressing the joy befitting the occasion of meeting a representative of the State.

"Alexander Ivanovich?" Ostap inquired, smiling even more radiantly.

"Quite so," confirmed Koreiko, kindling his joy as much as possible.

After this there was nothing else for the great schemer to do but to sit down on the chair and force a super-smile on his face. This done, he looked at Alexander Ivanovich. The millionaire clerk strained with all his might and produced—anything you like: tenderness, and rapture, and delight, and dumb worship—all because he was so fortunate as to meet a minion of the law.

This rivalry of smiles and emotions was reminiscent of one of the manuscripts of the composer Liszt, where on the first page is written, "Play fast," on the second, "Very fast," on the third, "Much faster," on the fourth, "As fast as you can," and on the fifth, "Still faster."

Seeing that Koreiko had reached the fifth page and that further competition was impossible, Ostap got down to business.

"I've come to you on an errand," he said less radiantly.

"If you please," remarked Alexander Ivanovich, his face becoming overcast.

"We want to please *you*."

"I am curious to know how."

By this time Bender's face expressed immeasurable sorrow. He put his hand into his pocket. Koreiko followed his movements with a face that was now completely funereal. Into the light of day appeared the tin box. But the cry of surprise that Ostap had expected was not forthcoming. The underground millionaire looked at the box with utter indifference. Ostap took out the money, carefully counted it, and pushing the package toward Alexander Ivanovich, said:

"Exactly ten thousand. Will you please sign a receipt for it?"

"You are mistaken, comrade," Koreiko said quietly. "What ten thousand? What receipt?"

"What do you mean? You were robbed yesterday evening, weren't you?"

"No one robbed me."

"What do you mean, no one robbed you!" Ostap became excited. "Yesterday evening by the sea! And they took ten thousand! The robbers were arrested! Sign the receipt!"

"So help me God, nobody robbed me," said Koreiko. A bright smile crossed his face. "Evidently this is a mistake."

Not yet realizing the full extent of his defeat, the great

schemer permitted himself to make a scene which he always afterwards remembered with shame. He insisted, became angry, pushed the money into the hands of Alexander Ivano-vich, and on the whole, as the Chinese say, lost face. Koreiko shrugged his shoulders, smiled courteously, but did not take the money.

"So you were not robbed?"

"No one robbed me."

"And no one took ten thousand from you?"

"Of course not! Why, what do you think? Where would I get so much money?"

"Quite right, quite right," Ostap said, cooling down. "Where could a petty clerk get such a lot of money? So you have no complaints to make?"

"None," replied the millionaire with a charming smile.

"And you're not suffering from indigestion?" Ostap asked with an even more charming smile.

"Not in the least. Do you know, I am a very healthy man."

"And you're not tormented by nightmares?"

"No, not at all!"

Then, as far as smiles were concerned, everything went according to Liszt: fast, very fast, much faster, as fast as pos-sible, and even faster yet. The new acquaintances parted as if they were enraptured with each other.

"Don't forget your police cap," said Alexander Ivanovich. "You've left it on the table."

"Don't eat too many pickles," Ostap advised, "or you might get the hiccoughs!"

"Good-by," Koreiko said, bowing with gay formality.

"Au revoir, au revoir," Ostap responded. "You're an inter-esting man. You have no complaints to make! Remarkable! Such luck—and still at liberty!"

And a fatuous smile still on his face, the great schemer went out into the street. He walked several blocks at a rapid pace, forgetting that he was wearing an official cap with the insignia of the city of Kiev, altogether out of place in the city of Chernomorsk. And not until he found himself in a crowd of respectable old men who were making a racket opposite the covered veranda of the Narpit Dining Room No. 68, did he recover and begin again quietly to estimate his chances.

While he walked back and forth ruminating absentmindedly, the old men continued to occupy themselves with their daily business.

These were strange, outlandish people for our epoch. Nearly all of them had on white piqué waistcoats and straw hats. Some of them even wore dilapidated old panamas. And of course all of them wore yellow starched collars out of which protruded their scrawny necks. Here in front of Dining Room No. 68, the former site of the famous Café Florida, gathered the remnants of Chernomorsk's pre-war business men: brokers who had been deprived of their offices, commission merchants who had withered away without commissions, grain agents, bookkeepers who had lost their minds, and similar riff-raff. At one time they had come here to close their deals. Now they were drawn to this sunny corner through habit and the necessity of wagging their old tongues. Every day they read the Moscow "Pravda"—they had no respect for the local press. And everything that happened in the world was regarded by the old men as a prelude to declaring Chernomorsk a free city. Some time ago—a hundred years ago—Chernomorsk had actually been a free city, and this had been so nice and profitable that the legend of *Porto-Franco* cast its golden sheen at the bright corner near the Café Florida until this day.

"Have you read about the disarmament conference?" one piqué waistcoat addressed another piqué waistcoat. "The speech of Count Bernsdorf?"

"Bernsdorf? A real head on his shoulders!" replied the waistcoat of whom the question had been asked, in a voice that suggested that he had become convinced of his conclusion on the basis of many years' personal acquaintance with the count. "But did you read about the speech that Snowden delivered at the meeting of the electors of Birmingham, that citadel of conservatism?"

"Why, what's the use of talking! Snowden has a smart head on him. Listen, Valiadis." He turned to the third old man in the panama, "What do you think of Snowden?"

"I'll tell you frankly," the panama replied. "I wouldn't advise anyone to put his finger in Snowden's mouth. Personally, I would not risk *my* finger."

And oblivious of the fact that Snowden would under no conditions permit Valiadis to put his finger in his mouth, the old man continued:

"But no matter what you say, I'll tell you frankly: Chamberlin also has a head on his shoulders!"

The piqué waistcoats shrugged their shoulders. They did not deny that Chamberlin also had a head on his shoulders, but they were pleased most of all with Briand. "Briand!" they exclaimed with heat. "There's a real head for you! With his project of Pan-Europe . . ."

"I'll tell you frankly, Monsieur Funt," Valiadis whispered. "Everything is settled. Beneš has already agreed to a Pan-Europe, but do you know on what condition?"

The piqué waistcoats gathered around closer and craned their scrawny necks.

"On the condition that Chernomorsk be declared a free city! Beneš! That's a real head! They have to sell their agricultural implements to someone, don't they? So we'll buy from them."

This idea caused the eyes of the old men to shine. They had been wanting to buy and sell for so many years!

"Briand! There's a head for you!" All of them sighed. "And Beneš also has a head on him."

When Ostap recovered from his thoughts, he noticed that an anonymous old man in a crushed straw hat with a greasy black band was firmly holding him by his coat. His four-in-hand necktie had slid to the side and the brass collar-button stared Ostap right in the face.

"But I tell you," the old man shouted into the ear of the great schemer, "MacDonald will not fall for that! He will never fall for that, do you hear?"

Ostap pushed the excited old man away and extricated himself from the crowd.

"Hoover! There's a head for you!" the old man shouted after him.

Ostap had arrived at a decision. He had considered all the four hundred honest means of obtaining money, and although among them were such gems as the organization of a joint stock company for raising a ship with a cargo of gold bullion that had sunk during the Crimean War from the bottom of the sea, or a large Easter celebration for the benefit of the prisoners of capitalism, or a concession for taking down old store signs, not one of these fitted the given situation. So Ostap had invented the four hundred-and-first method.

"I failed to take the fortress by storm," he thought. "I shall have to begin a regular siege. The principal premise has been established. The defendant has money. And judging by the fact that he refused ten thousand without blinking, he must have a lot of money. So, since the parties could not come to an agreement, the meeting continues."

He returned home, buying on the way a stiff yellow portfolio tied with shoe laces.

"Well?" they both asked him at once—Balaganov and Panikovsky who had awaited his return with impatience.

Ostap passed silently to the bamboo table, placed the portfolio before him, and in large letters wrote the following inscription: "The Case of Alexander Koreiko" . . . "Begun on June 25th, 1930" . . . "Finished ——th, 193—."

The foster-brothers looked at the portfolio over Bender's shoulder.

"What's inside of it?" asked the curious Panikovsky.

"Oh," said Ostap. "Everything is inside of this: palms, girls, Blue Expresses, the azure sea, a white steamship, a scarcely worn dinner jacket, a Japanese valet, a private billiard table, platinum teeth, socks without holes, dinners on pure butter fat, and, what is more important, my little friends, the fame and power of Money!"

And to the astonished Antelopians he disclosed an empty portfolio.

Chapter Fifteen

HORNS AND HOOFS

ONCE upon a time lived a poor private trader. He was a fairly wealthy man, the owner of a notion store located opposite the cinema "Capitoline." He traded quietly in underwear, laces, neckties, buttons and other small but profitable merchandise. One evening he returned home with a worried face. He went quietly to the cupboard, took out a whole cold chicken, and walking up and down the room, ate it all. When this was done, he again opened the cupboard, took a ring of Cracow sausage weighing exactly half a kilo, sat down on a chair, and, fixing his glassy eyes on one spot, slowly masticated the entire half kilo. When he stretched his hand out for the hardboiled eggs which lay on the table, his wife asked him in fright:

"What has happened, Borya?"

"Misfortune," he answered, shoving a hard rubbery egg into his mouth. "I have been frightfully taxed. You can't even imagine!"

"Then why do you eat so much?"

"I have to do something to take my mind off of it," the private owner replied. "I'm afraid."

And all through the night the private trader paced his room, which contained at least eight chiffoniers, and ate. He ate everything that was in the house. He was afraid.

The next day he rented half of his store to a trader in stationery supplies. Now in the same show window were neckties and garters, and a huge yellow pencil suspended by two pieces of string.

Then came times that were even worse. A third co-owner appeared in the store. He was a watchmaker who pushed the pencil a bit aside and took half the window to make room for a brass clock with a figure of Psyche but without a minute hand. And beside the pencil man, a watchmaker with a black magnifying glass stuck in his eye sat opposite the poor notion man who never stopped smiling ironically.

Twice again did misfortune descend upon the notion man. Into the store moved a plumber who immediately lighted a Primus for soldering purposes, and a strange merchant who had decided that in this—the 1930th year since the birth of Christ—the population of Chernomorsk was going to throw itself upon his merchandise—starched collars.

Then the once proud, refined sign of the notion man assumed an abominable appearance:

Notion Store GALANTPROM B. KULTURTRIGER	Watch Repairing of All Kinds GLAZIUS-SHENKER	KANZBUM Everything for the artist and the Soviet office worker LEV SOKOLOVSKY
	REPAIR of mains, lavatories, and basins M. M. FANATYUK	Exclusive Starched Collars From Leningrad KARL UKUSINEN

Customers would enter the store, which had once been neat, with trepidation. The watch maker, Glazius-Shenker, surrounded by wheels, his pince-nez and springs, sat under his clocks, among which was also a tower clock. Alarms rang frequently and resonantly. In the back of the store were crowds of school children on the trail of copy books which were difficult to obtain. Karl Ukusinen trimmed his collars with scissors, killing time while waiting for customers. And invariably, before the solicitous B. Kulturtriger had time to ask a customer, "What can I do for you?", the plumber Fanatyuk would strike a rusty pipe a thunderous hammer blow, and the soot of the blow torch would cover the delicate notions.

Finally this intricate combine of private dealers crashed. Karl Ukusinen drove away in a droshky with the merchandise that was anachronistic to his epoch. After him Galantprom and Kanzbum terminated the pursuit of the tax-collector by disappearing without leaving a forwarding address. Fanatyuk took to drinking; Glazius-Shenker joined the watch-maker's collective "New Time." The ribbed iron shutters dropped with a clatter and the interesting sign-board disappeared.

Soon, however, the shutters rose again, and over the former ark of the private dealers appeared a small, neat sign:

CHERNOMORSK BRANCH OF THE ARBATOV
OFFICE FOR THE COLLECTION OF
HORNS AND HOOFS

Any idle Chernomorskian who peeked into the store would notice that the shelves and counters had disappeared, that the floor was clean, that gleaming office desks were about, and that on the walls hung the customary notices about reception hours and the danger of handshaking. The new institution already had its counter as a rampart against the callers who, however, were not yet in evidence. At a small table, on which a yellow samovar puffed steam and weakly complained of its samovar fate, sat a messenger with a gold tooth. As he wiped the teacups, he sang irritably: "Oh, what wicked times are these! Oh, what wicked times are these! Men have lost their faith in God! Men have lost their faith in God!" A red-headed fellow wandered around behind the counter. Occasionally he would walk up to the typewriter, strike the keyboard with a thick, unbending finger, and then laugh uproariously. In the very back of the office, under the sign, "Department Chief," sat the great schemer, illumined by the light of an incandescent lamp.

The Karlsbad Hotel had been abandoned long ago. All of the Antelopians with the exception of Kozlevich had moved into Vasisualy Lokhankin's room in Magpie Village, despite its proprietor's protests. He pointed out that he had rented the room not to three, but only to one single, intellectual bachelor. "Mon Dieu! Vasisualy Andreyich," Bender had replied innocently. "Don't torture yourself. After all, of the three of us, I am the only intellectual, so we have kept to the terms of the agreement." To the landlord's further complaints Bender would reply philosophically, "Mein Gott, my dear Vasisualy! Perhaps herein lies the great homespun truth," which immediately quieted Lokhankin, particularly as soon as Ostap gave him twenty rubles. Panikovsky and Balaganov adapted themselves quickly and completely to Magpie Village, and their voices resounded with confidence in the general chorus of the apartment. Panikovsky was soon accused of wandering about at night and stealing the kerosene out of the Primus stoves. Mitrich did not miss an opportunity to reprimand Ostap for something to which the great schemer replied by poking him silently in the chest.

The office for the collection of horns and hoofs had been opened for many reasons.

"The investigation in the case of Koreiko may take a lot of time," Ostap said. "How long it will last, only God knows. And since there is no God, nobody knows. A horrible situation! Perhaps a year, and perhaps a month. At any rate, we need legal status. We must become a part of the great mass of office employees. The office will give us that status. Administrative activity has attracted me for a long time. At heart I am a bureaucrat and a blockhead. We will collect something very funny; for example, tea spoons, dog plates, or any kind of gadgets, or—horns and hoofs! Excellent! Horns and hoofs are needed for the comb and mouthpiece industry. Why can't it be an institution? In my little bag I have excellent blanks for all occasions, and a round rubber stamp."

The money which Koreiko had refused, and which the meticulous Ostap then felt he had the right to accept, was placed in a bank to the account of the new establishment. Panikovsky rebelled again and demanded a division of spoils, in punishment for which he was appointed to the low-paid and degrading office of messenger boy, which hurt his independent nature. Balaganov, on the other hand, was given the responsible post of expert on hoofs with a salary of 92 rubles. An old Adler typewriter was bought from a seedy intellectual in the market place and once more went to work.

The great schemer liked his new field of activity tremendously. Every hour he ran into the office with new purchases. He bought such intricate office machinery and supplies that the courier and the hoof-specialist oh'ed and ah'ed. There were hole-punchers, mimeograph presses, a duplicator, a screw-press, and a very expensive bronze inkwell with several little huts, each for a different color of ink. This work of art was entitled "Facing the Village," and cost a hundred and fifty rubles. All of these supplies were crowned by a cast-iron railroad conductor's ticket punch which Ostap requisitioned from the passenger department of the local railroad station. Finally Bender dragged in the branchy horns of a stag. Panikovsky, groaning and complaining of his low office, hammered them up over the chief's desk. Things went well—and even excellently. The establishment worked out its Five-Year Plan, indicating on the graph the excellent attainments for the past two years and pledging itself to fulfill its program long before the allotted time. Only one thing was lacking: the Antelope and its caretaker, Adam Kozlevich.

On the third day of the office's existence, a visitor appeared. To everyone's surprise it was the postman. He brought eight letters, and after gossiping a bit with the messenger, Panikovsky, went away. Among the letters were: three notices inviting a representative of the institution to appear immediately for conferences and sessions, all three notices emphasizing the fact that this appearance was obligatory; other communications from unknown but energetic establishments demanding all sorts of information, statistical data and other intimate details which had to be presented in innumerable copies, immediately and without fail.

"What does this mean?" Ostap cried. "Three days ago I was a free, rapacious eagle, flapping my wings wherever I wished, but now, if you please, I must present myself without fail. There is evidently a multitude of people in this city who are badly in need of Ostap Bender! However, who will carry on all of this correspondence with these friends? I shall have to readjust the budget and reconsider the question of personnel. We must have an experienced office manager and let her attend to such affairs."

Two hours later a new misfortune occurred. A peasant staggered in under a heavy sack.

"Who's in charge of the horns?" he asked, dropping his treasure on the floor.

The great schemer looked suspiciously at the visitor and his treasure. Examination revealed crooked, dirty horns, and Ostap regarded them with disgust.

"Not very good merchandise," the chief said dubiously.

"Come on, take another look at it!" The muzhik became excited and shoved a yellow horn under the nose of the great schemer. "A-1 quality, according to specifications!"

Since the merchandise was according to specifications, whatever the specifications were, it had to be bought. After that the muzhik drank tea with Panikovsky for hours, telling about village life and rousing in Ostap the natural irritation of a man who had just lost fifteen rubles.

"If Panikovsky lets in another horn-carrier," Ostap remarked after the visitor's departure, "Panikovsky will be minus a job. I'll fire him without advance salary. And anyway, we've done enough for the government and the Five-Year Plan. It's time to get down to our own business."

Hanging on the glass door a notice "Out for Lunch," the department chief took out of the closet a portfolio which presumably contained a blue sea and a white steamship, and striking it with the palm of his hand said:

"This is what will occupy our office. Right now this case hasn't a single document. But we'll get down to the bottom of it, even if it should necessitate sending Panikovsky and Balaganov to the sands of Kara-Kum or to Kremenchug for investigation!"

At this very moment someone tugged at the handle of the outer door. Outside the window paced an old man in a panama hat mended with white thread, and a wide pongee coat which revealed a piqué vest. The old man craned his scrawny neck and applied a large ear to the pane of glass.

"Closed! Closed!" Ostap cried quickly. "The collection of hoofs has been stopped temporarily."

The old man continued to make signs with his hands. If Ostap had not permitted the old man in the white vest to enter, perhaps this novel would have taken a different turn, and the remarkable occurrences which are about to be related would not have happened—those remarkable occurrences involving the great schemer, and in which the irritable courier, the carefree specialist in hoofs, and a number of other people, including a certain cold-blooded philosopher, the granddaughter of the old puzzle-maker, a famous civic leader, the chief of HERCULES and even a man who wrestled with his own feather bed participated.

But Ostap did open the door. The old man, smiling wistfully, staggered behind the counter and sank into a chair. He shut his eyes and sat silently in the chair for about five minutes. All that could be heard were short whistles which issued from his pinched nose from time to time. When all the employees of the office had decided that the visitor would never again be able to utter a word and had begun to consult in whispers how best to take his body out into the street, the old man raised his brown eyelids and said in a low voice:

"My name is—Funt—Funt."

"And do you suppose that is sufficient to justify your breaking into the office of a Soviet government establishment during the lunch hour recess?" Bender asked gayly.

"Here, you're laughing," the old man replied. "But my name is—Funt. I am ninety years old."

"Well, what do you want?" Ostap asked, beginning to lose patience.

But at this point Citizen Funt again sank into an inviolable silence that lasted a considerable time.

"You have an office," he finally said.

"Yes, yes. An office," Ostap encouraged him. "Go on, go on!"

But the old man merely stroked his knee with his hand.

"Do you see these trousers?" he pronounced after prolonged silence. "These are Passover trousers. There was a time when I put them on only for Passover, but now I wear them every day."

And in spite of the fact that Panikovsky slapped his back so that the words might come out without impediment, Funt again fell silent. He pronounced his words fast enough, but between his sentences there were intervals that lasted three minutes on an average. People who were unaccustomed to this peculiarity of Funt's could not endure conversing with him. Ostap was about to take Funt by his starched collar and show him the way out, when the old man again opened his mouth.

What is more, his discourse assumed such an entertaining character that Ostap managed to tolerate Funt's manner of carrying on a conversation.

"Don't you need a chairman?" Funt asked.

"What chairman?" Bender exclaimed.

"An official one—in a word, the chief of the establishment."

"I am the chief myself."

"In other words, you expect to do time yourself? Why didn't you say so in the first place? Why then did you take up two hours of my valuable time?"

The old man in the Passover trousers became exceedingly angry, foamed at the mouth, fumed, emitted explosive noises, but the pauses between his sentences did not diminish.

"I am Funt!" he said emphatically. "I am ninety years old! All my life I've done time for others! Such is my profession— to suffer for others!"

"Oh, so you are a professional figure-head!"

"Yes," said the old man, tossing his head boastfully. "I am Substitute-chairman Funt! I've always done time. At the time of Alexander the Second, the Liberator, at the time of Alexander the Third, the Peacemaker, at the time of Nicholas the Second, the Bloody." And the old man slowly bent back his fingers, counting the tsars. "At the time of Kerensky I also did time. At the time of Military Communism, I did no time, to tell the truth, because clean business disappeared and there was no work for me. But how I did time in the days of the NEP! How I did time in the days of the NEP! Those were the best days of my life. During four years I had less than three months of freedom. I married off my granddaughter Golconda Yevseyevna, and as dowry I gave her a concert piano, a silver bird and eighty rubles in golden ten-spots. And now I walk around and I cannot recognize our Chernomorsk. Where has everything gone? Where is private capital? Where is the First Society of Mutual Credit? Where, I ask you, is the Second Society of Mutual Credit? Where are the unincorporated companies? Where are the joint stock companies with mixed capital? Where are they all? Monstrous!"

This brief speech lasted a comparatively short time—a half hour. Listening to Funt, Panikovsky was touched. He took Balaganov aside and whispered with bated breath:

"Right away you can see that he is a man of the good old days. There are few of his kind left now, and soon none of them will be left."

And with a courteous flourish he brought the old man a cup of sweet tea.

Ostap dragged the substitute-chairman to his own desk, ordered the office closed, and began patiently to question the eternal prisoner who lay down his life for his friends. The substitute-chairman spoke with pleasure. If he had not taken such long rests between sentences, one might even say that he chattered without stopping.

"Don't you know a fellow by the name of Koreiko, Alexander Ivanovich?" Ostap asked, glancing at the portfolio tied with shoe laces.

"Don't know him," answered the old man. "Don't know him."

"And did you ever have any business with HERCULES?"

At the mention of HERCULES the substitute-chairman faintly stirred. Ostap did not even notice this movement, but if any piqué vest from Café Florida who had known Funt for a long time, had been in his place—for example, Valiadis—he would have thought to himself: Funt is terribly excited; he has simply lost control of himself!

How could Funt help knowing HERCULES when his last four convictions were directly connected with that institution? Several private joint stock companies had lived off HERCULES. There was, for example, one called "Intensifier." Funt was made the chairman of it. "Intensifier" received a large advance of money from HERCULES for the purpose of doing something connected with lumber—the substitute-chairman was not supposed to know what it was—and immediately it crashed. Somebody got the money, while Funt did six months. After "Intensifier" appeared a new organization called "The Laboring Cedar," again under the chairmanship of the presentable Funt. Naturally there was an advance from HERCULES for the delivery of seasoned cedars. Naturally there was an unexpected crash; somebody became rich, while Funt bore the responsibilities of chairman by doing time. Later there was "Saw Helper." An advance from HERCULES—a crash—someone took it all—Funt did time. And again—an advance from HERCULES—the "Southern Woodchopper"—Funt did time— someone got the treasure.

"But who got it?" Ostap demanded, walking all around the old man. "Who was actually behind all these enterprises?"

The old man silently sipped his tea and raised his heavy lids with difficulty.

"Who can tell?" he said mournfully. "They always kept it from Funt. All I had to do was do my time. This is my profession. I did time at the time of Alexander the Second, at the time of the Third, at the time of Nicholas Alexandrovich Romanov, at the time of Alexander Feodorovich Kerensky, and at the time of the NEP, and before the degeneration of the NEP, and during the degeneration, and after the degeneration. But now I am out of work and have to wear my Passover trousers."

For a long time Ostap continued to sift the words of the old man. He acted like a gold-pan that untiringly washes tons of mud and sand in order to find a few nuggets of gold at the bottom. He nudged Funt's shoulder, constantly awakened him, and even tickled him under his arms. With the aid of all these devices, he finally managed to find out that, according to Funt's opinion, behind all of these bankrupt business organizations there was undoubtedly some one person. As far as HERCULES was concerned, it had been milked of more than one hundred thousand.

"At any rate," the ancient substitute-chairman added, "at any rate, this unknown man has a head on him. Do you know Valiadis? Valiadis wouldn't put his finger into the mouth of this man!"

"But what about Briand?" Ostap asked with a smile, remembering the congregation of piqué vests in front of the former Café Florida. "Would Valiadis put his finger into the mouth of Briand? What do you think?"

"Not for anything in the world!" Funt replied. "Briand has a head on him." He moved his lips soundlessly for three minutes, and added, "Hoover has a head on him! And Hindenburg has a head on him. Hoover and Hindenburg both have heads on them!"

Panic gripped Ostap. The oldest of the piqué vests was about to sink into the morass of international politics. At any minute he might begin to speak about the Kellogg Pact, or about the Spanish Dictator Primo de Rivera, and then no power on earth could tear him away from this absorbing occupation. A mad gleam had already appeared in his eyes. His Adam's apple was beginning to quiver over the yellowed starched collar, auguring the birth of a new sentence, when Bender unscrewed an electric lamp and threw it on the floor. The lamp burst with the crack of a rifle shot, and only this deflected the attention of the substitute-chairman from international affairs. Ostap quickly took advantage of this.

"But didn't you see any representative of HERCULES?" he asked. "What about the business of advances?"

"I had business relations only with the HERCULES bookkeeper, Berlaga. He got his salary from them. But I don't know anything. They kept everything from me. People need me only for doing time. I did time under Tsarism, and under Socialism, and under the Hetman, and during the French occupation . . . Briand has a head on him!"

Nothing else could be squeezed out of the old man; but

even the little that he had said presented sufficient grounds for beginning an investigation.

"Here I sense the hand of Koreiko," Ostap thought. "But even if it isn't he, it's someone else who is well worth while."

The chief of the Chernomorsk Department of the Arbatov office for the Collection of Horns and Hoofs sat down at his desk and made a written record of the conversation with substitute-chairman Funt. He omitted, however, the disquisition about the relations of Valiadis and Briand.

The first page of the underground investigation of the underground millionaire was numbered, punctured in the proper places, and duly filed.

"Well, will you take on a chairman?" the old man asked, putting on his mended hat. "I see that your office needs a chairman. My price is not high: 120 rubles a month at liberty, and 240 in prison, a hundred per cent increase for damages."

"I suppose we can give you the job," Ostap said. "Make out your application and hand it to the hoof-specialist. To-morrow morning come to work. But don't be late. This is no 'Intensifier' and no 'Laboring Cedar.' We are very strict."

Chapter Sixteen

"JAHRBUCH FÜR PSYCHOANALITIK"

IN the Financial Accounting Department of HERCULES the working day began as usual at nine o'clock.

Kukushkind had lifted the hem of his coat in order to polish his eyeglasses, and was making ready to inform his fellow employees that working for the banking house of Sikomorsky and Tsesarevich was far pleasanter than for the Herculean Sodom and Gomorrah; Tezoimenitsky had turned toward the wall on his swivel chair, and had stretched forth his hand as usual to tear the sheet off the calendar; Lapidus Jr.'s mouth had opened to receive the piece of bread smeared with chopped herring—when the door opened, and on the threshold appeared none other than the Bookkeeper Berlaga.

This unexpected entrance provoked complete confusion in the Financial Accounting hall. Tezoimenitsky slipped on his swivel chair, and for the first time in many years the calendar sheet was not duly torn off. Lapidus Jr., forgetting to bite into his sandwich, bit empty air. Dreyfus, Chevazhevskaya, and Sakharkov were utterly astonished. Koreiko raised and dropped his head. And old man Kukushkind hastily put on his eyeglasses, forgetting to polish them—something which had never before happened to him in the thirty years of his career as an office employee.

Berlaga sat down at his desk as if nothing had occurred, and without replying to the subtle derision of Lapidus Jr., opened his books. .

"How is your health?" Lapidus persisted unabashed. "How is the medulla oblongata?"

"All well now," Berlaga answered without raising his head. "I don't even believe that this part of man's anatomy exists."

Until the recess for lunch the entire Financial Accounting Department was restless on its swivel chairs and cushions, tortured by curiosity. When the alarm bell rang out, the flower of the bookkeeping world surrounded Berlaga. But the fugitive barely replied to the questions. He took four of the most trustworthy aside, and, convinced that there was no outsider nearby, related his unusual adventures in the insane asylum. The fugitive bookkeeper embellished his account with a multitude of involved expressions and comments which are here deleted to attain greater continuity of narration.

THE TALE OF BOOKKEEPER BERLAGA RE-LATED BY HIM UNDER STRICTEST SECRECY TO BORISOKHLEBSKY, DREYFUS, SAKHARKOV, AND LAPIDUS JR. ABOUT WHAT HAPPENED TO HIM IN THE INSANE ASYLUM.

As is already known, Bookkeeper Berlaga fled to the insane asylum because he feared the housecleaning. His plan was to stay in this therapeutic institution through the troublous times and return to the HERCULES after the thunder had died down and the eight comrades with their little gray eyes had moved over to a neighboring establishment.

The entire plot was concocted by his brother-in-law. The latter found a book about the manners and habits of the insane, and after prolonged argument, of all the ideas, "delusions of grandeur" was selected.

"You won't have to do anything," the brother-in-law explained. "All that is necessary is to shout into everybody's ears: I am Napoleon! Or Emile Zola, or Mohammed, if you like."

"Can I be the Viceroy of India?" Berlaga asked wistfully.

"Why, of course, of course! A crazy man can be anything. Have you decided on the Viceroy of India?"

The brother-in-law spoke so impressively that one might take him for at least a junior physician of an insane asylum. As a matter of fact, however, he was an honest agent for the distribution of beautiful subscription editions of the State Publishing House, and in his little trunk all that remained of one-time commercial greatness was a Viennese derby with a white silk lining.

The brother-in-law ran to a pay-station telephone to call the ambulance, while the new Viceroy of India took off his *tolstofka* shirt, put on a nightshirt, and for good measure, poured a bottle of India ink of A-1 quality on his head. Then he lay down on the floor on his stomach, and, as soon as the hospital orderlies arrived, began to cry out:

"I am the Viceroy of India! Where are my trusty nabobs, my maharajahs, my abreks, my kunaks, my elephants?"

Hearing these delusions of grandeur, the brother-in-law dubiously shook his head; in his opinion abreks and kunaks did not enter into the sphere of activity of India's Viceroy. But the hospital orderlies merely took a wet towel, wiped the face of the bookkeeper, smeared with India ink of A-1 quality, and placed him in the ambulance. The enameled doors were slammed, the medical horn resounded, and the automobile carried Viceroy Berlaga to his new domain.

All the way over the sick man waved his hands and raved. Not once did he stop thinking with horror about his impending encounter with the first real madmen. He was very much afraid that the lunatics might not only hurt his esthetic sensibilities but perhaps even injure something more concrete.

The hospital proved quite different from Berlaga's conception of it. In a long light room men in blue robes sat on sofas, lay on beds or walked about. The bookkeeper noticed that the madmen almost never spoke to each other. They had no time to converse. They were thinking. They were thinking all the time. They had a multitude of thoughts. They strained to recall something. They strained to recall that most important thing of all on which happiness depends. But their thoughts would crash and the most important thing of all, flapping its little tail, would disappear. And again they had to ponder and try to understand: what has happened? Why has everything suddenly gone wrong when it used to be so fine?

A distracted, unhappy madman walked past Berlaga several times. Clutching his chin with his fingers, he walked on the same line from the window to the door, from the door to the window, back to the door, and again to the window. And so many thoughts rattled in his poor head that his other hand was constantly on his forehead as he hastened his pace.

"I am the Viceroy of India!" Berlaga shouted, looking around at the hospital orderlies.

The madman did not even glance in the direction of the bookkeeper. Wrinkling his face painfully, he again began to gather the thoughts that had been scattered by Berlaga's shouts. Just then a stunted idiot came up to the Viceroy and confidently putting his arm around his waist, uttered a few words in bird language.

"What?" the frightened Berlaga asked guardedly.

"Enna, benna, rabba, quinter, finter, jabbah," the unknown pronounced distinctly.

Berlaga uttered "Oi!" and retreated as far as he could from the idiot. While he was drawing away, he stumbled against a man with a lemonish bald spot. The latter immediately turned away to the wall and peered furtively at the bookkeeper.

"Where are my maharajahs?" Berlaga inquired, conscious of the need to uphold his reputation as madman.

Just then a patient who was sitting on a bed in the back of the room rose to his thin feet, as yellow as church candles, and shouted pathetically:

"Freedom! Freedom! To the pampas!"

As the bookkeeper later discovered, the man who wanted to go to the pampas was an old geography teacher, through

whose text-book young Berlaga had at one time become acquainted with volcanoes, capes, and isthmuses. The geographer had lost his mind quite unexpectedly. Glancing at the
map of both hemispheres one day, he could not find Behring
Strait. All day long the old teacher pored over the map.
Everything was in its place: Newfoundland and the Suez
Canal, and Madagascar, and the Hawaiian Islands with their
chief city Honolulu, and even the volcano Popocatepetl, but
Behring Strait was absent. And right there, bent over the
map, the old man went mad.[1] He was a goodnatured madman, quite harmless, but Berlaga was desperately frightened.
Every cry stabbed his heart.

"Freedom!" the geographer continued to cry. "To the pampas! Freedom!"

He knew better than anybody else in the world the meaning of freedom. He had been a geographer and he knew about
spaces which ordinary people occupied with dull affairs did
not even suspect. He wanted freedom; he wanted to gallop
through thickets on a sweating mustang.

A young woman doctor with sad blue eyes entered the
chamber and went directly to Berlaga.

"Well, how do you feel, my dear fellow?" she asked, touching the bookkeeper's pulse with her warm hand. "You feel
better now, don't you?"

"I am the Viceroy of India," he reported, blushing. "Give
me back my favorite elephant!"

"You are delirious," the woman doctor said kindly. "You
are in a hospital, and we shall cure you."

"Oh, oh, oh! My elephant!" Berlaga cried defiantly.

[1] According to the information obtained by the authors, there was really
no Behring Strait on the map which drove the poor geographer to insanity.
The absence of the Strait was due to the stupidity of the publishing house
"The Book and the Pole." The guilty ones were punished according to
their deserts. The chief of the publishing house was deprived of his position
and reduced in rank; the others were reprimanded and warned. I. I. and
E. P.

"But try to understand," the woman doctor said with greater kindness than ever. "You are not the Viceroy. All of this is delirium, do you understand, delirium!"

"No, it's not delirium," Berlaga objected, knowing that the first principle is to be stubborn.

"Yes, it *is* delirium."

"No, it is *not* delirium."

"Delirium."

"Not delirium."

The bookkeeper, seeing that the iron was hot, began to strike. He pushed the kind woman doctor away, and began to wail so appealingly that he excited all the patients, especially the little idiot, who sat down on the floor, and drooled:

"Un, deux, trois, quatre. Mademoiselle, joux ravatre."

And with satisfaction Berlaga heard the voice of the woman doctor saying behind his back to the orderly:

"Will you transfer him to those other three, otherwise he'll frighten the entire ward."

Two patient hospital orderlies led the quarrelsome viceroy to a small ward for the violently insane, where three men lay quietly. Only here did the bookkeeper begin to understand real insanity. As soon as the patients beheld the newcomer they exhibited extraordinary activity. A fat man rolled off the bed, quickly stood on all fours, and arching his back until it assumed the shape of a mandolin, began to bark intermittently and to scrape the hardwood floor with his hind paws in hospital slippers. Another flung a bed sheet around him and began to shout, "And thou, Brutus, hast sold thyself to the Bolsheviks!" This man undoubtedly imagined himself to be Caius Julius Cæsar. Once in a while, however, something would snap in his head, and getting things mixed, he would cry, "I am Henry Julius Zimmerman."

"Go away, I'm naked!" cried the third. "Don't look at me. I'm ashamed. I am a naked woman!"

And yet he was dressed like a man and even had a mustache.

The orderlies went away. Such fright possessed the Viceroy of India that he forgot to think of demanding the immediate return of his favorite elephant, maharajahs, trusty nabobs, as well as the puzzling abreks and kunaks.

"These three will make short shift of me," he thought, frozen with terror.

And he bitterly repented the scandal he had staged in the quiet ward. How marvelous it would be now to sit at the feet of the kindly teacher of geography, or listen to the little idiot chattering: "Enna, benna, rabba, quinter, finter, jabbah." However, nothing terrible happened. After the door closed, the mad dog yelped a few more times and, growling over his exertion, returned to his bed. Caius Julius discarded the sheet, yawned and stretched himself. The woman with a mustache lit a pipe, and the sweet odor of Soviet Capstan brought surcease to the quivering soul of Berlaga.

"I am the Viceroy of India," he declared, growing bolder.

"Shut up, numbskull!" Caius Julius replied lazily, and with the directness of a Roman added, "I'll kill you. I'll tear your heart out."

This remark of the bravest of emperors and warriors sobered the fugitive bookkeeper. He hid under the covers and, mourning his life full of alarums, began to doze.

At dawn, sodden with sleep, Berlaga heard strange words: "Here they've put a nut on our hands. It was so nice, the three of us, and suddenly . . . Now we'll have to bother with him. The first thing you know this damned viceroy will chew us all to pieces."

The voice of the speaker revealed to Berlaga that these words had been spoken by Caius Julius Cæsar. After a decent lapse of time, he opened his eyes and noticed that the dog-man was looking at him with lively interest.

"This is my finish," the Viceroy thought. "He's about to bite me!"

But the dog-man suddenly threw up his hands, and asked in a human voice:

"Tell me, aren't you the son of Foma Berlaga?"

"Yes," replied the bookkeeper, but suddenly remembering his rôle, cried:

"Return his trusty elephant to the unhappy viceroy!"

"Look at me," the dog-man invited. "Don't you really recognize me?"

"Misail Alexandrovich!" exclaimed the bookkeeper, on whom a great light was beginning to dawn. "What a meeting!"

Then the viceroy and the dog-man embraced heartily. The eyes of Misail Alexandrovich filled with tears.

"So you're not a madman?" Berlaga asked. "Why then do you play the fool?"

"And why do *you* play the fool? Listen to him! Give him elephants! Let me tell you, friend Berlaga, that for a good lunatic that viceroy idea is pretty weak."

"But my brother-in-law told me it was all right."

"Take me, for example," said Misail Alexandrovich. "Subtle play. Dog-man. Schizophrenic delirium, complicated by a maniacal depressive psychosis. And note, Berlaga, that a crepuscular condition of the soul goes with it. Do you think that was easy? I worked over the sources. Have you ever read Professor Bleyler's book 'Autistic Thinking'?"

"N-no," replied Berlaga in the voice of a viceroy who has just been deprived of the Order of the Garter and reduced in rank to an officer's orderly.

"Gentlemen!" cried Misail Alexandrovich. "He has never read Bleyler! Don't be afraid. Come here! He's as much a viceroy as you are a Cæsar."

The two remaining occupants of the small ward for the violently insane gathered around the newcomer.

"You haven't read Bleyler?" asked Caius Julius in surprise. "Excuse me, but with what materials *did* you prepare yourself?"

"I'll wager that he merely subscribed to the German journal 'Jahrbuch für Psychoanalitik und Psychopathologie'" suggested the mustached hermaphrodite.

Berlaga was disheartened, as if he had just been spat on. He stood meekly while the experts showered him with learned expressions that pertained to the theory and practice of psychoanalysis. They all agreed that Berlaga was in a bad way, and that the chief physician Titanushkin, whose return was expected from day to day, would expose him in five minutes. They did not divulge the fact that Titanushkin's return made them all feel sad.

"Perhaps I can change my delirium?" Berlaga suggested timidly. "Suppose I try Emile Zola or Mohammed?"

"Too late," said Caius Julius. "In the record of your illness you are recorded as a viceroy. And a madman cannot change his manias as he would change his socks. Now for the rest of your life you'll remain in the silly rôle of viceroy. We've been here a week and we know the rules."

An hour later Berlaga learned the details of his neighbors' infirmities.

The appearance of Misail Alexandrovich in the insane asylum was explained by a very ordinary turn of affairs in his life. He was a prominent Nepman who by chance had failed to pay the balance of 43,000 rubles income tax. This presented him with the prospect of an unavoidable journey to the North, while his affairs urgently demanded his presence in Chernomorsk.

Duvanov—that is, the man who simulated a woman—was apparently a petty sabotager whose fear of arrest was not entirely unfounded.

But such was not the case of Caius Julius Cæsar who in his

passport was designated as "the former attorney-at-law I. N. Starokhamsky."

Caius Julius Starokhamsky went to the insane asylum because of his lofty principles.

"In Soviet Russia," he said, draping himself in the sheet, "the insane asylum is the only place where a normal man can live. Everything else is super-Bedlam. No, I cannot live with the Bolsheviks. I prefer to live here with genuine madmen. At least they're not trying to build Socialism. Besides, here you can eat, while there, in their Bedlam, you merely work. But I refuse to exert myself for their Socialism. Here at least there is personal liberty, liberty of conscience, freedom of speech."

Seeing a hospital orderly pass, Caius Julius Starokhamsky shrieked: "Long live the Constituent Assembly! All to the Forum! And thou, Brutus, hast sold thyself to the commissars!" And turning to Berlaga, he added, "Did you see that? I can yell just what I like. But try and do it in the street."

All day long and the greater part of the night, the four "violently insane" patients played "Sixty-six" without 20 and 40, a subtle card game which requires self-possession, cleverness, purity of spirit and clarity of thinking.

In the morning Professor Titanushkin returned. He quickly examined all four and ordered them expelled at once from the hospital. They were helped neither by Bleyler, nor by the crepuscular condition of the soul complicated by a manic-depressive psychosis, nor by "Jahrbuch für Psychoanalitik und Psychopathologie." Professor Titanushkin did not respect simulators.

So they fled down the street, elbowing their way among the pedestrians. Caius Julius preceded the others pompously. After him hurried the female and the canine impersonators. In the rear the uncrowned viceroy dragged along, cursing his brother-in-law, and contemplating with horror the inevitable consequences of his wrong-doing.

After finishing this instructive tale, Bookkeeper Berlaga looked sadly first at Borisokhlebsky, then at Dreyfus, then at Sakharkov, and finally at Lapidus Jr. whose heads seemed to sway sympathetically in the twilight of the corridor.

"You see where your wild ideas brought you," the hard-hearted Lapidus Jr. pointed out. "You wanted to be rid of one housecleaning and got yourself into another one. And now you'll get it in the neck all right. Since you've been cleaned out of an insane asylum, you're sure to be cleaned out of HERCULES!"

Borisokhlebsky, Dreyfus and Sakharkov said nothing and slowly began to float away into the darkness.

"Friends!" the bookkeeper cried weakly. "Where are you going?"

But the friends had already departed as fast as they could. Their orphan asylum trousers flashed for the last time on the stairway and disappeared altogether.

"It's not ethical of you, Berlaga," Lapidus Jr. said coldly. "You have no business to drag me into your dirty Anti-Soviet scheme. Adieu."

And the Viceroy of India remained alone.

What have you done, Bookkeeper Berlaga? Where were your eyes, bookkeeper? And what would your father, Foma, have said if he had found out that in his declining years his son had yielded to a viceroyship? So this is where the strange connections with Mr. Funt, a chairman of many joint stock companies with mixed and impure capital, led you, book-keeper! It's frightful even to think of what old Foma would have said concerning the tricks of his favorite son. But old Foma has been lying a long time in the Second Christian cemetery under a stone seraph with a broken wing, and only boys who run in there to steal lilacs cast an incurious glance at the inscription: "Thy path has ended. Thine is now surcease from sorrow, F. Berlaga. Rest in peace." But perhaps the old man would have said nothing. Indeed, he could have said nothing because he himself had not led an exemplary life. He would have simply advised his son to be more careful, and in serious matters not to rely on his brother-in-law. Yes, indeed. You've got yourself into a dreadful mess, Bookkeeper Berlaga!

The sorrowful meditations that possessed the vice-regent of George V in India were interrupted by cries that came from the stairway.

"Berlaga? Who is asking for him? He's right there! Go right ahead, citizen."

The hoof specialist appeared in the corridor. Swinging his arms like a guardsman, Balaganov approached Berlaga and delivered a notice:

"Com. Berlaga: Upon receipt of this you are requested immediately to present yourself to clarify certain circumstances."

The message was written on the stationery of the Chernomorsk Department of the Arbatov Office for the Collection of Horns and Hoofs. The document bore the imprint of a round, rubber stamp, the context of which would have been rather difficult to decipher even if that attempt had occurred to Berlaga. But the fugitive bookkeeper was so crushed by the misfortunes that had befallen him that he merely asked:

"May I telephone home?"

"Telephone? Of course not!" the hoof expert said darkly.

Two hours later the crowd that stood at the cinema "Capitoline," waiting for the first show, and looked around for lack of something better to do, noticed that out of the doors of the office for the collection of horns came a man who fitfully clutched at his heart and slowly walked away. This was Bookkeeper Berlaga. At first he dragged his feet. Then he gradually increased his pace. He turned the corner, surreptitiously crossed himself and ran for all he was worth. Presently he was sitting at his desk in the Financial Accounting hall and frantically looking into the ledger. The figures spiraled and danced before his eyes. . . .

The great schemer closed the portfolio dedicated to the case of Koreiko, glanced at Funt who sat under the new inscription: "Chairman of the Managing Board," and said:

"When I was very young, very poor, and made my living at the Kherson fair by exhibiting a fat chesty monk whom I presented as the bearded woman—an explicable phenomenon of nature—even then I did not sink to such moral depths as this scoundrelly Berlaga."

"Pathetic, insignificant person," confirmed Panikovsky, serving tea to everybody. He was gratified by the discovery that there were people even pettier than he.

"Berlaga has no head on him," contributed the substitute-chairman with the deliberation peculiar to him. "His idea of a class world in industry . . ."

"That will do," said Bender. "We shall designate a special session to discover your views about MacDonald and other bourgeois statesmen. For the present we have no time. Berlaga really has no head on him, but he has informed us about the life and activity of self-exploding stock-companies."

Inexplicably the great schemer became gay. Everything went on well. No one brought in any more stinking horns. The work of the Chernomorsk Branch could be regarded as satisfactory, although the post delivered to the office a pile of new communications, circulars and demands, and Panikovsky had gone twice to the labor exchange in search of an office girl.

"Well!" Ostap cried suddenly. "Where is Kozlevich? Where is the Antelope? What kind of an establishment is this without an automobile? I must ride to conferences. Everybody is inviting me. They can't live without me. Where is Kozlevich?"

Panikovsky turned his head away and said with a sigh:

"Kozlevich is in a bad way."

"What do you mean 'in a bad way'? Is he drunk?"

"Worse than that," Panikovsky replied. "So bad that we were afraid to tell you. He's been befuddled by priests."

With these words, the messenger looked at the hoof expert, and both of them shook their heads sadly.

Chapter Seventeen

THE PRODIGAL SON RETURNS

THE great schemer did not like Catholic priests. He was
equally unfriendly to rabbis, lamas, orthodox priests,
muezzins, shamans, and other clerics.

"I myself have a tendency toward fraud and deception," he
said. "At the present time, for example, I am occupied with
the extortion of a large sum of money from a certain recalcitrant citizen. But I do not embellish my dubious activity
with the singing of hymns, with the roar of the organ, or with
foolish invocations in Latin or Old-Church Slavic. And anyway, I prefer to work without incense or astral bells."

And while Balaganov and Panikovsky, impatiently inter-
rupting each other, were describing the evil fate that had befallen the driver of the Antelope, the manly heart of Ostap
overflowed with anger and indignation.

The priests had caught the soul of Adam Kozlevich in the
yard of the inn where, in the midst of double-spanned German
carriages and Moldavian fruit carts, the Antelope stood on a
pile of manure. The priest Kuszakowski was in the habit of
coming there for spiritual conversations with Catholic colonists. When he beheld the Antelope, this cleric walked all
around it, touching each of the tires with his finger. He conversed with Kozlevich and discovered that although Adam
Kazimirovich belonged to the Roman Catholic Church, he
had not professed his religion for twenty years. "That's bad,
that's bad, *Pan* Kozlevich!" said Priest Kuszakowski and
went away, lifting his black skirts with both of his hands
and jumping across puddles that looked like foaming beer.

At daybreak, when excited petty speculators, crowded like sardines into the wagons, were leaving for the market in the little town of Koshara, Priest Kuszakowski appeared again. This time he was accompanied by another priest—Aloysius Moroszek. While Kuszakowski was elaborately greeting Adam Kazimirovich, Priest Moroszek attentively examined the automobile, and not only touched the tires but even pressed the horn, evoking the sound of the *matchish*. After this the priests looked at each other, advanced upon Kozlevich from both sides, and began to befuddle him. They befuddled him all day long. When Kuszakowski stopped, Moroszek began, and as soon as he paused to wipe the sweat from his brow, Kuszakowski fell again upon Adam. Sometimes Kuszakowski would lift his yellow index finger to heaven, while Moroszek told his rosary. At other times it was Kuszakowski who told the rosary while Moroszek lifted his index finger to the sky. Several times the priests sang quietly in Latin, and toward evening of the first day Adam Kazimirovich tentatively joined in the chorus. At this point both paters cast avid glances at the automobile.

After some time Panikovsky noted a change in the owner of the Antelope. Adam Kazimirovich spoke vaguely of the kingdom of Heaven. This was confirmed by Balaganov. Then the chauffeur began to disappear for long periods of time, and finally moved out of the inn.

"Why didn't you report to me?" the great schemer demanded indignantly.

They had wanted to report, but they feared the anger of the commander. They hoped that Kozlevich would recover his senses and return. But now all hope was lost. The priests had entirely befuddled him. Only the previous evening the messenger and the hoof specialist had accidentally come across Kozlevich. He was sitting in his automobile in front of the church. Before they could reach him, Priest Aloysius Moroszek came out of the church accompanied by a boy draped in lace.

"You understand, Bender?" said Shura. "All of them sat down in our Antelope! Poor Kozlevich took off his hat. The little boy tinkled a bell, and they drove away. It was simply pitiful to look at our Adam. We'll never see the Antelope again!"

The great schemer silently put on his captain's cap with its polished visor and turned his footsteps toward the door.

"Funt," he ordered, "you remain in the office. Under no circumstances should you accept horns or hoofs. When the mail arrives, throw it into the basket. The office girl will take care of that eventually. Do you understand?"

When the substitute chairman opened his mouth to reply (this happened exactly five minutes later), the orphaned Antelopians were already far away. At the head of the procession, the commander flew with gigantic steps. Occasionally he turned his head back over his shoulder and muttered, "They didn't take care of our delicate Kozlevich, the good-for-nothings! I'll repudiate all of them! Oh, how I hate these monks and priests!" The mechanic walked silently, pretending that these accusations did not refer to him. Panikovsky jumped up and down like a monkey, rousing his feeling of vengeance toward the abductors of Kozlevich, but a large cold frog lay upon his soul. He feared the black priests, in whom he acknowledged many magical powers.

In this formation the entire Branch for the Collection of Horns and Hoofs appeared at the entrance of the church. Before the iron grating woven of spirals and crosses stood the empty Antelope. The church was huge. It cut into the sky, sharp-edged as a fishbone. It stuck in the throat. Polished red brick, tiled roofs, sheet-metal weather vanes, bulging buttresses and beautiful stone statues that hid in niches from the rain—all of this erect, soldierly Gothicism flung itself at the

Antelopians. They felt small beside it. Ostap went to the automobile, sniffed the air, and said with disgust:

"Peugh! Nauseating! Our Antelope reeks with the odor of
tapers, collection boxes for the building of the temple, and
priests' boots. Of course it is much pleasanter to go out begging in an automobile than in a drozhky! Besides, it is free.
Well, I'm sorry, dear little fathers, our business is more
pressing!"

Bender walked into the churchyard, past the children who
were playing hopscotch on the chalk-smeared asphalt, and
went up the granite stairway that should have been in a bank,
to the doors of the temple. On the heavy doors, lined with
strips of iron, bas-relief saints were throwing kisses to each
other, pointing their hands in different directions, or entertaining themselves by reading thick books on which the conscientious woodcarver had inscribed Latin letters. The great
schemer pulled the door, but it did not yield. From within
came the plaintive sounds of a harmonium.

"They are bewitching him!" shouted Ostap, running down
the stairs. "I can hear the sweet tinkle of their dulcimer!"

"Don't you think we had better go away?" asked Panikovsky, turning his hat in his hands. "After all, it's the temple
of God. It's not nice!"

But paying no attention to him, Ostap went to the Antelope and began to press the horn impatiently. He played the
matchish until the clanging of keys was heard behind the
heavy doors. The Antelopians lifted their heads. Both sides
of the door swung back, and the joyous saints in their oaken
squares slowly disappeared into the depths of the temple. Out
of the darkness of the portal into the holy doorway walked
Adam Kazimirovich. He was pale. His conductor's mustache
was limp, and dangled tearfully below his nostrils. In his
hands he held a prayer book. On both sides he was supported
by the priests, on the left by Priest Kuszakowski and on the

right by Priest Aloysius Moroszek. The eyes of the holy fathers were drowned in unction.

"Hello, Kozlevich!" Ostap cried from below. "Aren't you sick of it yet?"

"How do you do, Adam Kazimirovich," Panikovsky cried jauntily, from behind the commander's back.

Balaganov raised his hand in greeting and made a wry face, which probably meant: "Adam, cut out this nonsense!"

The body of the Antelope's driver made one step forward, but his soul, lashed on either side by the penetrating glances of Kuszakowski and Moroszek, retreated. Kozlevich looked sorrowfully at his friends and dropped his eyes.

Then began a great struggle for the immortal soul of the chauffeur.

"Hey, you cherubim and seraphim!" Ostap shouted, challenging his enemies to a dispute. "There is no God!"

"Yes, there is!" objected Priest Aloysius Moroszek, protecting Kozlevich with his body.

"This is plain rowdyism!" muttered Priest Kuszakowski.

"There isn't! There isn't!" continued the great schemer. "And there never was! That is an anatomical fact!"

"I consider this conversation improper," Kuszakowski announced angrily.

"And you think to take the machine away is proper?" cried the tactless Balaganov. "Adam, they simply want to get the Antelope!"

The chauffeur raised his head and looked inquiringly at the priests. The priests did not know what to do and, swishing their silk cassocks, attempted to pull Kozlevich back. But Kozlevich resisted.

"Well, what about God?" insisted the great schemer.

The priests were obliged to begin the discussion. The children stopped jumping on one leg and came nearer.

"How can you say there is no God," began Aloysius Moroszek in a cordial voice, "when every living thing has been created by him . . ."

"I know, I know!" said Ostap. "I myself am an old Catholic and a Latinist: Puer, sozer, vesper, gener, liber, miser, osper, tener."

These Latin exceptions, memorized by Ostap when he was in the third grade of the private gymnasium of Iliadi, and which until now had stayed in his mind for no good reason, produced a magnetic effect on Kozlevich. His soul attached itself to his body, and as a result of this union, the chauffeur timidly moved forward.

"My son!" said Kuszakowski, looking with hatred at Ostap. "You are in error, my son. The miracles of the Lord prove to us . . ."

"Priest, stop flopping about!" the great schemer said severely. "I have performed miracles myself. Only four years ago I had occasion to be Jesus Christ for several days in one little town. And everything worked like a charm. I even fed several thousand believers with five loaves of bread. Of course, I cannot say that I really satisfied them, but you should have seen the queue!"

The dispute continued in this strange way. The gay, though unconvincing arguments of Ostap reacted in the liveliest way on Kozlevich. Color returned to his cheeks and his mustache began to rise gradually.

"Go go, go on!" Encouraging exclamations were heard outside the spirals and crosses of the grating, where a large crowd of the curious had gathered. "Tell them about the Pope, and about the Crusades!"

So Ostap told them about the Pope. He libeled Alexander Borgia for his improper behavior, remembered Seraphim Sarovsky for no reason at all, and particularly emphasized the Inquisition, which had persecuted Galileo. He was so carried away by his argument that he placed the direct responsibility for the fate of the great scientist upon Kuszakowski and

Moroszek. This was the last straw. When he heard of the terrible fate of Galileo, Adam Kazimirovich quickly put the prayer book down on a step and fell into the open embraces of Balaganov. Panikovsky was on the spot to pat the unshaven cheeks of the prodigal son. Joyous kisses filled the air.

"*Pan Kozlewicz,*" moaned the priests. "*Dokąd pan idzie? Opomiątaisie, panie!*"

But the heroes of the automobile race were already taking their places in the automobile.

"You see," Ostap cried to the dejected priests. "Didn't I tell you there is no God? It's a scientific fact. Good-by, Priests. Au revoir, Paters!"

Accompanied by the encouraging shouts of the crowd, the Antelope drove away, and soon the sheet-iron weathervanes and the tiled roofs of the church disappeared from their view. The Antelopians celebrated by stopping in a beer shop.

"Thank you, boys," Kozlevich said, holding a heavy mug in his hands. "I almost perished. The priests certainly had me befuddled, especially Kuszakowski. He's a sly devil. Believe it or not, he even made me fast! He said that if I wouldn't, I couldn't get to heaven."

"Heaven?" said Ostap. "Heaven is now in a state of neglect. This is a different epoch, a different slice of time. Angels want to come down to earth now. It is good on earth, because you have communal advantages here, and observatories where you can look at the stars while you listen to an anti-religious lecture."

After the eighth stein, Kozlevich demanded the ninth, raised it over his head, and sucking at his conductor's mustache, asked rapturously:

"Is there no God?"

"None whatever," Ostap replied.

"So there is no God? Well, here's how!"

So he continued to drink, pronouncing before each new mug of beer: "Is there a God? No? Well, here's how!"

Panikovsky drank as much as everybody else, but he expressed no opinion about God. He had no desire to become involved in this dubious argument.

With the return of the prodigal son and the Antelope, the Chernomorsk Department of the Arbatov Office for the Collection of Horns and Hoofs assumed the glitter it lacked before. At the door of the former combine of five private owners, a machine was now constantly on duty. It was not, of course, in a class with blue Buicks and sinuous Lincolns. It was even far below Fords. Still it was a machine, an automobile—an equipage, as Ostap was wont to say, which, in spite of all its faults, was still able to move along the streets without the aid of horses.

Ostap worked with abandon. If he had turned his abilities actually to the collection of horns and hoofs, the mouthpiece and comb industry would have been provided with raw materials to the end of the fiscal century. But the office chief was occupied with something else.

Having finished for the time being with Funt and Berlaga, whose communications, while exceedingly interesting, did not lead directly to Koreiko, Ostap delegated Balaganov to shadow, purely in the interests of business, the girl in whose company they had seen Alexander Ivanovich. A prolonged observation carried on by the hoof specialist led to the conclusion that there was little love lost between Zosya and Koreiko, and that the latter, to use Shura's expression, was wasting his breath.

"Where there is no love," Ostap commented with a sigh, "it is not customary to speak of money. We'll forget about the girl."

And while Koreiko was recollecting with amusement the crook in the policeman's cap who had made such a pathetic effort at third-rate extortion, the commander was driving all over town in a yellow automobile and unearthing all sorts of people whose existence the millionaire clerk had forgotten, but who well remembered him. Several times Ostap conversed by long distance with a private owner in Moscow, who became a part of the docket in the Department of Commercial Secrets. Now letters and telegrams came which Ostap quickly selected from the general mail, still generously supplied with invitations, notices, demands for horns, and reprimands because the office did not collect hoofs with sufficient energy. Some of these letters and telegrams reached the portfolio that was tied with shoe laces.

Toward the end of July, Ostap made up his mind to go to the Caucasus. The case demanded the presence of the great schemer in a small grape republic.

On the day of the chief's departure, something scandalous occurred. Panikovsky, who had been sent to the docks with thirty rubles to buy a ticket, returned a half hour later, drunk, without the ticket and without the money. He could say nothing in his defense, but merely turned out his pockets and laughed uproariously. Everything amused him: the rage of the commander, and the accusing glances of Balaganov, and the samovar that had been placed in his care, and Funt, who slept at the desk with the panama hat over his nose. But when Panikovsky looked at the elk horns, the pride and embellishment of the office, he was overcome by such laughter, that he rolled to the floor and promptly fell asleep with a joyous smile on his purple mouth.

"Now we have a genuine establishment," commented Ostap. "We have our own embezzler who, at the same time, is the drunken doorman. Both these types ensure the success of all our efforts."

During Ostap's absence Aloysius Moroszek and Kuszakowski appeared several times at the windows. As soon as Kozlevich saw the priests he hid himself in the furthest corner of the establishment. The priests would open the door, look inside, and call quietly:

*"Pan Kozlewicz! Pan Kozlewicz! Czy slyszisz głos oica nie-
bieskiego? Opamiątaisie, panie!"*

With these words, Priest Kuszakowski would raise his
finger to heaven while Priest Aloysius Moroszek told his
rosary. Then the clerics were invariably met by Balaganov,
who went out and silently displayed his fiery fist. The priests
went away, looking sadly over their shoulders at the Antelope.

Ostap returned in two weeks. The entire establishment met
him. From the high black wall of the approaching steamer
the great schemer regarded his subordinates with friendship
and kindness. About him lingered the odor of tender lamb
and Imeretinian wine.

In the Chernomorsk Branch, in addition to the woman
office worker who had been hired by Ostap, sat young men
in boots. They were students who had been sent from the
Animal Husbandry Technicum to get their practical training.

"That's fine," Ostap said sourly. "We pass the torch of
knowledge to the younger generation! But, dear comrades,
you will have to work hard here. You know, of course, that
horns, that is, growths covered with wool or hard, horny
layers, are adjuncts of the skull and are found principally
among mammals . . ."

"We know that," the students interrupted decisively. "What
we want is some practical training."

They rid themselves of the students by a complicated and
comparatively expensive method. The great schemer sent them
to the Kalmyk steppes to organize collecting stations. This
cost the office six hundred rubles, but there was no other way
out. The students might have interfered with the principal
enterprise. When Panikovsky learned what a large sum of
money the students had cost, he took Balaganov aside and
whispered irritably:

"And why don't I get sent away? I don't even get a vacation! I have to go to Essentuki for a cure. I don't even get a
day off, and I don't get any working clothes! No, Shura, I

don't like these working conditions. And anyway, I have discovered that they pay higher wages at HERCULES. I'll get a job as messenger there. Word of honor, I'll go away!"

In the evening Ostap again summoned Berlaga.

"On your knees!" Ostap cried in the voice of Nicholas the First as soon as he beheld the bookkeeper.

Nevertheless, the conversation was carried on in a friendly way and lasted two hours. Then Ostap ordered the Antelope to be at the entrance to HERCULES on the following morning.

Chapter Eighteen

ON LAND AND SEA

COMRADE SKUMBRIEVICH appeared on the beach with a brief-case under his arm. To the briefcase was attached a silver nameplate with one corner bent, and a large inscription to the effect that Yegor Skumbrievich had celebrated his fifth anniversary of service to HERCULES. His face was clean-cut, long, manly, like the smoothly shaven face of an Englishman on an advertising placard. Skumbrievich stopped at the board that indicated in chalk the temperature of the water, and freeing his feet with difficulty from the burning sand, went to look for a convenient place to undress.

The camp of the swimmers was thickly populated. Temporary shelters appeared in the morning only to disappear with the setting sun, leaving behind them the refuse of the camp—dry melon rinds, egg shells, bits of newspaper, which begin to lead a secret life on the empty nocturnal shore, whispering about something, and flying under the cliffs. In the morning, the boy whose business it is to keep the beach clean sweeps the camp with a new besom to which grains of oats still cling, and his jaw drops in fright at sight of the gnawed chicken bones. It suddenly seems that little children have been eaten here. The boy sniffs the air nervously. The sea smells of wild men and the tropics. And he does not doubt that at any moment a red *pirogue* will appear from behind the cliff and Jack London cannibals will disembark and make *kai-kai* of him.

Skumbrievich made his way among the tents of waffle-like towels, umbrellas, and sheets stretched out on sticks. Under these, girls in swimming suits hid themselves. Some of the men were also in swimming suits, but not all of them. Some of them were satisfied with fig leaves only; these, however, did not cover the biblical places but the noses of the gentlemen of Chernomorsk, to keep the skin of these gentlemen's noses from peeling. The men lay thus in the most abandoned poses. Occasionally, covering the biblical places with their hands, they would enter the water, take a dip, and run quickly back to the niches they had dug for themselves in the sand, so as not to lose a single cubic centimeter of the healthful sun bath.

The insufficiency of these citizens' clothes was more than made up for by a gentleman of an altogether different appearance. He lay apart from the large mass of bathers. He wore chrome leather button shoes and striped afternoon trousers, a buttoned-up coat, a collar, a necktie, a watch chain in his outer breast pocket, and a felt hat. A bushy mustache and cotton stuck into his ears completed his appearance. Beside him was a cane with a glass knob, stuck perpendicularly into the sand. He languished with the heat. His collar swelled with perspiration. Under the gentleman's arms it was as hot as in a smelter, and one could smell ore there. But he continued to lie, immovable. One such man may be found on any beach in the world. Who he is, why he comes, why he lies there completely dressed—nobody knows. But there are such people—one on every beach. He may be a member of some secret League of Fools, or a remnant of the once-powerful order of Rosicrucians, or an onanistic bachelor—nobody knows.

Yegor Skumbrievich sat down beside the member of the League of Fools and quickly undressed. The naked Skumbrievich decidedly did not resemble the clothed Skumbrievich. The arrogant Englishman's head sat on a white womanish body with sloping shoulders and a very broad behind. Swaying the latter part of his anatomy, Yegor walked to the water, touched it with the toes of one foot, and screamed. He dropped the other foot in the water, and screamed again. Then he made several steps, closed his ears with his thumbs, his eyes with his index fingers, and pinched his nostrils with his middle fingers, emitted a heartrending cry, and dipped four times in succession. Only then did he swim forward, swinging one arm at a time and turning his head with each stroke. And a gentle wave lifted Yegor Skumbrievich—the exemplary Herculean and prominent civic worker. Five minutes later, when the now-tired civic worker turned over on his back, his round globular belly bobbing on the surface of the sea, the Antelopian *matchish* resounded on the cliff above the beach.

Out of the machine stepped Ostap Bender, Balaganov, and Bookkeeper Berlaga, whose face displayed utter submission to fate. All three ran down and began to look for someone, unceremoniously examining the faces of the bathers.

"Here are his trousers," Berlaga announced finally, scuffing the sand before the clothes of the unsuspecting Skumbrievich. "He has evidently swum far away."

"Enough!" exclaimed the great schemer. "I have no intention of waiting any longer. I shall have to act not only on land but on sea."

He threw off his suit and shirt, under which swimming trunks appeared, and, swinging his arms, swam out. On the great schemer's breast was an azure tatoo representing Napoleon in a three-cornered hat and with a beer stein at the end of his stunted arm.

"Balaganov!" Ostap shouted from the water. "Undress and get Berlaga ready! We may need him!"

And the great schemer swam on his side, cleaving the waters with a bronzed shoulder and steering his course north by northeast, where bobbed the mother-of-pearl belly of Yegor Skumbrievich.

Before flinging himself into the deep, Ostap had to work very thoroughly on the continent. The clews had brought the great schemer under the golden letters of Hercules, and he had spent most of his time in that establishment. He was no longer surprised by rooms with alcoves and washstands, by statues that idled about stairway landings, nor by the doorman in the cap with a golden zig-zag who enjoyed talking about burial by fire.

Out of the muddled explanations of the despairing Berlaga had emerged the steady, "responsible" figure of Comrade Skumbrievich. He occupied a large two-windowed room in which foreign captains, lion tamers or wealthy students from Kiev had at one time stopped. On Skumbrievich's writing desk were two telephones and a messenger bell on a wooden rosette, itself indicating Yegor's important rank. Telephones rang frequently and enervatingly, sometimes alone, sometimes both together. But no one took off the receivers. Even more frequently the door would open, a clerk's shaven head would rapidly survey the room and disappear, yielding its place immediately to another head, not a shaven one this time but blonde and curly, or simply a bald one, lilac-colored like certain kinds of onions. But not even the oniony skull would remain long in the doorway. The room was empty.

After the door had opened for perhaps the fiftieth time that day, Bender looked into the room. Like his predecessors he turned his head from left to right, from right to left, and, like his predecessors, was convinced that Comrade Skumbrievich was not in the room. Arrogantly expressing his displeasure, the great schemer went from departments to sections, from sections to offices, asking all he met whether they had seen Comrade Skumbrievich. And in all of these places he received the identical reply: "Skumbrievich was here just a little while ago," or "Skumbrievich has just left."

The demi-responsible Yegor was one of those clerks whose number is legion: they have either "just been here" or "left a minute ago." Some of them cannot reach their offices throughout an entire working day. Such a man enters the vestibule of his establishment precisely at nine o'clock, and, full of good intentions, lifts his foot to the first step of the stairway. Great affairs await him. He has made arrangements for eight important rendezvous in his office, two large conferences and one small one. On his desk lies a pile of papers that demand immediate reply. In general, he has a multitude of affairs—too many for his working time. So the demi-responsible or the responsible citizen bravely lifts his foot to the marble step. But it is not so easy to put it down.

"Comrade Parusinov! One minute please!" A cooing voice lures him. "I want to discuss one little matter with you."

Parusinov is gently led away to a corner of the vestibule. And from that moment on, the responsible or demi-responsible worker has perished as far as his country is concerned: he passes from hand to hand. As soon as he discusses the "little matter" and runs up three steps, he is again stopped, led away to the window, or into a dark corridor, or to some deserted place full of empty boxes, and here something is explained to him, something asked of him, something is insisted upon, someone pleads with him to have something done out of turn. By three o'clock, however, he manages to reach the first landing. By five o'clock he manages to break his way to the second floor landing. But, since his office is on the third floor, and the working day is now over, he quickly runs downstairs and abandons the establishment in order to be on time for an interestablishment conference. And all this time his office is full of the din of telephones; the appointed rendezvous crumble; the correspondence lies without reply; and the members of two large conferences and one small one calmly drink tea and gossip about the mismanagement of the street cars.

These characteristics were further aggravated in the case of Yegor Skumbrievich by the social work to which he devoted himself with excessive zeal. Cleverly and profitably, he took advantage of the mutual and many-sided fraud which had unnoticeably become a part of HERCULES and for some reason was called "Civic Obligations."

"What's the matter with you, Comrade?" he would say, gliding along the corridors and stopping some fellow worker who could not manage to escape. "You are doing absolutely no social work! We'll certainly point that out in the wall newspaper."

The follow-worker would pull a long face, and thinking, "You low-down liar, you scoundrelly faker! You're not doing any work yourself and you're keeping others from working!", would reply:

"Well, you know how it is, Comrade Skumbrievich. I'm always planning to do some. I'm at your service. Give me some work to do. I'll be very glad."

"I'll put you down for our Mutual Patron Society," Yegor would say. "Come the day after to-morrow for the organizational meeting. It's about time to push this enterprise."

So the Herculean would sit at the meeting for three hours on end, listening to the loathsome chattering of Skumbrievich. Other Herculeans would sit with him. All of them wanted to grasp Yegor by his fat haunches and throw him out of the window from a respectable height. At times it seemed to them that there never was or never would be social work, in spite of the fact that they knew that a genuine social life existed beyond the walls of HERCULES. "There's an ape for you," they thought, mournfully turning a pencil or a teaspoon in their hands. "The damned careerist!"

But to find fault with Skumbrievich, to expose him, was beyond anyone's power. Yegor delivered the correct speeches about Soviet civic life, about cultural work, about vocational guidance, about various active circles. But behind all these passionate words there was—nothing. Fifteen circles, political, musical, dramatic, had been working out their respective plans for two years. Nuclei of voluntary societies, aiming to help the development of aviation, chemical knowledge, automobiling, horse-racing, road building, contact with the village, prisoners of capital, as well as the most rapid eradications of illiteracy, homelessness, religion, drunkenness, and godalmighty chauvinism, existed only in the swollen imaginations of the members of the respective local committees. And even the school of vocational guidance, the establishment which Skumbrievich considered his most distinguished attainment, was constantly being reorganized, which of course signifies that it was totally inactive. If Skumbrievich were an honest man, he probably would have said that all this work was a mirage. But in the local committees this mirage filled elaborate reports, and the district trade union organizations regarded the existence of these circles without the shadow of a doubt. They saw the vocational guidance school in the form of a large stone building in which stood school desks and an energetic teacher who diagrammed the growth of unemployment in the United States on the blackboard, while mustached students matured politically right before his eyes. Of all this volcanic ring of civic activities with which Skumbrievich surrounded Hercules, there were actually in operation only two smoldering cones: the wall newspaper, "The Chairman's Voice," which appeared once a month and was made up during working hours by the joint efforts of Skumbrievich and Bomze, and a veneered board with the inscription: "We stop drinking and challenge others to follow our example," under which, however, there was not a single name.

The chase after Skumbrievich over all the floors of Hercules turned Bender into a hundred devils. The great schemer could not find the famous civic leader. Here in the local committee he had spoken over the telephone just a little while ago; the transmitter was still warm and the fog of the social worker's breath had not yet disappeared. Here on the window sill still sat the man with whom he had just conversed. Once Ostap even caught the reflection of Skumbrievich in a mirror on the stairway. He dashed forward, but the mirror immediately cleared, reflecting merely a window with a distant cloud.

"Mother of mine, and all the powers that be!" exclaimed Ostap, breathing heavily. "What stupid, disgusting bureaucracy! Granted that our Chernomorsk Department also has its weak side . . . There are all sorts of deficiencies. But such as exist in HERCULES! . . . Am I right, Shura?"

The hoof specialist sighed laboriously like a pump. Again they found themselves in the cool corridor of the second storey, where they had already been at least fifteen times in the course of the day. And again, for the sixteenth time, they walked past the wooden bench which stood in front of Polykhayev's office.

Since morning, Engineer Heinrich-Maria Sause, a German specialist imported at great expense, had sat on the bench. He was dressed in an ordinary European suit, but his Ukrainian shirt with its Zaporozhian decorations bore witness that the engineer had been in Russia for about three weeks and had already had time to visit a handicraft store. He sat rigidly, his head resting on the wooden back of the bench, his eyes closed, like those of a man about to be shaved. One might have thought that he was dozing, but the foster brothers who had run past him more than once in search of Skumbrievich had had time to notice that the color on the immobile face of the guest from the distant land was constantly changing. In the beginning of the day when the engineer had taken the position at Polykhayev's doors, his face had been fairly rosy. Every hour it had flared more and more, so that by noontime it had assumed the color of sealing wax. It is quite possible that by this time Comrade Polykhayev had managed to reach the first landing of the stairway. After the noon recess the change of color continued in the opposite direction. The sealing wax color turned into scarlet fever spots. Heinrich-Maria began to pale; and by the middle of the afternoon, when the chief of HERCULES had managed to reach the landing of the second floor, the face of the foreign specialist had become as white as starch.

"What's happening to this man?" Ostap whispered to Balaganov. "What a gamut of suffering he is running!"

He had scarcely uttered these words when Heinrich-Maria Sause jumped from the bench and looked angrily at Polykhayev's door, through which came vague rings of the telephone. "Red tape!" he screamed in a high treble, and, flinging himself upon the great schemer, began to shake him by the shoulders.

"*Genosse* Polykhayev!" he cried, jumping before Ostap. "*Genosse* Polykhayev!"

He took out his watch, shoved it under Balaganov's nose, threw up his shoulders, and again flung himself upon Bender.

"*Was machen Sie?*" asked the bewildered Ostap, thus indicating a certain familiarity with the German language. "*Was wollen Sie* from a poor visitor?"

But Heinrich-Maria Sause would not desist. Continuing to grasp Bender's shoulder with his left hand, he pulled Balaganov nearer to him with his right hand and delivered to them an exhaustive and impassioned speech, while Bender looked impatiently around in the hope of catching Skumbrievich, and the hoof specialist hiccoughed softly, respectably covering his mouth with his hand and stupidly staring at the foreigner's shoes.

Engineer Heinrich-Maria Sause had signed a contract to work a year in the U.S.S.R., or, as the precise Heinrich pointed out, at HERCULES establishment. "Take care, Mr. Sause," he had been warned by his acquaintance, Doctor of Mathematics Bernhardt Herngross. "The Bolsheviks will made you work hard for their money." But Sause explained that he was not afraid of work and had long been looking for a wide field that would enable him to apply his knowledge of the mechanization of the lumber industry.

When Skumbrievich reported the arrival of the foreign specialist to Polykhayev, the chief of HERCULES ran back and forth under his palm trees.

"We can't get along another minute without him! What did you do with him?"

"I sent him to the hotel. Let him rest from the journey."

"Are you crazy? Let him rest!" cried Polykhayev. "We're paying real money for him, in *valuta!* To-morrow morning he must be here at ten o'clock sharp!"

The following morning at five minutes to ten Heinrich-Maria Sause, resplendent in coffee-colored trousers, and smiling at the thought of the wide field of activity, entered Polykhayev's office. The chief had not yet arrived. He had not arrived an hour later, nor two hours later. Heinrich began to languish. He was entertained only by Skumbrievich, who appeared from time to time and asked with an innocent smile:

"What! Hasn't *Genosse* Polykhayev come yet? Strange!"

Two hours later Skumbrievich stopped the lunching Bomze in the corridor and began to whisper with him:

"I simply don't know what to do! Polykhayev told the German to come at ten o'clock in the morning, but he himself has taken a trip to Moscow to arrange about our quarters. He won't be back for a week. Can't you help me, Adolf Nikolaievich? I have all these civic duties to perform. And we are in the midst of reorganizing our vocational guidance affairs. Sit down with the German and keep him busy somehow. We paid real money for him—*valuta!*"

Bomze smelled his daily cutlet for the last time, swallowed it, brushed off the crumbs, and went to meet the guest.

In the course of a week, Engineer Sause, guided by the courteous Adolf Nikolaievich, managed to examine three museums, to visit the ballet "The Sleeping Beauty," and to sit ten hours at a solemn meeting organized in his honor. After the session came an unofficial celebration, in the course of which certain Herculeans had a very gay time, shook their lafitte wine bottles, their Sebastopol vodka bottles, and turning to Sause cried, "Bottoms up!"

"Dear Tilly," the engineer wrote to his bride in Aachen,

"I've been living in Chernomorsk for ten days, but I have not yet begun work in the HERCULES establishment. I am afraid that these days will be counted out of the salary agreed upon in my contract."

However, on the fifteenth of the month, the pay clerk gave Sause his semi-monthly salary.

"Don't you think," said Heinrich to his new friend Bomze, "that I'm being paid money for nothing? I'm not doing any work."

"Cast out such dark thoughts, colleague!" cried Adolf Nikolaievich. "Still, if you like, I can arrange to give you a special desk in my office."

After this Sause wrote the letters to his sweetheart sitting at his own special desk.

"Dear little one, I am living a strange and unusual life. I do absolutely nothing, but I receive my money punctually, on the dates agreed upon. All of this surprises me. Tell our friend, Dr. Bernhardt Herngross, about it. He may find it interesting."

When Polykhayev returned from Moscow and learned that Sause already had a desk he was overjoyed.

"Well, that's splendid," he said. "Let Skumbrievich acquaint the German with his duties."

But Skumbrievich who at that moment had dedicated all his passionate devotion to the organization of a very powerful circle of harmonica players, pushed the German along to Adolf Nikolaievich. Bomze did not like it. The German interfered with his lunch, and was altogether too inquisitive about the nature of his duties. So Bomze gave him up to the Exploitational Department. But just then this particular department was reorganizing its work, which consisted of eternally dragging tables from one place to another, and Heinrich-Maria was sent to the Financial Accounting hall. Here, Arnikov, Dreyfus, Sakharkov, Koreiko, and Tezoimenitsky, who did not know the German language, decided that Sause was a foreign tourist from Argentine, and all day long they explained the Herculean system of bookkeeping to him, employing the alphabet of the deaf and dumb.

A month later the excited Sause caught Skumbrievich at the lunch counter and began to shout:

"I don't wish to receive money for nothing! Give me work! If this continues I shall complain to your boss!"

Skumbrievich did not like the final words of the foreign specialist's speech. He called for Bomze.

"What's the matter with the German?" he asked. "What's he fuming about?"

"Do you know what?" said Bomze. "I think he is simply quarrelsome. So help me God! All the man has to do is to sit at his desk, do absolutely nothing, receive a pile of money. And still be complains!"

"He really has a most quarrelsome nature," remarked Skumbrievich. "It's a pity he's a German. In cases like this we must apply repressive measures. I must tell Polykhayev about it. We'll chase him into a bottle pretty quick."

However, Heinrich-Maria himself decided to fight his way to Polykhayev. Since the chief of HERCULES was a prominent exponent of that type of worker who "left here a minute ago" or "was here just a little while ago," the attempt brought him only to the wooden bench and to the explosion, the victims of which were the innocent children of Lieutenant Schmidt.

"*Bureaucratismus!*" cried the German, passing in his agitation to the difficult Russian language.

Ostap silently took the European guest by the hand, led him to the complaint box that hung on the wall, and said as if speaking to a deaf and dumb person:

"Here! Understand? Into the box! *Schreiben, schrieb, geschrieben*. Write. Understand? I write, you write, he, she, it writes. Understand? We, you, they write complaints. And place in this box. To place! The verb 'to place.' We, you, they place the complaints . . . And nobody takes them out. To take out! I don't take out, you don't take out . . ."

But at this point the great schemer beheld the broad thighs of Skumbrievich a the end of the corridor, and without finishing the grammar lesson, ran after the elusive social worker.

"Courage, *Germania!*" Balaganov cheered the German, running after his commander.

But to Ostap's utter disappointment Skumbrievich disappeared again as if he had suddenly been dematerialized.

"This is sheer mysticism," said Ostap, turning his head. "A moment ago here was a man, and now he is no more."

In despair, the foster brothers began systematically to open one door after another. But Balaganov jumped out of the third room, his face distorted with fear.

"Waw, waw!" cried the hoof expert, leaning against the wall. "Waw, waw, waw!"

"What's the matter?" asked Bender. "Did anyone hurt you?"

"There . . ." muttered Balaganov, stretching forth a trembling hand.

Ostap opened the door and beheld a black coffin.

The coffin rested in the middle of the room on an office table. Ostap took off his captain's cap and walked on tiptoe to the coffin. Balaganov, terrified, watched him from the door. A minute later Ostap beckoned to him and showed him a large white inscription on the sides of the coffin.

"Do you see what is written here, Shura?" he said. " 'Death to Red Tape.' Does that quiet you?"

It was a splendid coffin for agitational purposes which the Herculeans dragged out into the street on state holidays, and with songs on their lips carried aloft throughout the city. Usually the coffin rested on the shoulders of Skumbrievich, Bomze, Berlaga, and Polykhayev himself, a democratic man and not ashamed to show himself with his subordinates in various processions and political carnivals. Skumbrievich pro-

foundly respected this coffin and attached great significance to
it. From time to time, putting on an apron, Yegor would
paint the coffin anew with his own hands and renovate the
anti-bureaucratic slogans, while in his office telephones were
roaring and screaming, and divers heads appeared at the
door, surveying the vacant room with sad eyes . . .

Still they could not find Yegor. The doorman in the cap
with the zig-zag informed Bender that Comrade Skumbrievich had been there a minute ago, had just left, and had undoubtedly gone to the beach, which would invest him, as he
put it, with a new charge of strength.

After shaking Kozlevich, who had fallen asleep at the
wheel, and taking Berlaga along in case of need, the Antelopians drove out of town.

Should we be surprised then that Ostap, thoroughly roused
by all that had occurred, wasted no time and went into the
water after Skumbrievich, not a bit embarrassed by the fact
that an important conversation about the unsavory joint stock
affairs had to be carried on in the Black Sea?

Balaganov carried out the orders of the commander with
precision. He undressed the docile Berlaga, brought him to the
edge of the water, and held him patiently around the waist
with both hands. It seemed that a very strenuous conference
was taking place in the water. Ostap shouted like a sea king.
The words could not be made out. But it was evident that
Skumbrievich was attempting to steer a course to the shore.
Ostap cut off his path and chased him into the open sea.
Then the voices became louder and one could hear separate
words: "Intensifier," and "Who took it then? Did the pope
of Rome take it?", "How should *I* know?"

Berlaga shifted his weight from one bare foot to the other,
leaving Indian footprints on the wet sand. Finally, from the
sea came the cry:

"Let him go!"

Balaganov dropped the bookkeeper into the sea and with incredible swiftness Berlaga began to swim dog-fashion, beating the water with his hands and feet. At sight of him, Yegor Skumbrievich dived head first into the water in terror.

Meanwhile the hoof specialist stretched out on the sand and lit a cigarette. He had to wait about twenty minutes. Berlaga was the first to come back. He squatted down on his haunches, took a handkerchief out of his trouser pocket, and wiping his face, said:

"Our Skumbrievich has confessed. He couldn't hold out against face-to-face testimony."

"Squealed, did he, the viper?" Shura asked goodnaturedly. And removing the cigarette butt from his lips between thumb and index finger, he clicked his tongue, and at the same time spittle flew from his mouth, like a torpedo.

Hopping on one foot and aiming the other into his trouser leg, Berlaga explained vaguely:

"I did not do it in the interests of verity, but in the interests of truth."

The second to arrive was the great schemer. He lay right down on his stomach and, pressing his cheek to the heated sand, gazed long and significantly at the blue Skumbrievich who was crawling out of the water. Then he accepted the portfolio from the hands of Balaganov, and wetting the pencil with his hand, began to enter into the case the new information he had secured with such strenuous effort.

A surprising transformation had come over Yegor Skumbrievich. A half hour before the waves had taken unto themselves a most active social worker, a man of whom even the chairman of the local committee, Comrade Niderlandyuk, would have said, "I don't know what others might do, but Skumbrievich will never fall down on us." And yet Skumbrievich had fallen down. And how he had fallen down! The small summer wave brought to the shore, not the splendid female body with the head of a shaven Englishman, but a shapeless wineskin filled with mustard and horseradish.

While the great schemer pirated in the open sea, Heinrich-Maria Sause, who had indefatigably waited for Polykhayev and finally had a very important conversation with him, emerged from HERCULES completely bewildered. Smiling strangely, he went to the post office and there, standing at the desk covered with plate glass, he wrote a letter to his bride in the city of Aachen:

"MY DEAR GIRL,
    I hasten to inform you of joyous news. At last my boss Polykhayev is sending me into production. But what surprises me, dear Tilly, is that here they call it, 'to chase you into a bottle' (*'Sagnat w boutilkou'*). My new friend Bomze told me that people are sent into production as a form of punishment. Can you imagine such a thing? And will our good friend, Doctor of Mathematics Bernhardt Herngross, ever understand it?"

Chapter Nineteen

THE UNIVERSAL STAMP

B Y twelve o'clock of the next day a rumor crept through
HERCULES that the chief had locked himself in his palm
hall with a visitor, and that for three hours he had not responded to the raps of Serna Mikhailovna nor to the calls
on the house telephone. The Herculeans were lost in guesses.
They were accustomed to leading Polykhayev under the arm
all day long in the corridors, seating him on window sills or
dragging him under the stairways, where all business was
settled. The supposition even appeared that perhaps the chief
had deserted the category of workers who "had just left," and
had joined the influential group of "shut-ins," who usually
penetrated into their offices early in the morning, locked the
doors, took the telephone receiver off, and thus barricaded
from the entire world, composed various reports.

But the work went on, papers demanded signatures, replies
and resolutions. Serna Mikhailovna would approach discontentedly and listen at Polykhayev's door, pearl balls dangling
from her large ears.

"It's a fact that has no precedent," the secretary said profoundly.

"But who is it? Who is sitting with him?" asked Bomze,
who emanated the mixed odor of eau de Cologne and cutlets.
"It is by any chance someone from the Inspection?"

"Why, of course not! I told you—just an ordinary visitor."

"And Polykhayev has been sitting with him for three
hours?"

"A fact that has no precedent," repeated Serna Mikhailovna.

"But what shall we do about it?" Bomze worried. "I must have Polykhayev's resolution immediately. I have a detailed report concerning the unfitness of the former quarters of Tin and Bacon for the conditions of work in HERCULES. I can do nothing without a resolution."

Serna Mikhailovna was surrounded on all sides by fellow workers. All of them held large or small papers in their hands. After waiting another hour, in the course of which the noise behind the door had not subsided, Serna Mikhailovna sat down at her desk and said with resignation:

"Very well, comrades. Bring me your papers."

From the closet she took a long wooden stand on which swung thirty-six stamps with fat lacquered heads, and dextrously extricating the necessary stamps out of this nest, she began to press them on the papers that could not endure delay.

The chief of HERCULES had long ago given up signing papers with his own hand. Whenever the occasion arose he would take a little stamp out of his vest pocket and, breathing lovingly upon it, would press above his title his violet facsimile. He approved this routine, and it suggested to him the thought that certain of the most frequently used resolutions could also be transferred to rubber.

Thus into the world appeared the first rubber adages:

"No objections. Polykhayev."

"I agree. Polykhayev."

"Splendid thought. Polykhayev."

"Put into operation. Polykhayev."

Having tested the new invention in practice, the chief of HERCULES came to the conclusion that it considerably simplified his work and needed further encouragement and development. Soon a new batch of rubber was put to work.

This time the resolutions were a bit wordier:

"To reprimand in the orders. Polykhayev."

"Make a public example of. Polykhayev."

"Throw to the periphery. Polykhayev."

"Dismiss without emoluments due on occasion of dismissal. Polykhayev."

The struggle which the chief of HERCULES was carrying on with the Communal Department concerning quarters inspired him with new standardized texts:

"I am not a subordinate of the Communal Dept. Polykhayev."

"What's the matter with them? Have they gone crazy? Polykhayev."

"Don't interfere with my work. Polykhayev."

"I am not your night-watchman. Polykhayev."

"I will not give up either the beds or the washstands. Polykhayev."

"The hotel belongs to us, and that's all!" Polykhayev."

"I am up to all of your tricks. Polykhayev."

This series was ordered in sets of three. He evidently foresaw a long struggle, and feared, not without foundation, that the rubber might soon wear out.

Besides these he ordered another set of resolutions for inter-Herculean needs:

"Ask Serna Mikhailovna. Polykhayev."

"Don't bother me. Polykhayev."

"Haste makes waste. Polykhayev."

Of course, the creative thoughts of the chieftain were not bounded exclusively by the administrative side of business. Being a man of broad views, he could not very well evade questions of current politics. And so he ordered a splendid universal stamp over the text of which he labored several days. This was a remarkable rubber thought which Polykhayev could apply to any occasion in life. Besides, it gave him the ability to respond immediately to all events, and freed him from the necessity of thinking painfully each time. The stamp was so conveniently constructed that it was sufficient

merely to fill in the spaces in order to get a resolution on the
topic of the day:

In reply to ....
....
...............we, Herculeans, like one man reply with:
(a) Raising the quality of production
(b) Increasing the productivity of labor
(c) Intensifying our fight against bureaucracy, procrasti-
nation, favoritism, and bootlicking
(d) Rooting out loafing
(e) Decreasing overhead expenditures
(f) General growth of trade union activity
(g) Refusal to celebrate Christmas, Easter, Trinity Day,
Annunciation, Epiphany, and other religious holidays
(h) Declaration of merciless war against indifference, hooliganism and drunkenness
(i) Joining, to a man, the society "Down with Routine"
(j) Beginning, to a man, to lead a new life
(k) Transferring, to a man, all our business correspondence
to the Latin alphabet

And also, we shall do all that will be required of us in the
future.

The dotted lines were filled in by Polykhayev in person,
depending upon the demands of the moment.

But now, while voices rumbled like a ventilator beyond
Polykhayev's door, Serna Mikhailovna worked energetically.
The stand on which the stamps were distributed according
to their size—from the very smallest, "No objections. Polykhayev.", to the very largest, the Universal Stamp—reminded
one of the very clever circus instrument on which a white
clown with a sun on the seat of his trousers plays "Angel's
Serenade" with little wooden hammers. The secretary picked
out approximately suitable stamps and decorated the papers
with them. Most frequently she used the very cautious rubber:

"Haste makes waste. Polykhayev.", remembering that this was her chief's favorite resolution.

The work went on without a hitch. The rubber proved an excellent substitute for the man. The rubber Polykhayev was in no way inferior to the living Polykhayev.

HERCULES was quite deserted, and barefooted scrub-women were walking over the stairway with their dirty buckets; the last typist, who had remained for an hour after work in order to copy for herself Esenin's lines beginning: "Dragging the gilded canvas of my verse, I want to tell you something tender," had departed; Serna Mikhailovna, tired of waiting, rose, and before going out into the street was beginning to massage her eyelids with cold cream—when the door of Polykhayev's cabinet quivered, opened, and out came Ostap Bender. He looked vaguely at Serna Mikhailovna and went on, swinging the yellow portfolio tied with shoe laces. After him, from under the cool shadow of the palms and magnolias, Polykhayev dived out. Serna glanced at her distinguished friend and without a word dropped into the square little cushion that softened the hardness of her chair. What a blessing that the fellow workers had already gone home and could not behold their chief at this moment! In his mustache lodged a pearly tear, like a bird in the branches. He blinked his eyes with remarkable rapidity and rubbed his hands energetically, as if he were attempting to obtain fire by the method customary among the savages of Oceania. He ran after Ostap, smiling shamefacedly and almost doubled over.

"What will happen now?" he muttered, running to one side and then to another. "I will perish! Tell me, my friend, my kind friend, won't I perish? How can I be calm?"

He wanted to add that he had a wife, children, Serna, children by Serna, and by another woman who lived in Rostov on the Don River; but all of this died in his throat and he kept still. Moaning tearfully, he escorted Ostap all the way to the vestibule. In the deserted building they met only two men. At the end of the corridor stood Yegor Skumbrievich. At the sight of the great schemer, he seized his jaws with both hands and retreated into a niche. Below on the stairway Bookkeeper Berlaga peeked out from behind a marble girl with an electric torch. He bowed slavishly to Ostap and even said, "How do you do," but Ostap did not respond to the greetings of the viceroy.

At the exit, Polykhayev seized Ostap by the sleeve and babbled:

"I didn't hide anything! Word of honor! Can I live in peace? Can I?"

"Man can have complete peace only from an insurance policy," replied Ostap, without slowing down his pace. "Any life insurance agent can tell you that. Personally, I don't need you any more. But the government will no doubt soon become interested in you."

Chapter Twenty

MAN PROPOSES . . .

In a small shop of artificial mineral waters on whose sign blue siphons were painted, Balaganov and Panikovsky sat at a white table. The hoof specialist chewed on a long cream puff, taking particular care not to push the cream out of the opposite end. With this food of the gods he drank seltzer water with "New-Mown Hay," a green syrup. The messenger drank salubrious mare's milk. Six empty bottles were already before him; he was carefully shaking the thick liquid out of the seventh. At the office that day the new girl office manager had paid out the salary on an order signed personally by Bender, so the friends were now enjoying the coolness that came from the Italian stone slabs of the stand, from the dark cylinders that held hissing water, and from the marble counter. A piece of ice had slid out of the closet and lay on the floor, shedding water. It was pleasant to glance at it after the weary appearance of the street with its short shadows, pedestrians prostrated by the heat, and dogs dazed with thirst.

"Chernomorsk is a good town," Panikovsky announced as he drank. "Mare's milk is good for the heart."

For some reason this remark tickled Balaganov. He squeezed his cream puff carelessly, and a thick sausage of cream oozed out; but the hoof specialist managed to catch it on the fly.

"Do you know, Shura," Panikovsky continued, "somehow I have stopped believing in Bender. He's doing something that's not regular."

"Well, well!" Balaganov said threateningly. "Nobody asked your opinion."

"No, seriously! I greatly respect Ostap Ibragimovich. He's such a remarkable man! Even Funt—you know how I respect Funt—said that Bender has a head on him. But I tell you, Shura, Funt is an ass. So help me God, he is such a fool! Just a pathetic, insignificant person! Mind you, I don't say anything against Bender, but there are some things about him that I don't like. To *you*, Shura, I'll tell everything, as if you were one of my family."

Since his last conversation with the Sub-inspector of Criminal Investigation, no one had addressed himself to Balaganov as a kinsman. Therefore he listened with satisfaction to the words of the messenger and thoughtlessly permitted him to continue.

"You know, Shura," Panikovsky continued, "I respect Bender very much. But I must tell you, confidentially, Bender is an ass. So help me God, he's a pathetic, insignificant person!"

"Hey, hey!" Balaganov warned him.

"What has 'hey, hey' to do with it? Just think. What is he spending our money for? Try to remember. Why all this foolish office? What expenditures! We pay Funt alone one hundred and twenty. And the office girl! Now they've sent two others. I saw them. And to-day they collected their salary. Why do we need it all? He says 'for the sake of legality.' To hell with legality if it costs all that money! And the elk horns for sixty-five rubles! And the ink well! And all the hole punchers!"

Panikovsky unbuttoned his coat, and the half-ruble shirt-front which was buttoned around the neck of the pact-violator rolled up like a piece of parchment. But Panikovsky was now so excited that he paid no attention to it.

"Yes, Shura! You and I receive a miserable emolument, while he swims in luxury. Why, I ask you, did he go to the

Caucasus? He says he went on business. I don't believe him. Panikovsky doesn't have to believe everything! And here I ran to the docks to get him a ticket! Mind you, a first-class ticket! This St. Petersburg dandy can't travel second-class! This is where our ten thousand is going. He talks over the long distance telephone and sends full rate telegrams throughout the entire world. Do you know how much a full rate telegram costs? Forty kopeks a word! *Any* word costs forty kopeks! While I have to deny myself the mare's milk which I need for my health. I am a sick old man. I tell you straight from the shoulder: Bender has no head on him!"

"Don't go too far," Balaganov remarked, wavering. "After all, Bender made a man out of you. Do you remember how you ran with the goose in Arbatov? Now you have a job, receive a salary, and are a member of society."

"I don't want to be a member of society!" Panikovsky suddenly screamed; then, lowering his voice, added, "Your Bender is an idiot! He started all these silly investigations when we can get the money to-day with our bare hands!"

Here the hoof specialist, thinking no more of his beloved chieftain, moved closer to Panikovsky. The latter, constantly unrolling his recalcitrant shirt front, told Balaganov of the serious experiment he had performed on his own responsibility.

On the very day that the great schemer and Balaganov were chasing Skumbrievich, Panikovsky left the office to old Funt, secretly penetrated into Koreiko's room, and taking advantage of the latter's absence, made a very thorough investigation. Of course he did not find any money there, but he discovered something better: dumbbells, very large black dumbbells, each one weighing about sixty pounds.

"Shura, I'll tell you everything, as to a member of my family. I have discovered the secret of those dumbbells!"

Panikovsky finally caught the tail of his lively shirt front,

attached it to a button on his trousers, and looked at Balaganov solemnly.

"What kind of a secret can it be?" the hoof expert asked
in disappointment. "They're ordinary dumbbells for exercise."

"Shura, you know how I respect you," Panikovsky said, his
voice trembling with excitement. "But you are an ass! Those
are gold dumbbells! You understand? Dumbbells of pure
gold! Each dumbbell sixty pounds! Together, a hundred and
twenty pounds of gold! I understood it at once. It simply
hit me between the eyes. I stood there before those dumbbells
and laughed like a madman. What a scoundrel this Koreiko!
He made himself gold dumbbells, painted them black—and
he thinks nobody will recognize them! But to you, Shura, I
speak as I would to my own relative. Do you think I would
have told you this secret if I could take the dumbbells by myself? But I am a sick old man, and the dumbbells are heavy.
And I appeal to you as to a kinsman. I'm not Bender; I'm
honest!"

"But suppose they aren't gold?" asked the favorite son of the
lieutenant, who wanted Panikovsky to dispel his doubts as
soon as possible.

"Well then, what are they, according to you?" the pact-
violator asked ironically.

"Yes," said Balaganov, blinking his red eyelashes. "Now
it's all clear. What do you think of that! An old man, and
he's discovered it all! While Bender doesn't do what he's
supposed to. He writes papers, takes trips . . . Still, let's give
him his share and be square about it, eh, what?"

"But why?" objected Panikovsky. "Everything for us! Now
we'll live beautifully, Shura! I'll get myself some gold teeth,
and I'll get married. So help me God, Shura, my honest,
honorable word! I'll get married!".

It was decided to secure the dumbbells without delay.

"Pay for the mares' milk, Shura," Panikovsky said. "We'll
settle our accounts later on."

At eleven o'clock that evening, the foster brothers, bent under the weight of two large dumbbells, walked in the direction of the Office for the Collection of Horns and Hoofs. Panikovsky bore his share with both hands, sticking out his stomach and puffing joyfully. Frequently he would stop, rest the dumbbell on the sidewalk and mutter: "I'll get married! My honest, honorable word, I'll get married!" The strong Balaganov carried the dumbbell on his shoulder. Occasionally Panikovsky could not turn a corner because the weight of the dumbbell pulled him forward. Then, with his free hand, Balaganov held Panikovsky by the scruff of the neck and gave his body the necessary direction.

They stopped at the door of the office.

"Now we'll each saw off a little piece," Panikovsky said in a business-like way. "And to-morrow morning we'll sell it. There is a watchmaker of my acquaintance, Mr. Biberkham. He'll give us the real price. Not as in the government store where they never give you a real price."

Just then the conspirators noticed a light behind the green curtains of the office.

"Who can be there at this hour?" Balaganov wondered, bending toward the keyhole.

At the desk, lit by the powerful light of a shaded table lamp, sat Ostap Bender, rapidly writing something.

"The author!" said Balaganov, laughing uproariously, and yielding the keyhole to Panikovsky.

"Of course," remarked Panikovsky, after he had his fill of peeking through the keyhole. "He's writing again! So help me, this pathetic man makes me laugh! But where will we saw off our pieces?"

And discussing with great spirit the necessity of selling two pieces of gold to watchmaker Biberkham on the very next morning, the two brothers lifted their loads and went off into the darkness.

In the meanwhile the great schemer was finishing the life

story of Alexander Ivanovich Koreiko. The bronze roofs of the five little huts that made up the ink well facing the village had been removed. Ostap dipped his pen at random wherever his hand landed, slid all over the chair, and scuffed his feet under the table. He had the exhausted face of a card gambler who, after losing all night, finally makes his stake at the break of dawn.

Ostap placed the last period, blotted the biography with a blotter whose handle was a silver bear, and began to gather the documents together. He took pleasure in keeping his documents in good order. For the last time he lovingly examined the depositions, telegrams, and various bits of information. The portfolio contained even photographs and extracts from various account books. The entire life of Alexander Ivanovich Koreiko lay in the portfolio with palm trees, girls, the blue sea, a white steamer, fast express trains, shining automobiles, and Rio de Janeiro, the magical city on the bay, populated by goodnatured mulattoes, most of whom wore white trousers. At last the great schemer had found the very individual of whom he had dreamed all his life.

"And there's no one who can appreciate my titanic labors," Ostap said sadly, rising and tying the fat portfolio. "Balaganov is very nice, but foolish. Panikovsky is simply a silly old man. And Kozlevich is an angel without wings. He does not doubt to this moment that we are collecting horns for the use of the mouthpiece industry. Where are my friends, my wives, my children? My one hope is that Alexander Ivanovich, whom I´respect, will appreciate my great labor, and will reward me, oh, poor man that I am, with half a million rubles! And yet . . . no! Now I will not take less than a million, or the good mulattoes will simply never respect me!"

Crackling palms and colored birds flitted through his mind. Ocean liners rubbed their sides against the piers of Rio de Janeiro. Clever Brazilian merchants busied themselves with coffee dumping before everybody's eyes. And in the open cafés the local young bloods were whooping it up with liquor and the tango.

"I will command the parade!" the great schemer exclaimed.

Putting out the light, he left the office and took the shortest path to the Street of Little Worries. Pale, compass-like legs of projectors stretched across the sky, descended, suddenly sliced a section of a building, revealing a porch or a glass-enclosed balcony and a couple petrified with surprise. Two small tanks with round mushroom-like hats drove around the corner, swaying and bumping Ostap with their caterpillar chains. A cavalryman, bending from the saddle, asked the pedestrian the nearest way to the Old Market. In one place artillery barred Ostap's way. He crossed the street, dashing through a narrow space between two batteries. In another place a militia-man was hurriedly nailing to the gates of a house a piece of wood with the inscription: "Gas Shelter."

Ostap hurried. The Argentine Tango urged him on. Paying no attention to what was happening about him, he entered Koreiko's house and knocked on the familiar door.

"Who's there?" he heard the voice of the underground millionaire.

"Telegram," replied the great schemer, winking in the darkness.

The door opened and he entered, his portfolio catching on the door jamb.

At dawn, in a gully far outside the city, sat the hoof special-ist and the messenger. They were sawing the dumbbells. Their noses were covered with iron filings. On the grass beside Panikovsky lay his shirt front. He had taken it off; it had interfered with his labors. Under the dumbbells the farsighted pact-violator had spread newspapers so that not one bit of the dust of the precious metal should be lost. From time to time the foster brothers regarded each other with dignity and sawed with renewed energy. The morning stillness was

broken only by the whistling of woodchucks and the screeching of the overheated files.

"What's the matter?" Balaganov said suddenly, stopping
work. "I've been sawing away for three hours, and still it
isn't gold!"

Panikovsky did not reply. He had made the discovery a half
hour before, and had continued to move the saw only for the
sake of appearance.

"Well, let's saw some more," redhaired Shura said gallantly.

"Of course we must saw," remarked Panikovsky, trying to
defer the moment of reckoning as long as possible.

He hid his face in the palm of his hand and through the
parted fingers watched the measured movements of Balaganov's broad back.

"I can't make it out," said Shura, when he had sawed the
dumbbell into two halves. "This is not gold!"

"Go on sawing! Go on!" gabbled Panikovsky.

But Balaganov, holding in each hand one half of the iron
dumbbell, slowly advanced upon the pact-violator.

"Don't come to me with that iron," screamed Panikovsky,
running away. "I despise you!"

But Shura swung on him, and, grunting with the effort,
flung a piece of the dumbbell at the intriguer. Hearing it
whistle overhead, the intriguer fell to the ground. The struggle between the hoof expert and the messenger was brief.
At first the angry Balaganov took delight in trampling upon
the shirt front; then he advanced upon its owner. As he delivered his blows, Shura chanted:

"Who thought of these dumbbells? Who embezzled the
office money? Who talked against Bender?"

In addition, the lieutenant's first-born remembered the violation of the Sukharev pact, which cost Panikovsky a few extra
blows.

"You'll pay me for this shirt front," Panikovsky cried
angrily, shielding himself with his elbows. "Bear in mind

that I will never forgive you the shirt front! You can't buy such shirt fronts nowadays!"

Balaganov wound up the fight by taking from his opponent an ancient purse containing thirty-eight rubles.

"This is for your mares' milk, you reptile!" he said.

They returned to the city joylessly. Shura stalked angrily ahead, and after him, limping on one foot and weeping lustily, Panikovsky dragged himself along.

"I'm a poor, unfortunate old man," he whimpered. "You'll pay me for the shirt front! Give me back my money!"

"You'll get it in the neck," Shura replied without looking around. "I'll tell Bender everything, you crook!"

Chapter Twenty-one

THE FALL OF MAGPIE VILLAGE

V ARVARA PTIBURDUKOVA was happy. Sitting at the round table, she joyously surveyed her menage. So much furniture stood in the room of the Ptiburdukovs that there was almost no free space. But even in the space that remained there was a sufficiency of happiness. The lamp cast its light beyond the window, where it quivered on a small green branch like a woman's brooch. On the table stood cookies, candies, and pickled fish in a round tin box. The tea pot had gathered to its crooked bosom all the coziness of the Ptiburdukov nest. It reflected the bed and the white curtains and the night stand. As for Ptiburdukov himself, sitting in blue pajamas opposite his wife—he was also happy. Blowing smoke through his mustache, he was hewing a toy country privy out of a piece of wood. It was highly detailed work. He had to saw the walls, put on a sloping roof, fix the inner mechanism, put glass in the little window, and attach a microscopic latch to the door. Ptiburdukov worked with passion. He regarded working with wood as the finest form of relaxation.

When he finished his labors, the engineer laughed gayly, slapped his wife's fat warm back, and pulled the box of pickled fish toward himself. At that moment a loud knock resounded on the door, the lamp quivered, and the teapot swayed on its wire pedestal.

"Who could be coming so late?" exclaimed Ptiburdukov, rising to open the door.

In the doorway stood Vasisualy Lokhankin. He was wrapped up to his beard in a white sheet which revealed only his hairy legs. To his breast he clutched the book entitled "Man and Woman," thick and embellished like an icon. Vasisualy's eyes wandered.

"Come in," the bewildered engineer invited, taking a step backward. "Varvara, what does this mean?"

"I come to live with you forever," replied Lokhankin in funereal iambics. "I hope to find my shelter here with you."

"What do you mean 'shelter'!" Ptiburdukov said, turning crimson. "What do you want, Vasisualy Andreyevich?"

"Sashuk, look! He's naked!" cried Varvara, after appraising the appearance of her erstwhile spouse. "What has happened, Vasisualy? Come in, come in!"

Lokhankin crossed the threshold with his bare feet, and muttering, "Misfortune! Misfortune!" began to pace the narrow limits of the crowded room. With the edge of the sheet he knocked the delicate handiwork of Ptiburdukov to the floor. Whereupon the engineer retreated to a corner, convinced that no good could be expected of this visit.

"What misfortune?" Varvara demanded. "Why are you dressed only in a bed sheet?"

"I come to live with you forever," Lokhankin bleated, pounding out a measured recitative with the regular beat of his yellow soles. "I come to live with you forever!"

"What are you raving about?" Varvara attacked her former husband. "Go home and sleep it off! Go away from here! Go away! Go home!"

"The home I had is now no more," quavered Vasisualy, shivering. "For it is now a pile of ashes. The fire, the fire it is that drove me here! I salvaged only this poor sheet, and this beloved book of mine. But since you are so cruel with me, I shall depart and place my curse on you."

Swaying mournfully, Vasisualy turned to the door. But Varvara and her husband stopped him. They begged his forgiveness, told him that they had not realized at once what had happened, and in general became busy. Into the light of the world appeared Ptiburdukov's new holiday suit, his linen and shoes.

While Lokhankin was dressing, the husband and wife conferred in the corridor:

"Where shall we put him?" Varvara whispered. "He cannot spend the night with us; we have only one room!"

"I'm surprised at you," said the good engineer. "A man has met with misfortune, and you are thinking only of your own comfort!"

When the husband and wife returned to the room, the iambics-monger was sitting at the table and devoting himself to the pickled fish with rapt attention. He had previously thrown two volumes of "Strength of Materials" off the shelf, and put the highly embellished "Man and Woman" in their place.

"How terrible! Did the entire house burn down?" Ptiburdukov asked sympathetically. "Horrible! Horrible!"

"I disagree with you. It was so fated," said Vasisualy, finishing his hosts' supper. "Perhaps from these flames I shall emerge transformed."

But he did not emerge transformed.

The Ptiburdukovs began to arrange night lodgings. They placed a small mattress for Vasisualy on that remaining floor space in which an hour before there had been sufficient happiness. They shut the windows and put out the light. Night entered the room. For about twenty minutes they lay in silence, turning over from time to time and sighing heavily. Then from the floor came the drawling whisper of Lokhankin:

"Varvara! Varvara! Listen, Varvara!"

"What do you want?" asked his former wife, annoyed.

"Why did you leave me, Varvara?"

Receiving no answer to this fundamental question, Vasisualy began to whine:

"You are a bitch, Varvara! You are a she-wolf! You she-wolf! Oh, how I despise you!"

The engineer lay rigidly in his bed, choking with anger and clenching his fists.

In the long chain of events that led to the destruction of Magpie Village, otherwise known as Apartment No. 3, the first link was Nobody's Grandmother. She burned kerosene in her attic, as is well known, because she did not trust electricity. After the flagellation inflicted upon Vasisualy Andreyevich, a considerable time passed without interesting occurrences, and the restless mind of Chamberlain Mitrich languished in forced idleness. It occurred to him then to ruminate upon Grandma's habits; and this disturbed him.

"The old woman will burn up the whole apartment some day!" he muttered. "Of course, *she* has nothing to lose. But my grand piano alone is worth two thousand."

Having reached this conclusion, Mitrich insured all of his movable property. Now he could be quiet and indifferent when he saw Grandma groan under the weight of the turbid bottle of kerosene, which she clutched to her breast as if it were a child. The first to learn of the foresight of Mitrich was Citizen Gigienishvili, who immediately interpreted it in his own way. He accosted Mitrich in the corridor and, clutching the former chamberlain's chest, said ominously:

"You want to set fire to the apartment, do you? You want to get your insurance, hey? You think Gigienishvili is a fool, hein? Gigienishvili understands everything!"

And that very day the excited lodger insured all his belongings for the maximum sum. This news spread terror throughout Magpie Village. Luzzia Franzevna Pferd ran into the kitchen, her eyes bulging.

"They'll set fire to us, these scoundrels! You can do what you like, citizens, but I shall take out insurance immediately.

We're doomed to be burned now. At least I'll get the insurance. I'll not go begging because of them!"

The next day the entire apartment was insured, with the exception of Lokhankin and Nobody's Grandmother. Lokhankin read "Fatherland," and noticed nothing, while Nobody's Grandmother had no more faith in insurance than she had in electricity. Nikita Pryakhin brought the insurance policy home, tied with a blue ribbon, and for a long time examined its water mark.

"This means, you see, that the government is assisting us," he said darkly. "Assisting the lodgers? Thanks! Well, as we like, so we'll do."

And hiding the policy under his shirt, Pryakhin went away to his room. His words instilled such fear in the lodgers that no one slept that night in Magpie Village. Dunya was tying up her things in bundles, and the other cotters went to spend the night with their acquaintances. In the daytime they all watched each other, and little by little began to take things out of the house.

Everything was clear. The house was doomed. It could not avoid going up in smoke. And actually, at midnight, the apartment flared up simultaneously in six different places.

The last to escape was Lokhankin, who had managed to cover himself with a sheet. With all his might he cried "Fire! Fire!" although he could surprise no one with this news. All the lodgers of Magpie Village were in quorum. The drunken Pryakhin sat on his little trunk with metal corners. He looked senselessly at the glimmering windows, chanting, "As we wish, so we'll do." Gigienishvili smelled his hands, reeking of kerosene, made a wry face after every whiff, and rubbed them against his trousers. The first tongue of flame darted out the window, and sparks began to spray from under the wooden cornice. The first window burst and fell with a clang. Nobody's Grandmother bayed gruesomely.

"The house has stood for forty years," Mitrich explained

with composure, walking among the crowd. "It has witnessed three régimes. It was a good house. But under the Soviet régime it burned. Such is the sad fact, fellow citizens."

The female part of Magpie Village gathered in one group and did not take its eyes off the fire. Flames burst from all the windows. Occasionally the fire would disappear, and then the darkened house seemed to jump back like the body of a gun after a discharge. But again the orange cloud would blaze forth, gayly illuminating Lemon Lane. It grew hot. It was impossible to remain any longer near the house, and the gathering removed itself to the opposite sidewalk.

Nikita Pryakhin, dozing on his little trunk in the middle of the street, suddenly jumped up, barefooted and terrible.

"True believers!" he cried, rending his shirt. "Citizens!"

He staggered away from the fire, dashed into the crowd and, shouting incomprehensible words, began to point at the flaming house. Confusion possessed the crowd.

"They have forgotten his child!" cried a woman in a straw hat.

Nikita was surrounded. He pushed the crowd away with his arms, trying to clear a pathway for himself to the house.

"It's lying on the bed!" Pryakhin screamed frantically. "Let me go, I tell you!"

Scalding tears rolled down his face. He struck the head of Gigienishvili, who barred his way, and dashed into the yard. A minute later he ran out carrying a ladder.

"Stop him!" yelled the woman in the straw hat. "He'll be burned up!"

"Go away, I tell you!" bellowed Nikita Pryakhin, placing the ladder against the wall and kicking back the young men in the crowd who attempted to catch his feet. "I won't let it be burned up! My soul is on fire!"

He kicked back with his feet, and crawled up toward a second-story window.

"Come back!" cried voices in the crowd. "What are you going after? You'll be burned up!"

"It's lying on the bed!" Nikita continued to shout. "A whole goose! And a whole bottle of vodka! Do you expect me to let it burn up, Citizens, True Believers?"

With unexpected skill, Pryakhin grasped the window sill, flung himself inside and disappeared, sucked in by the air. His last words were, "As we wish, so we'll do!" Silence fell upon the lane, broken only by the bells and horns of the fire department caravan. Firemen in unbending tarpaulin costumes and broad blue belts ran into the yard with axes.

A minute after Nikita Pryakhin committed the only heroic act of his life, a burning beam separated itself from the house and crashed to earth. The roof cracked, fell apart and dropped inside the house. A gleaming column rose toward the sky, as if a shell had been fired at the moon.

Thus perished Apartment No. 3, better known as Magpie Village.

Suddenly a thunder of hoofs was heard in the lane. In the light of the conflagration Engineer Talmudovsky flashed by in a droshky. On his knees lay a suitcase. Jumping up and down on his seat, the engineer bent forward to the *izvozchik* and cried:

"I'll never set my foot here again! At such a salary!"

And then his fat back, illumined by the conflagration and the firemen's torches, disappeared around the corner.

Chapter Twenty-two

"I WILL COMMAND THE PARADE"

"I AM dying of boredom," said Ostap. "Here I have been talking to you for two hours, only two hours, and I am already as sick of you as if I had known you all my life. With such a disagreeable character you might be a millionaire in America. But here a millionaire should be a bit more easy-going."

"You are insane," replied Alexander Ivanovich.

"Don't insult me," Bender remarked gently. "I am the son of a Turkish citizen, and therefore a descendant of the Janissaries. I will not spare you if you insist upon insulting me. The Janissaries know no pity, either for women, for children, or for underground Soviet millionaires!"

"Go away, citizen," said Koreiko, in the voice of a Herculean bureaucrat. "It is already almost three o'clock. I want to sleep. I have to go to work early."

"Right, right! I forgot!" Ostap exclaimed. "You don't dare be late for work. You might be fired without advance pay. Still, two weeks' salary is twenty-three rubles. With your economical ways, you can live a half a year on it."

"That is none of your business! Leave me alone. Do you hear? Get out!"

"But this economizing will be your undoing! Of course, it isn't safe for you to display your millions. However, you are overdoing it. Have you ever thought of what will happen to you when you finally have the opportunity to spend your money? Restraint is dangerous. A teacher of French of my acquaintance, Ernestine Yosephovna Poincaré, had never in her life drunk wine. And what do you think happened? At a party she was given a small glass of cognac. She liked it so much that she drank a whole bottle of it. And right there at the supper table she went mad! And there was one less teacher of French in the world! . . . The same may happen to you."

"What the hell do you want with me, anyway?"

"I want from you what my childhood friend, Kolya Osten-Baken, wanted from his childhood friend, the Polish beauty, Inga Zaiac. He wanted her love. And I, too, want love. I want you, Citizen Koreiko, to fall in love with me, and as a token of your regard, give me one million rubles."

"Get out!" said Koreiko quietly.

"There you go again, forgetting that I am a descendant of the Janissaries!"

With these words Ostap rose from his seat. Now the men faced each other. Koreiko's face was stormy, and white lights gleamed in his eyes. The great schemer smiled genially, displaying his white teeth. The enemies came close to the night lamp, and their gigantic shadows fell on the wall.

"I have told you a thousand times," said Koreiko, controlling himself, "that I have no millions and never had any. You understand? Do you understand? Well, then, get out! I shall lodge a complaint against you."

"You will never lodge any complaints against me," Ostap said significantly. "And I can go away. But the moment I come out on your Street of Little Worries, you will run after me, weeping. And you will lick my Janissary feet, begging me to return."

"What makes you think that I will beg you?"

"You will. It must be. As my dear friend Vasisualy Lokhankin is wont to say, 'Precisely in this lies the homespun truth.' Here it is."

The great schemer lay his portfolio on the table, and slowly untying its shoe laces, continued:

"But let's come to an agreement: no excesses. You must not

try to choke me. You must not attempt to throw yourself out
of the window. But the main thing is, don't die of a stroke.
If it should occur to you to die on the spot, I will be in a very
foolish situation. The fruits of long conscientious labor will
perish. Well, let's get down to business. It's no longer a secret
that you do not love me. I see that I shall never obtain that
which Kolya Osten-Baken obtained from Inga Zaiac, my
childhood friend. Therefore I shall not sigh in vain, and I
shall not attempt to put my arm around your waist. You may
consider the serenade over. The balalaikas are quiet now, and
so are the mandolins and the gilded harps. I am addressing
you as one juridical party to another juridical party. Here before you is a package that weighs three or four kilos. It is
being sold for—and it is worth—one million rubles—that same
million which, because of your greediness, you do not wish
to give me. Buy it!"

Koreiko bent over the table and read on the portfolio, "The
Case of Alexander Koreiko, begun on June 25th, 1930, finished August 10th, 1930."

"What nonsense!" he exclaimed, throwing up his hands.
"How perfectly absurd! First you come to me for money.
Then you invent some case. It's simply ridiculous!"

"Well, will you buy it?" insisted the great schemer. "The
price is not high. It is at a rate of only three hundred thousand
per kilo of the most remarkable information in the field of
underground commerce."

"What information are you talking about?" Koreiko asked
rudely, stretching his hand for the portfolio.

"The most interesting," replied Ostap, politely pushing
Koreiko's hand aside. "Information concerning your second,
more important life, which is so radically different from your
first—the forty-six-ruble one, the Herculean one. Your first
life is known to everybody. From ten to four you support the
Soviet system. . . . But of your second life from four to ten,

only I am informed. Have you estimated the significance of this situation?"

Koreiko did not reply. A shadow lay on his knitted brow.

"No," the great schemer said decisively. "You are not descended from a monkey like other people, but from a cow. You grasp things with great difficulty, like a split-hoof mammal. I tell you this as a specialist in cows and hoofs. And so, once again! According to my information, you are the possessor of seven or eight million. The portfolio is being offered for a million. If you do not buy it, I shall immediately take it to another place. There I shall receive nothing for it, not a kopek, but you will be finished. I tell you this as one juridical party to another juridical party. I shall remain the same poor poet and bigamist that I have always been, but to the very end of my days I shall rejoice that I have rid the world and society of a great skinflint."

"Show me the case," Koreiko said thoughtfully.

"Don't bother," remarked Ostap, opening the portfolio. "I will command the parade! You were informed of that by telegram in due time. Well now, the parade has begun, and, as you may notice, I am in command of it."

Alexander glanced at the first page of the case, and, seeing his own photograph pasted on it, smiled unpleasantly and said:

"I don't understand what you want of me. But I don't mind looking at it out of curiosity."

"I compiled it—out of curiosity," declared the great schemer. "Well, what do you say? Let's begin on *that* basis, which, after all, is perfectly innocuous. Gentlemen of the Jury, Alexander Ivanovich Koreiko was born . . . I suppose we may omit the happy childhood. In those days little Sasha had not yet occupied himself with commercial robbery. Further goes the rosy adolescence. We shall omit another page. And here is youth and the beginning of life. 'When I was handsome and twenty-two.' Here we may pause . . . out of curiosity. Page six of the case . . ."

Ostap turned page six, announced the contents of pages seven, eight, and further, inclusive of page twelve.

"And so, gentlemen of the jury, before you have passed the first important enterprises of my defendant; to wit: trade in government medicaments at the time of the famine and the typhus epidemic, and work in the Supplies Department, which led to the disappearance of the railroad train and the supplies directed to the starving Volga districts. All these facts, gentlemen of the jury, interest us from the point of view of pure, innocuous curiosity."

Ostap spoke in the atrocious manner of a pre-revolutionary attorney-at-law, who, catching hold of a little word, does not let it out of his teeth, and drags it after him through the ten days of a great trial.

"Likewise not altogether devoid of curiosity was the appearance of my defendant in Moscow in the year 1922 . . ."

Alexander Ivanovich's face maintained its neutrality, but his hands roved aimlessly along the table like a blind man's.

"Permit me, gentlemen of the jury, to ask you one question . . . of course, out of curiosity. What income could a man derive from two ordinary barrels filled with ordinary water? Twenty rubles? Three rubles? Eight kopeks, perhaps? No, gentlemen of the jury! To Alexander Ivanovich they brought four hundred thousand gold rubles, zero zero kopeks. True, these barrels had the significant title, 'The Industrial Artel of Chemical Products Revanche.' However, let us go further . . . pages forty-two to fifty-three. . . . The scene of action, a small trusting republic . . . azure sky, camels, oases, and dandies in golden Thibetan caps. . . . My defendant helps to build an electric station. I emphasize, he *helps*. Look at his face, gentlemen of the jury!"

Carried away by his own eloquence, Ostap turned toward Alexander Ivanovich and pointed his finger at him. But he did not manage the graceful semicircle which attorneys-at-law were wont to describe. Unexpectedly, the defendant seized the hand on the fly, and silently began to twist it. At the same time, with his other hand, the defendant tried to choke the throat of his attorney-at-law. For a half a minute the opponents bent each other back and forth, trembling and tense. Ostap's shirt flew open and revealed his tattoo. Napoleon was still holding the beer stein, but he was so red that he seemed to have had time to get drunk on it.

"Don't press my psyche!" said Ostap, tearing Koreiko away from him and taking a deep breath. "You're interfering with business."

"Scoundrel! Scoundrel!" whispered Alexander Ivanovich. "What a scoundrel!"

He sat down on the floor, twisting with the pain inflicted upon him by the descendant of the Janissaries.

"The session continues," Ostap remarked as if nothing had happened. "And as you see, gentlemen of the jury, the ice is breaking. The defendant has attempted to kill me. Of course . . . out of childish curiosity! He merely wanted to find out what is inside of me. I hasten to satisfy his curiosity. Inside of me is an honorable and very healthy heart, excellent lungs, and a gall bladder without a vestige of stones. I request that this fact be entered into the protocol. And now let us continue our play, as the editor of a humorous journal was wont to say, opening the regular meeting and severely regarding his fellow workers."

Alexander Ivanovich did not like this game. The business trip, from which Ostap had returned with the aura of young wine and youthful lamb, had left marked traces upon the course of affairs. Here was a copy of the verdict delivered after Koreiko's flight, here were copies of the plans of the combine, here were extracts from the profit and loss account, and here were photographs of the electric gully and of the movie stars.

"And finally, gentlemen of the jury, the third stage of activity of my quarrelsome defendant: modest office work at Hercules for society, and intensified underground trading activity for his soul. Merely out of curiosity, let us notice speculation in *valuta*, furs, little stones, and other compact objects of prime importance. And finally, let us pause to consider the series of self-explosive joint stock companies, under the flowery, provocative, coöperative titles, "Intensifier," "The Laboring Cedar," "Saw Belt," and "Southern Woodchopper." And behind all of these was *not* Mr. Funt, that prisoner of private capital, but my friend the defendant!"

At this point the great schemer again pointed at Koreiko, and this time described the effective flourish he had previously intended. Then with extravagant expressions, Ostap begged the imaginary court's permission to ask the defendant several questions, and waiting a minute out of respect, began:

"Did not the defendant have extra-official duties with the Herculean, Berlaga? He did not? Correct! Then with the Herculean, Skumbrievich? Also not? Wonderful! And with the Herculean Polykhayev?"

The millionaire clerk was silent.

"I have no further questions. Ugh, I'm tired and hungry! Tell me, Alexander Ivanovich, don't you happen to have a cold meat ball stored away somewhere? No? Surprising poverty if one takes into consideration the size of the sum which you, with the aid of Polykhayev, have extracted from good old Hercules! Here are Polykhayev's own explanations written in his own hand. He was the only Herculean who knew who was hiding behind the mask of a forty-ruble clerk. But even he did not fully realize who you are. But then, *I* know it! Yes, gentlemen of the jury, my defendant is a sinner. That has been proven. However, I shall permit myself to plead extenuating circumstances, on the one condition that the defendant buy my portfolio. I have finished. Thank you."

Toward the end of the great schemer's speech, Alexander

Ivanovich calmed down. Putting his hands in the pockets of his light trousers, he went up to the window. The young day, bedecked with street car bells, was already ringing in the city. Behind the palisades walked members of the Chemical Warfare Society, holding their rifles as if they were carrying shovels. Along the zinc cornice, their red claws scratching and constantly slipping, pigeons promenaded. Alexander Ivanovich, who had taught himself economy, put out the table lamp and said:

"So it was you who sent those foolish telegrams?"

"I," acknowledged Ostap. " 'Load oranges barrels brothers karamazov.' How was that?"

"Rather foolish."

"And the half-idiot pauper?" asked Ostap. "Wasn't he good?"

"A boyish prank. And the book about the millionaires also. And when you came in the guise of a Kiev investigator, I knew at once that you were a petty crook. To my regret, I was mistaken. Otherwise you would never have found me."

"Yes, you were mistaken. Anything might happen, to quote the Polish beauty Inga Zaiac a month after her marriage to the friend of my childhood, Kolya Osten-Baken."

"Well, now I understand the robbery. But the dumbbells? Why did you steal my dumbbells?"

"I did not steal any dumbbells."

"You're simply ashamed to admit it. Generally speaking, you know, you pulled some pretty silly tricks!"

"Quite possible," Ostap remarked. "I'm no angel. I have my weak points. However, we're talking too much. The mulattoes are waiting for me. May I have the money?"

"Yes, the money," said Koreiko. "But you see, it's not as simple as all that. The portfolio is a good one. I don't deny it. It's possible that I may buy it. But when you added up my fortune, you failed entirely to consider my expenditures and direct losses. A million is an excessively large figure."

"Au revoir," Ostap said coldly. "And please remain at home for half an hour. A splendid carriage with bars will call for you."

"That's no way to do business," said Koreiko with the smile of a merchant.

"That may be so," Ostap sighed. "But you know that I am not a financier. I am an independent artist and a cold philosopher."

"By what right should you receive this money . . . I earned it, but you . . ."

"I didn't only earn it, but I have even suffered! After the conversations with Berlaga, Skumbrievich and Polykhayev, I lost my faith in mankind! Isn't that alone worth a million rubles—faith in mankind?"

"It's worth it, it's worth it!" Alexander Ivanovich pacified him.

"Well then, shall we go to the corn bin?" Ostap asked. "By the way, where do you hold your cash? I don't suppose it's in a savings bank!"

"Let's go," Koreiko replied. "You'll see."

"Is it very far?" Ostap worried. "I can provide a machine."

But the millionaire declined the machine, declaring that it was not far to go and that it was much better to do it without extra pomp. He courteously let Bender out ahead of him, and followed him, taking a small package wrapped in newspaper from the table. As he went down the stairs, Ostap hummed, "Under the Sultry Sky of Argentine."

Chapter Twenty-three

A CHAUFFEUR'S HEART

O<small>N</small> the street Ostap took Alexander Ivanovich under the arm and both schemers walked rapidly in the direction of the railroad station.

"You're much better than I thought you would be," Ostap said in a friendly manner. "And that's the right way to be. One should part with money easily, without groans."

"A million is not too much for a good man," replied the clerk, apparently listening for something.

When they turned on Mehring Street, the baying sound of a siren rang through the city. The sound was long, wavy and mournful. On a foggy night such a sound produces an ill effect on sea-faring men, who immediately ask for an increase in wages because the service is so dangerous. The siren continued to moan. It was joined by land whistles and other sirens, more distant, and even more mournful. Pedestrians suddenly scattered, as if a rain storm were chasing them away. Everybody smiled and looked at the sky. The fat old women who sold sunflower seeds began to run, their stomachs sticking out and the little glasses jumping up and down among the merchandise in their wicker baskets. Across the street on a diagonal sped Adolf Nikolaievich Bomze and managed to get safely through the swinging doors of HERCULES. A squadron of reserve militia galloped by on horses of various colors. An automobile with a red cross flashed by. The street became suddenly empty. Ostap noticed that far ahead a small herd of piqué vests deserted the former Café Florida. Swinging their newspapers and panama hats, the old men began to run down the street. But before they reached the corner, a deafening cannon shot resounded. The piqué vests bent their heads, stopped, and immediately ran back, their pongee coats floating in the air.

The behavior of the piqué vests amused Ostap. While he was enjoying their curious gestures and jumps, Alexander Ivanovich unrolled the package he had taken from home.

"Scabby old fellows! Comic opera buffoons!" said Ostap, turning to Koreiko.

But Koreiko had disappeared. Instead, an astounding apparition with the glass eyes of a sea diver and a rubber proboscis, at the end of which was a khaki-colored tin cylinder, looked at the great schemer. Ostap was so surprised that he even jumped.

"What are these tricks?" he asked severely, stretching his hand toward the gas mask. "Citizen defendant, I call you to order!"

But at this moment a group of people in identical gas masks ran up, and amidst a score of the same rubber faces, it was impossible to find Koreiko. Clutching his portfolio, Ostap immediately began to examine the legs of the monstrosities. But just when he thought he had distinguished the orphan asylum trousers of Alexander Ivanovich, he was grasped under the arms, and a lusty young voice said:

"Comrade! You are poisoned."

"Who is poisoned?" Ostap cried, tearing himself away. "Let me go!"

"Comrade, you are poisoned by the gas," the orderly repeated gayly. "You are in a poison gas zone. Can't you see the gas bomb?"

On the pavement there was actually a box from which thick smoke was rapidly rising. The tell-tale trousers were far away. For the last time they flashed between two clouds of smoke and disappeared. Silently, passionately, Ostap tried to escape. He was held by six masks.

"Furthermore, Comrade, you are wounded by a fragment in your hand. Don't be angry, Comrade. Try to understand. You are aware that maneuvers are going on. We shall immediately bind your wound and carry you to the gas refuge."

The great schemer could not understand that resistance was useless.

A young Comsomol girl with a red cross on her apron ran up to him. She pulled bandages and cotton out of a tarpaulin bag and, knitting her brows to keep from laughing, bound the great schemer's arm outside his sleeve. When she finished this act of mercy, the girl laughed and ran off to the next wounded who meekly offered her his foot. Ostap was dragged to a stretcher. There a new struggle began, in the course of which the probosces swung about madly, and the first hospital orderly, in the loud voice of a lecturer, continued to rouse in Ostap social consciousness and other civic virtues.

"Boys!" muttered the great schemer while he was being strapped to the stretcher. "Boys, tell my deceased father, the Turkish citizen, that his favorite son, the former specialist in horns and hoofs, has died the death of the brave on the field of honor. The last words of him who perished on the field of honor were: 'Sleep, fighting eagles! Nightingale, nightingale, you little bird!' "

After this Ostap was carried away. He calmed down, concentrating his gaze on the sky, where a new bustle began. Thick, bright smoke rolled in clouds. High up in the air, translucent celluloid aeroplanes soared at weird angles. A ringing vibration came from them, as if they were all tied with tin threads. In the short intervals between cannon shots, sirens continued to bay.

Ostap had to endure yet another humiliation. He was carried past HERCULES. Clerks looked out of the windows of all four stories of the lumber enterprise. The entire Financial Accounting Department stood on the window sills. Lapidus Jr. was teasing Kukushkind, pretending he was going to push him down. Berlaga opened his eyes wide and bowed to the stretcher. In the window of the second story, against a background of palm trees, stood Polykhayev and Skumbrievich, clutching each other. Noticing the stricken Ostap, they whispered and quickly shut the window.

The stretcher stopped before a sign "Gas Refuge No. 34." They helped Ostap to rise, and when he once more attempted to escape, the orderly in charge again had to appeal to his civic pride.

The gas refuge was located in a house club. It was a long, light, cellar-like place with a silver ceiling from which models of military and mail planes were suspended on wires. At the rear of the club was a small stage with a back drop, on which two blue windows with a moon and stars and a brown door were painted. Under an inscription on the wall: "We wish no war, but we are ready to fight," bustled the piqué vests, the entire herd of which had been captured. On the stage a lecturer in a green military uniform was walking back and forth, glancing with displeasure at the door which was noisily permitting new groups of the poisoned to enter. He spoke with military precision:

"According to the character of their activity, military poisoning substances may be divided into the choking, the tear-producing, the generally poisoning, the festering, the irritating, and so forth. Among the tear-producing poisoning substances we note Chlorpicrin, Bromidic Benzyl, Bromeaceton, Chloracetophenon . . ."

Ostap turned his infuriated glance from the lecturer to the auditors. Young people gazed directly into the orator's mouth, wrote the lecture down in their note books, or busied themselves with rifle parts. In the second row, quite alone, sat a girl of athletic appearance who thoughtfully regarded the theatrical moon.

"A nice girl," Ostap decided. "A pity there's no time! What is she thinking of? I bet she isn't thinking about Bromidic

Benzyl. Ai, yai, yai! This morning, with that girl at my side, I could have gone away somewhere, to Oceania, to Fiji, to the Solomon Islands, or even to Rio de Janeiro . . ."

At the thought of the Rio he had lost, Ostap began to run back and forth in the refuge.

The piqué vests, numbering altogether forty, had recovered from their shock, adjusted their starched collars, and were talking heatedly about Pan-Europe, about the naval conference of three great powers, and about Ghandism.

"Have you heard?" one piqué vest was saying to another. "Ghandi has arrived in Dhandi?"

"Ghandi has a head on him," the other sighed. "And Dhandi, too, has a head on him."

An argument arose. Certain vests insisted that Dhandi was a city and could have no head. Others with insane stubbornness maintained the reverse. But all of them finally agreed that in the near future Chernomorsk would be declared a free city.

The lecturer frowned as the door opened again and into the refuge with a tremendous clatter burst—Balaganov and Panikovsky. The gas attack had overtaken them while they were returning from their nocturnal expedition. After the labor over the dumbbells they were as dirty as prowling cats. At sight of the commander the foster brothers dropped their eyes.

"Where have you been? At the archbishop's birthday party?" Ostap asked them darkly.

He feared their questions about the progress of the Koreiko affair, and therefore knitted his brows angrily and passed to an attack.

"Well, swan-brothers, where have you been, and what have you done?"

"So help me God," said Balaganov, pressing his hand to his manly chest. "It was Panikovsky who started it."

"Panikovsky?" the commander asked severely.

"My honest, honorable word!" wailed the pact-violator. "You know, Bender, how I respect you! These were Balaganov's tricks."

"Shura!" Ostap exclaimed with even greater severity.

"And you believe him?" the hoof expert reproved. "Well now, what do you think? Do you suppose I would have taken those dumbbells without your permission?"

"So it was *you* who took the dumbbells!" cried Ostap. "But why?"

"Panikovsky said that they were made of gold."

Ostap looked at Panikovsky. Only then did he notice that the half-ruble shirt front was missing under his coat and the light of the world shone on a bare chest. Without a word, the great schemer crumpled into a chair. He clutched the air with his hands and shook. Volcanic thunder burst from his throat, tears poured from his eyes, and blood-curdling laughter, which expressed all the fatigue of the night, all the disappointment of his struggle with Koreiko, so pathetically parodied by the foster brothers, reverberated in the gas refuge. The piqué vests trembled, while the lecturer continued to speak more loudly and distinctly than ever about chemical warfare.

Laughter pricked Ostap with a thousand Narzan needles and he already felt much refreshed and younger, like a man who has passed through all the stages of a barber shop: friendship with the razor, acquaintance with the scissors, a little shower of eau de cologne, and even the grooming of his eyebrows by a special little brush. A gleaming ocean wave broke over his heart, and he replied to Balaganov's question concerning affairs with the assertion that all was going splendidly if one were to leave out of consideration the unexpected flight of the millionaire in an unknown direction.

The foster brothers did not pay due attention to Ostap's words. They were overjoyed that their escapade with the dumbbells had gone off so easily.

"Look, Bender!" said the hoof expert. "Do you see the young lady sitting there? She's the one with whom Koreiko used to walk."

"So that is Zosya Sinitskaya!" Ostap exclaimed. "Well now, really! In the midst of the noisy ball, accidentally . . ."

He pushed his way to the stage, courteously interrupted the orator, learned that the gas imprisonment would continue for another hour and a half or two, thanked him and sat down opposite the stage beside Zosya. In a short time the girl was no longer looking at the painted window. Laughing with embarrassment, she was trying to tear her comb out of Ostap's hands. As for the great schemer—judging by the movements of his lips, he was talking without stopping.

Engineer Talmudovsky was dragged into the gas refuge. He fought for his freedom with two suitcases. His rosy forehead was wet with perspiration and shone like a buttered pancake.

"I can't do anything about it, Comrade," the orderly was saying. "Maneuvers! You entered the poison zone."

"But I was riding in a droshky!" the engineer protested. "In a dr-o-sh-ky! I am hurrying to the station in the interests of the Five-Year Plan! Last night I missed the train. Do you expect me to miss it again?"

"But, Comrade, have you no civic consciousness?"

"Why should I have a civic consciousness when I am driving in a droshky?" Talmudovsky shouted indignantly. He emphasized this fact strongly, as if riding in a droshky gave the rider immunity and deprived Chlorpicrin, Bromeaceton and Bromidic Benzyl of their poisonous properties. It is not known how much longer Talmudovsky would have quarreled with the members of the Chemical Warfare Society, had not a new arrival entered the gas refuge, who, judging by his gauze-swathed head, was also a wounded citizen. At sight of the new guest, Talmudovsky suddenly became quiet and dived deftly into the crowd of piqué vests. But the man in the gauze bandage immediately noticed the corpulent figure of the engineer and started in pursuit.

"At last I've caught you, Engineer Talmudovsky," he said ominously. "On what grounds did you desert the factory?"

Talmudovsky's tiny wild-boar eyes roved from side to side. Convinced that there was no escape, he sat down on his suitcases and lit a cigarette.

"I come to his hotel," the bandaged man addressed everyone. "And I'm told he's gone. 'What do you mean "gone"?' I ask, 'when he arrived only yesterday and according to contract must work a whole year?' 'He's gone,' they say, 'to Kazan, and he's taken his suitcases with him.' I thought then that all was over and that we'd have to go looking again for a specialist. But here I've caught him. There he is, sitting before you, smoking. You are a deserter, Engineer Talmudovsky! You are destroying industry!"

The engineer jumped from the suitcases with a cry, "*You* are destroying industry!" seized his accuser's waist, led him off to a corner and buzzed at him like a large fly. Soon fragments of sentences were heard from the corner: "Not on such a salary!" . . . "Go and find another one!" . . . "And what about traveling expenses?" The man in the gauze bandage looked sadly at the engineer.

The lecturer finished his instructions, having finally explained how to use a gas mask. The doors of the gas refuge opened, and the piqué vests, clinging together, ran back to "Florida." Talmudovsky had shaken his pursuer, won his freedom, and was yelling for all he was worth for a droshky. But the great schemer still chatted with Zosya.

"What a woman!" Panikovsky said enviously, going out into the street with Balaganov. "Ah, if only the dumbbells had been made of gold! My honest, honorable word, I would marry her!"

At the mention of dumbbells, Balaganov started to push Panikovsky with his elbow, but stopped just in time. In the doorway of the gas refuge appeared Ostap with the lady on his arm. He gazed at her with languishing eyes and bade her a lengthy farewell.

"What were you talking to her about?" Panikovsky asked suspiciously, when Zosya had smiled for the last time and departed.

"Nothing in particular," Ostap replied. "Well, you rough-necks, let's get back to business! We must find the defendant."

Panikovsky was sent to HERCULES, Balaganov to the lodging of Alexander Ivanovich. Ostap himself went to the railroad stations. But the millionaire clerk had disappeared. At HER-CULES his time card had not been taken out of the rack; he had not returned to his lodgings; and since the start of the gas attack eight trains with far destinations had departed from the stations. But Ostap had not really expected anything else.

"After all," he said, not too gayly, "there's nothing terrible about it. In China it would be rather difficult to find the man you need. There you have a population of four hundred mil-lion. But with us it is very easy. We have only a hundred and sixty million, and so it is three times as easy as it is in China. All we need is money, and that we have."

But when Ostap left the bank, he held in his hand only thirty-four rubles.

"This is all that remains of ten thousand," he said with inexplicable sadness. "And I thought we had a balance of six or seven thousand. How could it have happened? Everything was so fine! We were collecting horns and hoofs. Life was smiling at us. The earthly globe turned around especially for us. And suddenly . . . I understand! It's the supertaxes, of course! They have eaten up all the money!"

And he looked at the foster brothers accusingly. Panikovsky shrugged his shoulders as if to say, "You know, Bender, how I respect you. I always said that you were an ass." Balaganov stroked his curls in bewilderment and asked, "What is to be done?"

"What do you mean by 'what'?" Ostap cried. "The Office for the Collection of Hoofs and Horns, and the furnishings! Even the inkstand facing the village will be bought by any establishment, and joyfully, for a hundred rubles! And the typewriter, and the hole puncher, the elk's horns, the tables, the counter, the samovar, all of that can be sold. Finally, we have in reserve Panikovsky's gold tooth! Of course, it is not as large as the dumbbells, but still it is a molecule of that precious metal, gold."

The friends stopped in front of their office. Through the open doors were heard the lion-cub snarls of the students of the Animal Husbandry Technicum who had just returned from their trip, the sleepy muttering of Funt, and other unfamiliar basses and baritones of patently agrarian timbre.

"This is simply criminal!" the students cried. "We were surprised even then! Throughout the entire campaign they have collected only twelve kilos of unsorted horns!"

"You'll face the court for this!" thundered the basses and the baritones. "Where is the manager of the branch? Where is the hoof expert?"

Balaganov trembled.

"The office is dead," Ostap whispered. "It needs us no more. We shall go our way, bathed in sunlight, while Funt will be taken to a certain red brick house, to the windows of which, to satisfy some strange caprice of the architect, thick bars are attached."

The ex-chief of the branch office made no mistake. No sooner did the fallen angels remove themselves to the extent of three blocks from the office than they heard behind them the clatter of an *izvozchik's* equipage. In the equipage rode Funt. He would have looked altogether like the goodnatured grandfather who has finally come to visit his married grandson, if it were not for the militiaman who, standing on the step, held the old man's bony back.

"Funt has always done time," the Antelopians heard the low

hollow voice of the old man as the equipage passed. "Funt did time in the days of Alexander the Second, the Liberator, in the days of Alexander the Third, the Peacemaker, in the days of Nicholas the Second, the Bloody One, in the days of Alexander Feodorivich Kerensky . . ."

And counting the tsars and lawyers, Funt bent back his fingers.

"What shall we do now?" Balaganov asked.

"I ask you not to forget that you are living in the same sector of time as Ostap Bender," the great schemer said gravely. "I ask you to remember that he has a remarkable traveling bag that contains everything necessary to procure pocket money. Let us go home to Lokhankin's."

In Lemon Lane a new blow awaited them.

"Where is the house?" Ostap exclaimed. "Yesterday evening there was a house here!"

But there was no house. There was no Magpie Village. There was only an insurance inspector walking gingerly among the charred timbers. Finding in the rear of the yard a tin that once held kerosene, he smelled it and dubiously shook his head.

"Well, and what now?" Balaganov asked, smiling tearfully.

The great schemer did not reply. He was crushed by the loss of the traveling bag. The magic bag that contained the Hindu turban, and the announcement "The Seer Has Arrived," the doctor's apron, the stethoscope, had burned up. It was too sad for words.

"There you are," Ostap finally uttered. "Fate plays upon man as man plays upon a horn."

They wandered through the streets, pale, disappointed, stupefied with grief. Passersby pushed them, but they did not even protest. Panikovsky, who had hunched his shoulders on the occasion of the first blow in the bank, had not since lowered them. Balaganov twisted his red curls and sighed mournfully. And Bender walked behind them all, his head lowered, purring mechanically:

> "Ended, ended is the day of joys;
> Shoot me, little Zouave boys."

In this state they finally dragged themselves to the yard of the inn. At the back, the yellow Antelope stood under a shelter. On the porch of the inn sat Kozlevich. Blowing the liquid joyously, he inhaled hot tea from a saucer. His face looked like a red pot. He was obviously in the seventh heaven.

"Adam," said the great schemer, stopping before the chauffeur. "We have nothing left. We are paupers, Adam. Take us in. We are perishing."

Adam rose. The commander, degraded and poor, stood before him with his head uncovered. The lustrous Polish eyes of Adam Kazimirovich glistened with tears. He walked down the steps and embraced the Antelopians one after another.

"The taxi is free," he said, swallowing his tears. "Please sit down."

"But we may have to go far, very far away," said Ostap. "Perhaps to the end of the world, perhaps even further. Think it over."

"Wherever you like," replied the faithful Kozlevich. "The taxi is at your disposal."

Panikovsky wept, covering his eyes with his fists and whispering, "What a heart! My honest, honorable word, what a heart!"

Chapter Twenty-four

THE WEATHER FAVORED LOVE

EVERYTHING that the great schemer did in the days after the removal to the inn met with Panikovsky's disapproval.

"Bender is mad!" he said to Balaganov. "He is simply ruining us!"

And really, instead of trying to stretch the last thirty-four rubles and transform them into the necessary food, Ostap went to a flower store and spent thirty-five rubles on a huge bouquet of trembling roses. He borrowed an extra ruble from Balaganov to pay for it. In the midst of the flowers he placed a note: "Can you hear my heart beat?" Balaganov was ordered to take these flowers to Zosya Sinitskaya.

"What are you doing?" Balaganov cried, swinging the bouquet. "Why all this pretension?"

"It's necessary, Shura. It's necessary," Ostap replied. "I have a big heart, like a calf. And anyway, this isn't money. What we need is an idea."

Ostap sat down in the Antelope and asked Kozlevich to take him out of town.

"It is absolutely necessary," he said, "for me to philosophize in solitude about all that has happened, and make the necessary prognosis of the future."

All day long the faithful Adam drove the great schemer over the white seaside roads, past houses of rest and sanatoriums, where those who rested scuffled around in slippers, beat croquet balls with mallets and jumped in front of volley ball nets. Viola and cello sounds hummed in the telegraph

wires. Women dragged melons and egg plants in their carpet
bags. Young men with handkerchiefs on their hair, wet after
swimming, looked impudently into the eyes of the women
and delivered themselves of those pleasantries of which every
Chernomorskian up to the age of twenty-five has a full set.
Whenever two women passed, the young Chernomorskians
would say aloud, "That girl at the end is certainly a beauty!"
and then they would laugh heartily. They were amused because the girls could not decide for which one of them the
compliment was intended. Whenever they met a girl alone,
the wits would stop as if thunderstruck and smack their lips,
pretending to be madly in love. The young woman would
turn red, run across the road, dropping the egg plants, which
evoked hilarious laughter from the Lotharios.

Ostap reclined on the hard seat of the Antelope and thought.
It was impossible to get money from Polykhayev and Skumbrievich because the Herculeans had gone on vacation. The
mad Bookkeeper Berlaga did not count. One could not expect a good milking from him. Yet Ostap's plans and his big
heart demanded his sojourn in Chernomorsk. He himself
could not yet determine for how long.

Hearing a familiar funereal voice, Ostap glanced at the
sidewalk. Behind the row of poplars walked a couple no
longer young. The spouses were evidently bound for the shore.
Behind them Lokhankin dragged along. He carried a
woman's umbrella and a basket from which stuck a thermos
bottle and a dangling bath towel.

"Varvara," he moaned. "Listen, Varvara."

"What do you want, my sorrow?" Ptiburdukov asked without turning around.

"I must possess you, my Varvara."

"My, what a scoundrel!" remarked Ptiburdukov.

And the strange family disappeared in the dust of the
Antelope.

When the dust had settled on the ground, Bender saw a large glass studio against a background of sea and flowers. Plaster of Paris lions with dirty faces sat at the foot of a broad stairway. From the studio came the disturbing odor of banana oil. Ostap sniffed the air and asked Kozlevich to stop. He left the automobile and again began to inhale the life-giving odor.

"Why didn't I think of it before?" he muttered, pausing at the porte-cochère.

He looked intently at the sign, "The First Chernomorsk Motion Picture Studio," and stroking the warm mane of the stairway lion, and pronouncing the word, "Golconda!", quickly returned to the yard of the inn.

All night long he sat at the window sill and wrote by the light of the kerosene lamp. The wind which came through the window rustled the closely written papers. Before the author was a very unattractive vista. The delicate moon lighted—Lord knows what chambers! The yard of the inn breathed, stirred and snored in its sleep. Unseen horses tapped signals to each other in dark corners. Petty speculators slept in wagons on their pathetic merchandise. An untethered horse wandered over the yard, carefully stepping over the shafts, dragging its loosened bit and poking its head into the wagons in search of barley. It came up to the window of the author, and, placing its head on the window sill, looked mournfully at Ostap.

"Go away, go away, horse," remarked the great schemer. "Your mind cannot grasp this affair."

Before dawn, when the yard of the inn began to come to life and a little boy with a bucket of water walked among the wagons crying in a thin voice, "Who wants to water his horses?", Ostap finished his labors, took out of "The Case of Alexander Koreiko" a clean sheet of paper, and wrote on it the following heading:

```
"THE NECK"
Full-length picture
Scenario by
O. BENDER
```

At the First Chernomorsk Cinema Factory was the bedlam that can be heard only at horse fairs at the particular moment when everybody is earnestly endeavoring to catch the pickpocket.

At the entrance sat a guard. He severely demanded a pass from all comers, but when he received no pass he let them in anyway. People in blue berets collided with people in workmen's caps, ran up numerous stairways and immediately ran down the same stairways. In the vestibule they described a circle, stopped for a second, looked dumbfounded before them, and again ran up at a gallop as if they were being constantly belabored with a wet whip. Assistants, consultants, experts, administrators, directors and their assistants, illuminators, editors, title writers, elderly female scenario writers, keepers of commas, and preservers of the large iron seal ran by intently.

Ostap, attempting to walk through the cinema factory at his usual pace, soon noticed that he could not make himself a part of this whirling world. No one responded to his inquiries, no one stopped.

"I shall have to adapt myself to the adversary's peculiarities," said Ostap.

He began to run quietly, and immediately felt a bit easier. He even managed to exchange a few words with some female adjutant. Then the great schemer increased his speed and soon noticed that he had attained the necessary tempo. Now he was running nostril to nostril with the manager of the literary department.

"Scenario!" Ostap shouted.

"What kind?" asked the manager of the literary department, working away at a gallop.

"A good one!" Ostap responded, outracing his opponent by half a head.

"I am asking you what kind? Silent or talking?"

"Silent."

Adroitly throwing forward his legs in their thick socks, the manager of the literary department passed Ostap at a corner and shouted back, "Don't want it!"

"What do you mean you don't want it?" asked the great schemer, breaking into a heavy gallop.

"Just don't! There are no more silent films. Turn to sound films."

Both of them stopped for a split second, looked dumbfoundedly at each other, and ran off in different directions. Five minutes later, Bender, swinging his manuscript, ran between two galloping consultants.

"Scenario," Ostap announced, breathing heavily.

Both consultants, turning toward him as they galloped, addressed Ostap:

"What kind of a scenario?"

"Talking."

"Don't need it," the consultants answered, increasing their speed.

The great schemer lost step and began to gallop madly.

"What do you mean you don't need it?"

"Simply don't need it. There is no sound cinema yet."

In the course of half an hour of conscientious galloping, Ostap discovered for himself the ticklish situation of affairs at the First Chernomorsk Cinema Factory: the silent cinema operated no longer because of the beginning of the era of sound film, while sound film did not operate yet because of organizational deficiencies connected with the liquidation of the era of silent films.

In the thick of the working day when the run of assistants, consultants, experts, administrators, directors, adjutants, illuminators, scenarists, male and female, and keepers of the large iron seal attained the speed of the famous racing horse Krepysh, a rumor was spread that somewhere in some room sat a man who would immediately make a sound film. Ostap ran into the large office for all he was worth and stopped, struck by the silence. Beside a table sat a little man with a Bedouin's beard and a golden pince nez on a cord. Bending over, he was pulling a shoe off his foot.

"How do you do, Comrade," the great schemer said loudly.

But the man did not reply. He took off the shoe and began to shake sand out of it.

"How do you do," Ostap repeated. "I have brought a scenario."

The man in the Bedouin beard unhurriedly put on his shoe and silently began to lace it. When this was done, he turned to his papers and, shutting one eye, proceeded to trace a very fine scrawl.

"Why don't you say something?" Bender shouted with such might that the telephone receiver on the table of the cinema executive resounded like a clap of thunder.

Only then did the cinema executive raise his head, glance at Ostap and say:

"Please speak louder. I can't hear you."

"Write notes," suggested a consultant in a bright vest who ran past just then. "He's deaf."

Ostap sat down at the table and wrote on a piece of paper: "Do you make talking pictures?"

"Yes," responded the deaf man.

"I have brought you a talking picture scenario. It is called 'The Neck,' a popular tragedy in six parts," Ostap wrote quickly.

The deaf man looked at the note through his gold pince nez and said:

"Excellent! We shall immediately put you to work. We need new talent."

"Glad to coöperate. How about an advance?" Bender wrote.

"'The Neck' is just what we need," said the deaf man. "You sit here and I'll come right back. But don't you go away. I'll be back in exactly one minute."

The deaf man picked up the scenario for the picture "The Neck," and ran out of the room.

"We'll put you to work in the sound film group," he shouted, disappearing behind the door. "I'll be back in a minute!"

Ostap sat in the office for an hour and a half, but the deaf man did not return. Only when he went out on the stairway and merged himself in the general tempo, did Ostap learn that the deaf man had gone away in an automobile and would not return that day. And, furthermore, he would not return for a long time, because he had been suddenly assigned to the Uman district for cultural work among teamsters. But the most terrible part of it all was that the man had gone off with the scenario for the picture "The Neck." The great schemer managed to get out of the circle of the runners whose movements were constantly increasing, and dropped to a bench, falling on the shoulder of the doorman who sat there.

"Take me, for example," the doorman said suddenly, evidently developing a thought that had tortured him for a long time. "Terentyev, the assistant director, told me to grow a beard. 'You'll be Nebuchadnezzar, or perhaps Balthazar in the film . . .' By God, I've forgotten the name of it again! So I grew a beard, a regular patriarchal one. Now what in thunder am I going to do with a beard? The assistant director says there will be no more silent films, and, says he, 'You can't play in sound films because your voice is so unpleasant.' And so I sit here with a beard, God damn it, like a goat! I hate to shave and I'm ashamed to wear it. And so I have to live."

"And is there any filming going on?" asked Bender gradually recovering consciousness.

"What filming can there be?" the bearded doorman demanded. "A year ago last summer they made a silent film about Roman life, and to this day they cannot settle the criminal charges against them."

"Why is everybody running around?" the great schemer inquired, pointing to the stairway.

"Not everybody here is running around," the doorman remarked. "Comrade Suprugov doesn't run around. He's a real business man. I'm thinking all the time about going down to see him about my beard, to find out how I'm going to get paid for it—with a regular order or a special one . . ."

When he heard the word "order," Ostap went to Suprugov. The doorman had not lied. Suprugov did not gallop over the various floors, did not wear an Alpine beret, did not even wear foreign golf trousers. It was pleasant to rest one's gaze upon him.

He met the great schemer with extreme formality.

"I am busy," he said in the voice of a peacock. "I can give you only two minutes."

"That is all I need," said Ostap. "My scenario 'The Neck' . . ."

"Be brief," said Suprugov.

". . . my scenario 'The Neck' . . ."

"Come to the point! What do you want?"

". . . 'The Neck' . . ."

"Be brief! How much is due you?"

"That deaf fellow . . ."

"Comrade, if you don't tell me immediately how much is due you, I shall ask you to leave. I am busy."

"Nine hundred rubles," the great schemer muttered.

"Three hundred," Suprugov declared categorically. "Take it and go away. And bear in mind that you have stolen an extra minute and a half from me."

In a flourishing handwriting Suprugov wrote a note to the bookkeeper, gave it to Ostap, and like one possessed, seized the telephone receiver.

Coming out of the bookkeeper's room, Ostap shoved the money in his pocket and said:

"Nebuchadnezzar is right. There is only one business man here, and that is Suprugov."

In the meanwhile the running on the stairway, the circling around, the screams and bedlam at the First Chernomorsk Cinema Factory had reached its peak. The female adjutants bared their teeth. The assistant directors were leading a goat, exclaiming over its photographability. Consultants, experts and keepers of the iron seal collided with each other and laughed hoarsely. A woman messenger sped by with a pomelo in her arms. The great schemer was sure that he saw one of the assistants in blue pantaloons fly over the crowd and, turning a corner around the chandeliers, land on a cornice.

At that moment the vestibule clock rang out.

"Bam!" said the clock.

Screams, cries for help, and heartrending shouts shook the glass studio. Assistants, consultants, experts, and editors rolled down the stairs. There was a crush at the exit.

"Bammm! Bammm!" the clock beat out.

Silence crept out of the corners. The keepers of the large iron seal, the custodians of the commas, the administrators and the female adjutants had disappeared. For the last time the pomelo of the female messenger flashed by.

"Bammm!" the clock struck for the fourth time. There was no one left in the studio.

And in the doorway, the pocket of his coat caught on the brass handle, the assistant in blue pantaloons flapped and whined pathetically, and beat his little heels against the marble floor.

The working day had ended.

From a fishing village on the shore came the cockadoodle-doo of a rooster.

When the cash box of the Antelopians had been refilled with the cinema money, the reputation of the commander, somewhat tarnished by the flight of Koreiko, became brighter. Panikovsky was given a small sum for mares' milk and was promised golden jaws. Ostap bought a coat for Balaganov and a leather wallet that screeched like a saddle. Although the wallet was empty, Shura frequently took it out and peeped into it. Kozlevich received fifty rubles for the purchase of gasoline.

The Antelopians led a pure, moral, almost bucolic life. They helped the manager of the inn to keep things in order and became thoroughly acquainted with the prices of oats and sour cream. Panikovsky would occasionally go out into the yard, open the mouth of the nearest horse, examine its teeth with great concern, and mutter, "A good colt," although before him stood a good mare.

But the commander would be gone for days at a time, and when he reappeared at the inn he was gay and absent-minded. He sat next to his friends who were drinking tea in the dirty glass-enclosed porch, crossed a mighty leg with a red-brown shoe over his knee, and said amicably:

"Is life really so splendid, Panikovsky? Or does it merely seem so to me?"

"Where do you go mad?" the pact-violator asked enviously.

"Old man, that girl is not for you!" Ostap replied.

Balaganov laughed sympathetically and examined his new wallet, while Kozlevich tittered in his conductor's mustache. More than once he had driven the commander and Zosya along the seaside drive.

The weather favored love. The piqué vests asserted that such an August had not been known since the time of Porto Franco. The night revealed a pure telescopic sky, while the day rolled refreshing sea waves toward the city. Janitors traded at their gates in striped watermelons, while citizens squatted, squeezing the watermelons at both ends and listening for the desired crackle. In the evenings happy sweating football players returned from athletic fields. After them little boys ran in a cloud of dust. They pointed their fingers at the famous goal-keeper, and sometimes they would even lift him on their shoulders and carry him respectfully.

One evening the commander warned the crew of the Antelope that the next day there would be a large picnic outside the city and a distribution of presents.

"In view of the fact that a certain young woman will share our innocent pleasures," Ostap said significantly, "I request the gentlemen volunteers to wash their faces, brush up, clean up, and principally refrain from using any coarse expressions during the outing."

Panikovsky became terribly excited, begged three rubles from the commander, ran to the public baths, and spent the whole night cleaning and scrubbing himself like a soldier before a parade. He rose ahead of everyone and urged on Kozlevich. The Antelopians regarded Panikovsky with wonder and amazement. He was smoothly shaven and powdered until he resembled a cranberry in sugar. Every minute he pulled his coat around him and turned his neck with difficulty in his Oscar Wilde collar.

During the outing Panikovsky bore himself with great reserve. When he was presented to Zosya he bowed gracefully, but became so embarrassed that even the powder on his cheeks turned red. Sitting in the automobile, he put his left foot under him to hide his torn shoes, out of which peeked a large toe. Zosya wore a white dress with red embroidery. She liked the Antelopians very much. She was amused by the coarse Shura Balaganov, who combed his hair throughout the journey. Occasionally he would clean his nose with his finger, after which he invariably took out his handkerchief and languidly fanned himself. Adam Kazimirovich taught Zosya how to drive the Antelope, for which he also earned her regard. She was somewhat embarrassed by Panikovsky; she thought that he did not speak to her because of his pride. But most frequently of all her gaze rested on the features of the commander, so like the face on a coin.

When the sun sank, Ostap distributed the promised presents. Kozlevich received a watch charm in the form of a compass which perfectly suited his thick silver watch. Balaganov was presented with a volume of selected readings, and Panikovsky was given a pink necktie with blue flowers.

"And now, my friends," said Bender when the Antelope returned to the city, "Zosya Adamovna and I will promenade a bit. It is time for you to go back to the inn. By-by."

The inn was asleep. Balaganov and Kozlevich were practicing nasal arpeggios. But Panikovsky, the new necktie around his neck, wandered among the wagons, wringing his hands in dumb despair.

"What a woman!" he whispered. "I love her like a daughter."

Ostap sat with Zosya on the steps of the Museum of Antiquities. Along the square paved with lava rock young people walked, exchanging pleasantries and laughing. Behind a row of plane trees gleamed the windows of the International Seamen's Club. Foreign sailors in soft hats walked in twos and threes exchanging brief, incomprehensible remarks.

"Why did you fall in love with me?" Zosya whispered, touching Ostap's hand.

"You are lovely and wonderful," replied the commander. "You are better than anyone else in the world."

For a long time they sat silently in the black shadow of the museum columns, thinking about their little happiness. It was warm and dark, like between the palms of two hands.

"Do you remember I was telling you about Koreiko?"

Zosya said suddenly. "You know—the fellow who proposed to me?"

"Oh, yes," Ostap said absentmindedly.

"He's a very amusing chap," Zosya continued. "Do you remember I told you how unexpectedly he went away?"

"Yes," said Ostap more attentively. "He's very amusing."

"Just imagine! To-day I received a letter from him. Very amusing . . ."

"What!" exclaimed her lover, rising to his feet.

"Are you jealous?" Zosya asked slyly.

"M'm . . . A little. What does that dull fellow write you?"

"He's not a bit dull. He's merely a poor, very unhappy man. Sit down, Ostap. Why did you get up? Seriously, I don't love him at all. He wants me to come to him."

"Where? Where does he want you to come?" cried Ostap. "Where is he?"

"No, I shan't tell you. You're jealous. You may kill him."

"What are you talking about, Zosya!" the commander said casually. "I'm merely curious to know where people can make a living."

"Oh, he's far away. He writes that he found quite a good job. You know he made very little here. He is now working on the construction of the Turkestan Railroad."

"Where?"

"Upon my word, you are too curious! You mustn't be like Othello."

"So help me God, Zosya, you make me laugh! Do I look like that silly old Moor? I simply want to know on which part of the Turkestan Railroad one can find a job."

"I'll tell you if you really want to know," the girl yielded. "He has a job as a switchman in the Little Northern City. That is its only name. As a matter of fact, it is just a train. Alexander Ivanovich wrote about it very interestingly. This train lays down the rails, do you understand, and moves on along them. And another such little city moves to meet it from the south. Soon the two will meet. Then there will be an official union. All sorts of things are in the city, he writes, camels . . . Isn't it interesting?"

"Remarkably interesting," said the great schemer, walking back and forth among the columns. "Do you know, Zosya, it's time to go. It's very late. And it is cold. And anyway . . . let us go."

He lifted Zosya from the steps, led her out to the square, and hesitated, not knowing what to say.

"Aren't you going to see me home?" the girl asked in alarm.

"What?" said Ostap. "Oh, home! You see, I . . ."

"Very well," Zosya said haughtily. "Au revoir. And don't come to see me any more, do you hear?"

But the great schemer did not wait to hear anything else. He ran on for a block and then stopped.

"Lovely and wonderful!" he muttered.

He turned back, following his beloved. For about two minutes he ran under the black trees. Then he stopped again, took off his captain's cap, and paused for a moment.

"No, this is not Rio de Janeiro," he said finally. He made two more hesitating steps, stopped again, pulled his cap down and, no longer torn by doubt, ran to the inn.

That night the Antelope drove out of the gates of the inn-yard, its headlights shining feebly. The sleepy Kozlevich turned the wheel with difficulty. Balaganov fell asleep in the machine in the course of the brief preparations. Panikovsky moved his little eyes sadly, shivering in the raw night. His face still bore traces of the holiday powder.

"The carnival is over!" shouted the commander, when the Antelope drove under the railroad bridge with a clatter. "And now serious days begin!"

And in the old puzzlemaker's room, the "lovely and wonderful one" wept over a bouquet of withered roses.

Chapter Twenty-five

THREE ROGUES

T HE Antelope was unwell. It stopped even at easy ascents and helplessly rolled back. In the motor could be heard muffled rattles and shrill whistles, as if someone was being choked under the yellow robe of the automobile. The machine was overloaded. In addition to the crew, it carried large reserves of fuel. Gasoline gurgled in tins and jugs which filled all of the free space. Kozlevich shook his head, gave more gas, and looked despairingly at Ostap.

"Adam," said the commander. "You are our father. We are your children. The course is due East. You have an excellent navigation instrument in the watch fob compass. Don't lose the road."

The Antelopians had already ridden for three days, but only Ostap knew the final destination of this new journey. Panikovsky looked morosely at the fields of corn and whimpered:

"Why are we on our way again? What's the use of it all? It was so good in Chernomorsk!"

And remembering the splendid woman, he sighed and shivered. Besides, he wanted to eat. But there was nothing to eat. The money had come to an end.

"Onward!" cried Ostap. "Don't whine, old man. Golden jaws await you! A fat little widow! And a whole reservoir of mares' milk! I'll buy a little sailor suit for Balaganov and we'll place him in an elementary school. There he will learn to read and write, which is an absolute necessity at his age. And Kozlevich, our true Adam, will receive a new machine.

What kind do you want, Adam Kazimirovich? Studebaker? Lincoln? Rolls-Royce? Or Hispaño-Suiza?"

"Isotta-Fraschini," replied Kozlevich, blushing shyly.

"Very well, you shall have it! It shall be called Antelope the Second, or the daughter of Antelope, as you prefer. But now, don't lose courage. I shall provide plenty for you. True, my traveling bag has burned up. But there still remain the imperishable ideas. If the worst should come to the worst, we'll stop in some happy little town and stage a performance of a Sevillian bullfight. Panikovsky will be the picador! That in itself will rouse the morbid interest of the public, and consequently we'll have a good gate."

The machine moved along a broad dirt road marked by tractors. The chauffeur put the brakes on unexpectedly.

"Where shall we go?" he asked. "There are three roads."

The passengers crawled out of the machine and, stretching their numbed legs, walked a bit ahead. At the crossroads leaned a stone post on which a fat crow perched. The flattened sun was sinking behind the shaggy corn. Balaganov's narrow shadow fell toward the horizon. The earth was lightly touched by darkness, and an early star was prematurely signaling the approach of night.

Three roads lay before the Antelopians: an asphalt road, a highway and a byway. The asphalt was yet yellow with the sun. A blue mist hung over the highway. The byway, however, was entirely dark and lost itself immediately in a field behind the post. Ostap shouted at the crow, which became extremely frightened but did not fly away. Then he paced the crossroads thoughtfully and said:

"I declare the conference of Russian heroes open. There are present: Ilya Muromets—Ostap Bender; Dobrynya Nikitich—Balaganov; and Alyosha Popovich—the universally respected Mikhail Panikovsky!"

Kozlevich, taking advantage of the stop, had crawled under

the Antelope with a wrench, and was therefore not among the heroes.

"My dear Dobrynya," Ostap said. "Please stand on the right. Monsieur Popovich, please take your place on the left. Apply the palms of your hands to your foreheads and peer ahead."

"What is this nonsense?" exclaimed Alyosha Popovich indignantly. "I'm hungry. Let's go somewhere as soon as possible."

"Shame on you, Alyoshenka," said Ostap. "Stand as an ancient hero should stand, and think. Look how well Dobrynya behaves himself! At this moment you could write an epic about him! And so, my heroes, what road shall we take? On which of these rolls money, so necessary for our current expenditures? I know that Kozlevich would move along the asphalt road, because chauffeurs love good roads. But Adam is an honest man and therefore does not understand life. Besides, heroes are not interested in asphalt. It leads probably to some grain giant. We shall be lost in the noise of machines. We may even be crushed by some caterpillar or combine. And to die under a combine is rather dull. No, my heroes, we are not fated to drive along the asphalt road. Now, as for the highway . . . Kozlevich, of course, would not refuse that either. But believe Ilya Muromets, the highway won't do for us. Let them accuse us of backwardness, but we shall not take good roads. My nose predicts a meeting with tactless peasants from collectives and other such exemplary citizens. Besides they have no time for us. Over their socialized bailiwicks now wander multitudes of literary and musical brigades that are collecting materials for agrarian poems and truck gardening cantatas. There remains the byway, citizen heroes. Here is the ancient fabled way along which the Antelope will move. Here is the spirit of Russia. Here are the smells of Russia. Here still flies the glowing *zharptitsa,* and people of our profession may catch a few golden feathers. Here on his coffers sits Koshchei, who considered himself immortal, but who has now convinced himself to his horror that his end is at hand. But, my heroes, you and I will get something from him, especially if we present ourselves in the guise of wandering monks. From the point of view of road technique, this fabled way is terrible. But there is no other path for us. Adam! We are off!"

Kozlevich sadly drove the machine into the byway, where it immediately began to describe pretzels, sway from side to side and fling the passengers high into the air. The Antelopians caught at each other, swore under their breath, and knocked their knees against the hard tin cans.

"I want to eat," groaned Panikovsky. "I want a goose. Why did we leave Chernomorsk?"

The machine squealed, hopped out of a deep rut, and sank back into it.

"Hold it, Adam!" cried Bender. "No matter what happens, hold it! Let the Antelope but take us to the Turkestan Railroad, and we shall reward it with golden tires and ribboned swords!"

Kozlevich did not hear. Now and then the mad lurches tore the wheel itself out of his hands. Panikovsky continued to complain.

"Bender!" he cried hoarsely. "You don't know how I respect you! But you don't understand anything. You don't know what a goose is. Oh, how I love that bird! It is a remarkable fat bird, on my honest, honorable word! Goose! . . . Bender! . . . A wing! . . . The neck! . . . The drumstick! . . . Do you know how I catch geese, Bender? I kill a goose like a toreador, with a single blow. When I attack a goose, it's an opera! . . . 'Carmen'!"

"We know," said the commander. "We saw you at Arbatov. I don't advise you to try it again."

Panikovsky was silent, but a minute later, when a new lurch of the machine flung him into Bender's arms, his feverish whisper began again:

"Bender! She promenades along the road! . . . The goose!
. . . The remarkable bird promenades, and I stand and make
believe that it is no concern of mine . . . She approaches . . .
Presently she will hiss at me. These birds think they are
stronger than anything else. And therein lies their weakness.
Bender! Therein lies their weakness . . ."

The violator of the pact was almost singing.

"She approaches me and hisses like a phonograph. But I
am not a timid one, Bender. Someone else in my place might
run away, but I stand and wait. She approaches me and cranes
her neck—her white goose neck with its yellow beak. She
wants to bite me. Note, Bender, that the moral advantage is
on my side! It is *she* who attacks *me,* not *I* who attack *her!*
And then, in self-defense, I seize her . . ."

But Panikovsky did not finish his speech. A horrible,
nauseating crack resounded, and in a second the Antelopians
found themselves in the most varied poses along the road.
Balaganov's feet stuck out of a ditch. On the stomach of the
great schemer lay a tin of gasoline. Panikovsky groaned under
the weight of a spring. Kozlevich rose to his feet, and staggered several steps.

The Antelope was no more. On the road lay a disfigured
mass of rubbish. The brass intestines gleamed in the moonlight. The broken chassis lay in the ditch beside Balaganov,
who had just recovered consciousness. The chain crawled into
a rut like a reptile. In the silence that followed was heard a
thin tinkling, as a wheel, which apparently had been flung
far away by the explosion, rolled down, described a semicircle and fell softly at the feet of Kozlevich.

And only then did the chauffeur understand that everything was at an end. The Antelope had disintegrated. Adam
Kazimirovich sat down on the ground and seized his head
with his hands. Several minutes later the commander touched
his shoulder and said in a changed voice:

"Adam, we must go."

Kozlevich rose, but immediately sank into his former position.

"We must go," Ostap repeated. "The Antelope was a faithful machine, but there are many other machines in the world. Soon you will be able to select any one you like. Come, we must hurry. We must sleep somewhere, and eat, and get money for tickets. We have far to go. Come, come, Kozlevich. Life is beautiful, in spite of its drawbacks. Where is Panikovsky? Where is that goose-killer? Shura, lead Adam."

Kozlevich was taken by the arm. He felt like a cavalry man who, through carelessness, had caused the death of his horse. It seemed to him that now all pedestrians would laugh at him.

After the ruin of the Antelope, life immediately became complicated. It was necessary to spend the night in the open field. Ostap angrily fell asleep at once. Balaganov and Kozlevich fell asleep. But Panikovsky sat all night at the campfire and shivered.

The Antelopians rose with the dawn, but they could not reach the nearest village until four o'clock in the afternoon. All the way Panikovsky dragged along in the rear. He was lame. Hunger had given his eyes a feline gleam, and he complained unceasingly of his fate and of the commander.

When they reached the village, Ostap told his crew to wait on Third Street and go nowhere, while he went to First Street to the Village Council. He returned very soon.

"It's all arranged," he said gayly. "We shall immediately get quarters and a dinner. After the dinner, we shall rest in the hay. Do you remember the milk and hay? And in the evening we shall give a performance. I have already sold it for fifteen rubles, and I have received the money. Shura, you will have to recite something from your 'Selected Readings,' while I shall demonstrate anti-religious card-tricks, and Panikovsky . . . Where is Panikovsky? Where did he disappear?"

"He was here just a moment ago," said Kozlevich.

But behind a straw fence nearby they heard the cackling of a goose and a woman's scream. White feathers flew up, and into the street ran Panikovsky. It seemed that his true hand had failed our toreador, and he, in self-defense, had delivered an incorrect blow to the bird. The woman ran after him swinging a stick.

"Pathetic, insignificant woman!" cried Panikovsky, running out of the village.

"Saints preserve us!" Ostap exclaimed, without hiding his irritation. "That scoundrel has ruined our show. Let's run before they take away our fifteen rubles!"

In the meanwhile, the irate housewife caught up with Panikovsky and vented her rage on him with her stick. The pact-violator crawled on the ground, but the minute he was free, he jumped to his feet and ran away with unnatural speed. Having performed this act of revenge, the housewife triumphantly turned back. As she ran past the Antelopians, she threatened them with her stick.

"Now our artistic career is ended," said Ostap, walking rapidly out of the village. "The dinner, the rest—everything is lost."

They caught up with Panikovsky three kilometers away. He lay in the roadside ditch and complained loudly. From fatigue, fear and pain he had turned pale, and the red blotches indicative of his age had disappeared from his face. He was so pathetic that the commander canceled the punishment that had been prepared for him. Everybody regarded Panikovsky with disgust. Again he dragged himself in the rear of the column, moaning and wailing:

"Wait for me. Don't hurry. I'm old! I'm sick! I'm in a bad way . . . Goose! . . . Drumstick! . . . Neck! . . . Woman! . . . Pathetic, insignificant people!"

But the Antelopians had become so accustomed to the old man's complaints that they paid no attention to them. Hunger urged them forward. Never before had they found the world

so small and so inconvenient. The road stretched onward endlessly and Panikovsky fell further and further behind. The
friends had descended into a narrow yellow valley while the
pact-violator was still a dark dot on the top of a hill in the
green twilit sky.

"The old man is impossible," said the hungry Bender. "We
shall have to discharge him. Shura, go and bring that malin-
gerer here."

The disgruntled Balaganov went to carry out his mission.
While he was running up hill, Panikovsky's figure disappeared.

"Something has happened," said Kozlevich after some time,
looking at the crest of the hill where Balaganov was semaphor-
ing with his arms.

The chauffeur and the commander climbed up.

The pact-violator sprawled rigidly in the middle of the road
like a doll. The pink necktie lay crosswise on his chest. One
hand was twisted under his back. His eyes looked boldly at the
sky. Panikovsky was dead.

"Paralysis of the heart," said Ostap, for the sake of saying
something. "I can diagnose it without the stethoscope. Poor
old man!"

He turned away. Balaganov could not remove his eyes
from the corpse. Suddenly his face twitched, and he said with
difficulty:

"And to think that I beat him for the dumbbells! And even
before that, I fought with him!"

Kozlevich remembered the dead Antelope, glanced with
horror at Panikovsky, and began to chant a Latin prayer.

"Cut it out, Adam," said the great schemer. "I know everything you are going to do. After the psalm you will say, 'The
Lord giveth, and the Lord taketh away.' Then, 'We are all
in God's hands.' Then something else utterly devoid of sense
like 'After all, he's better off than we are now.' We don't need

any of that, Adam Kazimirovich. Before us is a simple problem. We must bury the corpse."

It was quite dark when a last resting place was found for the pact-violator. It was a natural grave washed out by rains at the foundation of a perpendicular flagstone. This flat stone had evidently stood a long time on the road. Perhaps at one time it bore the inscription, "Property of Retired Major Georgy Afanasyevich Volk-Lisitsky," or perhaps it was only a milestone from the time of Potemkin. But that was not important. Panikovsky was placed in the hole and covered with earth which had been dug up with sticks. Then the Antelopians lifted the flat stone and rolled it on the grave. Now the tomb was complete. By the light of match flares, the great schemer wrote an epitaph with a piece of chalk:

> Here Lies
> MIKHAIL SAMUILOVICH PANIKOVSKY
> A Man Without a Passport

Ostap removed his captain's cap and said:

"I was frequently unjust to the deceased. Was the deceased a moral person? No, he was not a moral person. He was an ex-blindman, usurper and goose-thief. He devoted all his powers to the task of living at the expense of society. But society did not want him to live at its expense. Mikhail Samuilovich could not endure this contradiction in views because his was an excitable character, and therefore he died. That's all."

Kozlevich and Balaganov were dissatisfied with Ostap's funeral oration. They would have considered it more appropriate if the great schemer had said a lot about the good deeds performed by the deceased in the interests of society, about his kindness to the poor, about his sensitive soul, about his love of children, and about all the other virtues that are ascribed to any deceased. Balaganov even went up to the grave to express all this himself, but the commander had already put on his cap and was disappearing at a rapid pace.

When the decimated ranks of the Antelopian army crossed the valley and climbed over a new hill, before them was a small railroad station.

"Here is civilization," said Ostap. "And perhaps a lunch counter, food! We shall sleep on the benches. In the morning we shall move toward the east. What do you think?"

The chauffeur and the mechanic said nothing.

"Why are you silent like bashful bridegrooms?"

"You know, Bender," Balaganov said finally, "I will not go. Don't be offended, but I have no faith. I don't know where we ought to go. All of us will perish there. I shall remain."

"This is just what I wanted to tell you," Kozlevich supported him.

"As you wish," Ostap remarked with sudden formality.

At the station there was no lunch counter. Only a kerosene lamp was burning. Two old peasant women slumbered on sacks in the waiting room. The entire railway personnel was wandering over the wooden station platform, looking with alarm into the gray dawn for a semaphore signal.

"What's the train?" Ostap asked.

"A special," the station chief answered nervously, adjusting his red cap with silver trimmings. "A private train! Held up for two minutes! Nothing must delay its departure!"

Thunder resounded, the wires trembled. Out of the commotion two wolves' eyes blazed, and a huge, shining train flew into the station. The broad windows of "soft cars" gleamed. Under the very noses of the Antelopians passed the bouquets and wine bottles of the dining car. Brakemen and porters jumped down with lanterns, and the platform suddenly filled with gay Russian talk and foreign speech. Along the cars hung cone-shaped arches and slogans: "Greetings to the heroes, to the builders of the Turkestan Railway!"

The special train and its guests were bound for the opening of the road.

The great schemer disappeared. A half minute later he reappeared and whispered:

"I am going. How I'm going, I don't know, but I'm going. Don't you want to come along with me? I'm asking you for the last time."

"No," said Balaganov.

"I will not go," said Kozlevich. "I can't."

"What will you do then?"

"What can I do?" Shura replied. "I'll become again one of the children of Lieutenant Schmidt, that's all."

"I'll put the Antelope together," said Adam Kazimirovich pathetically. "I'll find her, look her over and fix her up."

Ostap wanted to say something, but a prolonged whistle stopped him. He pulled Balaganov to him, patted his shoulder, kissed Kozlevich, waved his hand and ran for the train, the cars of which were already knocking together from the first pull of the engine. But suddenly he turned back, pressed into Kozlevich's hand the fifteen rubles for the show he had sold, and jumped on the step of the moving train.

Turning around, he saw in the lilac mist two small figures going up an embankment. Balaganov was returning to the unruly camp of Lieutenant Schmidt's children; Kozlevich was seeking the remains of the Antelope.

Part Three

A PRIVATE PERSON

Chapter Twenty-six

A PASSENGER ON A SPECIAL TRAIN

I N Moscow, at the asphalt platform of the Ryazan station, stood a short special train. It consisted of only six cars: a baggage car in which, contrary to custom, there was no baggage but food stores on ice; a dining car from whose windows peered a cook dressed in white; and administrative headquarters in a car which at one time had belonged to the singer Vyaltseva. Now, instead of the famous singer of "Everybody says that I am light-minded at times, everybody says that I love no one at all; but why then do I forget them all, and only one can I never forget?", rode representatives of the government and of the Council of Nationalities. The remaining three cars were for passengers. There on cushioned seats with severe striped slip-covers were distributed delegations of shock-brigade workers and foreign and Soviet correspondents. The train was ready to go for the meeting of the rails on the Turkestan Railroad.

The journey ahead was a long one. The shock-brigaders were hauling into the train traveling baskets with black locks dangling from iron loops. The Soviet press ran back and forth along the platform swinging lacquered rubberoid traveling bags. The foreigners watched the luggage porters, who were carrying their thick leather suitcases, trunks, and boxes covered with the colored labels of tourist bureaus and steamship companies. All the passengers had provided themselves with a book entitled "The Turkestan Railroad," on the cover of which was a camel sniffing at a rail. The book was being sold right there from a pushcart. The author of the book, the journalist Palamidov, passed several times by the cart, looking avidly at the purchasers. He was considered an authority on the Turkestan Railroad, and this was his third trip there.

The time for the train's departure approached, but the farewell scene in no way resembled the departure of an ordinary passenger train. There were no old women on the platform. No one pushed an infant out of the window to cast a parting glance at his grandfather. Neither was there a grandfather whose dim eyes usually reflect a fear of train draughts. And of course there was no kissing. The delegation of shock-brigade workers had been brought to the station by trade union dignitaries who had not had the time to discuss and decide upon the question of farewell kisses. Moscow correspondents were seen off by editorial workers, who are accustomed to do their bit on such occasions merely by hand-shaking. As for the foreign correspondents, who numbered thirty, they were going to the opening of the railroad in full marching order, with wives and phonographs, so that there was no one to see them off.

The members of the expedition talked more loudly than usual, pulled out their notebooks for no particular reason, and chided those who saw them off for not coming along on such an interesting journey. Journalist Lavoizian was particularly noisy. He was young at heart, but in his curls, like a moon in the jungle, gleamed a bald spot.

"It's disgusting to look at you!" he shouted to those who were seeing him off. "How can you possibly understand the significance of the Turkestan Railroad?"

If the hands of the tempestuous Lavoizian had not been occupied with a large typewriter in an oil cloth cover, perhaps he would have even thrashed one of his friends, so passionately was he devoted to the business of newsgathering. At that very moment he was longing to send a telegram to his newspaper, but there was nothing to send it about. Ukhud-

shansky, an editorial worker of a trade union newspaper, who
arrived at the station before everybody else, walked slowly
up and down the length of the train. He carried with him
"The Turkestan Region; A Complete Geographical Description of Our Fatherland; A Book for the Desk and for Travel
for Russian People," a composition of Semyonov-Tyan-Shan-
sky, published in the year 1903. He would stop a group of
those who were departing and those who were seeing them
off, and say with a certain satiric note in his voice:

"Are you going away? Well, well!"

Or:

"Are you staying behind? Well, well!"

In this manner he passed to the head of the train, and for a
long time, his head flung back, looked at the engine. Finally
he asked the engineer:

"Are you working? Well, well!"

Then Journalist Ukhudshansky went to his coupé, opened
the last edition of his trade union organ, and devoted himself
to reading his own article entitled: "Let Us Improve the Work
of Store Commissions," with a sub-title: "The Commissions
Are Not Reorganizing Properly." The article contained a report of a conference, and the relation of the author to the
event described could be expressed in one sentence: "Are you
conferring? Well, well!" Ukhudshansky read until the departure of the train.

One of those who were seeing people off, a man with a
pink plush nose and velvet temples, delivered a prophecy
which frightened everybody horribly.

"I know such journeys," he declared. "I've taken them
myself. Your future is clear to me. There are about a hundred
of you. You will ride for about a month. Two of you will be
left behind by the train at some small forsaken station, without
money and documents, and will catch up a week later, hungry
and bedraggled. Somebody's suitcase is bound to be stolen.
Perhaps it will be Palamidov's or Lavoizian's or Navrotsky's.

And the victim will complain all the way and will beg a shaving brush of his neighbors. He will return the shaving brush unwashed, and he will lose the mug. One of the travelers will die, of course, and the friends of the deceased, instead of going to the union of the rails, will be obliged to take his precious remains back to Moscow. It is very dull and disgusting to ride back with remains. Besides, some quarrel will begin along the road, mark my words! Somebody, perhaps even this same Palamidov, or Ukhudshansky, will commit some anti-social act and all of you will try him long and tediously, while he defends himself with screams and groans. I know it all! You are going away now in Moscow hats and caps, but you will return in Thibetan ones. The most foolish of you all will buy the complete outfit of a Bokhara Jew: a velvet hat trimmed with jackal, and a thick cotton blanket sewn into a robe. And of course, in the evenings all of you will sing 'Stenka Razin' in the train, and roar foolishly: 'And he threw her overboard into the proper wave.' Not only that, but even the foreigners will sing, 'Along the Volga, Mother of Rivers,' 'Sur Notre Mère, Volga,' 'Down Our Mother Volga'!"

Lavoizian became very angry and swung his typewriter at the prophet:

"You're envious!" he said. "We will not sing!"

"You'll sing all right, my darlings. That's inevitable. I know it."

"We will not sing!"

"You will! And if you're honest people, you'll immediately write me a postcard about it!"

Just then a stifled cry rang out. News-photographer Menshov fell from the roof of the baggage car. For several seconds he lay on the platform, holding the apparatus over his head. Then he rose, examined the shutter carefully, and again crawled up on the roof.

"Are you falling?" asked Ukhudshansky, appearing in the window with his newspaper.

"That's not a fall," the photographer said contemptuously. "If you had seen me fall from the spiral descent in the Park of Culture and Rest . . ."

"Well, well," remarked the representative of the trade union organ, and disappeared.

Crawling back to the roof and dropping to one knee, Menshov continued his work. A Norwegian writer who had already placed his things in his coupé and come out on the platform for a little walk, looked at him with an expression of the liveliest satisfaction. The Norwegian had light, childish hair and a large Varangian nose. He was so enthusiastic about the dashing photographic performance of Menshov that he felt the necessity of sharing his feelings with someone. He quickly approached an old shock-brigader from Tryokhgorka Factory, poked his index finger into his chest and exclaimed clearly:

"You!"

Then he pointed to his own chest, and with equal distinctness cried out:

"I!"

Having thus exhausted all the Russian words at his command, the writer smiled jovially and ran back to his car because the second bell had already rung. The shock-brigader also ran to his car. Menshov descended to earth. Heads began to shake, the last smiles appeared. A columnist in an overcoat with a black velvet collar ran by. When the tail of the train was already at the exit switch, two brother correspondents, Lev Rubashkin and Jan Skameikin, jumped out of the station dining room. From Skameikin's teeth dangled a wiener schnitzel. The brothers leaped like puppies, ran along the station platform, jumped to the ground covered with oil, and only there, among the ties, realized that they could not catch up with the train.

The train, running past Moscow in construction, began its deafening song. It pounded its wheels, laughed hellishly under bridges, and only when it appeared among the woods of country homes did it quiet down a bit and develop greater speed. It had to draw a considerable diagonal across the globe; it had to change provinces, and move itself from the cool central section to the heated desert—passing many large and small cities and overtaking Moscow time by four hours.

Toward the evening of the first day two messengers of the capitalist world appeared in the car of the Soviet correspondents: the representative of a free-thinking Austrian newspaper, Mr. Heinrich, and an American, Hiram Burman. They came to get acquainted. Mr. Heinrich was of small stature. Mr. Hiram wore a soft hat with turned-down brim. Both of them spoke Russian with fair purity and correctness. For some time everyone stood silently in the corridor, examining each other with interest. To give the conversation impetus, they began to speak about the Art Theater. Mr. Heinrich praised the theater, while Mr. Burman remarked evasively that, as a Zionist, he was interested principally in the Jewish problem in the U.S.S.R.

"But we have no such problem," said Palamidov.

"What do you mean there is no Jewish problem?" Hiram asked in astonishment.

"There isn't. It doesn't exist."

Mr. Burman became excited. All his life he had written articles for his newspaper about the Jewish problem, and to part with this problem was very painful.

"But aren't there Jews in Russia?" he asked cautiously.

"There are," Palamidov answered.

"Then isn't there also the problem?"

"No. There are Jews. But there is no problem."

The tenseness that had gathered in the corridor was somewhat dispelled by the appearance of Ukhudshansky. He was on his way to the washroom with a towel around his neck.

"Are you talking?" he asked, swaying from the rapid movement of the train. "Well, well!"

When he returned, clean and refreshed, with drops of water
on his temples, the discussion had embraced the entire corridor. Soviet journalists came out of their coupés. From the
adjoining car appeared several shock-brigaders. Two more
foreigners arrived, an Italian correspondent with a Fascist
medal that represented a Lictor's bud with a little hatchet,
and a German orientalist professor who was going to the
celebration on the invitation of VOKS. The front of the discussion was very wide—from the construction of Socialism
in the U.S.S.R. to berets for men, which were just becoming
fashionable in the west. And on all the points, no matter what
they were, there appeared differences of opinion.

"Are you arguing? Well, well!" said Ukhudshansky, disappearing into his coupé.

In the general commotion one could distinguish voices
raised in argument.

"If that's the case," Mr. Heinrich was saying, shaking the
Putilov worker, Suvorov, by his Russian shirt, "then why have
you merely prattled for thirteen years? Why don't you arrange
that world revolution which you talk about so much? You
can't do it, can you? Then stop this idle talk about it!"

"We have no intention of making a revolution in your
country. Make it yourself!"

"I? No! I will not make a revolution!"

"Well, it will be done without you! And without consult-
ing you!"

Mr. Hiram Burman was leaning against the leather-covered
wall, looking indifferently at the arguers. The Jewish question had fallen through some discussional crack at the very
beginning of the conversation, and other themes evoked no
emotion in his soul. From the group where the German professor was speaking very favorably about the advantages of
Soviet marriage over church marriage, the versifying column-

ist, who signed himself with the pseudonym, Gargantua, walked away and approached the thoughtful Hiram. He began to explain something to him with great heat. Hiram listened but was soon convinced that he could not make head or tail of it. In the meanwhile, Gargantua, continually adjusting Hiram's clothes, tying his necktie, brushing a piece of thread off his coat, buttoning and unbuttoning a button, was talking loudly, and, it seemed, even distinctly. But in his speech there was some incomprehensible defect which turned his words to hash. And what intensified the difficulty was that Gargantua loved to talk, and after every sentence demanded confirmation from the man with whom he conversed.

"It's true, isn't it?" he said, turning his head as if he were about to peck food with his large, fine nose. "It's correct, isn't it? Am I right?"

Palamidov couldn't make head or tail of it either, and, shaking his head, began to listen to the discussion that went on between the German orientalist and the train porter. The porter had long been trying to enter into the conversation, and only now had found an unemployed listener. Ascertaining the title as well as the name and surname of his listener, the train porter put the broom aside and began smoothly:

"I suppose you have heard, citizen Professor, that in Central Asia there is an animal called the camel. On his back he has two little hillocks, and a railroad man of my acquaintance, you've probably heard of him, Comrade Dolzhnostyuk, the baggage clerk, he sat down on this camel, between the hillocks, and hit him with a whip. The camel was a mean one, and so he began to press him between his hillocks until he almost choked him to death. Dolzhnostyuk, however, managed to jump down. He was a fighting fellow. You've heard of him, no doubt. And the camel spat on his coat, and the coat had just come back from the laundry . . ."

The evening's conversation died down. The meeting of two worlds ended satisfactorily. No quarrels resulted. The co-existence of two systems in the special train, the capitalistic and the socialistic, had to continue willy-nilly for a whole month. Mr. Heinrich, the enemy of world revolution, told an old traveling joke, and then everybody went to the dining car for supper, crossing from one car to another over the shaking iron platforms, shutting their eyes against the gusty draught. In the dining car, however, the two systems sat apart. Here at supper they appraised each other. The foreign lands, represented by correspondents of large newspapers and news agencies of the entire world, took quietly to vodka and glanced from time to time with frightful politeness at the shock-brigaders in boots, and the Soviet journalists, who, making themselves at home, appeared in bedroom slippers, and with collar buttons instead of neckties.

All kinds of people were in this dining car: Mr. Burman, the provincial from New York, a Canadian girl who had arrived from across the ocean only one hour before the departure of the train, and therefore still turned her head in bewilderment over a meat ball in a long metal plate, a Japanese diplomat, and another Japanese somewhat younger, Mr. Heinrich, whose yellow eyes laughed ironically at something, a young English diplomat with a slender tennis-player's waist, the German orientalist who had listened with magnificent patience to the train porter's story concerning the existence of a strange animal with two hillocks on its back, an American economist, a Czecho-Slovak, a Pole, four American correspondents, among them a pastor who wrote for a Y.M.C.A. paper, and a hundred-percent American woman from an ancient pioneer family with a Dutch name, who had acquired fame because she had missed her train at Mineralnyie Vody last year, and for purposes of publicity had hidden herself for some time under the railroad lunch counter (this event provoked a great deal of excitement in the American press; for three days articles appeared under sensational headlines: "A Girl of Ancient Family in the Clutches of Wild Caucasian

Mountaineers"; "Death or Ransom?"), and many others.
Some were hostile to everything Soviet; others hoped to solve
the riddle of Asiatic souls in the shortest possible time; and
still others attempted conscientiously to understand what was
going on, after all, in the land of the Soviets.

The Soviet land was noisy at its tables. The shock-brigaders
brought their food with them in paper packages, and dived
into the glasses of tea in their white Krupp-metal stands. The
more prosperous of the journalists ordered schnitzels, while
Lavoizian, suddenly overcome by an attack of Slavism, decided
not to lose face before the foreigners and demanded kidney
sauté. He did not eat the kidneys because he had disliked
them from infancy, but he blew up with pride notwithstand-
ing, and cast challenging glances at the foreigners. On the
Soviet side there were also various kinds of people: here was
a Sormovo worker sent on the trip by a general meeting, a
builder from the Stalingrad tractor plant who ten years ago
had lain in the trenches against Wrangel on the very field
where a tractor giant now stood, and a weaver from Serpuk-
hov, interested in the Turkestan Railway because it would
hasten the delivery of cotton to the textile regions. Here sat
also metal workers from Leningrad, miners from the Donets
Basin, a machinist from the Ukraine, and the leader of the
delegation in a White Russian shirt with a large Bukhara
star, received for fighting the Emir. How surprised the diplomat with the tennis-player's waistline would have been if he
had known that the small, polite versifier, Gargantua, had
been eight times prisoner of various Haidamak *atamans,* and
once had even been shot by the Makhnovites, an experience
of which he did not care to speak because he came out with
most unpleasant memories after having crawled from the
common grave with a broken shoulder. It is possible that even
the representative of the Young Christians would have
clutched at his heart had he discovered that Palamidov had
been chairman of an army tribunal, and that Lavoizian, in the

interests of newsgathering, had dressed up as a woman and thus penetrated a meeting of Baptist women, about which he wrote an extensive anti-religious correspondence, or if he knew that not one of the Soviet citizens there present baptized his children, and that among these sons of evil were even four authors.

Various people sat in the dining car.

On the second day, the words of the plush-nosed prophet came true. When the train, thundering and shouting, was crossing the Syzransk bridge over the Volga, the passengers of the special train began to sing a song about the Volga hero in grating city voices. While they sang, they tried not to look into each other's eyes. In the neighboring car the foreigners, who did not know what should be sung where, sang with inspiration a wandering merchant's song with the no less strange refrain "Ekh, ukhnem!" Nobody sent postcards to the man with the plush nose; they were too ashamed of themselves. Only Ukhudshansky held out. He did not join the general chorus. When the song storm possessed the train, he was silent, gritting his teeth tensely and making believe he was reading "The Complete Geographical Description of Our Fatherland." But he was severely punished. The musical paroxysm possessed him at night, far beyond Samara. At the stroke of midnight, when the unusual train was sound asleep, a quavering voice was heard from Ukhudshansky's coupé: "On the Volga there's a cliff; it is covered with wild moss." The journey had taken its own.

Later, when even Ukhudshansky was asleep, the door of the train vestibule opened. For a second the free thunder of wheels was heard, and into the empty, shining corridor, looking around him, came Ostap Bender. For a second he wavered. Then, sleepily waving his hand, he opened the very first door of the coupé. Under a blue night lamp slept Gargantua, Ukhudshansky and Photographer Menshov. The fourth berth, an upper, was empty. The great schemer did not stop to think.

Weakness from the prolonged wanderings, the irreparable losses, and the two-hours of standing on the steps of the car overcame him. He crawled up. Thence a beautiful vision presented itself to him. On the little table at the window, its feet sticking up like the shafts of a wagon, lay a white-bodied boiled chicken.

"I am following the uncertain path of Panikovsky," Ostap whispered.

With these words, he lifted the chicken up to his own level and ate it without bread or salt. He shoved the bones under the hard canvas bolster. Lulled by the creaking of the partitions, and inhaling the incomparable railroad odor of paint, he fell blissfully asleep.

Chapter Twenty-seven

"PERMIT A HIRELING OF CAPITAL TO ENTER"

A T night Ostap dreamed of the sad, shadowed face of Zosya, but later Panikovsky appeared. The pact-violator wore an *izvozchik's* hat with a feather, and, wringing his hands, was saying, "Bender! Bender! Do you know what a chicken is? It's a wonderful fat bird, a chicken is!" Ostap responded with angry bewilderment, "What chicken? But your specialty is goose!" But Panikovsky insisted, "Chicken, chicken, chicken!"

Bender awakened. Just over his head he saw a ceiling, arched like the cover of grandmother's trunk. At the great schemer's very nose swayed a baggage net. It was very light in the coupé. Through the half-open window streamed the hot air of the Ohrenburg steppe.

"Chicken," he heard from below. "Where's my chicken? There was no one else in the coupé besides us? Isn't that so? Permit me . . . But whose feet are these?"

Ostap shut his eyes with his hand, and immediately remembered with dismay that this was a habit of Panikovsky when threatened with danger. Removing his hand, the great schemer saw two heads on the level of his berth.

"'Are you sleeping? Well, well!" said the first head.

"Tell me, my dear fellow," the second head asked good-naturedly, "was it you who ate my chicken? Isn't that right? Isn't that so?"

Menshov sat below, his arms up to their elbows in a black photographer's bag. He was reloading the camera. His face was very thoughtful, as if he were roving under a skirt.

"Yes," Ostap said defiantly. "I ate it!"

"Thank you, thank you!" Gargantua exclaimed unexpectedly. "I didn't know what to do with it! It's hot, and the chicken would have spoiled. Am I right? I didn't want to throw it out. Isn't that so?"

"Of course," said Ostap guardedly. "I was very glad that I was able to do you this little favor."

"What newspaper do you represent?" asked the photographer, smiling languidly as he continued to poke in the bag. "You didn't get on at Moscow?"

"I see that you are a photographer," said Ostap, evading a direct reply. "I once knew a provincial photographer who even opened canned goods by red light, because he feared that otherwise they would spoil."

Menshov laughed. He liked the jest of the new passenger. And that morning no one asked the great schemer any embarrassing questions. He jumped down from the berth and, stroking his cheeks which were covered with three days' growth of beard, looked questioningly at the good Gargantua. The versifying columnist unpacked his suitcase, took the shaving tackle out of it, and stretching them forth to Ostap explained something at great length, pecking at unseen bird food with his nose, every moment demanding confirmation of his words.

While Ostap shaved, washed and cleaned up, Menshov, belted in his photographic paraphernalia, spread the news throughout the car that a new provincial correspondent was now in their coupé, and that he had caught the train during the night via airplane, and had eaten Gargantua's chicken. The story about the chicken caused great activity. Almost all the correspondents had taken along some food from home for the journey: cookies, meat balls, loaves of bread and hard boiled eggs. Nobody ate this food. The correspondents preferred to go to the restaurant. And before Bender could finish dressing, a stout writer in a soft childish coat entered his coupé. He placed twelve eggs on the table before Ostap and said:

"Eat. These are eggs. Since eggs exist, shouldn't somebody eat them?"

Then the writer glanced out of the window, looked at the warty steppe and said lugubriously:

"Desert—senseless! But it exists, and we must take it into consideration."

He was a philosopher. He listened to Ostap's expressions of gratitude, shook his head, and returned to his coupé to finish writing a story. Being a punctual man, he had firmly resolved to write one story a day without fail. He carried out this decision with the application of a model student determined to remain at the head of the class. Evidently he was inspired by the thought that since paper exists, shouldn't somebody write upon it?

Other passengers followed the example of the philosopher. Navrotsky brought pickled peppers in a jar; Lavoizian, cutlets with newspaper lines sticking to them; Sapegin, herring and cookies; and Dnestrov a jar of apple butter and pickled herring. Others came but Ostap closed the reception.

"I can't, I can't, my friends!" he exclaimed. "Here I do one man a favor, and everybody is rushing at me!"

Ostap liked the correspondents very much. He was glad to please them, but he had eaten so much that it was impossible for him to feel anything. With great difficulty he crawled into his berth and slept almost the entire day.

The third day of the journey began. The special train fretted with expectation. It was still a great distance from the Turkestan Railroad. Nothing noteworthy had happened but the Moscow correspondents, fidgety from the forced idleness, regarded each other suspiciously.

"Didn't someone find out something, and didn't he send it by fast wire to his paper?"

Finally Lavoizian could contain himself no longer and sent a telegram:

"passed ohrenburg stop exstack engine smoking stop everybody cheerful stop delegates trains discuss only turkestan railroad stop flash instructions aralsea lavoizian"

The secret was soon discovered, and at the very next station a queue formed at the telegraph window. Everybody sent short communications about the cheerful spirits and about the smoke which issued from the smokestack of the engine.

The broad field of activity opened for the foreign correspondents immediately after Ohrenburg, when they beheld the first camel, the first *yurta,* the first *kazak* with his sharp-edged fur hat and a whip in his hand. At a water tank where the train stopped unexpectedly at least twenty cameras were aimed at the camel. Here the exotics began: the ship of the desert, the freedom-loving dreams of the desert, and other romantic rot.

The American woman of old family emerged in round dark glasses. She was further protected from the sunlight by a green umbrella. In this outfit a gray-haired American took her picture for a long time with a hand movie camera. At first she stood beside the camel, then in front of it, and finally on it, taking her place between the hillocks about which the train porter had spoken with such feeling. The small, vicious Heinrich ran around among the crowd and warned everybody:

"You'd better look after her! She'll get stuck in the station by accident and there will be more headlines in the American press: 'Daring newspaper-woman in clutches of frantic camel!' "

The Japanese diplomat stood two paces from a *kazak*. They regarded each other in silence. Their slightly flattened faces, stiff mustaches, polished yellow skin, and swollen, narrow eyes were exactly alike. They would have passed for twins had not the *kazak* worn a sheepskin coat belted with a cotton sash, while the Japanese wore a gray London suit, and if the *kazak* had not begun to read only last year, while the Japanese had graduated twenty years before from two universities, one in Tokio and the other in Paris. The diplomat stepped back, bent his head to the sights of his camera, and clicked the shutter. The *kazak* laughed, jumped on his rough little horse and galloped away into the steppe.

But at the next station new elements entered this tale of adventure. Behind the station building lay red cyclindrical barrels of oil and gasoline and a new yellow wooden building, and before it, pressing their caterpillar chains heavily into the earth, stretched a row of tractors. On a cage-like stack of railroad ties stood a girl tractor-driver in black workman's pants and felt boots. Here the Soviet correspondents took their revenge. Holding their cameras on the level of their eyes, they began to approach the girl. In front of everyone crept Menshov. In his teeth he held an aluminum photobox, and his movements reminded one of a sharpshooter who was trying to run across out of the line. But if the camel had permitted his photograph to be taken with full consciousness of his right to fame, the girl was more modest. She endured about five photo-attacks calmly, then turned red and went away. The photographers then attacked the tractors. By a stroke of good luck, a line of camels could be seen on the horizon behind the scene. All of this, tractors and camels, would fit excellently into a picture entitled, "The Old and the New," or "Who Will Beat Whom?"

Ostap awakened before sunset. The train was still running through the desert. Lavoizian wandered through the corridors, urging his comrades to issue a special train newspaper. He had even thought of a title: "Full Steam Ahead."

"You call that a title?" remarked Ostap. "I once saw a newspaper published by a fire brigade which was called

'Where There Is Smoke There Must be Fire.' Well now, that was to the point!"

"You are a professional writer!" cried Lavoizian. "Confess that you are simply too lazy to write for the steering wheel of the train's public opinion!"

The great schemer did not deny that he was a professional writer. In case of necessity he could have explained without hesitation what organ of the press he represented on this train—the "Chernomorsk Gazette." But there was no particular necessity for this, because this was a special train and it was not visited by angry conductors with nickel-plated punches. Lavoizian was already sitting at his typewriter in the car of the shock-brigaders where his proposal had provoked bedlam. The old man from Tryokhgorka was already writing with an indelible pencil a notice concerning the necessity of organizing an evening for exchange of experiences and a literary reading. They were already looking for a caricaturist, and had already mobilized Navrotsky to organize a questionnaire on the subject of which enterprise represented by the delegates present had best carried out the plan for industry and finance.

In the evening a crowd of newspaper people gathered in the coupé of Gargantua, Menshov, Ukhudshansky and Bender. They sat very close together, six people to a berth. Heads and feet dangled from the top. The cool night refreshed the journalists who had suffered all day from the heat, and the slow, steady pulse of the wheels, which had not stopped beating for three days, disposed them to friendship. There was talk about the Turkestan Railway, reminiscences of editors and secretaries, stories about funny newspaper errors, and everybody made fun of Ukhudshansky because he lacked newspaper sense. Ukhudshansky raised his head high and answered in a superior manner:

"Are you jawing? Well, well!"

At the very height of the celebration appeared Mr. Heinrich.

"Permit a hireling of capital to enter," he said superciliously.

Heinrich made himself comfortable on the knees of the fat writer who groaned and thought stoically, "Since I have knees, should not someone sit on them? So here he is sitting."

"Well, how are you building Socialism?" the representative of the free-thinking newspaper asked flippantly.

It happened that all the foreign journalists on the train were accorded due respect and when addressed, their surnames were preceded with Mister, Herr or Signor. But the correspondent of the free-thinking newspaper was called simply Heinrich, was regarded as a windbag, and was not taken seriously. Therefore to his direct question Palamidov answered:

"Heinrich, don't exert yourself. You'll begin again to criticize the Soviet government. That is dull and uninteresting. And besides, we can hear it from any angry old woman in a queue."

"Not at all," said Heinrich. "I want to tell you a biblical story about Adam and Eve. Will you permit me?"

"Listen, Heinrich, why do you speak Russian so well?" asked Sapegin.

"I learned it in Odessa in 1918, when the army of General Von Beltz occupied that excellent city. At that time I bore the rank of lieutenant. No doubt you have heard of Von Beltz."

"Not only heard about him," said Palamidov, "but even saw him. Your Von Beltz lay in his gilded office in the palace of the commander of the Odessa military district with a bullet through his head. He had shot himself when he learned that a revolution had occurred in your fatherland."

At the mention of the word "revolution," Mr. Heinrich smiled coldly and said:

"The general was true to his oath."

"But why didn't you shoot yourself, Heinrich?" asked someone from the upper berth. "What did you do about your oath?"

"Well, will you listen to the biblical story?" the representative of the free-thinking newspaper asked irritably.

But for some time attempts were made to question him about his oath, and only when he became thoroughly insulted and threatened to leave, did they agree to hear his story:

MR. HEINRICH'S STORY ABOUT ADAM AND EVE

In Moscow, gentlemen, there was a young man, a member of the League of Communist Youth. He was called Adam. And in the same city there was also a young woman, likewise a member of the League of Communist Youth, who was called Eve. And once upon a time these young people went for a walk in the Moscow Paradise, the Park of Culture and Rest. I don't know what they talked about. Our young people usually talk about love. But your Adam and Eve were Marxists and it is possible that they talked about the world revolution. At any rate, it happened that in the course of their walk in the former Neskuchny Garden, they sat down on the grass under a tree. I don't know what kind of a tree it was, but it is quite possible that it was the tree of knowledge of good and evil. But Marxists, as you know, do not like mysticism. And so to them it probably seemed a simple mountain ash. As she talked, Eve tore a branch from the tree and presented it to Adam. Just then appeared a man whom the young Marxists, utterly devoid of imagination, recognized as the garden watchman, but it was more than likely the angel with the fiery sword. Swearing and grumbling, the angel brought Adam and Eve to the office to file a complaint against them for injuries inflicted upon the institution of public gardens. This paltry every-day occurrence deflected the attention of the young people from the elevated subject of politics. Adam saw that before him stood the lovely Eve, and Eve noticed that before her stood the manly Adam. And the young people fell in love with each other. Three years later they already had two sons.

Having reached this point, Mr. Heinrich suddenly fell silent, pushing his soft, striped cuffs into his sleeve.

"Well, what about it?" asked Lavoizian.

"Simply this," Heinrich said proudly. "One son is called

Cain, and the other Abel. After a certain time, Cain will kill
Abel, Abraham will beget Isaac, Isaac will beget Jacob and,
in general, the entire biblical history will begin over again
from the beginning. And no Marxism in the world can prevent it! Everything repeats itself. There will be a flood, there
will be Noah and his three sons, and Ham will insult Noah,
and there will be the Tower of Babel which will never be
finished, gentlemen. And so forth. Nothing new will happen
on earth. So you are fussing in vain about a new life!"

And, beaming with self-satisfaction, Heinrich leaned back,
crushing the fat good-natured writer with his narrow back.

"All this would be very interesting," said Palamidov, "if it
were supported by proof. But you can prove nothing. You
simply want it to be so. Nobody can forbid you to believe in
miracles. There's no need for that. Believe and pray."

"But have you any proof that it will be otherwise!" exclaimed the representative of the free-thinking newspaper.

"I have," replied Palamidov. "One of them you will see
the day after to-morrow at the meeting of the rails of the
Turkestan Railroad."

"Well, there you go again," Heinrich grumbled. "Construction! Factories! The Five-Year Plan! Why do you poke
all these things into my eyes? What matters is the spirit!
Everything will be repeated. There will even be a Thirty
Years' War, and a Hundred Years' War! And again people
who have dared to say that the earth is round will be burned
at the stake! And again poor Jacob will be duped and will be
compelled to work seven years without pay, after he has been
given the ugly, near-sighted wife Leah, instead of the full-
breasted Rebecca. Everything, everything will be repeated!
And as formerly the Wandering Jew will roam over the
earth . . ."

"The Wandering Jew will never wander again," the great
schemer said suddenly, regarding the gathering with a twin-
kle in his eye.

"And I suppose you can present proof for this in the course of two days!" Heinrich mocked.

"I can, right now," Ostap replied graciously. "If the company will permit, I shall relate what happened to the so-called Wandering Jew."

The company gladly permitted. Everybody prepared to listen to the story of the new passenger, while Ukhudshansky even remarked:

"Are you telling a story? Well, well!"

And the great schemer began.

OSTAP BENDER'S STORY OF THE WANDERING JEW

I will not remind you of the long and tedious history of that wandering Hebrew. I will only say that for about a thousand years this commonplace old man loafed over the entire world without registering in hotels, and annoyed citizens with his complaints about the high railroad fares, which compelled him to walk. He had been seen a multitude of times. He was present at the historical session where Columbus did not succeed in accounting for the advance sums he had taken for the opening of America. While still a young man, he had witnessed the burning of Rome. For about a hundred and fifty years he had lived in India, surprising the yogi with his longevity and his quarrelsome disposition. In a word, the old man could have told much of interest, if, at the end of every century, he had sat down and written his memoirs. But the Wandering Jew was illiterate, and besides he had a memory like a sieve.

Not long ago, the old man lived in the excellent city of Rio de Janeiro, drank cooling drinks, gazed at the ocean steamers, and walked in white trousers under the palms. The trousers he had bought by chance eight hundred years before, in Palestine, from some knight who had fought and won the Lord's Sepulchre, and they were still as good as new. But suddenly the old man became dissatisfied. He wanted to go to Russia, to the Dnieper River. He had been everywhere, on the Rhine, on the Ganges, on the Mississippi, on the Yangtse, on the Niger, and even on the Volga. But he had not been on the Dnieper. He wanted, as you see, to look at this broad river also.

Precisely in the year 1919, the Wandering Jew in his knightly trousers illegally crossed the Roumanian border. Is it necessary to add that around his stomach he had hidden eight pairs of silk stockings and a bottle of Parisian perfume, which a certain lady from Kishinev had asked him to deliver to her kinsmen in Kiev? During that stormy period, carrying contraband on the stomach was called 'to carry a poultice.' The old man had been taught this business very quickly in Kishinev. When the Wandering Jew, having carried out his mission, stood on the shore of the Dnieper, wagging his shaggy green beard, a man with yellow and blue officer's stripes and Petlurite shoulder straps, walked up to him and asked severely:

"A Jew?"

"A Jew," the old man answered.

"Well, come on," ordered the man with the officer's stripes.

And he brought him to a Kazak *ataman*.

"Caught a Jew," he reported, pushing the old man forward with his knee.

"Are you a Jew?" asked the *ataman* gayly.

"I'm a Jew," replied the wanderer.

"Here, stand him up against the wall!" cried the Kazak chieftain graciously.

"But I'm immortal!" cried the old man.

For two thousand years he had impatiently waited for death, but now he suddenly wanted very much to live.

"Shut up, Jew-face!" the forelocked *ataman* cried joyfully. "At him, boys!"

And the Wandering Jew was no more.

"That is all," concluded Ostap.

"I imagine, Mr. Heinrich, that as a former lieutenant in the Austrian army, you must be familiar with the habits of your friends, the Petlurites," Palamidov remarked.

·Heinrich did not reply, and immediately went out. At first everybody thought that he had been insulted, but on the next day it was discovered that the correspondent of the free-thinking newspaper had gone directly from the Soviet car to Mr. Hiram Burman, to whom he sold the story of the Wandering Jew for forty dollars. And from the very first station, Hiram transmitted Ostap Bender's story by telegraph to his newspaper.

Chapter Twenty-eight

THE PERSPIRING WAVE OF INSPIRATION

O N the morning of the fourth day the train turned east.
Past snow ranges—the Himalayan mountain spurs—
rolling thunderously across artificial constructions (bridges,
tubes for the drainage of spring waters, and the like), throwing a quivering shadow on mountain streams, the special
train passed through a town hidden under poplar trees and
for a long time squirmed around the side of a large snow
mountain. Unable to pass over the crest at one swoop, the
special train wove back and forth like a snake, attacked the
mountain from the right and from the left, turned back,
puffing, returned again, rubbed its dusty green sides against
the mountain, dodged about in every possible way, and finally
jumped out into freedom. Its wheels working energetically,
the train stopped importantly at the last station before the beginning of the Turkestan Railroad.

In cubes of astonishing sunlight, against the background
of aluminum mountains, stood an engine the color of young
grass—the gift of the station workers to the new railroad.

For a considerable time all was not well with us in regard
to gifts on celebrations and anniversaries. Usually the presents were either small, the size of a cat—a model engine—or,
on the other hand, some huge telegraph pole entirely out of
proportion. The painful metamorphosis of small objects into
large and vice versa, took much time and money. The useless
little engines gathered dust in office closets, and titanic chisels
carried on two vans idiotically gathered rust in the yard of the
establishment that had celebrated.

But the engine OV, brought out in advance of its schedule by a shock-brigade troop, was of normal size. The beautiful gift was immediately harnessed to the train and, bearing a placard "Let Us Unite the Rails," rolled to the southern source of the railway, the station Gornaya.

Exactly two years before the first blue-black rail manufactured by a Ural factory was laid there. Thence an endless stream of fiery rails had flowed. The railroad demanded more and more. Tent towns that moved to meet each other arranged a socialist competition and developed such tempos that it was difficult for the suppliers of materials to keep up with them.

That evening, at station Gornaya, illuminated by pink and green rockets, was so fine that the old-timers, had there been any, would of course have said that never before had they known such an evening. Fortunately there were no old-timers in Gornaya. As recently as 1928 there were not only no old-timers there, but no houses, no station building, no path laid down by the rails, and no wooden arch of triumph with flags waving on it, not far from which stopped the special train.

While a meeting was being held under the kerosene lamps, to which the entire local population gathered, news-photographer Menshov circled around the arch with two apparatuses, a tripod, and magnesium flash light pan. The photographer appreciated the arch and thought it would photograph well, but the train, twenty paces away from it, would come out too small. And if he were to take the picture from the other side of the train, the arch would come out too small. In such cases Mohammed usually comes to the mountain, understanding perfectly well that the mountain will not come to him. But Menshov did what seemed simplest to him. In the same nonchalant tone in which one asks someone to move in a street car, he asked the official to move the train under the arch. Moreover, he insisted that the engine stack must emit thick white steam, and that the engineer must look fearlessly out of the window into the distant spaces, shading his eyes with the palm of his hand. The railroad workers were taken by surprise, and thinking that this was necessary, satisfied his demand. The train pulled up to the arch with a roar; from the stack came the required steam, and the engineer, sticking his head out of the window, frowned furiously. Then Menshov caused such an explosion of magnesium that the earth trembled and dogs barked a hundred kilometers around. When he had taken the picture, the photographer thanked the railroad personnel and returned hurriedly to his coupé.

Late that night the special train was moving along the Turkestan line. When the population of the train was retiring for the night, Photographer Menshov came into the corridor, and, addressing no one, uttered plaintively:

"Strange, but it seems that I took a picture of that damned arch without a plate in the camera! Nothing came out!"

"That's all right," Lavoizian answered him with compassion. "It's a small affair. Just ask the engineer, and he will immediately turn back. In about three hours he will again be at Gornaya and you can repeat your photographing. As for the union of the rails—that can be postponed for a day."

"Devil of a lot I can take now!" the photographer said mournfully. "I've exhausted my supply of magnesium, or we'd certainly have to return."

The journey along the Turkestan Railway afforded much joy to the great schemer. Every hour brought him closer to the northern tent town and Koreiko. Besides, Ostap liked the passengers of the train. They were for the most part young people, gay, unaffected yet by the madness of bureaucracy which so distinguished his Herculean acquaintances. Only his lack of money prevented him from being completely happy. The provisions which had been given to him were eaten, now he needed cash for the dining car. At first, when his new friends asked him to come to dinner, Ostap would say that he had lost his appetite. But he soon understood that this could not continue. For some time he studied Ukhudshansky, who spent the entire day in the corridor looking at the telegraph poles and the birds that perched on the wires. A light satiric smile touched Ukhudshansky's lips. He threw his head back and whispered to the birds:

"Are you flitting? Well, well!"

To satisfy his curiosity, Ostap went so far as to acquaint himself with Ukhudshansky's article, "Let Us Improve the Work of Store Commissions." After this Ostap scrutinized the strange journalist from head to foot, smiled ominously, and sensing the familiar agitation of a sharpshooting hunter, shut himself in the coupé.

He left it three hours later, holding in his hands a large sheet covered with graphs that looked like a statistical report.

"Are you writing?" Ukhudshansky asked languidly.

"Especially for you," replied the great schemer. "I notice that you are constantly torn by the tortures of creative work. It is, of course, very difficult to write. Being an old editorial writer and, in general, an old hand at the pen, I know that to be so. But, my dear fellow, I have invented a little thing which frees you from the necessity of waiting until you are drenched in the perspiring wave of inspiration. Here! Look!"

And Ostap presented Ukhudshansky with a sheet on which was written:

THE COMPLETE CELEBRATOR

Indispensable manual for the composition of articles for gala occasions, feuilletons for state holidays, odes, hymns, and also poems for parades.

PART I—GLOSSARY

Nouns
1. Shouts
2. Workers
3. Dawn
4. Life
5. Beacon
6. Mistakes
7. Banner (flag)
8. Baal
9. Moloch
10. Myrmidon (fawner)
11. Hour
12. Enemy
13. Pace

14. Wave
15. Sands
16. Leap (bound)
17. Steed
18. Heart
19. Past

Artistic Epithets
1. Malicious
2. Vicious

Adjectives
1. Imperialistic
2. Capitalistic
3. Historical
4. Final
5. Industrial
6. Steel
7. Iron

Verbs
1. To flame
2. To fling (up)
3. To expose
4. To glow

5. To fly (up)
6. To decide (destinies)
7. To sing
8. To libel
9. To grit (teeth)
10. To threaten

Other Parts of Speech
1. Ninth
2. Twelfth
3. Let
4. So be it!
5. Forward!

(Interjections, prepositions, conjunctions, commas, rows of dots, exclamation points, parentheses, etc.)

N.B. Commas must be placed before "who," "which" and "if." Rows of dots, exclamation points, and parentheses—wherever possible.

PART II—Creative Part
(*Composed exclusively of words in Part I*)

I. EDITORIAL

The Ninth Wave

The Turkestan Railroad, that Iron Steed, which, scattering the sands of the future with its steely bound, decides the pace of history, exposing the regular, vicious gritting of the malicious enemy's teeth whom the ninth wave is already flinging up, threatening him with the twelfth hour, the last hour for the myrmidons of imperialistic Moloch, that capitalistic Baal; but, despite mistakes, may the banners of the beacon of industrialization glow and fly up, flaming under the shouts of the workers, before whom, to the tune of singing hearts, appears the dawn of a new life; forward!

2. AN ARTISTIC SKETCH—FEUILLETON

Let

Forward!

It flames under the shouts of the workers. . . .

It exposes the dawn of new life. . . .

The beacon!

Of industrialization!

Let us grant certain mistakes. Let us. Then how they glow. . . . How they fly. . . . How they fly up. . . . These banners! These flags! . . .

Let's suppose—the Baal of capitalism! Let's suppose—the Moloch of imperialism! Let's suppose!

But over the myrmidons is already flinging:

The final wave!

The ninth wave!

The twelfth hour!

Let them libel. Let them grit their teeth. Let the malicious, vicious enemy expose himself.

The historical pace is decided. The sands of the past are flung up with a steely bound.

This is—the "Iron Steed"! . . .

This is:

The Turkestan

Railroad!

"Hearts sing" . . .

3. LITERARY VERSE

(a) The Thirteenth Wave

Under the daily din hearts sing,
Like dawn the beacon flares.
The vicious enemy they fling—
The industrial fires he dares.
The iron steed is flying on
To sweep our Cleo's bound,
The worker's family bringing on
T' expose the errors found.
The final hour is flying up,
The ninth wave glows in glee.
The twelfth-elfth hour is in the cup,
Oh, Moloch-Baal, for thee!

(b) Eastern Variation

Under daily din the *ooryuk* blooms,
Like dawn the *keeshlak* flares,
While midst *aryks* and alley glooms
The *eeshak* forth he dares.

Asiatic Ornamentation

1. *Ooryuk* (apricots)
2. *Aryk* (canal)
3. *Eeshak* (ass)
4. *Plov* (food)
5. *Bai* (bad man)
6. *Basmach* (bad man)
7. *Shakal* (animal)

8. *Keeshlak* (village)
9. *Piala* (cup)
10. *Medresse* (theological school)
11. *Eecheeghee* (footwear)
12. *Shaitan* (devil)

13. *Arba* (wagon)
14. *Shaitan-Arba* (Central Asiatic R.R.)
15. You-me no savvy (expression)
16. Li'l-li'l (expression)

APPENDIX

With the aid of the materials in Part I following the methods in Part II may be composed also: novels, tales, poems in prose, stories, local color sketches, literary reporting, chronicles, epics, plays, political reviews, radio orations, etc.

When Ukhudshansky had acquainted himself with the contents of the document, his eyes, which until then had been dim, came to life. Before him, who had fed until now only upon reports of conferences, suddenly opened dazzling stylistic vistas.

"And for all of this—twenty-five *toogriks,* twenty-five Mongolian rubles," the great schemer said impatiently, suffering with hunger.

"I haven't any Mongolian ones," said the editorial worker of the trade union organ, clutching the "Complete Celebrator."

Ostap agreed to take ordinary rubles, invited Gargantua, whom he already called "friend and benefactor," and together they went to the dining car. He was given a carafe of vodka, a salad, and a large cutlet as heavy as a horseshoe. After the vodka, which produced light vertigo in his head, the great schemer mysteriously explained to his "friend and benefactor" that in the northern tent city he hoped to find a man who owed him a small sum. Then he would invite all the correspondents to a banquet. To this Gargantua replied with a long convincing speech, of which, as usual, one could not understand a word. Ostap called the head waiter, asked him if he had champagne and how many bottles of it, what other delicacies he had and in what quantities, and told him that he needed the information because in about two days he intended to give a banquet for his brothers of the pen. The head waiter declared that everything possible would be done.

"According to the laws of hospitality," he added for some reason.

As the train neared the place of the meeting of the rails, nomads increased in number. They galloped down the hills across the track in hats resembling Chinese pagodas. The special train thundered through dents in crags of porphyry, past the new three-ply bridge, which had been completed only the day before, and began to climb the crystal peak, made famous by the builders of the railroad who fulfilled all explosive and construction work in three months instead of the eight indicated by the plan.

Gradually the train began to gather to itself more and more of native life. The foreigners who had left Moscow in stiff collars that seemed to have been made of drugstone china, in heavy silk neckties and cloth suits, began to disrobe themselves. Heat won the day. The first to change the form of his dress was one of the Americans. Laughing with embarrassment, he walked out of his car in strange habiliment. He wore heavy yellow shoes, golf socks and breeches, horn-rimmed glasses, and a kind of Russian shirt worn by grain farming peasants, embroidered in cross stitch, and with a collar that buttoned on the side. As the heat increased the foreigners deviated more and more from European costume. Russian shorts, Apache shirts, Geisha shirts, open-neck sleeveless shirts, *tolstofka* shirts, pseudo-*tolstofkas*, and demi-*tolstofkas*, Odessa sandals, and Japanese clogs completely transformed the press workers of the capitalist world. They bore a remarkable resemblance to old-fashioned Soviet office workers, and one was tortured with the desire to "houseclean" them, to pry into their secrets, to find out what they had been doing before 1917, whether they were bureaucrats or procrastinators, and whether their families were Simon-pure.

Late that night, the indefatigable engine, hung with flags and garlands, pulled the special train into the station Gremyashchii Klyuch,[1] the place of the meeting of the rails. Motion picture operators lighted Roman candles. The chief of construction stood in the sharp white light, looking excitedly at the train. There were no lights in the cars. Everybody was asleep. Only the large square windows of the headquarters car were lit up. Its door opened quickly and a member of the government jumped to the ground.

The chief of the railroad took a step forward, saluted, and delivered the report which the entire country awaited. The Turkestan Railroad, which connected Siberia and Central Asia by direct line, was finished a year ahead of time.

When this formality had been carried out, the report given and accepted, two middle-aged, unsentimental men kissed each other.

All the correspondents, both Soviet and foreign, even Lavoizian who had impatiently sent a telegram about the smoke that came out of the engine smoke stack, even the Canadian girl who had sped at breakneck speed across the ocean—everybody was asleep. Only Palamidov rushed back and forth along the freshly-piled embankment seeking a telegraph. He reasoned that if he were to send a flash immediately it would appear in the morning edition. And in the dark desert he found the hastily constructed hut which housed the telegraph office. Chewing at his pencil, he wrote: "by starlight delivered report completion railroad stop eye witnessed historical kissing chief railroad member government palamidov"

The first part of the telegram was printed by the editor, but the kiss was eliminated. The editor explained that it was improper for a member of the government to kiss.

[1] The Thundering Key.

Chapter Twenty-nine

GREMYASHCHII KLYUCH

THE sun rose over the hills of the desert at 5 o'clock, 02 minutes, 46 seconds. Ostap rose one minute later. Photographer Menshov was already strapping his various photographic cases around him and assuming the appearance of a marsupial. He put on his cap with the visor backward, so that he might see better through the finder. The photographer expected a busy day. Ostap likewise expected a busy day, and, without washing, jumped out of the train. A yellow portfolio went with him. The trains that had brought guests from Moscow, Siberia and Central Asia formed streets and lanes. From all directions delegations had come to the platform. Steam engines hissed and the white steam clung to the large cloth slogan: "The Turkestan Railroad Is the First Child of the Five-Year Plan."

Everyone was still asleep. The cool wind whined through the flags on the empty platform. Ostap noticed that the clear horizon of the much-intersected locality was suddenly darkened with clouds of dust. Sharp-edged hats appeared over the hills on all sides. Thousands of horsemen, sitting in wooden saddles, were urging on their hairy little horses to the wooden arrow that stood on the very spot which two years before had been designated as the place of the future meeting of the rails.

Entire villages of nomads rode. Fathers of families moved on horseback; on horseback, male fashion, rode their wives; and even vicious mothers-in-law urged their true steeds forward, pricking them under the belly with their heels. The mounted groups swirled in the dust, flew across fields with their red banners, stretched out in their stirrups, and turning aside, curiously regarded the wonders before them. There were many wonders—trains, rails, the dashing figures of motion picture photographers, the caged dining room that had suddenly grown out of a bare spot, and the radio loudspeakers from which came a clear voice: "One, two, three, four, five, six," testing the readiness of radio operation. Two tent cities, two construction enterprises on wheels, with stores of materials, dining rooms, offices, bath houses, and living quarters for workers, faced each other before the platform, separated by only twenty meters of ties not yet covered by rails. "In this place the last rail will be laid, and the last spike will be driven."

At the head of the Southern City hung the placard "Let's Get the North," and at the head of the Northern one "Let's Get the South." The workers of both cities mixed in one crowd. They saw each other for the first time, although they had known of each other since the very beginning of the construction when they had been separated by a hundred and fifty thousand kilometers of deserts, cliffs, lakes and rivers. Competition in the work had hastened the meeting by one year. During the last month the rails had been laid at a run. North and South wanted to outdo each other and be the first to enter Gremyashchii Klyuch. The North had won. Now the chiefs of both cities, one in a black *tolstofka* shirt, the other in a white Ukrainian shirt, conversed peacefully at the arrow. On the face of the Northern chief, a smile twisted from time to time, against his will. He hastened to chase it away and praise the South, but again the smile lifted the mustache bleached by the sun.

Ostap ran to the cars of the Northern City. The city was empty. All of its inhabitants had gone to the stage, in front of which the musicians sat. Burning their lips against the hot metallic mouthpieces, they played an overture. Soviet journalists took the left wing of the platform. Lavoizian hung over the edge and begged Menshov to take a picture of him in action, but Menshov had no time for him. He was taking pictures of the railroad's shock-brigaders, separately and in groups, compelling the spike drivers to swing their hammers and the muckers to lean on their shovels. On the right wing were the foreign correspondents. At the entrance Red army men checked the invitational tickets. Ostap had no ticket. The commandant of the train had issued tickets according to a list on which the representative of the "Chernomorsk Gazette," O. Bender, was not inscribed. In vain did Gargantua beg the great schemer to come up, shouting, "Isn't it right? Isn't it so?" Ostap shook his head negatively, his eyes searching the platform on which heroes and guests found their places.

Sitting quietly in the first row was the timekeeper of the Northern tent city, Alexander Koreiko. For protection against the sun, he had covered his head with a triangular hat made of newspaper. He turned his ear slightly forward, the better to hear the first orator who had just come up to the microphone, when:

"Alexander Ivanovich!" shouted Ostap, putting his hands together like a megaphone.

Koreiko stood up and looked down. The musicians began to play "The International," but the wealthy timekeeper listened inattentively to the hymn. The absurd figure of the great schemer, who was running along the platform cleared for the last rails, robbed him of his sense of peace. He looked over the heads of the crowd, trying to decide whither to run away. But around him was the desert.

Fifteen thousand horsemen, who had galloped ceaselessly back and forth, fording the cold river a score of times, disposed themselves in cavalry formation beside the platform as the meeting began. But some, who were too proud or too bashful, spent the entire day on the top of the hills, not daring to come closer to the roaring, excited meeting.

The builders of the railroad celebrated their victory noisily, joyously, with shouts, music, and the tossing of their favorites and heroes in the air. The rails flew on the track with a clang. They were joined in a moment, and the workers who laid them down, workers who had beaten in a million spikes, yielded the right of the last blows to their leaders.

"According to the laws of hospitality," said the head waiter, sitting with the cooks on the roof of the dining car.

An engineer with the Order of the Red Banner pushed his large felt hat to the back of his head, seized the long-handled mallet, and, screwing up his face solemnly, hit straight at the ground. The friendly laughter of the spike-drivers, among whom were many strong ones who could knock a spike in at one blow, rang out. But the soft blows against the ground soon began to alternate with clangs testifying that the hammer at times came in contact with the spike. The secretary of the Regional Committee, members of the government, chiefs of the North and the South, and guests swung the mallets. The very last spike was beaten into the tie by the chief of the construction job.

Speeches began. They were given twice, in the Kazak and Russian languages.

"Comrades!" a shock-brigade spike-driver said slowly, trying not to look at the Order of the Red Banner, which had just been pinned to his shirt. "What's done is done, and there's not much to say about it. And in the name of our entire track-laying collective there is a request to the government to send us immediately on a new construction job. We've learned to work together well, and during the last months we have laid rails at the rate of five kilometers per day. We obligate ourselves to maintain and to raise this norm. And long live our World Revolution! I also want to say, Comrades, that many of the ties we received were faulty. We had to throw them away. That's bad business and must be set right!"

The correspondents could no longer complain of the lack of news. Speeches were written down. Engineers were caught by the waist and pumped for information, exact data, and figures. It became hot, dusty and busy. The meeting in the desert smoked up like a huge campfire. Lavoizian scribbled ten lines, ran to the telegraph, sent a flash, and again began to take notes. Ukhudshansky wrote nothing and sent no telegrams. In his pocket lay the "Complete Celebrator" which made it possible for him to compose in five minutes a splendid bit of correspondence with Asiatic ornamentation. Ukhudshansky's future was assured. And, therefore, with a more pronounced satiric note in his voice than ever, he told his fellow reporters:

"Are you working hard? Well, well!"

Unexpectedly, Lev Rubashkin and Jan Skameikin, who had been left behind in Moscow, appeared in the box of the Soviet journalists. They had been brought by an airplane that had arrived early that morning. It had landed ten kilometers away from Gremyashchii Klyuch on a natural airdrome beyond a distant hill, and the brother correspondents had only now dragged themselves thence on foot. Scarcely greeting anyone, Lev Rubashkin and Jan Skameikin pulled notebooks out of their pockets and began to make up for lost time.

The cameras of the foreigners clicked without stopping. Throats dried up from speeches and the sun. Everyone gazed more and more frequently beyond the cool river at the restaurant where the streaked shadows of an awning lay across long banquet tables on which were green bottles of Narzan mineral water. Beside it were soft drink stands to which the guests ran from time to time. Koreiko was tortured with thirst, but he held out under his childish three-cornered hat. The great schemer mocked him from the distance, raising over his head a bottle of lemonade and the yellow portfolio with the shoe laces.

At the table, beside the pitcher and the microphone, was a girl Pioneer.

"Well, little girl," the chief of the construction job said gayly, "tell us what you think of the Turkestan Railroad!"

It would not have been surprising had the girl suddenly stamped her foot and begun, "Comrades, permit me to summarize those attainments which . . .", etc., because we do have exemplary children among us who, with painful application, deliver two-hour speeches. But the Pioneer girl of Gremyashchii Klyuch immediately seized the bull by the horns with her weak little hands, and cried out in a thin childish voice:

"Long live the Five-Year Plan!"

Palamidov came up to the foreign professor of economics in quest of an interview.

"I am enraptured!" said the professor. "All of the construction work I have seen in the U.S.S.R. is grandiose! I have no doubt that the Five-Year Plan will be fulfilled! I shall write about it!"

A half year later he actually published a book about it, in which he proved in the first two hundred pages that the Five-Year Plan would be fulfilled by the time indicated, and that the U.S.S.R. would become one of the most powerful industrial nations. But on the 201st page the professor declared that precisely for that reason the land of the Soviets should be destroyed as soon as possible, because it would bring about the natural destruction of capitalistic society. The professor proved a much more business-like person than the windbag Heinrich.

A white airplane rose behind a hill. The Kazaks dashed away on all sides. The large shadow of the airplane flung itself across the platform and, dipping, ran into the desert. The Kazaks ran after the shadow shouting and lifting their whips. The motion picture operators excitedly began to grind their machines. It became even more chaotic and dusty. The meeting had come to an end.

"Here's what, comrades," said Palamidov, hurrying to the dining room with his brothers of the pen. "Let's agree not to write commonplaces."

"Commonplaces are disgusting!" Lavoizian supported him. "They're horrible!"

And on the way to the dining room the correspondents unanimously agreed not to write about Uzun-Kulak, which means Long Ear, which in its turn means "Telegraph of the Steppes." Everybody who has ever been in the east has written about it, and it is utterly unbearable to read about it any more. They also agreed not to write sketches entitled: "The Legend of Lake Issyk-Kuhl." There were enough commonplaces of an oriental turn.

Alone on the deserted platform, among cigarette butts, torn notes, and the dust brought in from the desert, sat Koreiko. He could not decide to come down.

"Come on down, Alexander Ivanovich!" Ostap cried. "Take pity on yourself! How about a drop of cool Narzan? Eh? Don't you want any? Then at least take pity on me! I want to eat. I won't go away anyway. Perhaps you want me to sing you Schubert's serenade entitled 'Come to me with thy light tread, my friend.' I can."

But Koreiko did not wait for that. Even without the serenade it was clear to him that he would have to surrender the money. Bending over and stopping at each step, he began to come down.

"Are you wearing a three cornered hat?" Ostap jested. "And where is your gray marching coat? You can't imagine how I missed you! Well, how do you do, how do you do? Perhaps we'll kiss each other, or perhaps we'll go immediately to the store room, into the cave of *Lechtweiss,* where you are hiding your *toogriks!*"

"Let's dine first," said Koreiko, whose tongue had dried up from thirst and scratched like a rasp.

"All right, let's dine. But this time without any nonsense.

Of course, you have no chance of escape. My boys are lying behind the hills," Ostap lied, just to make sure.

And remembering his boys, he became sad.

The dinner for the builders and the guests was given in Eurasian style. The Kazaks found their places on rugs, their feet folded under them, as is done by everybody in the east, and in the west only by tailors. The Kazaks ate *plov* from white bowls, washing it down with lemonade. The Europeans sat down at the tables.

Much labor, care and worry had been endured by the builders of the railroad during the past two years. But no less trouble had been caused by the solemn dinner in the heart of the desert. The Asiatic and European menus were long discussed. The question of alcoholic drinks brought forth a lengthy debate. For several days the management of the construction job resembled the United States before a presidential election. Partisans of the dry and wet problem entered the ring. Finally they resolved against alcoholic drinks. Then a new consideration arose—foreigners, diplomats, Muscovites! How could they be fed in the nicest way? In their Londons and New Yorks they were accustomed to various culinary excesses. And so it was decided to import from Tashkent the old specialist Ivan Osipovich. At one time he had been maître d'hôtel in the famous establishment of Martyanych at Moscow, but now he was spending his remaining days as manager of a restaurant near the Chicken Bazaar.

"Take care, Ivan Osipovich," he was told by the management. "We are depending on you. There will be foreigners. We have to make a good job of it, and rather elegant!"

"Take my word for it," muttered the old man with tears in his eyes. "What people I have fed in my day! I have fed the Prince of Württemberg! I don't even want any money. How can I refuse the opportunity of feeding people at least once more in the declining days of my life. I'll feed them this once and die!"

Ivan Osipovich grew frightfully worried. When he learned of the final decision against alcoholic drinks he almost fell ill. But he could not leave Europe without its dinner. The budget he presented was considerably cut down, but the old man whispered under his nose, "I'll feed them and die," and added sixty rubles from his own savings. On the day of the dinner Ivan Osipovich arrived in a cutaway that reeked of naphthalene. During the meeting he was nervous, looked at the sun from time to time, and shouted at the nomads who, from sheer curiosity, attempted to ride on horseback into the dining room. The old man waved his napkin at them and sobbed:

"Go away, Mamai! Can't you see what's going on? Oh, Lord! The sauce piquante will curdle! And the consommé isn't ready!"

Hors d'œuvres were already on the tables. Everything was served very beautifully and very expertly. Stiff napkins stood up like cones. On ice in glass plates lay the butter, twisted into boutonnières. The herrings held hoops of onions or olives in their mouths. There were flowers. Even the ordinary gray bread looked very presentable.

Finally the guests appeared at the tables. Everybody was dusty, red from the heat, and very hungry. No one resembled the Prince of Württemberg. Ivan Osipovich suddenly sensed the approach of disaster.

"I ask the guests' pardon," he said ingratiatingly. "Five minutes more and we shall begin to dine. I have a personal appeal to make to you. Please don't touch anything on the tables before dinner, so that everything may be done as it should be."

He ran away into the kitchen for a moment, pirouetting in worldly fashion, but when he returned, carrying a platter of fish on parade, he beheld a horrible scene: the table was being ravished. This failed to resemble Ivan Osipovich's plans for the ceremonial of acceptance of food to such an extent that he stood stock still. The Englishman with the tennis-player's waistline was nonchalantly eating bread and butter, while Heinrich was bending across the tables and pulling olives out of the herrings' mouths with his fingers. Everything was mixed up on the tables. The guests who had satisfied their first hunger were gayly exchanging impressions.

"What is this?" the old man asked in a faint voice.

"Where is the soup, papa darling?" cried Heinrich, his mouth full.

Ivan Osipovich did not reply. He merely waved his napkin and went away. Further cares he passed on to the shoulders of his subordinates. As the two schemers made their way to a table, a fat man with a nose that hung down like a banana, delivered the first speech. To Ostap's extreme surprise he recognized Engineer Talmudovsky.

"Yes! We are heroes!" Talmudovsky exclaimed, stretching before him a glass of Narzan. "Greetings to you, builders of the railroad! But what are the conditions of our work? Let us say, for example, our salaries? I am not arguing; the salaries at the railroad are better than in other places. But what about cultural conveniences? There is no theater! A desert! No canalization! No, I cannot work under such conditions!"

"Who is he?" the builders asked one another. "Do you know him?"

In the meantime Talmudovsky had already pulled out two suitcases from under the table.

"To hell with the agreement!" he cried, making his way to the exit. "What? Return the advance? We'll fight it out in court! We'll fight it out in court!"

And while he was pushing the diners with his suitcases, instead of "Pardon," he cried viciously, "We'll fight it out in court!"

Late that night he was rolling along in a hand car, having joined the railroad foremen who were riding on business to the southern end of the railroad. Talmudovsky sat astride his suitcases and explained to the foremen the reasons why an honest specialist could not work in that hole. Maître d'hôtel Ivan Osipovich was riding home with them. In his grief he had not even removed his cutaway. He was very drunk.

"Barbarians!" he cried, pushing his head out into the razor-like wind and shaking his fist threateningly in the direction of Gremyashchii Klyuch. "All that service for lousy swine! I fed Anton Pavlovich, the Prince of Württemberg! . . . I'll go home and die! Then they'll remember Ivan Osipovich! 'Serve a banquet table for eighty-four persons,' they will say. The lousy swine! And there'll be nobody to do it! There will be no Ivan Osipovich Trikartov! Dead! Gone to a better world where there is no disease, no grief, no sighs, but only life eternal. . . . Blessed me-mor-y . . ."

The old man chanted a requiem over himself, and the tails of his cutaway crackled like pennants in the wind.

Ostap did not let Koreiko finish his compote. He dragged him from the table to settle the account. They climbed a step ladder and crawled into the freight car where the office of the Northern tracklayers was located and where stood the time-keeper's folding bed. They shut the door.

After dinner while the passengers were resting, gathering strength for participation in the evening celebration, the columnist Gargantua caught the brother correspondents at a forbidden task. Lev Rubashkin and Jan Skameikin were carrying two pieces of paper to the telegraph. On one of them was the following brief information:

"urgent moscow steppe telegraph dash uzun hyphen kulak quote long ear unquote carried to villages news meeting rails main line rubashkin"

The second paper was written from top to bottom. It contained:

"legend lake issyk hyphen kuhl stop old kar hyphen kalpak ukhun bukheyev told me this legend permeated breathing ages stop two hundred thousand four hundred eighty five moons ago young fleetfoot like dzheiran paren mountain sheep unparen wife khan beauty sumburun passionately loved young nuker ai hyphen bulak stop great grief old khan when he discovered treason passionately beloved wife stop oldster prayed twelve moons then eyes tearful sealed beauty barrel attaching hunk pure gold weighing seven dzhasasyns paren eighteen kilos unparen flung precious burden mountainlake stop hence lake called issyk hyphen kuhl comma signifying quote heart beauty tends treasonward unquote skameikin"

"Isn't it so?" asked Gargantua, displaying the little papers he had confiscated from the brothers. "Am I right?"

"Of course! Scandalous!" replied Palamidov. "How did you dare to write that legend after all that had been agreed upon? According to you, Issyk-Kuhl means 'the heart of a beauty that tends toward treason and change.' But is it so? Didn't Kara-Kalpak Ukhun Bukheyev lie to you? Shouldn't it rather be translated: 'don't throw young beauties into lakes,' but instead 'throw the gullible correspondents who yield to the dangerous influence of exoticism'?"

The writer in the childish coat turned red. In his note books, Uzun-Kulak and two odorous legends garnished with eastern ornamentation were already duly inscribed.

"I don't think there's anything terrible about it," he said. "Since Uzun-Kulak exists, shouldn't somebody write about it?"

"But it's been written about a thousand times!" said Lavoizian.

"Uzun-Kulak exists," sighed the writer. "And one must take that into consideration."

Chapter Thirty

ALEXANDER IBN IVANOVICH

In the dark, hot freight car the air was as thick and heavy as in an old shoe. It smelled of leather and feet. Koreiko lighted a conductor's lantern and crawled under the bed. Sitting on an empty macaroni box, Ostap watched him thoughtfully. Both schemers were worn out by the struggle and regarded the event which Koreiko had feared extremely, and for which Bender had waited all his life, with an affectation of calmness. One might even have thought that the business was being transacted in a coöperative store, that the customer had asked for headgear and the clerk had negligently thrown out on the counter a sleazy cap of nondescript color. He doesn't care whether the buyer takes the cap or not, and the buyer is not excited, and merely to calm his conscience asks, "Haven't you any other?", to which he receives the customary reply, "Take it, take it! Pretty soon there won't even be this!", and both of them regard each other with utter indifference. Koreiko busied himself under the bed for a long time, evidently unfastening the cover of the suitcase and digging in it blindly.

"Hey, you, there on the schooner!" Ostap cried wearily. "What good luck that you don't smoke! To ask a cigarette from a tightwad like you would be utter torture. You would never offer a cigarette case, fearing that, instead of one cigarette, several would be taken. But you would dig in your pocket for a long time, opening the cover of the box with great effort and pulling out one, pathetic, crumpled cigarette.

You are a mean one! Why don't you pull out the whole suit-case?"

"Anything else?" growled Koreiko, stifling under the bed. He resented the odious allusion to the smoker.

He was pulling fat little packages out of the suitcase, and the nickeled tongue of the lock scratched his arms, which were bare to the elbow. For convenience he lay down on his back and continued to work, like a miner in a drift. Chaff and other straw trash, full of whiskers of grain and dust, flew out of the mattress.

"Oh, this is pretty bad," thought Alexander Ivanovich. "Pretty bad! Terrible! And suppose he chokes me now, and takes all my money away! It would be very simple. He'd cut me into parts and ship them by slow freight to various cities. And the head he'd pickle in a barrel of cabbage!"

The dampness of a cellar ran through Koreiko. He looked out from under the bed in terror. Bender dozed on his box, his head nodding toward the railroad lantern.

"But perhaps I shall send *him* by slow freight," thought Alexander Ivanovich gruesomely, continuing to pull out the packages. "To different cities; in strict confidence. What?"

He looked out again. The great schemer stretched out and yawned desperately, like a dog. Then he picked up the con-ductor's lantern and began to swing in, crying out:

"Station Khatsepetovka! Step out, citizen! We have arrived. By the way, I have entirely forgotten to tell you something. Perhaps you intend to cut my throat. I want you to know I'm opposed to it. And besides, I've been killed once already. There was a rattle-brained old man of good family, a former leader of the nobility, and later a clerk of the marriage bureau, by the name of Kisa Vorobyaninov. He and I were partners in a search for happiness that involved the sum of a hundred and fifty thousand rubles, and just before we came to a mutual agreement as to how we were to share the sum, yet unob-tained, the foolish old leader of the nobility slashed my neck with a razor. Oh, how vulgar that was, Koreiko! Vulgar and painful! Surgeons fought to save my young life, for which I am profoundly grateful to them."

Finally Koreiko crawled out from under the bed, pushing the packages of money to Ostap's feet. Each package was neatly sealed in white paper and bound with stout cord.

"Ninety-nine packages," said Koreiko in a tragic voice. "Ten thousand in each, in denominations of twenty-five *chervontsy*. You need not check it. I conduct business with the efficiency of a bank."

"But where is the one hundredth package?" the enthusiastic Ostap asked in dismay.

"I deducted ten thousand because of the robbery by the seashore."

"Well, that is sheer piggishness! The money was spent on you! Don't be a formalist!"

Koreiko, sighing, gave him the rest of the money, in exchange for which he received a yellow portfolio tied with shoe laces containing the story of his life. He burned the life-story right there in the iron stove, the stack of which went out through the roof of the car. In the meanwhile Ostap took one of the packages, tore open the cover, and, convinced that Koreiko was not deceiving him, shoved it into his pocket.

"But where is the *valuta?*" the great schemer asked capriciously. "Where are the Mexican dollars, the Turkish lire, the pounds, rupees, pesetas, centavos, Roumanian leis? Where are the Limitrophian latis, and zlotys? Let me have at least a part in *valuta*.

"Better take what you get," replied Koreiko, sitting before the stove and staring at the documents that were wrinkling in the fire. "Take it. Pretty soon there won't be even that. I don't keep any *valuta*."

"And so I'm a millionaire!" Ostap exclaimed in gay surprise. "The dreams of an idiot have come true!"

Suddenly Ostap grew sad. He was astounded by the dinginess of his surroundings. It seemed strange to him that the world did not change at that very moment, and that nothing, simply nothing had happened around him. And although he knew that in our stern times he could not expect any mysterious grottoes, barrels of gold and Aladdin's lamps, still he felt sorry about something. He was a bit bored, like Roald Amundsen when he was flying in the dirigible "Norge" over the North Pole, toward which he had been making his way all his life. He turned to one of his fellow-passengers and said calmly, "Well, here we are." Below him was broken ice, crevasses, frost, emptiness. The secret has been discovered; the goal has been reached. There is nothing else to do. One must change one's profession. But grief is evanescent, because before him is fame, honor and respect. Choruses resound; school girls in white capes line the way on either side. Old mothers of Polar explorers eaten by their companions—weep. National hymns are sung. Rockets flare. And the old king presses the explorer to his prickly medals and stars. . . .

The weakness of the moment passed. Ostap threw the packages into a little bag which Alexander Ivanovich graciously offered him, put it under his arm and rolled back the heavy door of the freight car.

The celebration was nearing its end. Rockets cast their golden fishing poles into the sky, reeling in red and green fishes. Cold fire sprayed the eyes. Pyrotechnic suns swirled. Beets burst into salads of glistening tomatoes and yellow asparagus. On a wooden stage behind the telegraph hut was a performance for the nomads. Some of them sat on benches, others watched the performance from their saddles. The horses neighed frequently. The special train was lighted from its tail to its head.

"Oh, yes!" exclaimed Ostap. "The banquet in the dining car! I quite forgot about it. What joy! Come, Koreiko! It is my treat. I am treating everybody! According to the laws of hospitality! Cognac with lemon, game dumplings, quenelle with champignons, old Hungarian wine, new Hungarian wine, champagne!"

"Quenelle! Quenelle!" Koreiko said angrily. "And then they'll put you in jail! I don't want to advertise myself."

"I promise you a supper in Paradise on a white tablecloth," Ostap insisted. "Come on! Forget your hermit life. Hurry! Drink your share of alcoholic liquors! Eat your twenty thousand meat balls! Otherwise strangers will come and eat your share of life. I'll fix you up in the special train. I'm one of them! And to-morrow we shall be in a comparatively civilized place. And there, with our millions . . . Alexander Ivanovich! . . ."

The great schemer wanted to load everybody with presents right away. He wanted everybody to be gay. Koreiko's funereal face dampened his spirits, and he began to persuade Alexander Ivanovich. He agreed that one should not advertise himself, but why should one starve himself? Ostap himself did not know why he needed the gloomy timekeeper, but having begun, he could not stop. He finally wound up by threatening him.

"You'll be sitting on your suitcase, and one fine day the Bony One will come for you, and hit you over the neck with his scythe! What a sight that will be! Hurry, Alexander Ivanovich, the meat balls are still on the table! Don't be a die-hard!"

After the loss of the million Koreiko was somewhat softer and more amenable to reason.

"Well," he said without assurance. "Perhaps I really should take an airing. Take a ride to Moscow. But of course, without any ostentation."

"Ostentation?! Two physicians, who are social workers, go to Moscow in order to visit the Art Theater and behold with their own eyes a mummy in a Museum of Fine Arts! Get your suitcase!"

The millionaires entered the train. Ostap swung his bag

carelessly like a censer. Alexander Ivanovich smiled foolishly.
The passengers of the special train walked back and forth,
keeping as close as possible to the cars, because the engine was
already being coupled. The white trousers of the correspondents gleamed in the darkness.

Under a sheet on Ostap's upper berth lay a man who was
a stranger to him, reading a newspaper.

"Well, get down," Ostap said amicably. "The boss has
come."

"This is my place, Comrade," replied the stranger. "I am
Lev Rubashkin!"

"You know what, Lev Rubashkin? I don't advise you to
cross me. Get out!"

The great schemer was impelled to strife by the perplexed
expression on the face of Alexander Ivanovich.

"What do you think of that?" the correspondent said
haughtily. "Who are you?"

"It is none of your business, dog! You've been told to get
down, so get down!"

Rubashkin began to scream, "Any drunkard who comes
here to raise Cain . . ."

Ostap silently grasped the correspondent's bare foot. Rubashkin's cries brought a crowd into the coupé. Koreiko
slipped out to the platform of the car.

"Are you fighting?" asked Ukhudshansky. "Well, well!"

Ostap, who had already hit Rubashkin over the head with
his bag, was seized by Gargantua and the fat writer in the
childish coat.

"Let him show his ticket!" the great schemer shouted for
all he was worth. "Let him show his sleeper receipt!"

Rubashkin, utterly naked, jumped from one berth to another, demanding the commandant of the train. Ostap, who
had entirely lost all connection with reality, also insisted on
calling out the administration. The scandal ended with great
unpleasantness. Rubashkin produced his ticket and his sleeper

receipt, and then, in a tragic voice, demanded the same from Bender.

"But I won't show it on principle!" declared the great schemer, hastily deserting the scene of action. "These are my principles!"

"Stowaway!" screamed Lev Rubashkin, jumping stark naked into the corridor. "I call your attention, comrade commandant! A stowaway rode here!"

"Where is the stowaway?" announced the commandant, whose eyes gleamed like a hunter's.

Alexander Ivanovich, who had hidden himself behind the platform in terror, peered into the darkness but could distinguish nothing. Near the train figures moved about, cigarette lights jumped, and voices were heard:

"Please be so kind as to show it"

"But I tell you I won't on principle!"

"Hooliganism!"

"Isn't it right?"

"Why shouldn't someone ride without a ticket?"

The buffer plates knocked close to the ground. Hissing, the air from the brakes ran past, and the lighted windows of the cars began to move. Ostap still blustered, but the striped seats with their baggage nets, train porters with lanterns, bouquets, and the fans on the ceilings of the dining car were already passing by him. The banquet with its champagne, with its old and new Hungarian wine was riding away. Game dumplings were torn from his hands and flew into the night. Quenelle, the delicate quenelle of which Ostap had spoken so warmly, forsook Gremyashchii Klyuch. Alexander Ivanovich approached Ostap.

"I shan't let this pass!" Ostap grumbled. "They have abandoned a correspondent of the Soviet press in the desert! I'll rouse public opinion! Koreiko! We are leaving on the very next express train. We shall buy all the places in the *wagon-lit.*"

"What are you talking about?" said Koreiko. "There is no express train. There are no trains from here at all! According to plans, operations will not begin for two months."

Ostap lifted his head. He saw above him the black Abyssinian sky, the wild stars, and he understood everything. But recollection of the proposed banquet which he had described to Koreiko gave him new strength.

"There's an airplane behind the hills," he remembered. "The one that arrived for the celebration. It won't leave before dawn. We shall have time."

In order to arrive on time, the millionaires moved at a broad dromedary pace. Their feet slid over the sands. Here and there burned the bonfires of the nomads. And to drag the suitcase in a sack was not merely tiring but extremely annoying. As they crawled up the hill from Gremyashchii Klyuch, dawn began to break from the other side, to the clatter of propellers. Bender and Koreiko ran down the hill, fearful lest the airplane would fly away without them.

Under the airplane's high wings that looked like roofs walked small mechanics in leather coats. Three propellers turned slowly, fanning the desert. On the square windows of the passengers' cabin swayed curtains trimmed with little plush balls. The pilot leaned idly against the aluminum step, eating a *pirozhok*, and drinking Narzan mineral water out of the bottle.

"We are passengers!" shouted Ostap, out of breath. "Two first-class tickets!"

Nobody replied. The pilot threw away the bottle and began to put on his gauntlets.

"Are there any places?" Ostap repeated, seizing the pilot's arm.

"We accept no passengers," said the pilot, grasping the railing of the ladder. "This is a special flight."

"I'm buying the airplane!" the great schemer announced quickly. "Wrap it up in paper!"

"Get out of the way!" shouted the mechanic, entering after the pilot.

The propellers disappeared in the fast swirling. Trembling and wobbling, the airplane began to make its way against the wind. The hurricane of air pushed the millionaires back to the hill. Ostap's captain's cap flew off and rolled toward India with such speed that one could have expected its arrival in Calcutta within not less than three hours. And it would have rolled thus into the principal street of Calcutta, its mysterious appearance evoking the attention of circles close to the intelligence service, if the airplane had not flown away and the hurricane quieted down. The ribs of the plane gleamed in the air and disappeared in the sunlight. Ostap ran after the cap which clung to a bush of *saksaul* and said:

"Transportation has slipped out of our hands. We have quarreled with the railroad. Communications by air are closed to us. On foot? Seven hundred kilometers! That is not inspiring. There remains only one thing: to accept Islam and advance on camels."

Koreiko said nothing about Islam, but he liked the thought of camels. The enticing glimpse of a dining car and an airplane had confirmed his desire to undertake the pleasure trip of a physician and social worker, of course, without any ostentation, but not without a certain dash.

The villagers who had arrived for the meeting of the rails had not yet departed, and the millionaires managed to buy the camels not far from Gremyashchii Klyuch. The ships of the desert cost them a hundred and eighty rubles apiece.

"How cheap!" Ostap whispered. "Let's buy fifty camels, or a hundred!"

"That's ostentation," replied Alexander Ivanovich darkly. "What would we do with them? Two are enough."

With shouts and cries, the Kazaks placed the travelers between the humps, and helped them to tie on the suitcase, the bag, and provision for the road—a skin of mares' milk and two sheep. At first the camels rose on their hind legs, causing the millionaires to bow low, and then on their front legs, and began to walk down the tracks of the Turkestan Railroad. The sheep, which were tied with ropes in the back, were very much afraid, dropping little balls from time to time, and bleating heartrendingly.

"Hey, Sheikh Koreiko! Alexander Ibn Ivanovich! Isn't life splendid?"

The sheikh did not reply. He happened to have drawn a recalcitrant camel and was beating it viciously across its mangy side with a *saksaul* stick.

Chapter Thirty-one

BAGDAD

FOR seven days the camels carried the two sheikhs through the desert. At the beginning of the journey Ostap's heart overflowed with joy. Everything amused him: Alexander Ibn Ivanovich, dangling between the camel's hillocks, and the recalcitrant ship of the desert which tried to evade its duties, and the bag containing the million, with which the great schemer struck the rebellious sheep to encourage them. Ostap called himself Colonel Lawrence.

"I am Emir Dynamite!" he cried, swaying on his high perch. "If we don't find decent food in two days, I shall rouse some tribes to rebellion. Upon my word! I shall appoint myself representative of the prophet and will declare a holy war, a *djikhad!* For example, against the Danes! Why did the Danes torture their Prince Hamlet? Under contemporary political conditions, even the League of Nations would be satisfied with such a pretext for war. So help me God, I'll buy a millions' worth of rifles from the English—they love to sell firearms to tribes—and march, march right into Denmark! Germany will let me through—on account of reparations. Can you imagine the invasion of tribes in Copenhagen? I shall ride on a white camel at the head of all! Ekh! There is no Panikovsky! How he would appreciate a Danish goose!"

But several days later, when only the ropes remained of the sheep, and the mares' milk had all been drunk, Emir Dynamite grew sad and muttered lugubriously:

"In the sandy wastes of the Arabian land, grew three proud palms . . . Why? . . . I can't understand!"

Both sheikhs became very thin, tattered, overgrown with little beards, and began to resemble dervishes from a poor parish.

"A little more patience, Ibn Koreiko, and we shall reach a little city that is no worse than Bagdad. Flat roofs, native orchestras, restaurants in eastern style, sweet wines, legendary damsels and forty thousand spits with *shashlyks* of Karsk, Turkish, Tatar, Mesopotamian and Odessa varieties. And finally, the railroad!"

On the eighth day the travellers reached an ancient cemetery. To the very horizon rows of semicircular graves stretched in waves of stone. The corpses were not buried there. They were placed on the ground and stone cowls were erected over them. A frightful heat beat upon the ashen city of the dead. The ancient East lay in its hot graves. The schemers slapped their camels and before long rode into an oasis. The city was lighted by green torches of poplars, reflected in square rice fields drenched in water. Cranes stood about, lonely, looking like gigantic globes on wooden pedestals. They began to meet little asses bearing fat riders in long robes, and bundles of clover.

They rode past little stores that sold powdered green tobacco and stinking conical soap that looked like tips of shrapnel. Tradesmen with white muslin beards busied themselves over sheets of copper, turning them into bowls and narrow-necked pitchers. Shoemakers dried small pieces of leather, painted with ink in the sun. Dark blue, yellow and azure tiles of mosques gleamed in a thin glassy light.

The millionaires spent the remainder of the day and night sleeping heavily and senselessly in the hotel. In the morning they bathed in white bathtubs, shaved, and went into the city. The cloudless mood of the sheikhs was spoiled by the necessity of dragging the suitcase and the bag with them wherever they went.

"I consider it my first duty," bragged Bender, "to acquaint

you with a magic cellar. It is called 'Beneath the Moon.' I was here five years ago and gave anti-abortion lectures. What a cellar! Semi-darkness, coolness, a masterly chef from Tiflis, a local orchestra, cold vodka, and dancers with tambourines and cymbals. Let's go there for a day. Even physicians interested in social work can have their little weaknesses. It's my treat. For the first time the Little Golden Calf is responsible for all!"

And the great schemer shook his bag.

However, the cellar, "Beneath the Moon," was no more. To Ostap's surprise, the street on which the tambourines and the cymbals had once rung out no longer existed. Here ran a straight European street which was being built up along its entire length. Fences stood here, alabaster dust hung over everything, and trucks heated the air that was already sufficiently incandescent without them. Glancing for a moment at the façades of gray brick and long sprawling windows, Ostap nudged Koreiko and said:

"There is still another place, kept by a man from Baku."

He led him to the other end of the city. But the poetic sign composed personally by the innkeeper from Baku no longer hung over the place:

> Respect yourself,
> Respect us.
> Respect the Caucasus,
> Visit us.

Instead, the sheikhs observed a cardboard placard in Arabic and Russian: "City Museum of Fine Arts."

"Let's go in," said Ostap sadly. "At least it will be cool. And furthermore, visiting the museums enters into the program of traveling physicians who are also social workers."

They entered a large room whitened with chalk, dropped their millions on the floor, and mopped their hot foreheads with their sleeves for a long time. There were only eight pieces in the museum: the tooth of a mammoth presented to the young museum by the city of Tashkent, an oil painting entitled "A Skirmish with the Basmach," two emir robes, a gold fish in a bowl, a showcase containing dried locusts, a porcelain statuette from the Kuznetsov factory, and finally, the model of the obelisk which this city intended to place in the main square. At the foot of the model lay a large, slender wreath tied with ribbons. It had been brought not long ago by a special delegation from a neighboring republic. But since the obelisk did not yet exist (the money assigned for it went for the construction of a public bath house, the need for which was much more pressing), the delegation, delivering the proper speeches, had placed the wreath upon the model.

The visitors were immediately approached by a youth whose shaven head was covered by a Bokhara cap made of a bit of carpet, and who, agitated as an author, inquired:

"What are your impressions, Comrades?"

"Not bad," said Ostap.

The young man was in charge of the museum, and without any hesitation began to talk about the difficulties which his child had to face. There was not enough credit. Tashkent had given them only the tooth, and there was no one to collect artistic and historical specimens. And the specialist had not yet arrived.

"If I had three hundred rubles!" cried the manager. "I should make a Louvre of it here!"

"Tell me, do you know the city well?" asked Ostap, winking at Alexander Ivanovich. "Couldn't you show us some of the sights? I used to know your city, but it has changed somewhat."

The manager was overjoyed. Shouting that he would show

them everything personally, he closed and locked the museum and led the millionaires to the very street on which a half hour previously they had sought the cellar "Beneath the Moon."

"Socialist Avenue!" he announced, inhaling the alabaster dust with pleasure. "Akh! What marvelous air! And what there will be here a year from now! Asphalt! Autobuses! Irrigation Institute! Tropical Institute! Well, if Tashkent dares this time not to give us scientific aid! . . . Do you know, they have so many mammoth bones! But they sent me only one tooth! And there is such an urge in our republic for the study of natural science!"

"Is that so?" remarked Koreiko, looking reproachfully at Ostap.

"And do you know," the enthusiast whispered, "I suspect that it is not a mammoth tooth! I believe that they gave us an elephant's tooth!"

"And what about those . . . cabarets of the Asiatic kind? You know, with tympans and flutes?" the great schemer asked impatiently.

"We've outlived those," the youth answered with equanimity. "We should have long ago wiped out that infection, that morass of epidemics! This spring we choked the last of them. It was called 'Beneath the Moon.' "

"Choked it?" Koreiko despaired.

"Word of honor! But instead we opened a kitchen-factory. European food! The plates are washed and dried with the aid of electricity. The curve of stomach diseases has gone down sharply."

"What's happening!" exclaimed the great schemer, covering his face with his hands.

"You haven't seen anything yet," said the museum manager, laughing modestly. "Let's have dinner at the kitchen-factory!"

They sat down in a carriage under a tasseled top, embroidered around the edge with blue, and drove away. Along the road the courteous guide compelled the millionaires to stick their heads out from under the baldachin every minute and showed them buildings that were already up, buildings in the process of construction, and places where buildings were going to be erected. Koreiko regarded Ostap with angry eyes. Ostap turned away and said:

"What a marvelous little native bazaar! Bagdad!"

"On the seventeenth of this month we shall begin to take it down," said the young man. "We shall have a hospital and a coöperative center there."

"And aren't you sorry to lose this exoticism? It's Bagdad!"

"Very beautiful!" Koreiko sighed.

The young man became angry.

"It's beautiful for you, the tourists, but we must live here!"

In the large hall of the kitchen-factory, in the midst of tiled walls, under ribbons of fly paper that hung from the ceiling, the travelers ate barley soup and small brown chops. Ostap inquired about wine, but received the exultant reply that not long ago a source of mineral water had been discovered near the city which excelled the famous Narzan in taste. As proof, a bottle of this water was demanded and drunk in grave silence.

"And how is the curve of prostitution?" Alexander Ibn Ivanovich asked hopefully.

"It has gone down sharply," replied the implacable young man.

"My, what's going on!" said Ostap with a false laugh.

But he actually did not know what was going on. When they rose from the table, it appeared that the young man had already paid for everybody. Under no circumstances would he accept money from the millionaires, assuring them that the day after to-morrow he would receive his salary anyway, and that until then he would manage somehow.

"Well, and how about entertainment? How does the city

entertain itself?" Ostap asked, this time without ecstasy. "Tympans, cymbals?"

"Don't you know?" the museum manager asked in surprise. "Last week our local Philharmonic Orchestra opened. Then there is a large symphonic quartette named after Bebel and Paganini. Let's go at once. I can't understand how I overlooked it."

After he had paid for the dinner it was impossible, for ethical reasons, to decline a visit to the Philharmonic. When they left, Alexander Ibn Ivanovich said rudely:

"Local phizharmonic!"

The great schemer turned red.

On the way to the hotel the young man suddenly stopped the carriage, forced the millionaires to get out, took them by the hand and, carried on wings of exultation, brought them on tiptoe to a little stone surrounded by a small wire enclosure.

"Here will stand the obelisk!" he said significantly. "The column of Marxism."

Bidding them good-by, the young man invited them to come frequently. The good-natured Ostap promised to come without fail, assuring him that never before had he spent such an enjoyable day.

"I'm going to the railroad station," announced Koreiko, when they were alone.

"Shall we go to another city for a good time?" asked Ostap. "In Tashkent we might be able to spend three days gayly."

"I've had enough," replied Alexander Ivanovich. "I'm going to the station to give up my suitcase for safekeeping. I'll get a job somewhere as a clerk. I'm going to wait for capitalism. Then I'll have a good time."

"Well, wait if you like," said Ostap rather ungraciously. "But I'm going away. To-day was a regrettable misunderstanding due to local deviations. The Little Golden Calf still has some power in our land!"

At the railroad station they saw the crowd of correspondents who, after the meeting of the rails, were making an excursion into Central Asia. They all surrounded Ukhudshansky. The possessor of "The Complete Celebrator" was turning around with self-satisfaction, exhibiting his acquisitions. He wore a velvet hat trimmed with a jackal's tail, and a robe made of a cotton quilt.

The predictions of the plush-nosed prophet continued to be fulfilled.

Chapter Thirty-two

THE GATES OF GREAT POSSIBILITIES

ON the sad and brilliant autumn day when gardeners in Moscow squares cut flowers and give them to the children, the chief son of Lieutenant Schmidt, Shura Balaganov, slept on a bench in the waiting room of the Kazan Railroad. He lay with his head on the small wooden crosspiece. His mangled cap was pushed over his nose. All evidence pointed to the fact that the mechanic of the Antelope and hoof expert was unhappy and poor. A bit of egg-shell stuck to his unshaven cheek. The canvas shoes had lost their shape and color and resembled Moldavian *postols*.

Swallows flew under the high ceiling of the hall which was illuminated by two lamps. Beyond the large, unwashed windows could be seen obstructions, semaphores and other articles indispensable to railroads. Porters ran out, and soon the population of the newly-arrived train streamed through the hall. The last to come in from the platform was a passenger in clean clothes. A light mackintosh, unbuttoned, revealed a suit in the tiniest, kaleidoscopic checks. The trousers fell in a waterfall over patent leather shoes. The foreign appearance of the passenger was completed by a soft hat, slightly tipped to one side. He did not take advantage of the services of the porters and carried his suitcase himself. The passenger walked lazily through the deserted hall and undoubtedly would have gone out of the station, if he had not suddenly noticed the pathetic figure of Balaganov. He narrowed his eyes, came closer, and for some time examined the sleeper. Then, carefully, with two gloved fingers, he lifted the cap from the face of the mechanic and smiled.

"Arise, Count! Great affairs await you!" he said, shaking Balaganov.

Shura sat up, rubbed his face with his hands, and only then recognized the passenger.

"Commander!" he cried.

"No, no," Bender remarked, protecting himself with the palm of his hand. "Don't embrace me. I'm a haughty man now!"

Balaganov capered around the commander. He could hardly recognize him. Not only was the suit changed, but Ostap was thinner, his eyes seemed distracted, and his face was covered with a colonial tan.

"You're brown!" Balaganov cried out joyously. "My, how brown you've become!"

"Yes, I've become brown," Bender announced with dignity. "Look at my trousers. Europe! A-1! And do you see this? The ring finger of my left hand is adorned with a diamond! Four carats! Well, what are *your* attainments? Are you still a son?"

"So, so," Shura stammered. "Mostly little things."

At the buffet Ostap ordered white wine and cookies for himself, beer and sandwiches for the mechanic.

"Tell me honestly, Shura, how much money do you need for happiness?" asked Ostap. "Only, be sure to figure in everything."

"A hundred rubles," replied Balaganov, regretfully tearing himself away from his bread and sausage.

"But no! You didn't understand me. Not just for to-day, but in general. For happiness! Is it clear? So that you will live well in the world."

Balaganov thought a long time, smiling timidly, and finally announced that for complete happiness he needed six thousand four hundred rubles, and with that sum he would live well in the world.

"Very well," said Ostap. "Here's fifty thousand."

He opened the square traveling case on his knees and gave Balaganov five white packages tied with stout cord. The mechanic immediately lost his appetite. He stopped eating, hid the money in his pockets and kept his hands there.

"Was it really on a little plate?" he asked in admiration.

"Yes, yes, the little plate," replied Ostap with equanimity. "With a blue border. The defendant brought it in his teeth. He wagged his tail for a long time before I agreed to accept it. Now I am in command of the parade! I feel fine."

The last words were not said with conviction.

The parade, to tell the truth, was not going very well, and the great schemer lied when he asserted that he felt fine. It would have been more just to say that he sensed a certain embarrassment, which, however, he would not confess even to himself.

A month had passed since the day he had parted with Alexander Ivanovich at the hand baggage room where the underground millionaire had deposited his little suitcase.

In the very first city which Ostap had entered, feeling like a conqueror, he could not find a room at the hotel.

"I'll pay as much as you like," the great schemer had said haughtily.

"Nothing can be done about it, Citizen," the clerk had answered. "The entire Congress of Soil Experts has arrived to examine the Experiment Station. All the rooms are reserved for the representatives of science."

And the polite face of the clerk expressed his respect for the Congress. Ostap wanted to cry out that he was more important, that he should be respected and honored, that he had a million in his bag. But he restrained himself and went out into the street, extremely irritated. All day he rode through the city in droshkys. In the best restaurant he languished for an hour and a half, waiting for the soil experts, the entire congress of which was dining, to rise from the table. That night at the theater the entire show had been sold out to the soil experts, and other citizens could not get tickets. Besides, Ostap would not have been admitted into the theater with a bag in his hand, and he had no place to put it. In order not to sleep in the street in the interests of science, the millionaire departed that evening, sleeping in a wagon lit.

In the morning Ostap found himself in a large city on the Volga. Yellow transparent leaves fluttered from the trees and swirled in spirals to the ground. Wind blew from the Volga. There were no rooms whatever in any of the hotels.

"Perhaps in a month," said the various hotel managers, bearded and non-bearded, mustached and clean-shaven. "Until they fix up the Third Section at the electrical station, you won't find a room. Everything is taken by the specialists. And after that there will be the District Congress of the League of Communist Youth. We can't do anything for you."

While the great schemer stood at the high counters of the clerks, engineers, technicians, foreign specialists and members of the League of Communist Youth, delegates to the Congress hurried up and down the hotel stairways.

And again Ostap spent the day in a droshky, impatiently waiting for the express train where he could wash himself, rest and read a newspaper.

The great schemer passed fifteen nights in various trains going from one city to another, because nowhere could he find a room. In one place a blast furnace was being erected, in another an ice plant, in a third a zinc factory. Everything was filled with people of affairs. In the fourth place a Pioneers' camp meeting frustrated his plans, and in the room where the millionaire could have passed a pleasant evening with a woman companion, children were playing. In the course of his wanderings, he acquired property, bought a suitcase for his million, articles for traveling, and generally equipped himself. He had begun to consider a long, peaceful journey to Vladivostok, estimating that the trip there and back would take three weeks, when suddenly he felt that if he were not to touch ground immediately he would die of some strange railroad disease. And he did what he had always done when he had been the happy possessor of empty pockets. He began to pretend that he was somebody else, telegraphing ahead that an engineer or a physician-social-worker, or a tenor, or a writer was coming. To his surprise, rooms were found for all people who came on business, and Ostap rested from the long jolting on trains. On one occasion he had to present himself as a son of Lieutenant Schmidt in order to find a room. After this episode the great schemer fell into unhappy rumination.

"And this is the path of the millionaire!" he thought bitterly. "Where is the respect, where is the honor, where is the fame, where is the power?"

Even "Europe A-1," about which Ostap bragged to Balaganov—the suit, the shoes and the hat—had been bought in a commission shop and despite excellent quality had a flaw. They were not things made for him, not his own. They had been cast off by somebody else. Someone had worn them, perhaps only for an hour, or for a minute. Still, someone had worn them before. He was also aggrieved that the government paid no attention whatever to the pitiful state of millionaires, but distributed worldly goods according to plan. And in all ways, it was very bad. The station chief did not salute him as, in the old days, he had saluted any merchant with a capital of fifty thousand. The city fathers did not present themselves at his hotel. The press did not rush to interview him, and, instead of photographs of the millionaire, they printed the portraits of shock-brigaders who were earning a mere hundred and twenty rubles a month.

Every day Ostap counted his million, and still there was a million minus some small trifle. He did all in his power,

dined several times a day, drank precious wines, distributed
fantastic tips, bought a ring, a Japanese vase, and a skunk
fur coat. He had to make a present of the fur coat and the
vase to his valet de chambre because he did not like to be
bothered with large things while traveling. Besides, he could
have bought many more vases and fur coats whenever he
needed them. Still, he spent only six thousand throughout
the entire month.

No! The parade was decidedly not a success, though everything was in place. The troops of the line had been sent
out in time, all the units had arrived according to schedule,
the orchestra was playing. But the regiments did not look
at him. Not for him did they shout "Hurrah!" not for him
was the band master swinging his arms. However, Ostap did
not surrender. He placed great hope on Moscow:

"But what about Rio de Janeiro?" Balaganov asked excitedly. "Shall we go?"

"The devil take it!" Ostap said with unexpected anger.
"It's all a figment of the imagination! There is no Rio de
Janeiro! And there is no America! And there is no Europe!
And there is nothing! The waves of the Atlantic Ocean break
on Shepetovka[1]!"

"Well, well, well," Balaganov sighed.

"A certain doctor explained everything to me," Ostap continued. "The rest of the world is a myth about life beyond
the grave. He who goes abroad never returns!"

"It's simply a circus!" exclaimed Shura, understanding noth-
ing. "Ekh! What a fine time I'll have now! Poor Panikovsky!
Of course, he violated the pact . . . Well, God be with him!
How the old man would have enjoyed this!"

"I propose to honor the memory of the deceased by rising,"
said Ostap.

The foster brothers rose and stood in silence for a minute,

[1] Shepetovka, like Negoreloye, is the last border point on Soviet Russia's
western frontier.

looking down at the broken cookies and the unfinished sandwich.

The oppressive silence was broken by Balaganov.

"Do you know what happened to Kozlevich?" he said. "It's a regular circus. He actually put the Antelope together and is working in Chernomorsk. He sent me a letter. Here . . ."

The mechanic took the letter out of his cap.

"How do you do, Shura," wrote the driver of the Antelope. "How are you getting along? Are you still a son of Lt. Sch.? I'm getting along fine but I have no money. And after the overhauling, the machine has become temperamental and works only one hour a day. I'm fixing it all the time, and I simply can't stand it any more. The passengers are constantly complaining. Perhaps, dear Shura, you could send me an oil pipe, even if it's not a new one. I simply can't get it anywhere here at the market. I'm sure you can find it at the Smolensk market in the place where they sell old locks and keys. But if you're not getting along, come here and we'll manage somehow. My stand is at the corner of Mehring Street—at the Exchange. Where is O. B. now? Yours respectfully, Adam Kozlevich. I forgot to write that I was visited at the Exchange by the priests Kuszakowski and Moroszek. There was a scandal. A. K."

"Now I'll run out and try to find his oil pipe," Balaganov said solicitously.

"Don't bother," Ostap replied. "I'll buy him a new machine. Let's go to the Grand Hotel. I've reserved a room by telegraph for the conductor of a symphonic orchestra. As for you, we'll have to get you some clothes, wash you up, and give you a complete overhauling. Shura, before you are opening the gates of great possibilities!"

They went out on Kalanchev Square. There was no taxi. Ostap refused to ride in a droshky.

"That is the carriage of the past," he said with disgust.

"You cannot go far in it. Besides, tiny mice live under the cover!"

They had to take a street car. It was crowded. It was one of those cars infected with squabbles which frequently circulate throughout the capital. The squabble is usually begun by some vengeful old woman during the morning crush when people are bound for work. Gradually all the passengers in the car are involved in the squabble, even those who get there a half an hour after the beginning of the incident. The old woman has got out long ago; the cause of the squabble has long been forgotten; but the cries and the exchange of insults continue, and new detachments of passengers enter the wrangle. And in such a car, swearing doesn't stop until late into the night.

The excited passengers quickly separated Balaganov and Ostap, and soon the foster brothers dangled in different parts of the car, crushed by chests and baskets. Ostap hung on a strap, with difficulty pulling out the suitcase which was constantly being carried away by the flux. Suddenly, drowning the street car altercation, a woman's howl was heard from the side where Balaganov swayed:

"I've been robbed! Hold him! There he is!"

All heads turned. Enthusiasts, choking with curiosity, began to fight their way to the scene. Ostap glimpsed the dumbfounded face of Balaganov. The mechanic himself did not understand what had happened, but he had already been seized by the hand in which he firmly clutched a woman's cheap purse with a little brass chain.

"Bandit!" cried the woman. "I turned away and he . . ."

The possessor of fifty thousand had stolen a purse that contained a tortoise shell powder box, a trade union book, and one ruble seventy kopeks in cash. The car stopped. The enthusiasts pulled Balaganov to the exit. As he passed Ostap, Shura whispered bitterly:

"How did it happen? I did it mechanically."

"I'll show you—mechanically!" said an enthusiast with a portfolio and pince nez, lustily hitting the mechanic's neck.

Through the window Ostap saw a militia man quickly join the group and lead the criminal along the middle of the street.

The great schemer turned away.

Chapter Thirty-three

THE HINDU GUEST

IN the four-cornered, hedged-in yard of the Grand Hotel could be heard kitchen noises, the hissing of steam, and the cries, "Two teas for number sixteen!" but in the white corridors it was as calm and quiet as in the switchboard room of an electric station. In a hundred and fifty rooms slept the congress of soil experts, who had returned from the journey; thirty rooms had been dedicated to a delegation of foreign merchants who were trying to solve the sore subject: "Is it profitable to trade with the Soviet Union?" the best suite of four rooms was occupied by a famous Hindu poet and philosopher; and in a small room reserved for the conductor of the symphonic orchestra slept Ostap Bender.

He lay on the plush cover, fully dressed, pressing the suitcase with the million to his chest. During the night the great schemer had inhaled all the oxygen that the room contained, and the remaining chemical elements could be called nitrogen only out of politeness. The room was permeated with soured wine, malodorous meat balls, and something else that was inexpressibly vile. Ostap moaned and turned over. The suitcase dropped to the floor. Ostap quickly opened his eyes.

"What was that?" he muttered, making a grimace. "Swaggering in the dining hall! And even worse than swaggering! Fooh! I behaved like a merchant of the Second Guild. My God, I hope I didn't insult those present! Some fool cried, 'Soil experts, arise!' And then he wept and swore that, in his heart, he himself was a soil expert. Of course that was I! Yes, but why did I do it?"

And he remembered that yesterday, deciding to begin a

life that suited a millionaire, he had resolved to build himself a house in Moorish style. The morning passed in grandiose dreams. He imagined a house with minarets, a doorman with the face of a statue, a small drawing room, a billiard room, and some kind of a conference room. In the Soviet Land Department the great schemer learned that he could obtain a piece of land. But everything crashed in the Building Office. Down went the doorman, his stone face thundering, the golden conference room swayed, and the minarets fell to pieces.

"Are you a private person?" the millionaire was asked.

"Yes," Ostap replied. "I am distinctly individualistic!"

"I regret to inform you that we build only for collectives and organizations."

"Coöperative, social and economic?" Ostap asked bitterly.

"Yes, for them."

"And what am *I* to do?"

"You build for yourself."

"Very well. But where will I get stones, casement window bolts? Where will I get even skirting boards?"

"Find it somehow, although it is difficult. All the supplies have been distributed according to the demands of industry and the coöperatives."

This was probably the reason for his disgraceful swaggering that night.

Still lying down, Ostap took out his notebook and began to count up his expenditures since he had received the million. On the first page was a memorable inscription:

Camel	180 r.
Sheep............	30 r.
Mare's Milk	1 r. 75 k.
Total	211 r. 75 k.

It did not improve as he went on: a fur coat, railroad tickets, again a ticket, three turbans bought for a rainy day, droshky fees, a vase, and all sorts of trash. Not counting the fifty thousand he had given to Balaganov, and which had brought him no happiness, the million was still there.

"They simply will not let me make large investments!" Ostap exclaimed indignantly. "They won't let me! Perhaps I ought to begin to lead an intellectual life like my friend Lokhankin. After all, I have already acquired material wealth. I must now accumulate some spiritual wealth, little by little. I must immediately find out the meaning of life!"

He remembered that girls were crowding in the vestibule of the hotel all day, hoping to speak with the visiting Hindu philosopher about the soul.

"I'll go to the Hindu," he resolved. "I'll find out what's the point of it all. This, of course, is decadent, but there is no other way out."

Dressed as he was, in his crushed suit, and taking the suitcase along, Bender went down to the first floor and knocked at the door of the great man. He was met by an interpreter.

"Is the philosopher receiving?" Ostap asked.

"It depends whom," the interpreter replied politely. "Are you a private person?"

"No! No!" the great schemer said in alarm. "I represent a coöperative organization."

"Are you with a group? How many of you are there? Because, you know, it is very difficult for the Master to receive individual persons. He prefers to converse . . ."

"With a collective!" Ostap finished. "You see, the collective has delegated me to decide a very important question of principle concerning the meaning of life."

The interpreter went away and returned in five minutes. He pulled back the portières and said pompously:

"Enter, coöperative organization desiring to learn the significance of life."

In an easy chair with a high, uncomfortable, carved back,

sat the great philosopher and poet in a brown velvet robe and a turban of the same material. His swarthy face was delicate and his eyes were black, like a sub-lieutenant's. His beard, broad and long, covered his chest like the shirt front of a swallow tail. A stenographer sat at his feet. Two interpreters, a Hindu and an Englishman, stood at either side.

At the sight of Ostap and the suitcase, the philosopher began to fidget in his chair and whispered something excitedly to an interpreter. The stenographer began to record it rapidly, while the interpreter turned to the great schemer.

"The Master wishes to know whether the stranger is carrying songs and sagas in his suitcase, and whether he intends to read them aloud, because many songs and sagas have already been read to the Master and he cannot listen to any more of them."

"Tell the Master that I have no sagas," Ostap replied respectfully.

The black-eyed old man seemed more worried than ever, and speaking rapidly, pointed his finger with fear at the suitcase.

"The Master asks," began the interpreter, "whether the stranger intends to move into his room, because never before has anyone come to him for a reception with a suitcase."

And only after Ostap had reassured the interpreter, and the interpreter had reassured the philosopher, did the tenseness pass and the conversation begin.

"Before replying to your question about the significance of life," said the interpreter, "the Master wishes to say a few words about popular education in India."

"Please convey to the Master," Ostap declared, "that the problem of popular education has perturbed me since childhood."

The philosopher closed his eyes and began to speak in measured tones. Throughout the first hour he spoke English, but during the second hour he spoke Bengalese. At times he sang in a quiet, pleasant voice, while once he even rose and, raising his cassock, made several dance movements which apparently represented the play of school children in the Punjab. Then he sat down and again shut his eyes, while Ostap listened long to the translation. At first Ostap shook his head politely, then he looked sleepily at the window, and finally began to amuse himself by fingering the change in his pocket, admiring his ring, and even winking quite openly at the pretty stenographer, which caused her to scratch with her pencil faster than ever.

"But how about the significance of life?" asked the millionaire, snatching at the opportunity.

"First of all, the Master wishes to acquaint the stranger," explained the interpreter, "with the extensive materials which he has gathered while informing himself of the condition of popular education in the U.S.S.R."

"Please convey to his honor," Ostap replied, "that the stranger has no objections."

And again the machine was wound up. The Master spoke, sang Pioneer songs, displayed a wall newspaper with which he had been presented by the children of the 146th Labor School, and once even wept. The interpreters talked simultaneously, the stenographer wrote, and Ostap absentmindedly trimmed his finger nails.

Finally Ostap coughed aloud.

"Do you know," he said, "it is not necessary to translate any more. Somehow I have begun to understand the Bengal language. But when he begins to speak about the significance of life, then you may translate."

When Ostap's insistent desire was repeated to the philosopher, the black-eyed old man became excited.

"The Master says," declared the interpreter, "that he, himself, has come to your country in order to learn the significance of life. Only where popular education is placed on the heights that it is placed in your country, does life become significant. The collective . . ."

"Good-by," the great schemer said quickly. "Please convey to the Master that the stranger begs permission to depart immediately."

But the philosopher was already singing in a tender voice, "The March of Budyonny," which he had learned from Soviet children. And Ostap departed without permission.

"Krishna!" cried the great schemer, running around his room. "Vishnu! What's going on in the world? Where is the homespun truth? Am I a fool that understands nothing? And life passes foolishly, unsystematically? A real Hindu, if you please, knows everything about our extensive country, while I, like an operatic Hindu guest, repeat by rote one and the same thing: 'Uncounted lie the flaming diamonds in rocky treasure troves.' How vile!"

That day Ostap had his dinner without vodka, and for the first time left the suitcase in his room. Then he sat quietly on the window sill, watching with interest the ordinary passersby as they jumped like squirrels into autobuses.

At night the great schemer awakened suddenly and sat up in bed. It was quiet. Through the keyhole the melancholy strains of the "Boston" drifted from the restaurant.

"How did I ever forget it!" he exclaimed angrily.

Then he laughed, turned on the light and quickly wrote a telegram:

"Zosya, I was mistaken. I want to come. Reply Moscow, Grand Hotel."

He rang and asked that the telegram be sent immediately.

In the buffet room, the corridor servant acquainted himself with the contents of the telegram and, coming to the conclusion that the business was not urgent and could be attended to in the morning, fell asleep.

Zosya did not reply. And there was no response to other telegrams composed in the same desperate and lyric manner.

Chapter Thirty-four

FRIENDSHIP WITH YOUTH

THE train was bound for Chernomorsk.

The first passenger took off his coat, hung it on the brass hook of the baggage net, pulled off his boots, lifting his fat feet one after the other, almost to his very face, and put on slippers with tongues.

"Have you ever heard the story of a certain Voronezh land surveyor who proved to be a kinsman of the Japanese Mikado?" he asked, smiling cautiously.

The second and third passengers came closer. The fourth passenger was already lying on the upper berth under a prickly, raspberry-colored blanket, petulantly turning over the pages of an illustrated magazine.

"Haven't you really heard it? It was talked about a lot at one time. He was an ordinary land surveyor—had a wife, one room and a salary of a hundred and twenty rubles. His family name was Bigusov. He was an ordinary man . . . well, in no way remarkable, and, if you like, between you and me, rather boorish. One day he came back from work and in his room he found a Japanese in an excellent suit, between you and me, in eyeglasses, and, if you please, in snakeskin shoes, which was the latest fashion. 'Is your surname Bigusov?' the Japanese asked. 'Yes,' replied Bigusov. 'And your name and patronymic?' 'So and so,' he replied. 'Correct,' said the Japanese. 'In that case won't you please take off your *tolstofka* shirt. I have to examine your naked body.' 'With pleasure,' he complied. Well, speaking strictly among ourselves, before the Japanese could examine the body,

he immediately noticed the birthmark. You see, Bigusov had
a large birthmark on his side. The Japanese looked at it
through a magnifying glass, turned pale and said, 'I congratu-
late you, Citizen Bigusov, and permit me to deliver this
package and letter.' His wife, if you like to know, opened
the package and there, speaking among ourselves, was a
double-edged Japanese sword, lying in wood shavings. 'Why
do I get the sword?' asked the land surveyor. 'Read the
letter,' he says. 'It's all explained there. You are a Samaurai.'
Here it was Bigusov's turn to become pale. Voronezh, if you
like to know, is not a very large city. Speaking among ourselves, what treatment can you expect them to give a Samaurai? Only the worst! But it couldn't be helped. Bigusov
took the letter, broke the fourteen wax seals, and read it.
What do you think? It appeared that exactly thirty-six years
before a certain Japanese half-prince was passing through
Voronezh province incognito. Well, of course, between us, his
highness got mixed up with a Voronezh girl and had a child
by her, also incognito. And he even wanted to marry her,
but the Mikado forbade it in a coded telegram. The half-
prince had to go away and the child remained illegitimate.
And this child was Bigusov. And so after the passing of many
years, the half-prince was dying and, as if to spite him, he
had had no legal children. There was no one to whom to
pass the heritage, and besides, a famous family was perishing,
which was the very worst thing for a Japanese. Well, it
occurred to him to remember about Bigusov. And so this
man struck a piece of good luck. Right now, they say, he is
already in Japan. The old man died, and Bigusov is now a
prince, a kinsman of the Mikado, and moreover, speaking
among ourselves, he has received a million yen in cash. A
million! And to such a fool!"

"If I could get a million rubles," said the second passenger,
twisting his legs, "I'd show them what to do with a million!"

In the passage between the two upper berths appeared the

head of the fourth traveler. He looked attentively at the man who knew what to do with the million, and saying nothing, again covered himself with the magazine.

"Yes," said the third passenger, unsealing the railroad wax-paper package containing two individual zweiback, "there are various things that happen in the field of monetary circulation. The uncle of a certain young lady in Moscow died in Warsaw and left her a heritage valued at a million, and she didn't even know about it. But abroad they found out about it, and a month later a quite respectable foreigner appeared in Moscow. This darling resolved to marry the girl, before she could learn of her inheritance. But she had a fiancé in Moscow, quite a nice young man from the Chamber of Weights and Measures. She loved him very much and naturally did not want to marry the other fellow. But the foreigner simply went crazy over her. He sent her bouquets of flowers, candy, and rayon stockings. It was later discovered that the foreign darling did not come on his own, but had been sent by a joint stock company which had been organized especially to exploit her uncle's estate. They even had an investment capital of eighteen thousand zloty. This representative of theirs simply had to marry the girl and take her abroad. A very romantic story! Can you imagine the state of mind of the representative? Such responsibility! And besides, he had taken the advance and he could not account for it because of that Soviet sweetheart. And there in Warsaw it was a nightmare! The stockholders waited, worried, the stocks fell! And the whole thing ended in a crash. The girl married her Soviet sweetheart, and so she never even found out about it."

"There's a fool for you," said the second passenger. "If I only had a million!"

And in agitation he even pulled the zwieback out of the hands of his neighbor and ate it nervously.

stallment plan. He resolved to maintain his authority. And then began the sad music. Dostoyevskyism: 'On the one hand, I admit, but on the other hand, I emphasize.' But what was there to emphasize? What a backboneless wagging of the tail! And so our Bubeshko had to write another letter!"

The passengers began to laugh again.

"But even there, he did not say a word about his opportunism. And he took to writing. Every day another letter. They wanted to start a new department in the newspaper for him. 'Corrections and Denials.' And he knows that he's got himself into a muddle, wants to crawl out, but he himself has started such a hullabaloo that he can't do it. The last time he got to the point where he wrote: 'So and so . . . I recognize the error while I consider the present letter insufficient.'"

When Ostap returned from washing himself, the new passengers were still laughing. The coupé had been swept, the beds made, and the porter was going away, holding a bundle of sheets and blankets under his chin. The young men were not afraid of draughts. They opened the window in the coupé and, like a sea wave enclosed in a box, the autumn wind rolled and tossed in the coupé. Ostap put the suitcase containing the million on the baggage rack, and sat down beneath it, regarding his new neighbors good-naturedly. They accustomed themselves to life on an international car with ardor. They looked frequently at the mirror on the door, jumped up and down on their seats, testing the resistance of the springs, commented favorably on the quality of the polished red scrollwork, and pressed all the buttons. From time to time, one of them disappeared for several minutes, and upon his return whispered with his comrades. Finally, a girl appeared in the doorway. She wore a man's beaver coat and gymnasium slippers bound about her ankles with ribbons, in the ancient Greek manner.

"Comrades," she said decisively, "this is piggishness! We

also want to ride in luxury. We must change places at the very next station."

Bender's traveling companions raised a threatening racket.

"Never mind, never mind! All of us have the same rights as you have," the girl continued. "We've already cast the lots. Tarasov, Parovitsky and I won. Clear out to the third class!"

Out of the commotion that arose, Ostap understood that a large group of polytechnic students were returning on this train to Chernomorsk from their summer factory practice. There was not enough room for everybody in the "hard" cars, and so they had had to buy three tickets in the wagon lit with its elaborate carvings.

The girl remained in the coupé and the first three removed themselves with belated dignity. In their places Tarasov and Parovitsky immediately appeared. They began at once to jump up and down on the seats and press all the buttons. The girl jumped busily with them. Less than a half hour later the first trio re-appeared in the coupé. They were drawn back by nostalgia for the lost magnificence. After them, with embarrassed smiles, appeared two more, then another one with a mustache. The turn of the mustached one to ride in luxury was to come only on the second day and he could not hold out. His appearance evoked particularly excited cries and brought the train porter to the scene.

"What's going on here, Citizens?" he said officiously. "What is the meaning of this crowd? Get out, all of you from the 'hard' car! Otherwise, I'll go to the chief!"

The entire group was struck dumb with fear.

"These are guests," the girl said sadly. "They only came to visit us for a while."

"It's against the rules," said the train porter. "Go away! Clear out!"

The mustached one was backing toward the exit, when the great schemer interfered in the conflict.

"What's the matter with you, papa?" he said to the train porter. "Passengers ought not to be lynched without special necessity. Why apply the letter of the law with such exactitude? You must be more hospitable. Do you know how it's done in the East? Come on, I'll explain it all to you right away—all about hospitality!"

After he had conversed with Ostap in the corridor, the train porter was so permeated with the spirit of the East that he no longer contemplated exiling the group, even brought it nine glasses of tea in heavy metal holders, and his entire reserve supply of individual zwieback. And he would take no money.

"According to the Eastern custom," Ostap said to the gathering. "According to the laws of hospitality, in the words of a certain worker in the culinary sector."

The good offices were performed with such ease and simplicity that they could not be refused. The zwieback packages crackled as they were being torn open. Ostap played the host and distributed the tea, and soon became friendly with all the students, including the girl student.

"I have long been interested in the problem of universal, equal, and secret education," he gossiped joyously. "Not long ago I even discussed the matter with a Hindu philosopher and enthusiast, a man of such extreme learning that, no matter what he says, his words are immediately recorded on a phonograph record. And since the old man likes to talk—he has that little vice—eight hundred carloads of records have accumulated, and now they're making buttons out of them!"

Beginning with this free improvisation, the great schemer took a zwieback in his hand.

"This zwieback," he said, "is removed by one step from a grinding stone. And that step has already been taken."

The friendship, warmed by this sort of pleasantry, developed very quickly, and soon the whole crowd was singing a popular song under Ostap's direction:

"Peter, called the Great (poor Pete!)
Had no kith and had no kin,
Just a snake and one old nag,
This was all his family."

By evening Ostap called them all by their first names, and with some of them he used the familiar "thou." But much of what the young people talked about he did not understand. Suddenly it seemed to him that he had become frightfully old. Before him sat Youth, somewhat coarse, straightforward, and shamelessly naïve. He had been quite different at twenty. He confessed to himself that when he had been twenty he was much more many-sided, but much worse. He did not *laugh* then, but merely laughed *at* something. But these young folks laughed for all they were worth.

"What is this fat-faced youth rejoicing at?" he thought with sudden irritation. "Upon my word, I'm beginning to envy them!"

Although Ostap was undoubtedly the center of attention, and his speech flowed without a hitch, although the attitude of those around him was the very best, it lacked the admiration of Balaganov, the cowardly submissiveness of Panikovsky, and the devoted love of Kozlevich. One sensed in the students the superiority of people in the audience over the showman. The man in the audience listens to the citizen in swallow tails, sometimes laughs, and sometimes lazily applauds him, but in the end he goes home and forgets about the showman. And after the show, the showman comes to the Actor's Club, sits mournfully over his meat ball and complains to a fellow member of the Actor's Association, a comedian from a comic opera, that the public does not understand him and that the government does not appreciate him. The comedian drinks his vodka and likewise complains that nobody understands him. But what is there to understand? The witticisms are old, and the method is old, and it is too late to relearn things. It all seems clear.

The story of Bubeshko, who had underestimated the plans, was told again, this time especially for Ostap's benefit. He went with his new friends to the "hard" car to persuade a girl student, Liuda Pisarevskaya, to come and visit them, and chatted on so pleasantly that the bashful Liuda came along and took part in the general uproar.

The friendship had developed to such an extent that, toward evening, as he walked along the platform of a junction station with the girl in a man's overcoat, the great schemer brought her to the last exit semaphore, and there, to his great surprise, poured his heart out in pretty, banal phrases.

"You understand," he explained to her. "The moon, the queen of the landscape shone. We were sitting on the steps of the Museum of Antiquity. And I felt that I loved her! But that very evening, I had to go away, and the whole affair was broken up. She was hurt, it seems. I am positive she was hurt."

"You were sent away on a business trip?" the girl asked solicitously.

"M'm—yes. Sort of a business trip. Well, not exactly a business trip, but a very pressing affair. Now I'm suffering! I'm suffering foolishly and majestically!"

"That's not so terrible," said the girl. "Switch the excess of your energy to another circuit for executing some labor process. Saw wood, for example. There is such a tendency nowadays in love."

Ostap promised to switch his energy, and although he could not imagine how sawing wood could take the place of Zosya, still he felt better. They returned to the car with a mysterious air, and later went out into the corridor several times to whisper about unrequited love and about the new tendencies in that field.

In the coupé Ostap continued to do his best to win the favor of the company. And he attained it. The students regarded him as one of them, and the coarse Parovitsky hit Ostap on the back with all his might and exclaimed:

"Come to our polytechnicum! By God! You'll get a stipend of seventy-five rubles! You'll live like a god! We have a table with meat every day! Then we'll go to the Urals to practice!"

"I've already graduated from one higher institution of the humanities," the great schemer answered hastily.

"What are you doing now?" asked Parovitsky.

"Working along the financial line."

"Have you a job in a bank?"

Ostap suddenly looked satirically at the student and said distinctly:

"No, I have no job. I'm a millionaire."

Of course this declaration in no way involved Ostap. Everything could be converted into a jest. But Parovitsky began to laugh with such vehemence that the great schemer was hurt. He was possessed by the desire to astonish his fellow travelers, to evoke great admiration among them.

"How many millions have you?" asked the girl in the gymnasium slippers, urging him on to a gay reply.

"One," said Ostap, pale with pride.

"Not very much!" declared the chap with the mustache.

"Not much! Not much!" they all cried.

"It's enough for me," Bender said solemnly.

With these words, he lifted his suitcase, clicked the nickeled locks and threw all of his possessions on the seat. The flat packages of paper lay in a sprawling mound. Ostap bent one of them. Its cover cracked with the snap of a card.

"There's ten thousand in every package. Is that enough for you? There's slightly less than a million here. Everything is in place . . . Signatures, silk threads and water marks."

Everybody was silent as Ostap put the money back in the suitcase and threw it on the baggage rack with a gesture that seemed regal to him. Again he sat down, leaned back, placed his feet apart and looked at the group.

"As you see, the humanistic studies also bring forth fruit," said the millionaire, inviting the students to share in his fun.

The students were silent, examining various buttons and hooks on the ornamented walls of the coupé.

"I live like a god," Ostap continued, "or like a demi-god, which, after all, is the same thing."

After waiting awhile, the great schemer moved restlessly and exclaimed in the friendliest tones:

"Why did you devils suddenly become sad?"

"Well, I have to go," said the chap in the mustache thoughtfully. "I'll have to go back and see how things are."

And he fled from the coupé.

"A remarkable thing," Ostap remarked. "This morning we weren't even acquainted, but now we feel as if we have known each other for ten years. Is it because the fluids are acting?"

"How much do we owe for the tea?" asked Parovitsky. "How many did we drink, comrades? Was it eight glasses or ten? We'll have to ask the train porter. I'll be back right away."

Four more, overwhelmed by a desire to help Parovitsky settle their account with the train porter, went out with him.

"Suppose we sing something?" Ostap suggested. "Something solid. For example, 'Priest Sergei, Priest Sergei!' I have a marvelous Volga bass!"

And without waiting for a reply, the great schemer began to sing hastily, "Down the little river, down the Kazanka, the dove-colored drake floated by." When it was time to join in the chorus Ostap swung his arms and stamped his foot like a conductor, but no roaring voices joined in. Only one, Liuda Pisarevskaya, out of sheer timidity, chirped, "Priest Sergei, Priest Sergei!" but she stopped immediately and ran out into the corridor. The friendship was dying before his eyes. Soon only the goodnatured, sympathetic girl in gymnasium slippers remained in the coupé.

"Where did they all run to?" asked Bender.

"Indeed," whispered the girl, "I have to find out."

She ran alertly to the door, but the unfortunate millionaire caught her by the hand.

"I was joking!" he muttered. "I'm a worker! I'm the director of a symphonic orchestra! I'm the son of Lieutenant Schmidt! My father is a Turkish subject! Believe me!"

"Let me go," the girl hissed.

The great schemer was alone.

The coupé shook and creaked. The spoons turned in the empty glasses, and the entire flock crept slowly to the edge of the table. In the doorway appeared the train porter, holding a pile of blankets and sheets under his chin.

Chapter Thirty-five

THE COLUMN OF ATMOSPHERE

T HE roofs rattled in Chernomorsk and draughts wandered over the streets. The unexpected attack of a northeaster chased the tender Indian summer into garbage boxes, gutters and the protuberances of house. There it died among charred maple leaves and torn street car tickets. Cold chrysanthemums drowned in the bowls of flower vendors. Green shutters of closed kvass stands banged. Pigeons mourned: "Ooomroo, oomroo."[1] Sparrows warmed themselves as they pecked at hot manure. Chernomorskians struggled against the wind, lowering their heads like bulls. The piqué vests were worse off than the others. The wind tore their stiff straw hats and panamas and rolled them along the clean-swept street to the boulevard. The old men ran after them, puffing and indignant. The sidewalk storms pushed the pursuers with such vehemence that at times they outran their headgear and came to a stop leaning at the wet feet of a bronze figure of a Catherinian notable that stood in the middle of the square.

Ship-like creakings issued from the Antelope as it rested at its stand. If previously Kozlevich's machine had evoked gay astonishment, it now inspired pity. The left rear fender was tied on with rope, a considerable part of the windshield was replaced with plywood, and instead of the horn that had played the *matchish* and which had been lost during the catastrophe, a nickeled chairman's bell hung on a string. Even the steering wheel, on which rested the honest hands of Adam Kazimirovich, was somewhat bent to the side. On the side-

[1] Meaning: "I'll die, I'll die." C. M.

383

walk, beside the Antelope, stood the great schemer. Leaning against the side of the machine, he was saying:

"I have deceived you, Adam. I cannot present you with an Isotta-Fraschini, nor a Lincoln, nor a Buick, nor even a Ford. I cannot buy you a new machine. The government does not regard me as a purchaser. I am a private person. The only thing I can do is to look through the advertisements in the paper and buy you a bit of trash like our Antelope."

"Why do you talk that way?" Kozlevich objected. "My Lauren-Dietrich is a good machine. If I could only have an oil pipe, I wouldn't need any Buicks."

"I have brought you the pipe," said Ostap. "Here it is. But this is the only way, dear Adam, in which I can help you to mechanize transportation."

Kozlevich rejoiced at the pipe, turned it over and over in his hands, and began to attach it immediately. Ostap pushed the bell which produced a chairmany ring, and began passionately:

"Do you know, Adam, here's a bit of news. A column of air, weighing two hundred and fourteen kilos, presses upon every citizen."

"No!" said Kozlevich. "But why?"

"How—why? It's a scientific, medical fact. And recently I have found it extremely oppressive. Think of it! Two hundred and fourteen kilos! It presses twenty-four hours a day, and especially at night! I don't sleep well. What?"

"Nothing. I'm listening," Kozlevich said kindly.

"I feel very bad, Adam. My heart is too big!"

The driver of the Antelope hummed while Ostap continued to chatter.

"Yesterday in the street an old woman stopped me and asked me to buy an everlasting wick for a primus stove. Do you know, Adam, I didn't buy it. I don't need an everlasting wick! I don't want to live forever! I want to die! I have all the banal symptoms of being in love: absence of appetite, sleeplessness, and the maniacal urge to compose verse. Listen to what I wrote last night by the guttering light of an electric lamp: 'I recollect a wondrous instant; and you appeared before me then, beloved, like a passing shadow, like the spirit of pure beauty.' Good, isn't it? Talented! And only at dawn, when I was finishing writing the last lines, did I remember that this verse had already been written by A. Pushkin. Such a blow delivered by one of the classics! Eh?"

"No! No! Continue," said Kozlevich sympathetically.

"So I live on," continued Ostap with a quaver in his voice. "My body is registered in Hotel Karlsbad, while my soul plays truant. It doesn't even want to go to Rio de Janeiro. And to top it all, I'm being oppressed by the column of atmosphere."

"Have you called on her?" asked the simple Kozlevich. "Have you called on Zosya Adamovna?"

"I shan't go," said Ostap. "I am proud and modest. The Janissaries have stirred within me. I sent that good-for-nothing three hundred and fifty rubles' worth of telegrams from Moscow and didn't receive even a half ruble's worth of reply. *I* did that! *I!* With whom housewives, houseworkers, widows, and even a woman dentist, have fallen in love! No, Adam, I will not go! Good-by."

Kozlevich looked for a long time after the departing Ostap, then thoughtfully started his motor and moved on.

The great schemer returned to the hotel, pulled the suitcase containing the million from where it lay under the bed beside a pair of worn-out shoes. For a while he looked at it stupidly. Then he took it by the handle and went out into the street. The wind seized him by the shoulders and dragged him to the seaside boulevard. There it was deserted. No one sat on the white benches, carved during the summer with lovers' inscriptions. In the outer harbor, passing the lighthouse, a low freighter with thick, straight masts was departing.

"Enough!" said Ostap. "The Little Golden Calf is not for

me! Let him who wishes take it! Let him play the millionaire to his heart's content!"

He turned around and seeing no one about, threw the suitcase on the gravel.

"Help yourself!" he invited, addressing the black maples and bowing.

He walked along the path without looking back. At first he walked slowly, at the pace of a promenader. Then he put his hands in his pockets, because they suddenly began to disturb him, and quickened his pace in order to overcome his wavering. He compelled himself to turn the corner and even to sing a little song. But a minute later he ran back. The suitcase lay in its former place. However, from the opposite side, bending forward and stretching out his hands, a middle-aged citizen of ordinary appearance was advancing upon it.

"What do you want?" cried Ostap from the distance. "I'll show you how to grab other people's suitcases! Can't even leave it here for a second! Preposterous!"

The citizen shrugged his shoulders discontentedly and retreated. And again Bender dragged along with the Little Golden Calf in his hand.

"What's to be done?" he mused. "How can I dispose of the accursed treasure which enriches me only with moral torments? Shall I burn it?"

The great schemer paused at this thought with satisfaction.

"There happens to be a fireplace in my room. I'll burn it in the fireplace! That's magnificent! The act of a Cleopatra! Into the fire! Package after package! Why should I bother with them? And yet, it's foolish. Burning money is sheer ostentation! But what can I do with it, except get some Nepmanish food? Silly situation! The manager of a Museum thinks he can build a Louvre for three hundred rubles! Any collective of water-workers, or some coöperative corporation of playwrights could build half a skyscraper for a million, with a flat roof for open-air lectures! But Ostap Bender, descendant of Janissaries, can do nothing with it. There you have the hegemony of the class crushing a lonely millionaire!"

Musing on what to do with the million, the great schemer ran along the garden paths, sat down on the cement parapet and angrily looked at the steamer that swayed beyond the breakers.

"No, I shall have to forget the conflagration. To burn money is cowardly and ungraceful! I must think of some effective gesture. I might found a stipend in the name of Balaganov for students of correspondence courses in radio-technique! I could buy fifty thousand silver spoons and out of them smelt a statue of Panikovsky on horseback and place it on his grave! Perhaps I could incrustate the Antelope with mother-of-pearl! And perhaps . . ."

Suddenly struck by a new thought, the great schemer jumped down from the parapet. Without hesitating another minute, he left the boulevard and, bravely weathering the pressure of frontal and side winds, went to the postoffice. There, at his request, the suitcase was sewn in burlap and bound crosswise with stout rope. A package appeared, simple in appearance, such as the postoffice receives by the thousands every day, and in which citizens send lard, jam or apples to their relatives.

Ostap took an indelible pencil, waved it excitedly in the air, and wrote:

Valuable
To the People's Commissar of Finance
Moscow

The parcel, flung by the hand of a hefty postal clerk, crashed on a pile of oval bundles, sacks and boxes. Shoving the receipt in his pocket, Ostap saw his million, in a pile of

other packages, carried away on a little wagon into the adjoining hall by a lazy old man with white streaks of lightning
in his buttonhole.

"The meeting continues," said the great schemer. "This
time, without the participation of the representative of bewildered landed proprietors, O. Bender."

For a long time he stood under the arch of the postoffice,
torn between approval of his act and regret. The wind blew
under his mackintosh. He felt cold. And he remembered with
bitterness that he had never bought a second fur coat.

A girl stopped for a second directly in front of him. Tossing
back her head, she glanced at the shining face of the postoffice
clock and went on. She wore a rough little coat, shorter than
her dress, and a blue béret with a childish pompon. With her
right hand she tried to hold down the bottom of her coat that
was being blown by the wind. The commander's heart missed
a beat, even before he recognized her as Zosya. He followed
her over the wet paving stones, involuntarily maintaining a
certain distance. Occasionally the girl would be hidden from
him by passersby, and then Ostap would step into the street,
peering sideways at Zosya and deliberating the main points
of the explanations that would take place.

At the corner Zosya stopped before a notion stand and
began to examine men's brown socks that swung on a rope.
Ostap patrolled not far away.

At the very edge of the sidewalk two men with portfolios
were engaged in heated conversation. Both of them wore top-
coats which revealed white summer trousers.

"You left HERCULES just in time, Ivan Pavlovich," said one
of them, pressing the briefcase to his chest. "There's havoc
there now! They're cleaning them out like beasts!"

"I hear everybody in town talking about it," the other
sighed.

"Yesterday they were house-cleaning Skumbrievich," the
first one continued with evident relish. "You couldn't break

your way in. At first everything was quite proper. Skumbrie-vich told his biography so that everybody applauded him. 'I was born,' he said, 'between the hammer and the anvil!' He wanted to emphasize with this that his parents were black-smiths. Then someone in the audience asked, 'Tell me. Don't you remember? Wasn't there a mercantile house "Skumbrie-vich and Son"? Ironmongers? Aren't you that Skumbrie-vich?' And the fool goes and says, 'I'm not Skumbrievich; I am the son.' You can imagine what will happen to him now! The first degree of punishment is assured!"

"Yes, Comrade Weintorg. It's simply terrible! And who's being cleaned to-day?"

"Oh, to-day is a big day! To-day—Berlaga! You know—the one who tried to save himself in the insane asylum. And after that, Maestro Polykhayev himself. And that viper, Serna Mikhailovna, his morganatic wife! She didn't give anybody in HERCULES a chance to breathe. I'm going this evening two hours before it begins; otherwise I'll never push my way through! Besides this, Bomze . . ."

Zosya walked on, and Ostap never found out what became of Adolf Nikolaievich Bomze. This, however, in no way an-noyed him. The initial sentence of the conversation was now ready. The commander quickly caught up with the girl.

"Zosya," he said. "I have arrived: it is impossible to brush this fact aside!"

He delivered this sentence with belligerent jauntiness. The girl drew back, and the great schemer understood that he had assumed the wrong tone. He changed his intonation, spoke rapidly and volubly, complained of circumstances, said some-thing about youth not having passed as he had imagined it in his tender years, that life had proved to be coarse and low, like a bass key.

"Do you know, Zosya," he said finally. "Every man, even a member of the Party, is subject to the pressure of a column

of atmosphere that weighs two hundred and fourteen kilos.
Have you ever noticed it?"

Zosya did not reply.

They were walking past the cinema "Capitoline." Ostap
glanced diagonally across to the side where the office founded
by him had been located during the summer, and whistled
quietly. Across the entire building stretched a broad sign:

```
┌─────────────────────────────────────────────┐
│                                               │
│      STATE TRUST HORNS AND HOOFS              │
│                                               │
└─────────────────────────────────────────────┘
```

Typewriters and the portraits of government leaders could
be seen in all the windows. At the entrance, a triumphant
smile on his face, stood a dashing messenger, infinitely
superior to Panikovsky. Through the open gates with the
sign: "Main Warehouse," drove three-ton trucks loaded to the
top with horns and hoofs according to specifications. It was
evident that Ostap's child was going along the right path.

"This class hegemony is certainly driving forward," Ostap
said ruefully. "Even my frivolous idea is being utilized for its
purposes, while I have been pushed aside, Zosya. Do you hear?
I have been pushed aside. I am unhappy."

"What a lugubrious lover!" Zosya exclaimed, turning to
Ostap for the first time.

"Indeed," Ostap said. "I am a typical Eugene Onyegin, and,
at the same time, a knight deprived of his heritage by the
Soviet government."

"A fine knight *you* are!"

"Don't be angry, Zosya. Consider the column of atmosphere! It seems to me that it presses upon me with greater
force than on other citizens. This is because I love you. And
besides, I am not a member of a trade union. That's another
reason."

"Also it's because you lie more than other citizens!"

"That is not a lie. It is a law of physics. And yet, perhaps there really is no column, and all this is only my imagination."

Zosya stopped and began to pull off a glove the color of gray stockings and of the same texture.

"I am thirty-three years old," Ostap hastened to add. "The age of Jesus Christ. But what have I done until now? I have created no religion. I have wasted my disciples. I have not brought the dead Panikovsky to life, and only you . . ."

"Well, good-by," said Zosya. "I am going to the restaurant."

"I am also going to dine," announced the great schemer, glancing at the sign: THE MODEL TRAINING FOOD TRUST F.Z.U. AT THE CHERNOMORSK STATE ACADEMY OF SPATIAL SCIENCES. "I'll eat some model soldiers' *shchi* in this academy. Perhaps I'll feel easier then."

"This restaurant is only for members of the trade union," Zosya reminded him.

"Well, then I'll just sit."

They went down three steps. In the rear of the model training trust, under a palm as green as the roof of the building, sat a black-eyed young man who was regarding the menu with dignity.

"Pericles!" Zosya cried from the distance. "I bought you socks with double heels! Let me introduce you. This is Femidi."

"Femidi," repeated the young man, heartily squeezing Ostap's hand.

"Bender-Zadunaisky," the great schemer replied rudely, comprehending at once that he had come late to the feast of love, and that the double-heeled socks were not merely the simple product of some coöperative artel of pseudo-invalids, but the symbol of a happy marriage, legalized by the bureau of vital statistics.

"What! Are you also Zadunaisky?" Zosya asked gayly.

"Yes, Zadunaisky. You, too, are no longer Sinitskaya. Judging by the socks . . ."

"I am Sinitskaya-Femidi."

"For twenty-seven days already," remarked the young man, rubbing his hands.

"I like your husband," said the knight bereft of his heritage.

"I like him myself," Zosya replied provokingly.

While the newlyweds were eating sailors' *borshch,* raising their spoons high and exchanging glances, Ostap glowered at the cultural placards hung on the walls. On one of these was written: "Do not distract yourself with conversation while eating. This interferes with the proper secretion of gastric juices." Another was composed in verse:

> "Beverages with fruit flavors
> Bring us carbohydrates' favors."

There was nothing to be done. He felt that he ought to leave, but he was prevented from doing so by an unexpected shyness.

"In this sailors' *borshch,*" Ostap remarked nervously, "swim the remains of a shipwreck."

The Femidis laughed goodnaturedly.

"What is your line of work?" Ostap asked the young man.

"I am secretary of the iso-collective of railroad painters," replied Femidi.

The great schemer began to rise slowly.

"Oh, a representative of a collective. I might have expected that. However, I shall no longer distract you with conversation. It would interfere with the proper secretion of your gastric juices, which are indispensable to health."

He departed without bidding them good-by, bumping against the corners of the tables, moving in a straight line to the exit.

"The girl was stolen!" he muttered as he walked along the street. "She was stolen right out of the stall! Femidi!

Nemezidi! The representative of the collective, Femidi! Stolen from the private trader millionaire . . ."

And at that moment it occurred to Bender with painful clarity that he no longer had his million. He kept thinking about it as he ran, pushing the passersby aside with his hands as a swimmer pushes aside the water in a contest to establish a world's record.

"Here is another Apostle Paul for you!" he whispered, jumping over the flower beds in the city garden. "Goody-goody! Son of a bitch! Damned Mennonite! Accursed Seventh Day Adventist! Fool! If they have already sent the package, I shall hang myself! Such a Tolstoian deserves to be killed!"

Slipping twice on the tiled floor of the postoffice, the great schemer ran up to the little window. There stood a small, forbidding, silent queue. In his excitement Ostap was about to shove his head into the little window, when the citizen who stood first in line nervously raised his sharp elbow and crowded the newcomer back. The next citizen in line likewise raised his elbow, as if he had been wound up, and the great schemer found himself further away from the desired window. In utter silence, elbows were raised and lowered until the insolent one found himself in his proper place—at the end of the queue.

"I only . . ." Ostap began.

But he did not continue. It was useless. The queue, gray, stony, was as implacable as a Greek phalanx. Everyone knew his place and was ready to die for his small rights.

Only after forty-five minutes had elapsed did Ostap put his head into the window of the postoffice and vehemently demand the return of his parcel. With complete equanimity, the clerk returned the receipt to Ostap.

"Comrade, we never give parcels back."

"What! Have you sent it already?" the great schemer quavered. "I brought it only an hour ago."

"Comrade, we never give parcels back," repeated the postal clerk.

"But it is *my* parcel," Ostap said ingratiatingly. "Do you understand? It is mine. I sent it, and I want to take it back. You see, I forgot to put in a jar of preserves. Quinces! Please do me a favor. My uncle will be frightfully disappointed. You see . . ."

"Comrade, we never give parcels back."

Ostap looked around, seeking aid. Behind him stood the queue, silent and forbidding, knowing all the rules, including the one that parcels are never given back.

"I want to put the jar in," Ostap babbled. "Quinces!"

"Comrade, send the jar in a separate parcel," said the clerk softly. "It won't hurt your uncle any."

"But you don't know my uncle!" Ostap exclaimed excitedly. "And besides, I'm a poor student. I have no money. I ask you as a public-spirited citizen!"

"See for yourself, comrade," said the clerk in a tearful voice. "How will I look for it now? There are three tons of parcels here!"

But at this point the great schemer began to talk such pathetic nonsense that the communications worker went into another hall to look for the poor student's parcel. The queue, which until then had been silent, immediately raised a hue and cry. The great schemer was reviled in every possible manner for his ignorance of the postal laws, while in her indignation one woman citizen even pinched him.

"Never do it again," the postal clerk warned him severely, returning the little suitcase to Bender.

"I'll never do it again!" the commander declared. "Upon my word of honor as a student!"

The wind knocked on the roof, the lamps swayed, shadows moved over the earth, and the rain cut across the rays of automobile headlights.

"Enough of psychological excesses!" Bender cried joyously.

"Enough of suffering and self-torture! It is high time to begin a hard-working bourgeois life. To Rio de Janeiro! I shall buy a plantation and import Balaganov as a monkey! He'll pluck the bananas for me."

Chapter Thirty-six

THE KNIGHT OF THE ORDER OF THE GOLDEN
FLEECE

A STRANGE man walked at night through the marshes that led to the Dniester. He was enormous, shapeless. A skin-tight, hooded raincoat enveloped him. Past clumps of reeds, under straggling fruit trees, the strange man moved on tiptoe, as if he were in a bedroom. From time to time he stopped and sighed. Then, within his coat one could hear a tinkling as of metal objects clashing together. And following this, each time, a delicate ringing hung on the air. Once the strange man tripped over a wet root and fell on his stomach. This brought forth the noise of knightly armor falling on a hardwood floor. For a long time the strange man lay still, peering into the darkness.

The March night was full of sounds. Drops, like liquid from a medicine dropper, fell from the trees and struck against the ground.

"Accursed platter!" whispered the man.

He rose and walked without mishap to the Dniester itself. He lifted his coat, slid down the embankment, and, slipping on the melting ice, ran toward Roumania.

Throughout the winter the great schemer had made his preparations. He had bought United States dollars with their portraits of white-wigged presidents, gold watches and ciga-rette cases, wedding rings, diamonds, and other precious articles.

Now he carried them himself—seventeen massive cigarette cases with monograms, eagles, and engraved inscriptions:

"To the director of the Russo-Carpathian Bank and benefactor, Yevsey Rudolfovich Polufabrikant, on the day of his
silver wedding anniversary, from his appreciative fellow-em-
ployees."

"To Privy-Councilor M. I. Svyatotatsky, on the conclusion
of the Senatorial investigation, from the ranking officers of the
Chernomorsk Municipality."

But heaviest of all was a cigarette case with the dedication:
"To the Constable of the Alexeyev District from grateful Jews
engaged in commerce." Under the inscription was a flaming
enameled heart punctured with an arrow which, of course,
was to symbolize the love of the Jews engaged in commerce
for the constable.

In all his pockets he had strings of wedding rings, rings set
with precious stones, and bracelets. On his back, in three rows,
twenty pairs of gold watches hung on stout cords. Some of
them ticked irritatingly, and it seemed to Bender that insects
were crawling over his back. Among a number of presentation
watches was one whose inscription on the watch-cover testi-
fied: "To my beloved son, Seryozhenka Kastraki, on the day
he passed the examinations for his diploma."

The winter had passed in heavy labor. The great schemer
had obtained only four hundred thousand rubles' worth of
diamonds. Of *valuta,* including some dubious Polish and
Baltic money, he had managed to secure only fifty thousand's
worth. With the rest of the money he had had to buy heavy
things. It was especially difficult to move about with a gold
platter on his stomach. The platter was large and oval, like
the shield of an African chieftain, and weighed twenty
pounds. The mighty neck of the commander bent under the
weight of an archbishop's cross with the inscription: "In the
name of the Father, the Son, and the Holy Ghost," which had
been bought from a former arch-deacon, Citizen Samoo-
blozhensky. Over the cross, on an imposing ribbon, hung the
Order of the Golden Fleece, a molten lamb.

After much bargaining Ostap had succeeded in buying this medal from a rare old man who might have been a grand duke at one time, or perhaps the chamberlain of a grand duke. The old man continually raised the price, pointing out that such a medal was possessed by only a few people in the world, and most of them crowned heads.

"The Golden Fleece," muttered the old man, "is given only for the highest valor."

"Mine happens to be the highest," Ostap had replied. "That is why I am buying the lamb—only because it is a scrap of gold."

But the commander was pretending. He had liked the medal at once and had decided to keep it for himself as the order of the Little Golden Calf.

Urged on by fear and the expectation of imminent gunfire, Bender ran to the middle of the river and stopped. He was oppressed by gold—the platter, the cross, the bracelets. His back itched under the watches. The tails of his coat were drenched, and weighed several *poods*. With a groan Ostap tore off the coat, threw it on the ice, and went on. Now he revealed a fur coat, a large, most unusual fur coat, perhaps the most unusual article of clothing Ostap wore. He had been building it for four months, building it like a house, preparing charts, gathering materials. The fur coat was double, the finest red fox within, genuine seal without. The collar was of sable. It was a remarkable fur coat, a super fur coat, with chinchilla pockets that were full of medals for the rescue of the drowning, crosses to be worn about the neck, and golden bridges—the latest attainment of dental technique! Above the great schemer's head rose a hat, no, not a hat—a beaver tiara.

This remarkable load was to secure an easy, happy-go-lucky life for the commander on the shores of the warm ocean, in the city he had dreamed of since childhood, among the potted palms and figs of Rio de Janeiro.

At three o'clock in the morning the refractory descendant

of the Janissaries stepped on the strange foreign shore. There also it was quiet, dark; there also it was spring, and drops yearned from the branches. The great schemer laughed aloud.

"Now, a few formalities with the sympathetic Roumanian *boyars,* and the path is clear. I think that two or three medals for the rescue of drowning persons will put color into their drab life on the border!"

He turned toward the Soviet side, and, stretching his plump sealskin hand into the waning darkness, said:

"Everything should be done according to form. Form No. 5: farewell to the fatherland. Well, what of it? Adieu, great land! I do not like to be at the head of the class and receive special grades for attention, application and deportment. I am a private person and am not obliged to evince enthusiasm for silos, trenches, and towers. For some reason, I am but slightly interested in the problem of the socialist transformation of man into an angel and a depositor of a savings bank. On the contrary, I am interested in the pressing question concerning the careful treatment of the personalities of lonely million-aires . . ."

Here the farewell to the fatherland according to formula No. 5 was interrupted by the appearance of several armed figures in whom Bender recognized the Roumanian border guards. The great schemer bowed with due dignity. Then, clearly and distinctly, he pronounced a sentence he had specially learned for the occasion:

"Triascu Romania mare!"

He glanced ingratiatingly into the faces of the border guards which could scarcely be seen in the half-darkness. It seemed to him that the border guards were smiling.

"Long live great Roumania!" Ostap repeated in Russian. "I am an old professor who has run away from the torture chambers of the Moscow Cheka. So help me God! I scarcely managed to get out. I greet you . . ."

One of the border guards came close to Ostap and pulled

off his fur tiara. Ostap stretched his hand toward the head-gear, but the border guard silently pushed him away.

"But!" the commander said goodnaturedly. "But, but! Hands off! I shall complain about you to the *Sfatul-zery*, to the large *Khuruldan!*"

Then another representative of civilization began deftly, with the agility of an experienced lover, to unbutton Ostap's great, almost incredible super fur coat. The commander re-sisted. With this movement a large bracelet flew from one of his pockets and rolled over the ground.

"Bracelet!" screamed the border guard officer, dressed in a short coat with a dog-skin collar and large metal buttons.

"Bracelet!" cried the others, flinging themselves upon Ostap.

Entangled in the fur coat, the great schemer fell to the ground. Immediately he was aware that the precious platter was being pulled out of his trousers. When he rose he saw that the officer, an inhuman smile on his face, was weighing the platter in his hand. Ostap clutched at his property and tore it from the hands of the officer, whereupon he received a blinding blow in the face. Events developed with military swiftness. The fur coat handicapped the great schemer, and he fought with his enemies on his knees, pelting them with medals for the rescue of drowning persons. Then he suddenly sank into inexplicable ease which permitted him to deliver to the enemy a number of fatal blows. He discovered that this ease was the result of the hundred-thousand-ruble fur coat being pulled off of him.

"Oh, what treatment!" Ostap cried in a piercing voice, look-ing around him wildly.

There was the moment when he leaned against a tree and swung the gleaming platter on the heads of his attackers. There was the moment when the Order of the Golden Fleece was being pulled from his neck, and the commander flung his head back and forth like a horse. There was also the moment when, raising high the archbishop's cross with the inscription:

"In the name of the Father, and the Son, and the Holy Ghost," he cried out hysterically:

"Exploiters of hardworking people! Leeches! Myrmidons of capital! Vipers!"

Pink saliva ran from his mouth. Ostap fought for his million like a gladiator. He flung off his enemies, and rose from the ground, looking before him with a darkened gaze.

He came to on the ice, with one boot and without his fur coat, without the cigarette cases embellished with inscriptions, without the collection of watches, without the platter, without the *valuta,* without the cross and diamonds, without the million. The officer with the dog-skin collar stood on the high bank and looked down at Ostap.

"Accursed *Siguranza!*" cried Ostap, lifting his bare leg. "Parasites!"

The officer slowly drew out a pistol and pulled back the hammer. The great schemer understood that this meeting had come to an end. Bending over, he hobbled back to the Soviet shore.

A white fog, like cigarette smoke, rose from the river. Opening his hands, Bender saw a flat brass button, the tufts of somebody's coarse black hair, and the medal of the Golden Fleece, miraculously preserved in battle. The great schemer gazed stupidly at the trophies and remains of his wealth, as he moved forward, slipping on holes in the ice and writhing in pain.

Suddenly the surface of the ice wavered under a mighty, prolonged blow like a cannon shot. A warm, dew-laden wind was blowing. Bender looked under his feet and saw a large green crack in the ice. The ice plateau on which he found himself swayed and began to crawl into the water.

"The ice is breaking!" the great schemer cried in horror. "The ice is breaking, gentlemen of the jury!"

He began to jump over the ice floes that were drifting apart, hurrying with all his might in the direction of the land from which he had parted with such disdain only an hour before. The fog lifted, pompously, deliberately, disclosing the bare marshes.

Ten minutes later a strange man, bareheaded and with one boot, crawled out on the Soviet shore. Addressing no one, he said aloud:

"No ovations are necessary. I did not become a Count of Monte Cristo. I shall have to qualify as a janitor!"

Moscow, October 3, 1931.

THE END